MW01064281

Running Wild Novella Anthology, Volume 3

Book 2

Edited by Barbara Lockwood
and Lisa Diane Kastner

These are works of fiction. Names, characters, places, and incidents either are the product of the author's imagination or are used fictitiously. Any resemblance to actual persons, living or dead, events, or locales, is coincidental.

Published in North America and Europe by Running Wild Press. Visit Running Wild Press at www.runningwildpress.com Educators, librarians, book clubs (as well as the eternally curious), go to www.runningwildpress.com for teaching tools.

ISBN (pbk) 978-1-947041-40-0
ISBN (ebook) 978-1-947041-41-7

Printed in the United States of America.

Contents

CIRCUITS END

By Rasmenia Massoud

Won't Sleep Better Alone

The end of together is a special kind of pain. There's a change in the light of a person's eyes when they realize the connection is about to be severed. Dreams of future adventures and joy are annihilated. The glimmer of adoration is crushed, replaced by shadows of defeat, betrayal, and relief. Their normal everyday is about to be forever altered. If you pay close attention, you can look past their eyes, to a room inside of them where the person they're about to become without you walks in.

Walter never believed I meant it when I threatened to leave, when I demanded that things change. He couldn't change. I'd grown bored and he couldn't fix it. But tonight, there's no doubt it's genuine. All those other times, I was only talking. Unsatisfied, unsure, and unhappy talking. Longing for more out of life, but too spineless to do anything about it besides making idle threats and lazy complaints. This time, though, it's as real and normal as doing laundry, or stopping to fill up on gas. A task I have to do; keep on going.

I hadn't planned on it playing out this way. I assumed he'd seen it coming. He wanted to go out for pizza. There we were, leaning over our greasy, cheesy, cholesterol pie, talking about work and coworkers and a whole lot of nothing, when he starts rubbing my thigh under the table. He said something about repairing a transmission in some old lady's car. I told another boring anecdote about me and my best friend Lucy getting pissed off about something in the circuit board shop we work at. He kept rubbing, moving his hand farther up my thigh and before I had time to think anything through, I heard the words as though they were coming out of someone else's mouth.

"I'm moving out."

"What?"

"Maybe we should talk about this at home."

"What the fuck, Axeline? What are you talking about?"

My timing could have been better. Riding home in the awkward silence born from my abruptness and Walter's confusion was the longest mile and a half I've ever traveled.

Now, sitting on the ugly blue couch with big pink flowers, I say nothing because any of my words in this moment are hurtful, no matter how much I try to soften them. In this tiny old house, which in a few days, will no longer be my home, I see him process the hurt I'm inflicting on him. My muscles are wound tight. I regret giving up cigarettes. Now would be a good time for a dose of nicotine. Chemical stress relief. As Walter's comprehension is wrapping around my clichéd breakup platitudes, his spine seems to melt. Elbows on his knees, his head in his hands, shaking, silently saying, "no" for eternal seconds until he finally looks up and says, "How could you do this to me?"

"I'm not doing anything to you. I'm doing this to us. For me." I pick at the frayed armrest that Tocki has been using as a scratching post for the past few years.

"You're doing this for yourself? That's fucking selfish." He's been drifting between devastation and anger all night. I know I should let him ride it out and say nothing, but I've never been good at seizing an opportunity to be silent.

"I'm doing it for you, too. Do you want to live with someone who doesn't want to be with you anymore? Asking me to do that is selfish."

I wish I could say anything other than the things I'm saying. I want to think and speak and be better words. Words that are profound or witty, or at least something comforting, to make this situation beautiful and bittersweet instead of sad and awkward, but I don't know how to create perfect moments in any situation.

I want to make this moment more, but it isn't anything other than what it is: a scene that's been played out countless times by countless people who have grown bored with one another's company. I'd like to give voice to it, and tell Walter that this whole scene is ridiculous and unnecessary, that we both know it's over and the two of us sitting here like a couple of puppets spouting off breakup lines we've heard in movies a thousand times is diminishing each of us and prolonging our further individual evolution.

Not that Walter is one for personal evolution. He's only a few crow's feet changed from the day we met a dozen years ago. That's the problem. He's the same, I'm someone else, even if I don't know who that is.

I want to say better things, but rather than taking the risk of making things worse, I sit on the couch and watch Walter vacillate between anger, sadness, and acceptance. Again and again, all night, he drifts through the waves of his emotions and I watch without throwing any lifeline, waiting for him to start swimming. When he seems to have exhausted himself, Walter sits up straight and pulls the elastic hair tie from his ponytail. He smooths his sandy brown hair and ties it back again. He picks up a lighter from the coffee table and flick, flick, flicks it again. Tap, tap, tap on the table. He twists the corner of his mustache. Walter's been fidgety since the day I met him. I always wondered why he'd never taken up a cigarette habit.

His nervous energy stops. "Axeline, you were my world."

"You should have been your own world."

"That's bullshit."

"You'll be okay."

He stands up and drops the lighter on the table. "That's a cruel thing to say. And you know it."

"I didn't mean it to be cruel." Why can't I say things better?

He shakes his head again and looks at the ceiling. He laughs and I catch a flicker in his eyes that says he's concocted some clever barb to jab me with, but instead it's, "You're bullshitting yourself. You know that, right?"

"I'm not bullshitting myself about anything. I know what I want." I grab the lighter. I pick up the bong from the coffee table and hit it.

"We already have what other people want. We have a house. We have a relationship. We have history. You want a ring on your finger? We can do that."

"Gawd, no. That's not at all what this is about." I pass the bong to him. "I need to try life on my own. I'm thirty fucking years old and I feel like an old married person, like I missed out my twenties."

Walter exhales a cloud of smoke toward me, sets the bong down on the table and holds his hands up. "Oh, I'm so sorry that I robbed you of your youth."

"You didn't rob me of anything. I should've worded that better. I meant that I don't think we're moving in the same direction anymore. I mean, aren't we just friends at this point?"

What I'm seeing in him might be defeat, or it maybe acceptance. Too often, they look like the same thing.

"I thought we were going until the end of the ride," he says.

"I did, too. For a while, anyway."

"Well… twelve years is a pretty good run, I suppose. When were you planning on moving out?"

"Next weekend. I found a place."

He slumps over again, elbows on his knees and nods. "You already found a place? You've been looking for a place behind my back?" He rubs his face, then pulls out the hair tie, sits up and reties it again. "Well, all right then. Whatever."

I pull back the curtain next to the couch. "The sun's coming up. It's already tomorrow."

Walter starts fidgeting with the lighter again. "You wanna get some food? One last breakfast?"

Beyond the tears, I have a clear view of the person who Walter will be without me. A healthy person who doesn't need me, who only thinks of me on rare occasions when his memory is prompted by a familiar scent that he can't quite place, or hears a song I love.

I look long and hard at a Walter I don't recognize, a stranger born of my decision to leave him. Out of nowhere, the fear hits me and I wonder how long it will take before I learn to sleep in a bed alone.

So Much Work

"So, that's it, then? You just told him you're moving out, and that's it? It's over?" Lucy drops her keys on the picnic table and starts digging around in her purse. Every morning begins the same way. I show up on time, swipe my badge and head to the parking lot behind the building where I wait for Lucy to arrive. She's always late, but it's not like anyone around here ever gets fired or written up for anything.

I nudge her arm. "Dude. You should at least go inside and clock in first."

She twists her straight black hair up into a bun on the top of her head and then lights a smoke. "No way. Joe's gonna jump on my ass and he'll nag at me as soon as I walk through that door. I'll just be late. Fuck it. I wanna hear the rest of this. So what'd Walter say, then?"

I shrug. "Not much. We went and got breakfast."

She shakes her head, laughs and rolls her eyes. "You are the only two people I've ever met who could break up after almost a dozen years together, then go sit around at the fuckin' Waffle House."

"Yeah, it was emotional, but dull. It's fitting, I suppose." I reach for her cigarette. She draws her arm back.

"Fuck off. You quit."

"I did, but I only want a drag."

"Well, you can't have one. Who gets Tocki?"

"He was my cat way before I even met Walter, so he's coming with me."

"It's about time you got it over with. Now you can move on with your life." She takes a drag and adjusts her bra strap.

Lucy is everything I'm not. Long black hair halfway down to her ass that's never had a split end or a fly away. I've can't even grow my dull brown frizz past my shoulders. Lucy's petite, curvy and confident. When we stand side by side, she's the one people notice first. They don't see the gangly, duck-footed mess standing next to her. Her grandparents emigrated here from Mexico and don't speak any English, so she's bilingual, too. She married her high school boyfriend and they had Abigail right after graduation. I shacked up with my dad's mechanic for twelve years and now I'm a single lady with a cat. Even in high school, when we were two kids barely acquainted with one another who were still trying to figure out who we wanted to be, Lucy was more of a person than me.

"This is crazy shit, man. I still can't believe you guys are done. I mean, you've been saying it for a couple of years, but now it's really real and I can't picture either one of you as single people."

"You knew me when I was single."

"Yeah, but we weren't friends then. It doesn't count."

A car pulls into the lot. Lucy crushes her cigarette on the brick wall and tosses it in the trash, which has only caught on fire once that I'm aware of. Neither one of us says anything as we watch some long-legged kid with curly black hair step out of a small powder blue Datsun. The driver's side door creaks as he slams it shut. We don't even bother to pretend we aren't staring at him. He lumbers toward us, hands in pockets, slouching, his long dragging feet on the blacktop as though they were too heavy to lift off the ground.

"Dude," Lucy says. "Who the fuck is that guy? A new sales rep?"

"Too young to be a sales rep. And his car's way too shitty."

She nudges my arm. "When I was on my way out the door on Friday, Joe said something about a new guy starting today. I bet that's him."

"Are you fucking kidding me? He's wearing a button-up shirt. And it's tucked in. Who does that?"

"Yeah, tucking in is weird, man."

Now he's close enough to hear us, so we shut up, making it obvious that we're talking about him.

"How's it going?" He straightens and pulls a hand from the pocket of his jeans. Instead of holding it out for a shake, he waves. "Is Neil around?"

Lucy tosses her keys in her bag and slings it over her shoulder. "Yeah, he's in there. I'll take you to him. You the new guy?"

"I'm the temp guy."

"Good for you." She opens the door. "I've never been a temp anything."

Joe carries a wooden rack of boards into my room and sits down in one of the empty chairs that is almost never empty because no one ever uses the break room. It's either the parking lot, or my room, and since I work in here, I think that means everyone else is taking more breaks than me. It's not as though this room is more comfortable than the kitchen, or the picnic table outside, but it's in the center of the shop. You can see everyone pass by as they emerge from the office with paperwork, or head toward the plate shop with armfuls of panels for electroplating. You can see down the hall to the yellow room where Lucy works, and the big, noisy room with the drill machines. All day long, I sit in a glass cube situated in the heart of this noisy, stinking, factory, listening to the cheap radio on the shelf that only receives three stations.

Joe sets the rack down and runs his hand along the finished green circuit boards, then back again. That clacking noise. "Neil wants these inspected by four o' clock so I can run 'em up to Loveland for electrical test by five."

We all do this same dance with Neil and Joe every goddamn day. Neil gives us a deadline that we can only meet with the aid of a time machine and will not accept any finished product with a single flaw, of which there are always several due to everyone's attempt to defy the normal order of minutes and hours in a day.

Joe seems to be everywhere at once, while never doing much of any specific thing except for talking. Joe is always talking, telling stories about anything and nothing. Neil aggravates everyone with his impossible demands and incessant questions. He's ignorant about how things get done and he's so immersed in stress that it's clogged his ears, and he can't listen. Neil's annoying, but easy to blow off because we all have more experience than him. Neil's just some rich guy who moved out west and bought a business without knowing a damn thing about how to run the place or deal with the people.

Joe doesn't know much more than Neil, but he's friendly enough that nobody minds. We all realize that poor Joe would have a hard time finding another job that would let him come in reeking of stale beer and looking like an extra from *Wayne's World*. He does a good job of sucking up to Neil and running around as his messenger, acting as a buffer between Neil and the rest of us, which is nice, because someone's got to do it. His brown nosing benefits us all and serves the greater good. The world needs tiny acts of heroism like the ones Joe performs every day to ease some of the pressure from our mundane, blue collar lives.

"Joe, it's after three. There must be two-hundred boards there. It ain't happenin'. It'll go faster if you help me."

"Yeah, okay. Your job is so fucking boring, though."

I grab a small pile of boards from the rack, and turn on my halo lamp. "Yeah. My job *is* fucking boring."

My fucking boring job is to look for mistakes. Keeping my face in front of the magnifying glass of that halo lamp, staring at circuitry. Repairing flaws. Realizing that nothing can ever be perfect. Taking things back to Lucy or Barry to inform them that they've shat the bed and will have to stay late to do the job over again. Nobody likes to see the QC inspector entering their work room. Unless I'm empty handed, then they're a little more welcoming.

Joe is telling me some weird story about the time he single-handedly prevented a major firefight at a convenience store when Neil walks in with the temp guy. Neil rubs his bald head, adjusts his bifocals and asks Joe if he'll be in Loveland by five o' clock, and then comes over to take a gander at a few of the boards as if he understands what he's looking for. He lifts his head and flinches with surprise as though I appeared from thin air.

"Hey, Axel. You meet Gavin, yet?" He turns on his heel toward the awkward young man standing in the doorway.

"Gavin? You mean the temp guy?"

"What?"

"Nothing. Never mind. I met Gavin. Sort of. Hi, Gavin."

Again, he waves. Instead of speaking, he grimaces and leans against the wall.

Neil sets the boards down and darts out of the room in a weird spontaneous way that makes me think some ghost none of us can hear is shouting out his name.

"So, what's up, Gavin?" Joe doesn't look away from the little green circuit board in his hand. "Neil giving you the tour?"

Gavin shakes his head. "He said he wants me to sit in here for a while to get a feel for what you guys do."

"Why?" I turn around in my spinny chair. "What're you going to be doing here?"

"Accounting."

"Accounting? What in the hell does that have to do with what we're doing out on the floor?"

"Yeah, uh… I have no idea." His curly black hair pokes up in all directions and I wonder if he's as young as he looks, or if he just needs a haircut. He sits down, folds his arms across his chest and stretches his legs out, crossing them at the ankles. His eyes are bright green and close together. We've said so little to one another, but looking into those eyes, I feel judged. For what, I don't know.

Joe, who seems oblivious to the conversation, drops the board he's been inspecting, removes his thick, tinted glasses and starts cleaning them on his sleeveless, collarless AC/DC t-shirt. "Hey, do either one of you know of an ancestral method for sharpening a katana?"

"Oh, yeah," Gavin says, picking up a black marker from the table. "I do."

"No shit?" Joe puts his glasses back on. The expression behind them, it's something between disbelief and pleasant surprise. I don't think Joe's accustomed to receiving serious responses to his bullshit.

"Nope. No shit." He removes the cap from the marker and sniffs it. "Wait." He points the marker at Joe, tilts his head and says, "You do know a samurai, or a master, right?"

In this moment, I have no concern whatsoever for Neil's impossible deadlines, the hundreds of boards I have to inspect, the demise of my relationship or the fact that I have to move with my aged cat to a lonely apartment this weekend. Nothing else matters except for this absurd conversation taking place in my workroom.

"Oh, yeah. Of course." Joe nods.

"Okay, great." Gavin leans forward in his chair. "So, here's what you do, then."

I'm captivated as Gavin the temp accountant proceeds to give Joe a strange list of instructions involving the collection of certain kinds of rocks, tree branches and fabrics, what rituals to perform with his samurai and how to light the "ancestral fire". At the end of it, Joe looks confused.

"Wait. Where am I supposed to find those stones?"

Gavin points toward the back of the building with his marker. "I saw some out back behind the building next to the parking lot. I noticed because I thought about taking some home for my own katana."

"Right on. I'm gonna go check that out." Joe stands up and drops the board he'd been inspecting on the table.

"Dude," I say. "What about electrical test by five?"

"I'll come back, don't worry. It's only a twenty-minute drive to Loveland, anyway."

He hurries out of the room and I turn to Gavin, who's sniffing the marker again. "You don't own a katana."

"You don't know. I could own a katana."

"You're a terrible person." I take the marker from him and toss it on the table.

"But, it was funny, right?" He nods, looking pleased with himself. "You thought it was funny."

"You don't know what I thought."

"Sure I do. You smirked. You're amused."

Maybe I smirked. Maybe he's not wrong. I can't tell if he's a comedian, or an asshole, If I'm repulsed or charmed is just as much of a mystery, but trying to figure it out feels like too much of an effort.

"Look," I say. "Joe talks a lot of shit. It's what he does."

"He's a loser. You know it. I know it." Gavin tilts his head, looking pensive. "Not sure if he knows it, though."

"I'm pretty sure loserdom is subjective," I say.

"What?"

"Never mind. Joe's a good guy."

I change the topic to the dull subject of my boring fucking job, explaining to Gavin the Temp Accountant how circuit boards are made. I tell him about everyone else's boring fucking job; how Joe's wife Debbie obtains the artwork from a client and how the holes are drilled into panels of copper and fiberglass that Lucy puts an image on. How Barry stands on his goddamn feet for ten hours every day silk screening solder mask on them and all about the poor bastards electroplating in the back who stand around a bunch of chemical tanks all day, dunking panels in a variety of toxic soup.

I explain to Gavin how it isn't supposed to be as sloppy as all this, that other board shops have newer equipment, newer facilities, better air conditioning and more employees, but he doesn't show much interest in any of it.

"Damn. Your give-a-shitter isn't processing any of this. You really are a temp, aren't you?"

He nods. "I'm just here for the summer. I'm taking a break from school."

I'm about to ask him for more details because someone going to school and working here isn't a common thing, but Lucy bursts in, flinging the door open and laughing her ass off. She closes the door and drops in the chair next to mine. She grabs my arm.

"Okay," she says. "What the fuck. Why is Joe outside digging around in the gravel?"

Gavin tells her about his brilliant prank and I'm defeated when Lucy laughs even harder and tells Gavin how hilarious he is. My defeat hardens to full-on aggravation when she decides to invite him to go have a beer with us after work.

Fucking Lucy, man.

Committed

The owner of The Bit of Billiards understands the importance of location. Every day, all of us cogs from Circuit's End along with all the other employees of Sunset Industrial Park have to pass by the bar on our way home. Many of us don't pass by. We stop and drink. Working as a mindless cog day in and day out makes you thirsty.

The three of us seat ourselves at a little round table close to the bar. Lucy and I each order a Fat Tire. Gavin inquires as to why this bar serves Guinness instead of Murphy's. Lucy waves her hand, tells him not to be a beer snob, that this is Longmont, Colorado; there are too many local beers available to be pissing and moaning about some old Irish shit. Finally, he orders a 1554 and mutters something about Belgium, but I'm not listening.

When we all have our beers, Lucy pokes me in the arm. "Carlos has to work on Saturday, but I'm gonna borrow his truck so I can help you move."

"You're moving?" Gavin leans back in his chair. "Where are you moving to?"

"To another apartment here in town." No more details. I don't know him well enough for details.

Lucy turns to Gavin. "She's moving in to her own place. She broke up with her boyfriend this weekend." Lucy, on the other hand, has decided I do know him well enough for details. Fucking Lucy, man.

"Oh. Sorry." He grimaces, tilts his head, then busies himself pouring his beer into his glass.

"After twelve years. She told him she's moving out, then they went out for breakfast. Can you believe that shit?"

"Nice, Luce. Tell the dude my whole life story like I'm not even sitting here."

She turns to me and blinks slowly. "Don't worry. I will, if you stop interrupting."

Gavin shrugs. "I'll help you move."

"I met you this morning. We haven't known each other long enough to be moving friends." Lucy has decided Gavin and I are acquainted enough for details, but no way are we familiar enough to be moving friends.

"I know you're a good breaker upper."

Lucy laughs. "That's because she spent two years thinking about it before she did it."

Gavin looks me in the eye. "You must've been committed. I admire people who are able to commit to something."

I wonder if he's making a snide, backhanded compliment, but the way he's smiling at me feels sympathetic. Warm. Lucy shouts at someone over by the pool tables and leaves us to go talk to whoever it is because she knows half of Longmont. Gavin leans forward and says, "I think it shows fortitude to stick with something, even when you know deep down that it's over."

His nonsense about fortitude conjures an image in my mind of a fish bouncing in the dirt, reaching out with its dying, gasping fish lips for a chance of life while its eyes say that it knows death is right in front of him. All the stupid, gasping fishes in the world have more fortitude than I ever will.

What he's mistaken for fortitude was in reality, fear of change. It took me two years to find the courage to hurt Walter. Fortitude had nothing to do with anything, but I'm not not about to correct him.

"You sound like someone who's never been in a long-term relationship," I say.

"I haven't. I'm only twenty-one."

"That's not much of an excuse." I point toward the pool tables. "Lucy was a married mother long before she was that old."

His reply is silence. We're both aware of the fact that his twenty-one is different from the twenty-one Lucy and I and everyone else at Circuit's End lived through. I don't bother asking for any details. Not because I don't know him well enough. Because I don't care. Nothing Gavin can tell me about his life is going to interest me. Either he shat the bed somewhere along the line and he's more of a loser than he thinks he is, and that's why he's working with us, or he's a tourist, slumming for the summer. Or maybe it's neither one of those things and I just don't want to hear about the lives of college kids who tuck in their shirt and bitch when the beer isn't European enough.

Lucy comes back and sits down, a little out of breath for some reason. She tells us some gossip about the person she was talking to over at the pool tables, and then starts asking me about my paintings.

"They're not paintings, exactly." I wave at the server, hoping that ordering another round will be distracting enough to take the topic away from me and onto something else equally dull but less awkward for me.

"Okay, well your fucking ghost or spirit masks or whatever they are. You gonna keep making them?"

"I don't see why not. All the other details of my life won't change."

Lucy tilts her head and one corner of her mouth pulls down, which is a tacit way of telling me that I'm bullshitting myself. Great. First Walter. Now Lucy. I don't know me, but they do. Gavin is interested, asking me about painting. When Lucy tells him that I should sell them instead of hoarding them in a closet, he's even more intrigued. The way he leans forward and smiles as he probes and questions me could be flattering, if not for the cold green eyes that make me feel like I'm under a microscope. As though learning that the factory monkey can play with a paintbrush is fascinating.

The need for beer refills is the diversion I had hoped for. Gavin asks how long Lucy and I have been friends, why we went to the same school and work at the same job.

"Dude," Lucy says. "PCB workers are almost like carnies, you know? If you quit or get fired from one board shop, you move on to the next one. Most of us know each other, or know of one another. We all wander around from board shop to board shop. Me and Axel both worked at Redstone Circuits in Boulder at the same time, too. We didn't even really become good friends until Redstone."

Lucy pulls her hair down, twists it all back up into a shiny black knot on top of her head and tightens it. Effortless and perfect. "What about you?" She juts her chin out at Gavin. "What're you doing out among the riffraff, college boy? You're not even from around here, are you?"

Gavin shakes his head. "Nah. Not too far, though. Moved here from Cheyenne. I'm taking business economics at CU, but I wanted an easy job for the summer."

I shake my head and lean back in my seat. "Why in the hell would you want to spend your summer working in a board shop, inhaling chemicals and listening to machinery all day long?"

He takes a drink of his beer and smirks. "Just to help out Neil. He's my uncle." Gavin shrugs. "And I was interested in seeing how the other half live, you know?"

"The other half?" Lucy leans forward, bursting with a laughter so great that you can see all of her teeth.

"Chrissakes, man," I say to Gavin over the sound of Lucy's hysteria. "You really oughta get out more."

Closet

My dad found Tocki underneath the wooden deck of our house when I was twelve. He'd been working on his motorcycle in the garage when he heard the distressed mewing and went searching, knowing there was a wounded animal nearby. I was curled up on the ratty gray couch watching TV when he came flying through the door with this tiny, furry mess in his arms.

"Go get a towel from the bathroom." He wrapped it around the cat and handed the bundle to me. "Hold on to him. Not too tight. We're gonna go run him down to the animal hospital."

"Is he gonna die?" A wave of panic shot through me. I didn't know what to do if he died in my arms, or if he were to suddenly freak out and bite my face, injecting me with a mouthful of rabies.

"I dunno, Kid." My dad squeezed my shoulder and grabbed his keys from the kitchen counter. "He looks pretty bad off. We're gonna help him anyway."

On the way to the animal hospital, the cat barely moved at all. His breathing was steady and a couple of times, I thought I heard him purring. One of his ears had been torn and kept twitching. Blood had matted his black and gray fur and had dried on his face. I couldn't take my eyes off of him. I was afraid that if I did, some sort of spell or invisible lifeline might be broken, causing his breathing and purring to cease. Tocki must have believed in it, too, because he never stopped looking at me, either.

The vet told us it was most likely a dog that had gotten a hold of Tocki, that he was lucky to be alive. The vet cleaned him, stitched him up and said he'd be taken to an animal shelter. My dad rubbed his beard, which was still mostly dark brown at the time, and he looked hard into my eyes. I kept waiting for him to tell me something, but instead, he turned to the vet and said, "Nah, it's all right. We'll take him home with us."

The vet tried to explain to my old man that this was a stray cat. He was young, but likely too feral to make a good pet. The vet didn't know my dad. His mind was already made up. My old man, he looked at the vet and in his low, gravelly monotone said, "I'm sure he'll fit right in."

On the way home, Tocki sat between us on the bench seat of my dad's truck, cone of shame around his neck, bits of fur shaved off and replaced with bandages.

"He's your cat," my dad said.

"Okay."

"You feed him, scoop his shit and make his vet appointments."

"Okay."

Then he did something strange. He laughed and said, "Your mom always hated cats."

I believed him because I had no reason not to. I had no evidence or memory of the contrary. I didn't know much about her, and I thought he knew everything about anything, including her. I was only certain about one thing when it came to my mother. I knew she was lousy at goodbyes. When I was in the third grade, I arrived home from school one day to find a note saying that she went to live somewhere else and I never saw or heard from her again.

Tocki may have been a stray until the day my old man found him under the deck, but he never strayed from me. After he came to live with us, he never even showed any interest in venturing outside again. He ended up with a few scars and a weird-looking ear, and was like a little brother to me. Even my hard-assed, motorcycle-riding father looked content when he'd fall asleep in his reclining chair with Tocki curled up and purring away on his chest.

When I left that house six years later to live with Walter, Tocki came with me, curled up in a laundry basket in the backseat of my ugly brown Oldsmobile. And when I brought him here a few weeks ago, to this tiny one-bedroom apartment, he wandered around, confused and restless until I threw his little blue cat bed on the floor. He snuggled himself inside it like that bed was all he needed in the whole world. I envied him.

We've been living in this place for almost a month, but we're still surrounded by stacks of hastily packed boxes and bare walls. Every day, when I come home from work, I look around at these stark white surroundings and realize that alone, I don't have much of a life to display. Digging around in boxes and albums, there's only photos of my life with Walter, nothing that says who I am without him. Nothing to symbolize my tastes or interests. Nothing that proves I am someone, even if I'm with no one.

I come across a few photos of me and Tocki, so I pull a couple of Walter photos out of their frames and replace them. They're the wrong size for the frames and once I hang them, I'm certain this is the type of decor that would be in the house of that crazy cat lady on *The Simpsons*, but I don't care. If that's where I'm headed, I don't see any alternative to embracing it with both hands. After all, I made this choice.

Then I think, "Oh, Walter is going to crack up when I tell him I'm turning into that crazy cartoon cat lady," because a brain can take a while to catch up to the fact that a person you were connected to is no longer there.

There's photos of my father. My old man riding his bike. Standing next to his bike. Working on his bike. Polishing his bike. More pictures of him with that goddamn Shovelhead than his daughter. I find an old one with the two of us that I like and even though he and I haven't spoken for almost twelve years, I hang it up. Then I walk away, change my mind, come back and take it down, then hang it on the wall again. I stand there staring at it, thinking I should just go to the fucking mall and get some cheap, cheesy paintings of random barns and bridges and shit. Things that have no emotional weight to them, because decorating an apartment and unpacking memories is exhausting. My apartment will look like the waiting room of a dentist's office, but I can deal with this by telling any possible future guests that medical waiting rooms are one of my many interests. People find others fascinating if they're into quirky shit.

I consider this for a few minutes, then decide I can't pull off quirky charm, so fuck it.

Between the pages of an old album that makes dry crackling sounds when I open it is a picture of my mother. It's the only photo I have of her, and if I didn't come across it every so often, I would have already forgotten what she looked like. Which is the very reason my father saved this one photo and made me keep it. A few months after she left, he emptied the house of every reminder of her. Every single one except for me and this photo. The old man, he said I should remember my mother's face. Who knows why he says shit like that. I didn't care much either way at the time, but every few years, when I look at it, I want it less and less, then I have a brief internal debate about throwing it away. The face I'm looking at belongs to a stranger. A stranger who didn't want to be anything else to me. A stranger with a hard mouth and cold eyes who I never sought to know or forgive. There's a sort of freedom to be gained by forgetting your mother's unhappy face. You don't have to grow older and watch yourself turning into her. You get to grow into yourself.

But, I'm not ready for absolute freedom, so I stick the photo back in the album, slam it shut and drop it in a box that I shove into the closet. Right next to the box labeled "masks" and on top of a box of books about the Old West. When Walter and I had guests, they'd see the bookcase and assume the Old West magazines and biographies of Billy the Kid and Wild Bill Hickok belonged to Walter. I don't know what in the hell they were thinking. He never cracked open anything besides automotive manuals or boring car magazines.

I open a box of books with the intention of unpacking, but this only leads to me scattering books all over the floor, revisiting each one, geeking out on the old stories, remembering the time when I was still in junior high and I rode on the back of the old man's bike; we went down to Golden and rode up Lookout Mountain to see Buffalo Bill Cody's grave.

I decide that sitting among a pile of dusty books on the floor of my apartment would be better with beer, so I start drinking and lose track of the time. Tocki comes wandering in, yowling and chiding me for being late with the dinner service. His voice is hoarse; his mews are raspy. The delicate way he lowers his bony little butt to the floor and lays down is so cautious and fragile. His paws resting on a hardcover history of the Lincoln County War. I run my fingers along his back. The fur above his tail is always greasy and sticking up because he hasn't been able to clean back there for a long time. He can't bend that way anymore. I leave the books and empty beer bottles scattered on the floor of my lonely little bedroom, scoop up my feline brother and take him to the sleeping bag which is laid out on floor of our tiny living room. I grab what's left of last night's rotisserie chicken and turn on the TV.

We sprawl out and eat cold chicken until it's just the two of us and a clean chicken carcass laying there. Then Tocki creeps down to the foot of the bag and snuggles himself inside it like cold chicken and a sleeping bag on the floor is all he needs in the whole world. I envy him.

Go With It

I come back from scarfing down another crappy drive-thru lunch in my car, and walk in on Joe and Debbie fighting in my room. Scraping by week to week at a sad job where I'm sitting on my ass in a room that has more windows than walls. Not a fucking one of them lets me look outside, but lets everyone in the shop who passes by peer in as though I were boxed up in some stinking blue collar aquarium. All day long, people walking by, knocking and tapping things on the glass, pressing their fat asses up against it because everyone thinks the pressing ham gag never gets old. Day in, day out, the stink of solder mask and fumes from the toxic chemical soup in the electroplate area fill everyone's lungs, not to mention the flux that goes straight up my nose. Benefits are the absolute minimum Neil can get away with, no bonuses. Ever.

And now his goddamn brain trust is engaging in one of their white trash marital spats at my table.

I'm still holding my greasy fast food bag, so I reach in and grab a few hot sauce packets. I fling them in the direction of the bickering, which catches them both off guard. Most of them hit Debbie and one sticks in her curly blonde hair for a moment before it falls to the floor. She takes a step backwards, squishes the thing and shoots cheap taco sauce across the shiny speckled gray and white tile.

"Nice, Axel. Real fucking professional." She steps over the mess in an elegant way that reminds me of the ballerina hippos in *Fantasia* and sulks away.

"What's up with her?" I squat down and wipe up the sauce with a taco napkin.

"Aw, she's just... you know." Joe waves his hand up over his head, then turns around and leans over some paperwork on the table.

"Everything all right?" I'm not asking because I care, but because I'm curious. Debbie is a boring woman, but she's nice enough. I don't notice her much during the day. In spite of her massive size, she's not visible all that often. For as long as I've worked here, she's been sitting in the front office, noshing and gossiping, surfing the internet and declining in health. Every time I take a good look at her, she seems a few pounds heavier, her eyes a deeper shade of bloodshot. Her skin, a more alarming shade of sallow.

"Yeah, it's all good. Just not seeing eye-to-eye on something."

"Okay, man."

"You know, we get along great most of the time, but sometimes, me and Debbie, we have violent fits. Total knock-down drag-outs. This one time, she lunged at me with a knife. I held my arm in a classic defense stance. I should have used a disarming technique. Anyway, I was bleeding, but I remained silent. Then I told her 'Look at this. This does nothing to me. Nothing.' Every time, after she spazzes out like that, she'll bust out crying in my arms. Love is crazy. Hot and cold, you know?"

I think back on various arguments that Walter and I had, but couldn't bring to mind a single incident where bleeding or cutlery was involved. Knowing what a shit talker Joe is, I decide his account of passionate domestic violence is worth blowing off, even if listening to it makes me feel kind of awkward and wondering if I've been missing out on some incendiary fireworks in my love life.

Then I wonder if one day the two of them will passionately stab one another at work. I hope it won't be here in my room.

"Shit. I just remembered a thing I have to talk to Lucy about." I start for the door, thinking I've made a quick escape.

Joe snaps his fingers. "That's what I meant to tell you."

"What?"

"She had to go home for the day. Something about her kid being sick or something."

I'm sure it's bullshit, that she got tired of being at work and decided to take off. Sometimes Abigail has an indisputable illness, but now and then, Lucy uses motherhood as a get-out-of-work-free card. I know this because she told me about it one night after a couple of kamikaze shots at The Bit of Billiards.

"So, I was wondering," Joe says, "if you'd mind taking over Image for the rest of the day while she's gone."

"Oh, you've got to be fucking kidding me, dude."

"No kid. It's backed up to high hell in there and you're the only person here with any experience at Image. I mean, besides me. And I'm busy."

Fucking Lucy, man. "Why do you even bother asking if I mind when I obviously have to go back there and do it?"

He shrugs. "Bein' polite."

Defeated, I head to the back of the building to the Image room. There's one narrow window too high to see out of that makes the room look like it was designed to be a prison cell. It's covered with a clear sheet of yellow Mylar. The fluorescent lights in the ceiling, those are yellow, too. Yellow, yellow everywhere, so that every motherfucker who walks in here or works as an Image technician in a circuit board shop looks like they have jaundice. It's Green Lantern's worst nightmare. This room, it's not for claustrophobes, either. The exposer machine, which is basically a giant camera, takes up half of the room. The other half is occupied by a lamination machine which was outdated several years ago. Most board shops, they have automatic machines. Put a stack of copper-coated fiberglass panels on one end, they come out the other end with a nice, smooth sheet of blue or green film on the surface. The internal parts of the machine are hot, but the rest of the room is always a cool 72° Fahrenheit.

Not our machine. Our machine is an archaic piece of shit that requires the user to stand in front of the 300°F rollers, slicing each sheet of film with a goddamn razor blade and delivering plenty of cuts, burns and wafting poison laminate fumes. This room, it's yellow and always hot, but it has a stereo, so I change the station from Lucy's lame classic rock and set the dial to the indie station that no one here listens to except me. I crank up Nick Cave singing a weeping song and stew in my disdain for my job, telling myself how I'm fed up with shit and first thing Monday morning, I'm calling in sick and finding another job. But it's not the truth. It's just the angry, frustrated nonsense I tell myself to fuel even angrier, frustrated nonsense. It took me years to even find the words to end my relationship. I'm sure it'll take me a few more years to muster up another dose of courage to quit my job. The only reason I'm here and not at my previous job is because they had the good sense to fire me. Maybe they knew if they didn't take the initiative and shit-can me, I'd never go anywhere. Neil would never do anything decent like firing me.

I'm deep in my self-pity trance, sweating and slicing film with a razor blade when Gavin comes in. He points at the stereo. "Really?" He raises his eyebrows in the form of a question. "I had you pegged as more of a butt-rock or klan-rock type of music fan."

"Well, that's what you get for pegging people."

"You're probably right. Mea culpa. So, how's the new digs?"

I shrug. "All right, I guess. I'm still unpacking and getting situated. Thanks again for helping with the move, by the way." In truth, I'm not thankful, since Gavin showed up late, then only helped Lucy and me empty one truckload before suddenly remembering some baby cousin's birthday party that he had to fuck off to. Lucy said carrying a box of dishes up a flight of stairs was too much for him. I gave him the benefit of the doubt, because I didn't mind him leaving us alone. But throwing a "thanks again" for his half-assed effort from a month ago somehow feels like something meaningless to say to fill in a silence since he is standing here chatting with me for whatever reason.

"Yeah, no problem. Let me know the next time you move and I'll be there. At least to carry a box or two." He grins and I notice for the first time that his smirk is just on one side of his face and am annoyed at myself for finding it cute. Then I giggle and want to punch myself in the throat.

"So," he says. "When're you getting out of here today?"

"I dunno. Four. Maybe four-thirty. Why do you query, sir?"

"I was wondering if you wanted to stop by the bar, maybe have a quick beer after work."

"It's Friday. Better make it more than just 'a quick beer'."

"Aces." He gives two thumbs up in a dorky manner befitting the front office accounting nerd that he is. "Come shout at me in the office when you're ready to clock out."

He walks out, hands in pockets, slouched over, the toes of his big clown feet pointing outward. I wipe the sweat off my forehead, turn the stereo up, and continue slicing.

My phone rings and I hate myself for not turning the ringer off before passing out last night. It's Saturday morning, so when I see the screen telling me it's Lucy calling and that it's just after eight o'clock in the morning, I answer it and say, "I am going to murder you," because a simple "hello" is not appropriate for occasions such as this.

"Yeah, yeah," she says. "Murder me in Deadwood, then."

"What the hell are you talking about?"

"I'm talking about a road trip. Carlos is taking Abigail down to Colorado Springs to hang out with his parents for a week next month. That means free time. And you're turning into one of those weird, lonely cat ladies. So, we're going on a road trip."

Whenever Lucy's in-laws want to spend time with their son and their granddaughter, it's always with the understanding that the visit will not include their daughter-in-law. I was never quite able to grasp the reasons why, only that it had something to do with Lucy being a devil. Or a whore. Or a devil-whore of some kind.

"Luce, no way is Neil gonna let us both have the same week off."

"Ah, fuck that bald-ass diptard. He can hire a temp, or have Joe fill in. There's not a whole helluva lot he can do about it. It's not like he'll fire us. Come on. You know you want to. I can play black jack. You can get your nerd on with all your goofy-ass cowboy bullshit."

"Calamity Jane," I say.

"What the fuck?"

"Calamity Jane. She wasn't a cowboy."

"Whatever. Fucking nerd. We're going. It's either this or Vegas."

"Gross. No way am I going to Vegas. Okay, fine. We're going."

I talk to her for another minute that feels like an hour, then end the call, hang my arm off the edge of the bed and let the phone drop to the floor. I let my eyes close again, wishing the sandy, gritty eyelids away. Then I hear the buzzing to my left. Buzz. Buzz. Buzzzzzzzzzzzzz. Then the giggling.

Opening my eyes and leaning on my elbows, I squint at Gavin, wielding a purple dildo and his lopsided smirk. Dark curls hanging in his close set green eyes. "What's this?" He wants to know as he starts to climb on top of me.

"Oh, that's a magical device. If used often enough, it can help to prevent you from making foolish decisions."

"Wow. Last night was a foolish decision? Show me how this works."

"You're so smart, you show me how it works."

Clean

Tocki is curled up on Gavin's lap, oblivious to the bouncing caused by Gavin's *King of the Hill* induced laughter. His long feet are up on my coffee table, one hand stroking Tocki's back while the other stuffs pretzels into his mouth. There's a hole in his white tube sock and pretzel crumbs on his white undershirt. I've never been with a guy who wears an undershirt.

"This is a good one." He points at the TV. "It's the one where Hank and Ladybird dance."

"Okay, are you sure you two will be all right?" For an instant, it occurs to me that perhaps my father experienced similar feelings of uneasiness when he'd take off for one of his weekend-long bike runs when I was a teenager. Only for an instant, because then I think, as often as he left me and Tocki alone, he mustn't have been too worried about us.

"We'll be fine." Gavin gently sets Tocki on the cushion next to him. He brushes pretzel dust off himself and onto my floor. He ambles over to me. "We're gonna miss you, though." He wraps one hand around my waist and the other around my back, pulling me toward him. "Work is going to be boring without you there."

"Speaking of, you sure nobody knows that you're staying here with Tocki while we're gone?"

"Oh, I told everyone. I told 'em that we're doin' it, too." He dry humps my leg like a dog.

"Hilarious."

"Yeah. I'm joking. But not about missing you."

During the past month, Gavin's been at my place more than his own. Almost every night after work, I find excuses to ditch Lucy or anyone else who wants to stop for a drink or a bowl after work. Gavin never fails to come up with clever and creative stories to tell his uncle Neil about how he spends his evenings. Every morning, one of us is always late for work so that we never arrive at the same time. There is a voice inside of me that is awake and mature, shouting at me about being irresponsible, about being cruel and careless with a young kid's feelings and using human beings as sex toys. It's often muted by the fists of another voice that just wants to get laid by someone under forty with clean hands that aren't covered in engine grease.

When I catch him staring at me with schoolboy crush painted all over his face, I know I'm doing the wrong thing. When I'm thinking up new lies about how I spend my free time or at work pretending to feel like Gavin's just some arrogant, dorky little shit, the wrong thing prickles through my veins and skin strong enough to tense my muscles. Each day this happens, and each day I push it all out of my mind with more rum and Gavin's dick because my boxes are finally unpacked. My walls are finally decorated and I'm sleeping in my bed in my bedroom like a grown-up in her own home instead of in a sleeping bag on the living room floor like a squatter making a temporary pit stop.

I push it away because his sense of adventure seems to make up for his lack of experience, so even though it's doomed, I figure when the end comes, he'll be able to take it. He'll find some awkward, studious girl who makes sense standing next to him. And I'll meet another Walter, another guy with sweat and dark smudges on his face at the end of the day who's still into Nugent, loud cars and bimbos with damaged hair because other than a haughty naive kid, I haven't attracted the interest of anything other than carbon copies of my father. Then again, I haven't been trying to meet anyone else. I'm not sure I know how to do that. Sometimes, at the bar with Lucy, she'll tell me, "Hey, that guy's checking you out. Make sexy eyes at him." I give it a whirl, then see the guy's expression morph from flirtatious to confused. According to Lucy, my sexy eyes stare too long, don't blink enough, and say, "I want to eat your skin."

In the parking lot outside the front window of my apartment, Lucy's black Chevy pickup growls low and steady. She gives the horn a quick bleep. I nuzzle Tocki one more time and hurry outside, trying to ignore the imagined invisible thread pulling at me from deep inside my gut, commanding me to go back inside my apartment.

We leave Longmont behind and enter I-25 when Lucy asks who'll be cat sitting Tocki during the week we're in Deadwood. I tell her a neighbor's taking care of everything and without hesitation, she asks which one. Not because she's prying, but because she's making the normal sort of conversation that regular people make when they're not hiding their boss's nephew in their apartment. My mind does a rapid flip through mental photos of the few random neighbors I'd seen during the short time I've lived there. It occurs to me that I haven't met a single person in the building and that the few people I've seen might not even live there.

Lucy, in her observant and gregarious existence, likely knows my neighbors better than I do.

"Is it Creepy Sexy Mormon Guy?" Lucy's so tiny, the way she wraps both arms around the steering wheel of her truck, she always looks like a child pretending to drive like a grown-up.

"Who?"

"You know. That weird but good-looking Mormon dude who lives across the hall from you? In the gross sweater vest? 'Member? We shot the shit with him for a few the day we moved you in."

"Oh, uh… no, not that guy. It's a lady."

"What? Not the call girl with the C.C. Deville hair?"

"Who? Seriously, Luce. How in the fuck do you know all these people?"

She leans back in the driver's seat, turns away from the road for a moment and curls her lip. "Jesus, what crawled up your ass? We need to find you some dick in Deadwood, or what?"

"No. I'm getting plenty of dick, thanks."

"Whoa. What? Are you and Walter getting back together? Where'd you find a dick?" Now she's about to go full-on bobble head, from me to the road. To the road to the rearview to me.

It's too much. I've never been good at seizing an opportunity to be silent. Lies have always been too complicated for me. They require too much work, so I stumble into a fit of logorrhea about all the time I've been spending with Gavin, the lame bullshit excuses I'd been giving her for not hanging out with her as much, the fact that he was in my apartment when she came to pick me up and how he'll be staying there the entire week we're gone. I confess my awareness of doing a wrong and stupid thing and I admit that I would even feel embarrassed to be seen out in public with Gavin in a couple situation, especially if we ever ran into Walter. I go on and on for miles and miles. When I come up for air, Lucy giggles and shakes her head.

"It's about time you came clean, because you two are both lousy bullshitters."

"So you were just fucking with me about Creepy Sexy Mormon Guy."

"Of course I was fucking with you. Did you really think I wouldn't notice what was going on with you two? Duh. We work together. We spend all day together." She slaps my thigh. "Besides, I know you, Chica."

Fucking Lucy, man. The mother and the sister I never had. Can't get anything past her.

Don't Wanna Cry

During dinner on the night we arrived, Lucy said, "Getting high and drinking gets me too fucked up now."

"Yeah, I can't party like that anymore, either," I shook my head. "It has to be one or the other because I'm too old for that shit, now. My body can't take it."

"Well, not so old, unless you're hung over. I think the severity of the hangover directly correlates with age. But, yeah. Definitely too old for that stupid shit."

We have one night of vacation left and are no longer too old for stupid shit. We are now the appropriate age for all manner of stupid shit. Lucy hasn't fallen out of control with the blackjack. I don't even understand the game, so I end up wandering with a Long Island Iced Tea in my hand, dicking around with a few slot machines after I grow bored of watching her play. I don't mind keeping myself entertained in the casinos and Lucy doesn't complain when I drag her to the cemetery to make gravestone rubbings, even though I have to keep correcting her every time she says Buffalo Bill instead of Wild Bill.

I'm hunched over in front of a nickel slot machine, a few nickels in my fist and a beer in the other hand when Mr. Perfect Stubble with movie star shiny black hair sits down on the stool next to mine as if it belongs to him. His grey button-up shirt is unbuttoned enough to make it clear I'd like what's underneath, but not low enough to declare, "sleaze bag." Whatever his flaws, they aren't on the outside. Spotless clothes. Perfect, clean fingernails. He's a well put-together guy who spent a lot of time and money to look this way and probably has a good job. Physically, he's out of my league, so I still read "sleaze bag."

He asks if he can buy me a drink and 'm not sure how to respond, so I do the cowardly thing and fall into affable mode. I smile, let him buy me another Long Island and tune out the small talk he's spewing at me because I'm distracted by the realization that I'm not sure if time spent with Gavin is because of a relationship, or if I'm still single. If I am single, it's a problem. I don't know how to manage that because I'm thirty years old and haven't been untethered in almost a dozen years. That train of thought drops off a twinge of guilt; I wonder if I'm cruel because it'd be nice to be seen sitting across from a guy like this in a restaurant instead of Gavin, with his unkempt hair curling into his disturbing green eyes and lanky, boyish body.

Yet, looking at this stranger who looks as though he ought to pose in an ad for men's cologne, I can't sweep the image Gavin, sitting on my couch with my cat clean from my mind.

I laugh and nod and sip my drink until Lucy rescues me and fills in any awkward gaps in the conversation with her magical gift of feeling comfortable while chatting up total strangers. Shooting the shit and boozing are going at a good pace. The realization hits me that we'll be stuck with this guy for the rest of the night, but then he tells us he has to go meet up with his buddy. There's some idle talk about meeting up later, but I assume we'll blow him off.

I'm feeling drunk, but not enough to stop caring yet, so random bits of my life reel before my eyes. The worst fragments float around in my inebriated mind and bring me down until the brightness of the casino becomes overwhelming. I don't understand how to be a single adult. I don't know my mother. I missed my twenties. I never attended college; never had that college experience people say is so important. I haven't spoken to my father in years. My cat is old and looks sick. I hate my job. My boss is an 80s reject who thinks he's the last fucking samurai.

Lucy and I go outside because she wants to smoke. I talk her into giving me a cigarette because when she's wasted, it's easy to convince her that it's not a big deal I quit. I tell her Tocki is old and not doing well. I'm not sure how much longer he'll be around. I'm scared. I tell her this thing with Gavin freaks me out. I start crying a little. I wonder why I ever quit smoking because this feels so much better even though it's assaulting my throat and making me cough.

"What the fuck, dude," Lucy holds both her hands up, displaying the palms. "You need to chill out, for real."

"I know. Sorry."

"And, c'mon. Don't worry. Tocki is tough. And you're allowed a rebound fling. Don't let it stress you out."

"A fling? Maybe it's not a fling."

"Oh, really?" She throws her head back and laughs, showing her straight, impeccable teeth. I run my tongue along my own crooked teeth and recall my father telling the dentist that braces are a waste of money. "Man, you're drunk. Why would you want to get serious about some dopey college kid right after you finally found balls enough to leave Walter and be on your own? Why can't you just enjoy it?"

Everything she's conveying to me, the laughing, the head shaking, none of it is wrong. I know this, but I feel myself resisting all of it, wanting her to be wrong.

"Yeah, I know," I say. "But he's fun. Frustrating, but fun."

"And he's decent in bed?"

"Yeah. I mean, I think so. I don't have a lot to compare it to."

"So, have fun while it lasts, until something better comes along. You told me one of the reasons you left Walter was because you felt like you missed your twenties and wanted to have your own life. Now you have it. You have no idea how much I fucking envy you."

"Why would you envy me? You already have what everybody wants. A husband, a kid, a house. All that shit."

"That's not what everybody wants. You think I wanted to be a mom? It just happened. It's hard. And back in the day, in high school, Carlos was awesome. He was hot, he was funny. Now he makes my fucking skin crawl. If I was in your shoes, man... I sure wouldn't waste it."

"Dude. Carlos looks like Enrique Iglesias. He's still hot."

"Ugh. He's hot when you don't live with him."

"I thought you were digging being a mom."

"I never said that." She shakes her head and lights a new cigarette from the old one. She wobbles for a moment, recovers then crushes the butt. "You have no idea. For real. I just wanna run away from home all the fucking time."

What I hear isn't that Lucy wants to run away. What I hear is all runaway mothers confessing that they didn't want to be a mom. That they didn't care about their kids. The only female friend, the mother and the sister I never had, is the same breed as my own mother. I wonder where the sacred nurturing mothers are that other people write songs and stories about.

"Yeah," I wave my hand at her. "Runaway from home like you're doing right now?"

"What? We're just hanging out like we always do."

"You ran away from home. Instead of spending time with your kid, you're here getting shitfaced with me."

"Yeah. Today."

"That's fucked up."

Her face changes from soft happy drunk to belligerent. "Why is that fucked up? You act like I'm never going back home."

"Well, don't you miss her?"

"Of course I miss her."

"I haven't seen you call home."

"Jesus, Axel. All our other road trips, you were never a bitch like this. I don't have to defend my parenting skills to you." She walks off and goes back inside the casino. My first thought is not to chase after her, but to find more smokes because she has taken the cigarettes with her. I know she's pissed at me, but feel like there's a good chance she'll get over it soon enough, so I decide to embark on a quest to obtain my own pack of cigarettes, convincing myself that I won't smoke more than one or two because I quit smoking.

When I return to the casino, I'm feeling good. I've had a moment to reflect on how I'd almost descended into being a crying drunk and risen above it to happy drunkie. It warms me like only a tiny internal triumph can. I've had a couple of smokes, walked off some of the confusion and frustration and am ready to find Lucy so we can go back to normal.

I wander around the blackjack tables, but fail to locate her. I make my way through the entire casino and then figure she must have said "fuck it" for the rest of this night and gone back to our room. I pause near the bar for a moment, considering one more Long Island before heading to the motel. That's when I see Gray Shirt and his sleek black hair, leaning down, his hands on Lucy's face, pushing his tongue down her throat.

"Are you kidding me, Luce?" I put my hand on her shoulder. "Okay, dude. We need to go."

"Go? I'm not gonna go shit." Lucy's been passing the time with Captain Morgan while I was out on my cigarette quest. Her drunk level has far surpassed mine.

Gray Shirt is laughing, stroking the stubble on his cheek.

"Go shit? Really?" I turn to Gray Shirt. "You can see how hammered she is. And she's married."

"Settle down." His tone isn't playful. It's commanding. "She's fine."

"I'm not fucked up, bitch. You're fucked up." Lucy pokes her finger at my arm, but her aim is off and she jabs it into my armpit instead. If that wasn't weird enough, she does it a second time.

"You're not wasted? You're finger banging my armpit."

"Oh, shut the fuck up."

The debate escalates from there. It doesn't take long for the bartender to come over and kick us out. Gray Shirt giggles until his face is red and tears well in his eyes. When I turn to flip him off as we leave, he doesn't see it because he's too busy wiping hysterical laughter from his cheeks.

Come Back Home

Across the table from me, the large magnifying glass of the halo lamp Joe's using distorts his face like an evil funhouse mirror. We're touching up flaws in a small stack of circuit boards with skinny paintbrushes. Each of us holds a tiny paper cup like the ones you put ketchup in, but ours are filled with green solder mask. This is the only fragment of my job I find relaxing. Holding a paintbrush. Looking for what went wrong. Correcting the mistakes.

"Hey, have you ever taken one of those IQ tests online?" Joe moves his head away from the lamp. His face returns to its normal size.

"Nah. Why?"

"Me and Debbie both did one last night. Scared the shit out of ourselves."

"Taking an IQ test scared you?"

"Yeah. We both scored like, really high. We weren't prepared for that." He lowers his voice and leans forward. "It said I'm one of the hundred most intelligent people on Earth. That's like, you know, too much responsibility. What am I supposed to do with that?"

The best response I can come up with is, "Wow."

"That probably means I'm on my final incarnation." He tilts his head, looking pensive.

"You believe in reincarnation?"

He leans back in his chair and runs his fingers along the sides of his head, tucking the hair back behind his ears. "Of course. You know, it's like, once you reach a certain level of intelligence, there's no more to learn, so that's your final one. I'm on my final one, I think. People often tell me so."

"Damn, Dude. You should put it to good use. You could wander the world like Caine in *Kung Fu*, or *The Incredible Hulk*, using your intelligence for good and helping the downtrodden."

"I know, right?"

"What was your score, anyway?"

"Well, I got a 436. Debbie got a 300. Not bad, but still pretty good."

"Um… are you sure about the accuracy of those tests?"

He shrugs. "Well, it said it was the actual IQ tests."

Joe keeps on with his talk about intelligence and responsibility and I don't know what else because I'm just painting, smiling, and nodding, inserting a grunt or a "yeah" to feign listening. Even though his words are entering my mind, it doesn't absorb them. My brain is still hanging out on my pillow at home. It's stuck in two hours ago, minutes before Gavin and I got out of bed. We said nothing. We didn't touch. Heads on our pillows, we lay there only looking in one another's eyes for a long time. It wasn't strange or sexy or uncomfortable, but it was different. It was connecting and touching in a way I never imagined could exist and now the experience clung to me, its claws deep in my mind and chest.

Joe's asinine babble is too much to take today, so when he finally stops talking for a breath, I make a run for it. I walk back to the yellow room and grab Lucy. When I enter the room, she lets out an exasperated sigh and shakes her head. She's in a complaining mood. It happens at least once a week where Luce goes on a tangent about her in-laws, Neil or Joe nagging at her, or the heat and yellow lighting in her room.

We head out to the parking lot and she starts venting about everything wrong with the day. Neil is crawling up her ass. Debbie is nagging and asking stupid questions. The laminating machine in her room took a shit again. The air is full of the distinctive dead stench from Longmont Foods less than a mile away. That's the smell of Longmont. All Longmonsters recognize it. The stink emanating from hundreds of dying turkeys. It's why no one in this town eats any of the Longmont Foods products they sell in the grocery store. I light a cigarette. Lucy frowns. Her disappointment is silent, but heavy. She lights her own. We sit down on a short stack of wooden pallets. Lucy tucks a loose strand of hair behind her ear and says, "Dude. Did you tell Gavin about what went down our last night in Deadwood?"

"Yeah. Some of it. The short version."

"What the fuck? Why would you do that, Bigmouth?"

"We were just talking. He won't tell anyone."

Lucy leans forward and wraps her arms around her knees. "I'm not worried about that. It's just that now he knows something about me."

"A lot of people know things about you. You talk a lot."

"Yeah, but it's not the same. He's giving me weird looks. He's judging." Her expression softens. She tilts her head. "How long are you two going to keep this shit up?"

"What? What shit?"

"Do you see a future with Gavin? He's a kid, Axel. And don't even give me that, 'he's mature for his age' bullshit because he isn't. He's a childish snob for his age."

"Aw, come on." I don't feel like listening to this and the firm mother tone her voice has taken on makes it even more intolerable. "You just don't know him." I hear how feeble this sounds. Before I spoke the words out loud, I was sure it was a much stronger defense.

"I know enough. And I know what you tell me. Like how he was insulting your music? Snobby. Douchebag."

A couple of days ago during our lunch break, I'd told Lucy about the night before, when Gavin had ransacked my CD collection, analyzing and providing commentary on everything he found.

"Really?" He held up my Enya CD. "Enya? Why do you have an Enya CD?"

"I owe an explanation as to why I have it? Because I like it. It's nice background music when I'm high or painting my masks."

"Oh my gawd. You're like one of those new-agey stoner goofballs."

Taking it as a light-hearted jab, I laughed.

He continued through the CDs. "Velvet Underground. Nice. Sting. Ugh. Garbage. Good. The Cure. Okay. Queen? QUEEN? Are you kidding me? First Enya. Now, fucking Queen?"

"Queen is the best band of all time. Watch your mouth."

Sitting on my living room floor, surrounded by plastic CD cases, he held up my copy of *A Day at the Races* and said, "You're serious? This is your favorite band of all-time? The one you would choose if you could only listen to one band for the rest of your life?"

"Yep."

"Jesus." He set the CD on the pile and shook his head. He grimaced.

"Well, what about you? What's your all-time favorite band?"

Like the answer should have been obvious, he shrugged and said, "Nirvana," and continued his analyzing and critiquing until he'd gone through almost everything.

Now Lucy is holding that incident in front of my face. "Think about it," she says. "He wasn't being superficial or curious. He was dissecting you. Knocking you down. Criticizing things you love like that, he's criticizing you. Picking apart your music collection and telling what is okay to like and what isn't? He's picking apart and judging your life experience; what makes you You. Fuck that. That is not okay. Eye rolling instead of accepting another person's tastes is immature and snobbish."

"I dunno. I didn't take it like that." I'm lying. I was aware when I watched him opening up the cases, explaining to me what made this one good or what made another one terrible, that I was watching someone who was still trying to find who they are, who was aggressively stating strong opinions about music or movies in order to create and establish an identity.

Lucy shakes her head and laughs. "Please. You're not that dumb. I wish you'd love yourself better than that. I can't understand why you won't. This isn't you."

A car pulls into the parking lot behind me. In a panic, I drop my cigarette and crush it with my foot. I turn and see Debbie getting out of her and Joe's Jeep. She gives us a quick "hey" and goes inside.

"You're still afraid Gavin's gonna catch you smoking?" Lucy says.

"Yeah. Kind of."

"Dude. Doesn't he smell it on you?"

"I wash my hands after. I chew gum and rub lavender oil in my hair."

"That's why you've been reeking of flowers lately? For fuck's sake. That's too much effort just to keep a secret you don't even need to keep. If it weren't for him, you wouldn't have even started again."

"That's got nothing to do with him."

"Yeah, I know. But it kind of happened around the same time, so I want to blame him."

We debate going back inside, but neither one of us feels like going back to work just yet and no one has come out to yell at us for staying out longer than we should. We share another smoke around the corner of the building where we can't be seen from any of the windows. That's when I decide to ask Lucy why she doesn't leave Carlos, why she doesn't leave her kid behind with him and run away to be on her own.

"Because I'm a coward," she says. "I'm afraid of what can happen or who I'll be when things change. If it always stays the same, I don't have to be afraid. Right now is always easier than the future. Besides, he and Abigail are still in the Springs with his parents. I haven't had to think much about him lately."

"They're still there? I thought it was just for a week?"

"Me, too." Lucy closes her eyes and leans back against the brick wall. "Guess he had a change of plans."

A Girl Like You

"You never tell me anything." Gavin takes another bite of barbecue rib. It's strange to me how much barbecue sauce he's managed to smear on his face. It's a complete turn off, but he was enthusiastic when he'd ordered the all-you-can eat platter because he's some kind of weirdo who's never eaten barbecue ribs before, so I make an effort to conceal my revulsion.

"There's not much to tell. You keep probing, asking me to tell you things, like I'm supposed to vomit out my entire life story over baby back ribs and chicken fingers." I squirt more ketchup onto my plate. "People learn about one another over time. You don't need to push and pry."

He's searching for a specific thing, but I have no idea what it is. I'm under scrutiny, being tested and dissected. Or maybe he wants to find something wrong with me. Funny, coming from a guy who can't overpower a barbecue rib.

"I'm not prying. I'm just curious about what you're not telling me."

"About what? Are you under the impression that I'm lying to you? Hiding something from you? There's a lot I'm not telling you. It's okay to learn about a person's inner life organically instead of demanding an info dump over dinner. Being in a relationship means respecting boundaries and letting one another move at their own pace."

He tears open one of the towelettes that stink of cheap furniture polish and begins cleaning himself up. "Oh. I wouldn't know."

"What you mean?"

"I've never had an actual relationship."

"You've got to be kidding."

"No. I went to prom with someone. I had a one-nighter with a girl at a party my housemates and I had last year, but I never dated. Didn't seem important."

"What changed?" I point at my cheek to show him where he missed some sauce.

"Nothing." He wipes his face again, and lets the soiled towelette fall onto the table. "It still doesn't seem important, but I met you. Both of my brothers dated in high school. Now they're married to those same girls."

"See? I had no idea that you have brothers. You told me when it came up. Stellar example. Really fucking stellar."

Siblings are a significant detail to leave out. An even bigger detail if you're insisting another person lay themselves bare, but I decide to let it go. I'm about to point this out when he says, "You never asked." He dips a fry in my ketchup. "I have two. Gale and Gary."

This new information is too ludicrous. I can't help but laugh. "Your names all start with a 'G'?"

"Yeah. I guess my parents like things neat. They're funny. They're both PhDs. Kind of dorky types. Grew up Mormon. You know how it is, the whole educated, squeaky-clean, conservative home environment."

"No. I don't know."

I feel as though I should defend my life and my parents' lack of college degrees. My lack of a college degree. With all the disappointment and disdain I harbor for the mother who abandoned me, I feel even more indignation at the idea of someone belittling her who hasn't earned it by being personally wounded by her. My estranged, alcoholic father comes forth in my mind. I don't feel outrage or resentment, only wistful and protective.

I'm confused, unsure if this is Gavin's doing, or if it's me making me feel this way. I've dropped down into a place where I'm small and inadequate. I want to blame someone for me being in this place. I want to rage and break the walls of this place. But I swallow it down, longing for a me that existed only a short time ago, a version of me who never seized an opportunity to be silent. Here, where I'm sulking and need her to speak.

Back at my apartment, we walk in to discover that Tocki has been sick everywhere. I clean up the puke puddles while Gavin opens the bottle of cheap merlot we picked up on the way from the restaurant. He pours the glasses and sits on the couch while I search the apartment for Tocki, who I find hiding under the bed with my camping gear.

He lets me scoop him up. I remove my sweatshirt and snuggle him up in it, then carry him out to living room. Holding Tocki in my lap, I sit on the floor and take a sip of the wine. It does not taste good. I would prefer a beer, but Gavin insisted on buying a bottle of wine on the way home, blathering on about Colorado wineries versus Californian wineries, and something about vines or soil or sun and I was too uninterested to argue for Colorado breweries. Echoes of our dinner conversation muted any of my opinions on beverages. Tonight I feel more white trash than normal and decided one night of pretending to appreciate wine might help me work my way back up to low self esteem.

"Seriously?" Gavin's eyes are on the swaddled old feline in my lap. "You're aware of the fact that he's not an infant, right?"

"No, he's not an infant, thankfully." I give Tocki little scratches around his scarred ears. The left one poking straight up, taller than the right ear that's missing its top bit of skin. He pokes my hand with his nose, gives me a lick, then nestles deeper into the sweatshirt and starts purring. "He's more like a tiny old man. I need to take him to the vet tomorrow."

"Axel…" Gavin sets his wine glass on the coffee table, leans forward on the couch and clasps his hands together.

"What?"

"Well, he's such an old cat. He's not looking so good. And he smells pretty bad."

"Whatever. I said I'm taking him to the vet tomorrow."

"Yeah, I know. It's just that maybe you should start thinking about—"

"No. That's between me, Tocki and the vet. I've had this cat for almost two-thirds of my life. You want to poke and prod about my past? You want me to tell you things? Okay, here: my mother bailed on us when I was eight. I never saw her again. I grew up with my dad, who was a good father. For a while. Then he stopped being a good dad because he's also a drunk who likes women and motorcycles. I haven't spoken to him in more than ten years. When he decided it was time for his trashy girlfriend to move in, he also decided it was time for me to move out. Or maybe he was pissed because I'd started dating one of his friends. He partied too much and his repair shop went under. He lost his house. He bailed on me. This old, smelly cat has been the one constant in my life for almost twenty years. So, there you go. Now you know more things about me."

Gavin leans back on the couch. "I can't believe you just said that to me." He shakes his head.

"What? You wanted me to tell you things about my life, so I did."

"That's between you, Tocki and the vet? Like my opinion doesn't even matter?"

"Why would you be part of any decisions about my pet? I only met you a few months ago. Did you even hear anything else? Or were you stuck on that?"

He runs his bony hands through his unkempt hair. "Oh, I heard. You were dating your dad's friend? Who does that?"

"Jesus. My dad introduced me to Walter. Walter was my dad's transmission guy. They worked together. It's not as though he's the same age as my dad. They weren't high school buddies. Who cares how we met? It isn't even any of your business; it's irrational for you to be so judgmental about it."

"Did you date any other friends of your dad?"

"Wow. That's a tacky question. No, I didn't. But even if I had, it wouldn't be any of your business."

"Of course it would."

I take a big sip of wine, not caring any more how bad it tastes, or how to sip wine like wine instead of beer. "Just because you're fucking me, that doesn't give you the right to know and critique everything I've ever done with my vagina. It's bad enough you think it's acceptable to do that with my music collection."

He runs his hands through his hair again, making it poof out and curl in all directions. His crazy hair is a barometer for his composure. "It does give me the right. It's like, if you buy a car, you have the right to know how many miles are on it."

"Okay." I set my glass down on the coffee table. "My twat is not a used car. When I buy a car, I prefer someone else drives it first and tunes it up to get the lemons and glitches out of it. Life is hard. People are more complicated than junk in a car lot. Surely you can deal with your insecurity about your lack of experience with women in a way that's less assholish."

He stands up. "Oh, so now I'm an asshole."

"Yes, Gavin. You're being an asshole."

"I don't think I am."

"Well, you're wrong."

"I don't think I'm wrong."

"Of course you don't." I can't look at him. If I see the smugness, my composure will vanish. Tocki starts wiggling, trying to reach his neck. I remove his collar, decorated with faded fish skeletons and a tiny jingle bell. I scratch his neck and he relaxes again.

Gavin pours himself another glass of wine and after a long silence, says, "I think I'd rather be with someone who has more education and less life experience." He makes this statement with the same casual tone a normal person would use to announce that they need to buy some new socks.

"I think I'd rather be with someone who has more everything."

"Okay. That's it." He stands up and pulls on his jacket. "I can't do this anymore."

"Do what? Follow through with the fight you started?"

He stands at the door with his hand on the knob long enough that the moment becomes awkward, then turns and gives me a hard stare with his head tilted in a surreal, melodramatic way that makes me wonder if he's emulating some damaged, passionate couple from a bad movie. I sit on the floor, hoping he'll finish playing this whole scene out soon so that I can have a cigarette. He turns back to the door, takes a deep breath, shudders, and exhales loud enough for me to hear. I assume he's going to leave then, but he inhales again, so I look away and sip my wine to keep from laughing and making this whole scene even worse.

At last, he manages to leave and I lock the door behind him. I lay Tocki in his bed, but he only rests there for a few minutes before wandering back to his hidey hole among the camping gear. I'm not sure what to do with myself, so I stand there smoking, staring at the empty cat bed. A situation like this feels unnatural on my own. The shadow underneath a storm cloud of impending grief is no place to dwell alone. But I can't call any of the people who I feel should be here staring at the empty cat bed with me.

The only person I feel like calling is Lucy, but it's been tense the past few days with her constant lecturing and mothering and growing disdain of Gavin. I know if I call her, she'll come. She'll cry and smoke and drink and talk with me, but at some point she'll mention Gavin. All I want right now is someone to lie to me, to tell me Tocki is going to be okay, not someone speaking the truth about how wrong I am.

Paradise Cove

The singer is tall, his shiny blond hair falling in waves around a sharp, mustached face like a Viking head carved out of wood. He smiles and gives me a nod as he walks past my table on his way to the tiny platform in the corner that serves as a stage. The more I drink, the more I let his gesture go to my head and decide he was flirting with me. This is what happens if you're at a bar other than your usual place without a friend to talk you down. Your brain misfires and lets your body do stupid shit. Nobody is there to stop you. I could have gone to The Bit of Billiards, but decided going to a new place would lessen the risk of running into someone I know. Besides, this one is within staggering distance from my apartment. The wooden sign outside announcing this place as *Paradise Cove* is barely noticeable from the street, with a single light pointing at it. Almost as though they don't care much if anyone comes inside. That appeals to me. Anyway, I've lived alone for a couple of months, now. It's about time I become better acquainted with the neighborhood.

The acoustic Viking sings alone with his guitar. Everything he plays is terrible folk music; angsty, outcast, and heartbroken. Songs about solitary journeys and memories of better times. I think about leaving, knowing I should be home on the other side of the road with my poor old sick cat, but the thought of being alone with all that loss makes it hard to breathe. I remember how Tocki insisted on hiding himself away under the bed and reason that he'd understand if I left him alone a little while longer.

I'm doodling ghost-like faces on a bar napkin when someone sets another bottle of 90 Shilling in front of me. I start to say that I hadn't ordered another beer, but instead of the waitress, the Viking folk singer casts a tall shadow over my table and slides the beer toward me with his calloused fingers.

"Can I buy you another beer?" He smiles and I notice his blond soul patch for the first time.

"Looks like you already did. Thanks." I point at the wooden chair across from me. "Wanna sit?"

"Don't think I've ever seen you in here before, have I?"

"No. I just moved in nearby. It's walking distance, so I figured I'd come in and check it out."

"Glad you did." He holds out his hand. "I'm Marc."

I shake his hand. "Axel."

"Axel?"

"Short for Axeline. I inherited it from some old timey relative from Scandinavia who died making the trek out west with a bunch of other settlers. Or so I was told."

"That's a great story." He leans back in his chair and opens his arms wide. "Abandoning the past. Embarking on adventure, seeking a new life." He hunches over table and points at me with his beer bottle. "You carry the legacy of a daring explorer in your appellation. Embrace it." He sees my doodle napkin and holds it up. "Phantoms of bygone progenitors, perhaps?"

I feel my face pull into a smile and realize it's the first one I've worn all day. "Hey," I hold my bottle up. "Next round's on me."

Marc clinks the mouth of his bottle against mine. "Well, I'm not gonna say no to that."

It only takes a couple of tequila shots to make going back to my place seem like a good idea. Marc doesn't notice the two empty wine glasses on my flea market coffee table. He walks right past them to the bookcase, which isn't an actual bookcase, but a thing I cobbled together with wooden palettes and crates from the Circuit's End parking lot because spending money on a trip to Deadwood with Lucy made more sense than buying furniture.

"Wow. You read all these?" He folds his long limbs and sits down cross-legged on the floor in front of the books. I open a couple of beers, hand one to Marc and sit next to him.

"Most of 'em." I point at a stack on the floor. "That's my to-read pile."

"Not much of a fiction reader, are you?"

"Made up stories never did it for me. I need real adventures. Genuine tragedy. True survival. Factual stories about breathing flesh and bone people who came before. Who lived big. How they dealt with being alive and human. Life today is so mundane. So easy."

"Is it, though?"

"Well, not for everyone, I suppose."

Marc pulls a biography of Billy the Kid from the shelf, looks it over and holds it up to me. "This young man's life is a fascinating tale, steeped in adventure and mystery. It's also — if you peer through the cracks between the myth and excitement — a story about loss, a damaged child, violence, scheming politicians, and lives cut short. Modern dilemmas. Stories about legendary figures from the past are important, but only if we view those characters as living beings existing in a present moment, not a historical film or diorama."

"I've never met anyone who talks like you."

"Well, my daring explorer, I've never met anyone who talks like you."

I'm trying to come up with a clever response when he asks to use the bathroom. While he's in there, I put the wine glasses in the sink. A tiny surge of anger at the thought of Gavin rises up, fluttering and warm in my chest. I push it back down, then go to the bedroom and peek at Tocki under the bed. He's snuggled against a sleeping bag, curled up asleep with his head on his paws. I stroke the top of his head. He opens his eyes halfway, licks my finger, then closes them again.

I stand up and find Marc standing in the doorway of my bedroom. He's not looking at me. His attention is on the pile of painted masks in the corner of the room.

"Holy shit. What are those?"

"Oh, um… these mask things that I paint sometimes. It's something to do."

He turns to me with eyes wide and mouth agape. "Why do you belittle yourself and your art? You carry the name of a courageous pioneer through the world. You have the capacity and compulsion to create inside of you. Be proud. Wave your flag."

"Yeah," I say. "I think that's something I need to work on."

"Hey." He shrugs. "We all have something we need to work on. Everyone's fucked up and afraid. That's not the important part. The unfucking, the decoding and rewiring, that's the interesting part of the ride."

Following the circuitry. Searching and repairing.

Marc empties his beer and sets the bottle on the windowsill. He takes mine from my hand, sees that it's empty and places it on the window next to his. He takes my face in his hands. He kisses me like I've never been kissed by anyone and I'm granted a reprieve from my loneliness, my anger and impending grief until dawn.

When I open my eyes, I find Marc sitting on the floor, hunched over, with one hand under the bed.

"His name's Tocki," I prop myself up on an elbow and rub my face.

"That's a good name." Marc pauses for a moment. "He's a tired old guy, isn't he?"

"I'm taking him to see the vet this morning. Sorry if my sick cat weirded you out."

He laughs and pushes his wavy blond hair away from his chiseled Viking face. "No, no. Not at all. He's not embarrassed about it, so I'm sure as hell not, either."

I get out of bed, check on Tocki, then make some coffee. I ask Marc if he'll stay and have a cup with me. He accepts and I'm relieved. Not because I think picking up a stranger in a bar is going to lead somewhere and not because I want it to, but something about his accepting demeanor puts me at ease. Listening to Gavin's immature insults and judgements has left me angry and ashamed. Ashamed when I know I don't deserve to feel this way. I've done nothing to feel ashamed for and I don't need his approval for fucking someone back when Gavin was still in grade school. It doesn't matter if my twat has five or five hundred miles on it, he doesn't have the right to judge what I've done and where I've been. I know this. Still, his criticism takes up space in my mind and I resent it, knowing it will turn to rage because that space belongs to me and Tocki right now, not some snobby college fuck who hasn't yet learned the basics of being a boyfriend.

Sipping coffee at my kitchen table, as if he can hear my inner monologue, Marc asks, "So, you have a boyfriend?"

I think about the two wine glasses in the sink. "Why do you ask that?"

He shrugs. "Saw some guy clothes in your room."

Fucking Gavin. Using my building's laundry room, storming off in a fit, then leaving his clothes here. What a little shit. "Oh. Yeah. No. Well, he's not my boyfriend. He's… I don't know what he is. Definitely not my boyfriend. I'm sorry. I just, I met you at a weird time in my life."

Marc shrugs. "Our entire lives are weird times. The good news is, there is a day fast approaching where you will look back at this particular weird time and these things will no longer matter." He smiles, nods and sets his cup down. He gives me his phone number, asks me to call, or to come into the bar to see him again. He wishes me luck and courage for Tocki's visit with the veterinarian. He takes my face in his hands again. "Axeline. You carry the legacy of a daring explorer in your appellation. Embrace it." He leans down, kisses my forehead, and then he's gone.

The woman at the animal hospital strokes Tocki's head between his battle-scarred ears. I want to hear every word she is saying to me, but she cuts in and out, her explanation fragmented by the barks and howls of an unhappy dog on the other side of the door. What I hear is broken sentence shards that say things like, kidney failure, loss of appetite and dehydration. She's not suggesting euthanasia to me. I'm grateful because I'm realistic enough to see that's where this situation is heading, but greedy enough to want more time. The I.V. in his arm will give me that, but I can't keep bringing him back here every few days for intravenous life.

"If he eats, drinks and maintains some regular activities, that's a good thing." She lowers her chin toward her chest. But, if he stops being able to do those things, you need to bring him back here, okay?" She says this with the stern yet gentle tone of a mother bargaining with her young child. Now she's suggesting euthanasia and I feel a little less grateful and a little more scared.

After I bring Tocki back home, I let him eat whatever he wants. Potato chips. Fine. Yogurt. Sure, here you go, Little Guy. I try to call Lucy, but she's not answering. I'm cross-legged on the floor, with open packages of bologna and orange-colored, imitation cheese slices, rolling them together and noshing on them like some white-trash delicacy while Tocki curls up on my lap, lifting his head for the occasional sniff of my food. I look at the phone sitting on the dingy gray carpet next to me and wonder if I should call my father. Letting him know Tocki is almost ready to tap out is the right thing to do. I try Lucy again instead. I don't call my dad. I don't leave a message on Lucy's voice mail because I know as soon as I open my mouth to say anything to anyone, the deluge will come.

I need it to come. I need it to come, but know the weight of it will smother me. I can't face it alone.

I pick the phone up again and wonder if my father would comfort me, if he would take on a terse tone with me; if he'd answer the phone at all. If he would be the father I loved and admired, or the father who wounded me and let me down. I imagine different possible scenarios, letting each one play out, deciding on the perfect response to each possible situation.

Then I call Gavin.

When You See the Light

A guy reeking of weed is holding two red plastic cups of beer, asking if I want one. His head is shaved and his scalp shines with blond fuzz. A ratty backpack hangs from his broad shoulders. Everything about him strikes me as smooth and round with no sharp edges; his wide blue eyes are easy-going and pleasant.

"You look thirsty." He winks and hands me a cup. He says his name is Rog. This is the first time I've been to Gavin's house when there were other people in it. The two other times I'd been here, all the other housemates were out. I don't know a single person here aside from Gavin, but for some reason, none of these people seem to notice how out of place I am. College students. Twenty-somethings. People who wear fucking sandals and backpacks to keg parties. They're nice to me. If they think I'm odd, if they have any clue at all that I'm an uneducated factory worker, they're not letting it show. I go along with it and act as though I belong, even though I have no backpack and my shoes look like I stole them from a janitor.

I make small talk with Rog for a few minutes before mentioning I'm there with Gavin.

"No way." He shakes his head. "You? And Gav? For real?"

"Yeah. Why? Is that weird?"

"Weird? Oh, no. Uh... not weird. You just struck me as a more, uh... like you'd be into a more... well, someone more—"

"Yo, you two delinquents talking about me?" Gavin appears from nowhere as if he'd just teleported into the spot next to me.

"Just getting acquainted with your girl, man." Rog taps his plastic cup against Gavin's.

Gavin gives us a proper introduction which leads to Rog laughing and shaking his head in disbelief. "Axel? Like, Axl Rose? As in, where do we go, where do we go, now?" He does a slithering, snake-like dance. "For real?"

"For real." I nod, take a sip of the beer he brought me, then add, "I carry the legacy of a daring explorer in my appellation."

Gavin scrunches his face in a way that reminds me of a bag of dried prunes. He shakes his head. Rog tilts his and leans in closer. "Say what, now? Axl Rose was an explorer?" The way he smiles is as smooth and round as the rest of him.

"Nah." I shake my head. "The ancestor my parents named me after. Axeline. She was a pioneer back in the day."

"No shit? That's awesome." Rog looks at Gavin, but points at me with his red plastic cup. "No way is this your girlfriend, Dude."

Gavin and I exchange a brief look of confusion. Should I be offended? Should he? Before either one of us can respond, Rog hits Gavin with a playful nudge in the shoulder. "No way could you score a chick this cute and this cool." He turns to me. "Is he blackmailing you? Holding you hostage? Blink once for 'yes' and twice for 'no'."

I can't help but laugh. Not because his humor is so hilarious, but because his demeanor is fun and affable and I'm flattered. Walter's friends had all been kind enough to me, but in the same way that anyone would be kind to anything. Whenever they complimented Walter on his good fortune in the relationship aspect of his life, it was no different than the way they complimented his car or a well-behaved pet. A part of me is also aware of a smug sense of satisfaction. Someone is acknowledging that I can do better than Gavin. That he isn't as entitled to as much as he believes. That I'm better than him. I wonder if Gavin is offended, but if he is, he doesn't show it. Instead, he finds an excuse to break away from the conversation, claiming he has to look for someone outside.

The night rolls on. With the darkening skies and increasing blood-alcohol level, I'm feeling better and better. I hadn't felt like going out at all when I called Gavin after Tocki's appointment with the vet, but he'd convinced me. He didn't tell me there would be a keg party taking place at his house, only that he and his roommates were getting some beer, having a get-together and it would take my mind off things. It didn't sound fun, but sitting at home alone with myself sounded worse. Off and on throughout the night, Gavin and I wander away from one another. I cross him a few times, playing host and telling stories. At one point, I find him with a few other people, standing around the desk in his bedroom, showing off his music collection, which is just a list of files he's downloaded. When he starts blathering on about Sonic Youth, I back out of the room before he notices me, but end up backing up into a person, trapping myself in the doorway.

"Oops. Sorry." I turn around and bump into a large Asian girl standing behind me. Long black braids streaked with blue frame the sides of her scowling face. She's wearing cat-eye glasses and blue eyeshadow. I haven't worn blue eyeshadow since junior high. If I tried to do it now, no way I would look as cool and hip as this girl.

"Who are you?"

"Axel. I'm here with Gavin." I gesture with my red plastic cup toward the bedroom where Gavin is busy having a debate with someone about Thurston Moore.

"You're here with Gavin. Really. What, like you're on a date?"

Maybe saying I'm with someone in a crowded house full of drunk college students makes me sound like an old person. I don't know how to be at this party. "A date? No, no. I mean, he invited me. We work together."

"Oh. Yeah." She laughs. "You're the barfly he's fucking."

At best, this girl loathes me. At worst, she doesn't even think I'm worth loathing. "Sorry." I shake my head. Every nerve and muscle vibrate, anticipating an escalation of aggression. "Have I done something to you? Who are you?"

"Who am I?" She shakes her head, then stares at the ceiling for a moment. "You have got to be kidding me." She turns and stomps down the hallway, almost knocking Rog into the wall.

"Hey, Trace," he says, but she blows past him without acknowledging his presence. He looks at me, shrugs and walking toward me, says, "I guess you met Tracey."

"She never told me her name, but yeah, I guess I met Tracey. Kind of a cranky type, or what?"

Rog looks past me, into the bedroom. "She lives here. She and Gavin... well, I don't know what the deal is there, exactly, but—"

"It's okay." I hold my hand up. "I don't need to know."

"Cool. So, what's your story, then? You doing some kind of postgrad program?"

So much for blending in.

Gavin stands hunched over his desk, face awash in laptop glow. One hand clicks the mouse repeatedly, the other, still holding his shirt, leans on the desk. On the other side of the door, the party buzzes on. At some point between my awkward mingling and his smug music debates, we ended up alone in his room, which led to locking the door and making out. It was the only thing to do once we were alone. Talking seems pointless and risky.

Gavin clicks a few more times. "Uh... I don't know what you feel like listening to."

"I'm telling you, it doesn't matter." I lean on my elbows, dangling my feet over the edge of his stupid twin bed. "Whatever is fine."

He stands up straight, looks at me, eyes squinting and top lip curled up in confused disdain. "What the hell is that?"

"I don't know. What the hell is what?"

He shakes his fistful of shirt in frustration. "Have an opinion. Don't you have any opinions?"

"What a retarded fucking question. Of course I have opinions. As far as which one of your shitty music files I want you to click on before we screw in your room during a party like fucking high schoolers, no. I have no opinion. I give absolutely no shits. And for the record, an actual grown-up man would give no shits, either. Only middle school boys waiting for their balls to drop and a single chest hair to come in need to use their deluded ego about their musical taste to get hard when they've got a woman on their stupid little twin bed, or have any sort of identity at all."

He grabs a fistful of his wild hair in each hand, making his mop of brown curls fluff out in an even bigger mess. His cheeks are mottled with the red blotches of boozy anger. "I can't believe you called me a retard. What kind of person still calls someone a retard?"

Now I have no idea what we're talking about. I only know he's looking for a fight and I've given him one. I'm staring at him, trying to decide if I should humor him, or put my janitor shoes back on and storm out, back home to my old, tired cat and my fear of impending grief. I want to jump up, continue my tirade about his assholery and exit in a terrific scene of womanly rage and fire, but instead, it's Tracey and her pissed off fist hammering on the other side of the door that break the silence and steal my thunder.

She's screeching Gavin's name in a drunken fury. I start putting my shoes on. Gavin stands there, slack jawed and holding his stupid shirt. Tracey, she keeps pounding and yelling, taking her emotions out on the bedroom door.

"Okay." I sigh, defeated and deflated. "I'm outta here. You need to take care of this. Sort out whatever is going on with you and this girl."

"She's just one of my housemates. She gets kind of crazy."

"Yeah. I bet she does. So do I. I'm sure the next one will, too."

"Hey, hey." Gavin reaches out with his long arms, puts his hands on my shoulders. "It's not like that. She and I messed around a few times. Just drunk stuff." He laughs. "She let me do her in the butt. Who wants to be with a girl who gets drunk and lets you in her butt the first time you're together?"

"Oh my god." I get to my feet. "I'm leaving. I didn't come here so you could use me to mess with that poor girl's head."

More people have gathered on the other side of the door, attempting to talk Tracey down. I no longer feel old; I feel like the only adult in the house. I don't want to walk through that mess, so I procrastinate for a moment, hoping it gives them time to move away from the door and go on with their lives.

"You don't have to go." Gavin pulls me to him. "We can still pick up where we left off."

I push away. "I'm going home. I'll see you at work"

"Oh. Going home to your dead cat?"

"He's not dead. He's sick." I wonder how much Gavin's had to drink tonight, if any of this is booze talking, but I know better. This cruelty has been living in his bones all along. Every time I let him touch me. Every time he slept in my bed and ate my food and looked into my eyes and touched my face.

It doesn't matter. Turning around and leaving this room before I can't stand to look at myself again is all that matters. The other side of the door doesn't matter. Getting to the door does.

"Fuck," Gavin says. "Remind me not to make you the executor of my 'do not resuscitate' order."

"Chrissakes, Gavin." I open the door. "You're a real class act."

On the other side of the door, at the end of the hall, Tracey is flanked by a couple of girlfriends. Her cool blue cat eyes are only slightly smeared, but red with tears and inebriation. The three of them stop talking and put all their attention on me. One of the girls wears her brown hair in a ponytail and a sloppy sheen of shimmery pink lip gloss. She smiles and apologizes for interrupting Gavin and me. I don't smile back and tell her nobody interrupted anything.

"You don't belong here," she says.

"You're right. I don't." I turn to Tracey. Hip, cool, fiery, heartbroken Tracey. "You can do better."

I let my janitor shoes carry me out into the night where my lousy brown Oldsmobile waits. I light a cigarette and feel a twinge of regret at picking up such a bad habit again. That thought is a spark, igniting in my mind a series of regrets. The most painful of all, giving myself a fresh start in my life and wasting it on some inexperienced, narcissistic kid who has contempt for every human being he touches.

I'm driving and sobbing, following the circuitry of my self-sabotage. Searching for the mistakes, the flaws. Considering means of repair. I tell myself that nobody interrupted anything. The fresh start, it's still happening. I can still salvage it. The unfucking. The rewiring. The correcting and painting over the damaged circuitry is the interesting part.

I tell myself this the whole way home. But, I keep sobbing, anyway.

All at Once

The first thing out of Lucy's mouth is, "You had more than two choices. You had more options besides stay home alone and cry, or run to that idiot accounting boy who doesn't give two shits about you. You should've left a message. I would've called you right back. I would have come and sat with you and Tocki. You shouldn't have gone to that stupid party. When did you become such a low self-esteem, masochistic girl?"

I wonder if that's what I've become. It doesn't sound quite right, but I can't come up with any defense at the moment. These things Lucy's saying, they're the truth. She's going on and on and on. Fucking Lucy, man. She's right about everything, but being correct about mistakes that I've already made isn't doing any good. It's only doing bad. The time on the dashboard of Lucy's car says we still have ten minutes left on our lunch hour. I know the clock is wrong, it's always wrong, but I decide to go with it and light another cigarette with my already lit one. I flick the butt into the rocks where Gavin sent Joe digging a few months ago. I feel guilty for littering. I feel guilty because I didn't stick up for Joe more on that first day when Gavin teased him. I feel guilty for thinking of myself. For being a bad pet owner. A bad friend. For wasting years of Walter's time. For needing Lucy to parent me. I almost feel guilty for being a bad employee, but I'm not sure this job deserves that. I inhale flux and formaldehyde all day long and Neil likes to linger near the time clock every day between four and five so he can give people grief when they clock out at their scheduled time. Having a life outside of this place is frowned upon below a certain pay grade.

Lucy continues to lecture me. She's looking in the rearview, wiping little flakes of mascara from under her eyes with her pinky finger, adjusting her bun of thick dark Latina hair, rattling off phrases like, "be more self aware," "more self respect," and "focus on priorities."

"Jesus," I say. "I don't need a mother right now. Get off me. Go mother your fucking kid instead of me for a change."

I feel guilty for talking. For judging and trying to masquerade as a halfway decent person. I see the heat rising in Lucy's face, the twitch in her eye that comes before she lets slip the dogs of outrage. I deserve it. I ready myself for it, but it doesn't come. She turns away, nods, and pulls the keys from the ignition, drops them in my lap.

"Lock it up when you finish your smoke." She steps out of the car and heads back inside, leaving me there alone with my shame, without the luxury of her anger. Fucking Lucy, man. The sister and the mother I never had. Maybe parents teach us how to be in the world. To love, to be a friend, to care and watch over another living thing. Or maybe they just teach us to be assholes.

Following the circuitry. Searching and repairing. Unfucking and rewiring. That's where the fun is.

Back inside, Joe and Neil sit at my table. Neil's leaning back, his blue short-sleeve, button-up shirt is wrinkled. Half the collar is up, the other half is down. His arms are folded across his chest. He's nodding along to some of Joe's nonsense.

Joe's holding his arm out, displaying it to Neil. "And that's how come I've never broken any bones at all. They're twenty or thirty percent stronger than a normal person's bones. Not even a toe or finger or anything like that."

"Sounds like a nice advantage to have," Neil says. I can't tell if he's humoring Joe, or if he's expressing genuine fascination.

"Are you fucking kidding me?" I drop my bag on the table. "Can we just have one goddamn day without having to listen to these far-out stories?"

Neil holds his hand up and leans forward. "Okay, now. I don't think that's a very professional way to speak to your supervisor."

"Professional. As if there's anything professional about this place or my supervisor. It's a joke and you know it. You couldn't even hire a real accountant."

Neil stands. "Actually, uh, that was something Joe and I, uh, wanted to talk to you about." He shoves one hand into his pocket and pushes his glasses up with the other. Wire frames. The lenses are covered with a thin film of dust. Chin on his chest, eyes locked on the floor, he says, "We do have some regulations regarding interactions with coworkers. Uh, as far as, you know, relations between employees, certain decorum and uh… what's acceptable, or, uh… professional."

"There's that word again." I pick my bag up off the table, sling it over my shoulder. I turn to Joe, who's not looking at me or Neil, but down at the table. "Joe and Debbie are married. Barry the screener fucked the receptionist in the bathroom and you're talking to me about decorum? Fuck this."

"Now, wait." I hear Neil saying, but I don't turn around. I head straight back to Lucy's room. She's there, filling out some paperwork. I hand her the keys to her car.

"I gotta go. I can't be here. I can't talk to anyone anymore. I just keep screwing it up." I feel the dam inside me breaking, so I look up at the ceiling as though this is an effective method to prevent an outpouring of emotion. "I just need to go home and be with Tocki."

"Hey." Lucy's hands on my shoulders. "Hey, Axel? Look at me. Look. At. Me."

I risk looking down. Something in Lucy's eyes that forgives me for being an asshole, that understands, hammers at the dam, makes that tingle in my nose and eyes that lets me know the deluge is about to come. Fucking Lucy, man. Always been more of a person than me. The woman who loves me best. Better than I deserve. Taking care of me like only sisters and mothers can.

"Go straight home," she says. "I'm right behind you, as soon as I can duck out of here, okay?"

I nod, because even with so many words in my head, I can't speak any of them.

"Straight home. And don't leave. I'll be there."

I just make it out the back door to the parking lot when I run into Joe. I start a feeble attempt to stammer out an apology, but I can't focus on a coherent sentence, so it all comes out as a weird mix of regretful sentence fragments.

"Don't worry about it." He says this without looking me in the eye, sounding so stung and embarrassed that now I feel even worse.

"You're not a loser, Joe."

He scrunches his face, lets out a tiny laugh and shakes his head. "I know that."

"I have to go."

"Well, wait. Neil wants to talk to you."

"No. I'm sorry, man. I can't talk. I can't be here anymore. I'm going."

I get in my car and pull out of the lot, not looking in the rearview, even though I'm certain I'll never be coming back.

Lose You

My tiny apartment is filling with a death smell. The failure of Tocki's insides has created a stink that's subtle at first, filling the place room by room, but becomes overwhelming when I get close to him. His black and gray fur, once slick and shiny in his fierce alley cat days, sticks out in dull tufts. We're sitting on the floor, Lucy on one side of him and me on the other, talking to him, to each other, petting him and helping him take little sips of water. He can't take little sips by himself anymore. He can't walk anymore. Can't eat. Can't use the litter box.

Lucy strokes him, looks up at me with her tear-rimmed eyes. "We have to take him soon, Pal."

"I know. I can't just yet." I'm trying to breathe. I think of the first time I took him to the vet's office with my father. When he was feral and scrappy. When I was only twelve years old and building an adult version of me in my imagination that would never exist. When I was still a priority in my father's life. I give him a little scratch on his torn ears and his eyes open, slowly close, and then open again. My stomach heaves and a big ugly sob comes out of me. "I'm still trying to get myself ready. I need to gain some composure first. Talk about something else."

"Okay." Lucy stands up, goes to my sink and fills a glass with water. She hands it to me and sits down on the floor again, strokes the back of my head once. "Here's something else: Carlos left me."

"What? Why?"

"Why? Because it's over. It's been over. His parents call me *puta* behind my back. And he tells me about it. He doesn't defend me; he just tells me about it. He hasn't mentioned anything about divorce yet, but he will. He's moving down to the Springs with his parents."

"Shit. I'm sorry, Luce. What about Abigail? You think you guys'll share custody or something?"

Lucy, leaning against the wall, pulls her knees up to her chest and looks down at Tocki. Wrinkles on her forehead appear and she pushes her lips together. For a moment, I think she's not going to answer me. Then she says, "I dunno. I think I might let Carlos have custody."

"Luce, come on. Think about that. His parents will poison her against you and he won't do anything to stop it."

"Yeah. Maybe."

I wish I could say anything other than this. I want to think and speak and be with better words. Words that are a profound solution or capable of healing, but I don't know how to create perfect moments in any situation.

I'm searching that person inside myself who knows how to comfort another person. I want the right thing to say that will shake her up, light a fire under her ass and make her want to fight for her kid, but I don't know what words can make a mother fight for her child. I guess my father didn't either.

"Here's the thing," she says, "I hate being a mother. I love my daughter. Abigail is an amazing little person. But from day one, I've been drained by the constant need, the crying, the sleepless nights, the sticky fingers, and shitty pants. The questions, the arguing, the snotty noses and running through the house knocking things over. I'm not allowed to tell those things to anyone. I'm not allowed to hate being a mother. I'm expected to love being a mother and to be good at it because I'm a woman. A Mexican woman from a Catholic, Mexican family. I'm a piece of shit because I don't want to be a mother. You're a piece of shit because you aren't one at all. All of us are expected to spawn and be saintly mommies, and fuck it, Axe. I hate it. I suck at it. And there's nothing else to be done. Maybe she's better off."

For years, I've watched Lucy fight anyone. She put herself out there time and time again, ready to defend herself, or anyone else, never choosing silence over speaking her mind. Now, sitting here on my dirty floor, next to my dying cat, she's so small and resigned to defeat.

The scene is too much for me to handle and I fall apart again. For a few minutes, Lucy cries with me and we start getting messy about it. I don't have any tissues, so I go to the bathroom and bring out a roll of toilet paper. Then I'm holding Lucy's hand, petting Tocki with the other.

"I haven't been paying enough attention to what's been going on with you," I say.

"No. You haven't. But, that's over now, right?"

"Totally over."

"Good. Because I need help with this, Axe."

"You've got it." I give her hand a squeeze. "You can come live with me."

"Well, of course I'm gonna come live with you. Not here, though. This place is a shithole."

Through the snot, sobs, and tears, we laugh. "It is," I say, "but that bar across the road? There's dudes there."

Another laugh. Sniffing. More nose blowing on toilet paper. "Dudes? What dudes?"

"Okay. I totally forgot to tell you this with everything else going on. I went there the other night after Gavin pissed me off. I had a few and kind of hooked up at that bar."

"Kind of? Kind of fucked a rando?"

"Not a rando. He was the acoustic guitar folk singer guy."

"Oh. For fuck's sake." Lucy lets out a normal, loud, Lucy laugh that shows all her perfect teeth. "A dive bar folk singer rando."

"Okay, yeah. But, if you stick a Gandalf hat on him, he sort of looks like a young wizard. He has a soul patch."

"Oh my god. A folk wizard. With a freaking soul patch. How young of a folk wizard?"

"I dunno. Late thirties. Forty, maybe."

"Well, that's more like it. You gonna see him again?"

"Maybe. He seems pretty great and weird in a really nice way, but… I'm not sure another man is what I need in my life right now. When I left Walter, I had this fantasy that I'd be the priestess in the tower on the hill with my feline familiar, surrounded by books, creating art; becoming strong and wise."

"You're getting to that." Lucy says. "It just takes time."

"Yeah. But I'm losing my feline."

"I know." Lucy squeezes my hand.

I look down at Tocki and remember the day my old man found him under the house, how he looked at me in the vet's office. The way I couldn't take my eyes off him because I was afraid that if I did, some sort of spell or invisible lifeline might be broken, causing his breathing and purring to cease. Whatever spell it was, Tocki must have believed in it, too, because he never stopped looking at me, either. From that moment, we were in this thing together. For almost twenty years, we were in this thing together. The way he's looking at me now tells me there is no magic spell. No invisible lifeline. He's ready to tap out whether I like it or not.

We were in this thing together, but now it's the end of the ride. The end of together.

One last trip to the animal hospital, and we'll end the way we began.

"I think we have to take him, now," I say.

The end of together is a special kind of pain.

Long Time Nothing New

I'm clearing a space on my home made junk bookshelves for Tocki's urn. Broke, no job since I walked out of Circuit's End a few weeks ago, but spending what I had left on his cremation made sense. Lucy loaned me some cash for the urn. When I find another job, I'll buy him his own shelf. Make a sacred space, just for him. Or, maybe I'll find some more wooden palettes from a parking lot somewhere and make him something. Strong, worn, wood with marks and scratches. With character beaten into them. That'd suit him better than some brand new piece of shiny garbage made from dressed-up particle board. Tocki wasn't a fancy cat. Tocki was good and true and loving, covered with scars and lumps from living a real life.

When I find another job. I have no skills aside from being a no-ambition factory cog. There's a fantasy I have of sitting at a desk, in a place where the room temperature is comfortable and no one is so sad and starved for attention that they need to tell ridiculous stories of katana swords and unbreakable bones. A place where I don't feel like a peasant, but am not so important that I have to be responsible for a group of people, or will even be noticed by anyone who is important. A place where no one knows me. Another board shop, you bring in your experience and your reputation. They know your story before they know you. They've judged you before you speak. The only way to be free is through strangers. The only way to be who I want to be is to be no one.

The want ads have nothing. Pizza delivery. Which I considered, but am certain I will hate. Night stocker. Data entry. I can't type well enough for that. At least, I don't think I can. Lucy said I should go to a temp agency and let them do the work of searching for me. They might even help me learn some office skills. I'm still thinking about it. I'll end up going in the long run. I could find a gig with another board shop in a minute. I don't want to, even though I can't keep the thought from popping up in my mind over and over again. It's the easy way out. I've always sucked at job hunting and this is a quick fix solution. The lazy path to a paycheck and more of the same banal bullshit. Easy is what I've always done. Easy brought me to this moment and all I want is for this moment to be over. I want the future, but the future isn't always easy to come by.

I want different. I want new, but have no idea how to achieve it. I want big, brave changes like the night I told Walter I was leaving. Other people make this look so simple. I can't even dress myself in a way to make a job interviewer look at me with a normal facial expression.

My phone rings and I consider not answering it, but seeing Walter's name on the screen piques my curiosity.

"How are things across town, Sir?"

"Hey, Axe. All right. All good. How're things with you?"

"Me? I'm good. Not a lot going on."

"You sure about that?"

"Who've you been talking to?"

"This is me, Axe. I know you. If something's going on, you can still talk to me. You know that, right?"

"Tocki died."

The silence is long and I'm afraid of having to repeat that phrase, but then Walter says, "Oh, shit. Axe, I'm so sorry. He was a special little guy. Can I do anything?"

"Nah. Thanks. It was a couple weeks ago. He liked you."

"I liked him. He was a character."

Another long silence. I'm about to open my mouth to deliver some feeble excuse for why I have to end the call. Walter clears his throat. I sense the real reason for the phone call is coming, so I wait a moment until he comes out with it.

"Listen, Axe. Why I called… Donnie came by yesterday. He asked about you. I didn't give him your number or your new address because it didn't feel like my place, but he wants to see you."

"He said that?"

"Well no. I mean, he did in his way. He's your old man. You know how he is. He was surprised as hell when I told him you'd moved out."

"Yeah, I never told him anything. I still haven't talked to him. Sorry you got stuck in an awkward moment."

"Oh, hey. It's no big deal. I figured you two still weren't talking. He didn't leave me a number; just said he was still living at the same place up in Loveland."

Like Walter said, he's my old man. I know how he is. I know he has a phone, but would rather make me drive twenty minutes to his crappy apartment instead of letting me off the hook with a quick phone call. I could blow him off, but I won't, even though I'm confident that seeing him will fix nothing and won't make me feel any better.

"Okay, I'll think about taking a drive up there if I can find the time."

"Working lots of O.T. these days?"

"I'm actually between jobs right now." I try to sound casual, the way a person might sound who can afford to be between jobs. Like some

51

snobby fuck taking a sabbatical.

"What happened to C.E.?"

"Oh, you know. Time to move on." I step over to the window and pick up the pack of cigarettes from the windowsill. I take one out and hold it, but don't light it, in case Walter can hear the flick of the lighter through the phone. He knows I'm unemployed and that I've lost my pet. I don't need him to find out that I've started smoking again, too. Even when we split from someone amicably, we have to save face. That's important for some stupid reason.

"A lot of that going on lately, eh?"

There's a silence I feel a burden to fill with something clever, but I'm learning more and more lately that I'm not all that clever and not half as cool as I thought I was several months ago. A powder blue Datsun pulls into the parking lot. Gavin steps out and looks up at the window where I'm standing. I immediately take a step back, hoping he didn't see me.

"Hey, Walter. I gotta take off. A friend of mine just showed up. Thanks for calling and delivering the message, though. It's good to hear from you."

"No problem. Axeline, listen, if you need anything—"

"I know. You too."

"I know."

As soon as I end the call, Gavin's fist is at my door. I can't tell which is louder; the pounding on the door or in my chest. I go to the back of my apartment, into the bedroom, as far as I can get from that door. I still have a view of the parking lot from my bedroom window. Four parking spots away from Gavin's Datsun sits my car. I panic, wondering if he knows I'm in here, if I should answer the door.

The last thing I want is to see his smug face. To hear his snide voice and all the insults it inevitably brings. I have no idea if he came to start a fight, or if he just wants to get laid. It doesn't matter. He's a mistake I made. A mistake I'm not going to carry around anymore.

The pounding continues for a few minutes. When it stops, I hear men's voices murmuring on the other side of my door. Gavin arrived alone, so I figure it must be one of my neighbors who got tired of the ruckus he brought. A few seconds later, I see Gavin stomping through the parking lot. He folds his long body into his ridiculous tiny car and drives away, trying to peel out on the pavement in a car too weak for such a big gesture.

There's a dead car in the far corner of the parking lot where my father lives. A rusty brown Saab with busted out windows and no tires. It's been sitting in that corner, next to the unpainted fence, gathering blowing dust and leaves since my dad moved in here twelve years ago. Ever since his business went belly-up, he lost our house, and told me I had to move out.

"You're almost eighteen. You oughta be finding your own place by now," he said.

"You told me I could stay here until I finished school."

"Graduation is in a few months. Then you're finished."

"No, I enrolled in some classes at Front Range. I'll have two more years of school after graduation."

"Where?"

"The community college." I'd told him my plans already. He had already agreed to everything, telling me that it was a good idea. My part-time job at the gas station up the road didn't pay much, but it would pay some of the tuition, and he'd offered to help me out with the rest.

"Oh. Well, you can still do that, but I'm selling the house and renting a place with Marla. Why don't you move in with that boyfriend of yours?"

"That boyfriend of mine? Walter works for you. It's not as if you've never met him. And who the fuck is Marla? I haven't even met Marla."

"Watch your mouth. You're an adult. You can figure all this stuff out for yourself."

I learned about my dad losing the business and the house from Walter. My father, he didn't tell me anything. I put off my classes and found a full-time job at a circuit board factory. Walter found another job working on transmissions for someone else. I didn't go to my graduation because Walter and I were moving into a rotting apartment next to the cemetery. I never met Marla.

Now, I'm sitting behind the wheel of my car, staring at this sad, discarded Saab that someone once needed and took care of, and I wonder how people decide all of a sudden that something valuable can be tossed aside.

The old man's apartment is on the second floor of this green brick building. The place looks more like a prison than a place where people come to live willingly. I've only been here once before, but I can't see that anything has changed. The swimming pool, surrounded by a wire fence and dry, brown grass is still empty. Between the pool and the building is a tiny patch of lawn with a couple of picnic tables and barbecue grills. They look like they've been used recently. Someone left a pair of dirty tongs and a twelve-pack box full of empty cans near one of the tables. A few people have the doors of their apartment open. TV and chatter faintly comes out of a few of them, but it's quiet for the most part and aside from a woman with wiry gray hair wandering around in the dead courtyard, I don't see anyone.

"Hey, little girl." The woman is looking at me, smiling. A few of her teeth are missing and she's gripping a fistful of something.

"How you doing?" I keep walking toward the stairs, hoping she isn't trying to lure me into some small talk.

"Good. Who are you?"

"Donnie's kid."

"Donnie from upstairs? He ain't got any kids. Not yet."

I stop, two steps up. "He's got a kid. I'm his kid."

"You're too big to be a kid."

"You just called me a little girl."

"Yep." She holds up her fist, opens it and shows me the cigarette butts she's holding.

"What the hell is that?"

"Cigarette butts. I've only picked up twelve so far."

"Okay, well… good on you." I turn and trot up the stairs to the second floor, deciding that if this crazy lady keeps talking and showing me garbage, I'm going to pretend I don't hear anything.

I knock on the door. It opens right away. Standing in front of me is a woman in sweat pants and a baggy MC-5 t-shirt. She has big, brown eyes and wild copper hair spiraling in perfect curls all around her freckled, heart-shaped face. She looks to be about the same age as Gavin.

"Oh, sorry," I say. "I thought Donnie Cleveland lived here. Did he move?"

"No, he still lives here. He'll be back in a few minutes. Who are you?"

I start to turn away. "Can you tell him that Axel stopped by?"

"Axel?" She steps out the door, reaches her hand out toward me. "Wait. He'll be back in a few. Hang out for a minute? Have a beer or coffee or soda or something."

"He told you about me?"

"Of course he did. Sorry I didn't recognize you. All the pictures I've seen of you, you were still a little kid." She smiles, holds out her hand. Purple fingernail polish. "I'm Kelly. Will you please wait?"

I shake her soft, small hand. "Yeah, um… sure. Why not."

Inside the apartment, it's dream catchers and plants everywhere. Snake plants. Mother-in-law tongue. Aloe vera and umbrella plants. Boring southwestern style bric-a-brac that can be found in every single gift shop in the state. As soon as I walk through the door, there's the couch. The same ratty gray couch I used to lay on while watching TV with Tocki when we were growing up. Oak coffee table. Matching television stand. The view outside the window looks out onto the forgotten swimming pool and the roof of another run-down apartment building. Beyond that, the abandoned sugar mill with all its creepy broken windows. It's the exact living room set up I grew up with, only smaller and with a worse view. Shrunken and condensed to fit into a smaller life.

I pass the tiny living room and go straight to the kitchen table. Different table. Our old one never would've fit in this cramped space. This one looks as though it belongs in a diner, or cafe. Small and square with a solid metal base instead of four legs.

Kelly offers me a beer, but doesn't sit at the table with me.

"How old are you?" I twist the cap off my beer. "Sorry, I mean, if you don't mind me asking."

"No, it's okay." She scrunches her nose. "I'm thirty-two."

"Oh."

Kelly sits down. "It's weird, right? Me only being a couple of years older than you? It's weird."

"Yeah, it's weird. But, don't worry about it. It could be weirder. I actually thought you were much younger."

"Oh, man." She shakes her head. Lets out a little laugh. "That would've been weirder. Thanks, though."

A key jingles in the doorknob and Kelly jumps up out of her seat. "Shit. I accidentally locked him out again." She opens the door and in walks my father. The color has been completely washed from his beard. It's all white. Flecks of black and brown run through the silvery white on his head. His tattooed arms, sunburned and a little less defined than they were the last time I saw him. His eyes, still green, have lost their brightness. Dim and tired, lined with deeper crow's feet than I've seen on him, but he still looks strong and hard. The light may have gone out somewhere inside of him, but nothing else has changed. Same chain wallet and leather vest with its dirty and worn patches from various motorcycle runs and fallen comrades. Same big hands, streaked with dark engine grease stains, hard and calloused.

He looks at me, blinks and closes the door behind him. "Hey, Kid."

"Hey, Dad."

Kelly turns to me, then back to my old man. "Oh, I almost forgot. I need to talk to Lennie across the way for a minute. I'll be back in a few."

My dad's hard, dim face softens, becomes perplexed. "Lennie? What the hell you need to talk to him for?"

It occurs to me that he doesn't want her to leave. He's afraid to be alone with me. He needs the buffer to keep the conversation light and superficial. Kelly turns to me, and smiles. "I hope we'll get to talk some more before you take off."

"Yeah," I say. "Me, too." The way she smiles at me, though, gives me the sense that she knows what a coward my dad is when it comes to honest conversation with his daughter. She might be another one of the old man's bimbos, but maybe not. Something tells me she isn't.

She leaves. My dad comes to the kitchen, offers me a beer; seeing I already have one, grabs one for himself, pops it open and sits down.

"Heard you and Walter split up."

"Yeah. It was time."

"It was time. Jesus." He shakes his head, and takes a swig of his beer. "You sound like your mother."

"Well, not much more I can say about it than that. Some things have an expiration date."

"Everything has an expiration date."

For what feels like hours, we say nothing. The only sounds in the room are beers being sipped. It's no more than a few seconds, but it's a silence so heavy, it kills all the sound in the room. All sound everywhere. No sound comes in from outside. The whole building, the whole town, and everything in the world stops and is frozen by our silence.

When I can't take it, and I finally feel strong enough to break it, I say, "Tocki died."

"Shit. I'm sorry, Kid." His face softens again, and I see a man I used to know. A man I admired, who put me on a pedestal. We were everything to one another. I see a glimpse of him, and I long to reach out and hold it, make him stay, but I know I can't. It's merely a passing image that will soon fade.

"Yeah, me too. He was everything to me. And now he's gone forever."

"You know, you look more and more like your mother as time goes by." He leans forward, rests his elbows on his knees and folds his hands together.

"Is that why you like me less and less as time goes by?"

It happens again where the void between us sucks the sound and motion out of this small apartment, out of the entire crappy green brick apartment building. All of Colorado and the whole world stopped by the deafening nothing that sits between father and daughter at this tiny kitchen table.

I wonder why I came here. I know I wanted something else to happen, a magical reunion between father and daughter that would heal every other wound I'd inflicted on my life. I wanted to be everything in my father's eyes again and I wanted to see regret in those eyes when he looked at me. I knew none of it would happen, but I drove here and put myself through this scene anyway. Sometimes, we need so much to be loved by those who didn't love us well enough that the longing short circuits our brains and turns us into fucking idiots.

Inside of me, the words are flying around in my mind, ricocheting off one another. How he could have been the hero in my life after my mother left us. How I thought I was okay with her leaving because I had him, but with each year that I grew into my adult body, he went on more and more road trips with his biker buddies. He drank more. Got into trouble more. Brought more women around. He failed me because he couldn't live with me reminding him of the woman who left him; couldn't have me in the way of the women he brought around trying to forget her.

The words come, they want to scream at him for robbing me of the future I had planned for myself. For pulling those plans out from underneath me because he couldn't keep his shit together enough for us to have a home. The words come, but I can't get them out of my head. My mouth won't work, can't form the sounds of anything honest and necessary.

My speech can only manage short phrases of nothing important, so I take my phone out of my pocket and look at the screen, pretending I don't already know what time it is. "It's almost five o'clock." I stand up. "I should take off."

"Kelly's pregnant."

"What? Is it yours?"

"Of course it's mine. You're gonna have a little brother or sister."

"She doesn't look pregnant."

"She wears it well. Hides it all under my old t-shirts."

"You know, she's my age."

"She's a couple years older."

"Oh my god. I'm sorry, I've got to go. It was good seeing you, Dad."

Downstairs, Kelly is sitting at one of the picnic tables with the cigarette butt lady and a skinny man wearing a baseball cap and no shirt. He looks as though he was formed out of driftwood and old shoe leather.

"You taking off?" Kelly's smile is soft and sympathetic.

"Yeah, I've got somewhere I need to be."

"Okay. I'll walk you to your car."

Once we're away from her strange, scraggly neighbors, she says, "How'd it go?"

"Not great. You don't look pregnant."

She pulls the baggy shirt tight around her belly. "There's a baby bump hiding under here."

"Did you tell him to contact me about this? Doesn't seem like he would do it on his own."

"I felt like you should know." She shrugs, brushes some of her coppery ringlets away from her face. "I want my kid to know his or her sister."

Part of me wants to jump in my car, slam the gas and never look back. The same part of me that regrets coming here. Then I look over at that discarded Saab, its interior rotted and cracked, bits of trash and beer bottles on its floor. Kelly's big brown eyes, the freckles on her cheeks.

"Okay," I say. "But next time, just call me yourself. We don't need to go through him."

Future Life

My cubicle is small. I have to be careful when rolling my chair back to stand up, or else I'll hit the wall behind me. Carl sits on the other side of that wall. Carl wears a different color sweater vest every day. He eats candy bars and drinks diet soda. The other day, he used the word "gosh" sincerely, without a trace of irony. Every morning, when he walks past my cubicle with his can of diet soda, he smiles and says, "Good morning, Axeline!" or, "How are ya today, Axeline?". I like Carl.

I feel out of place here, but I think the notion of me being an outsider weirdo is an idea that exists in my own head. Everyone else working in this office, they either don't notice me, or they're nice to me. I'm not sure how long I'll be here. The woman at the temp agency who sent me here a few months ago told me I'd probably be able to work here full time as long as I didn't make any major screw ups.

"You don't have many skills for office work," she'd said. "You'll have to start at entry level."

I nodded. "That'll be okay. I don't mind." It was the truth. I don't mind having to learn everything all over again. The things I know, they're useless to me now.

I make the same amount of money, because Neil didn't pay us shit.

Lucy moved in with me. To celebrate our new roommate status, I took her to Paradise Cove. I introduced her to Marc and we all had a few beers. "You should come work here," he said. "I can get you a waitress job today if you want it. You could walk to work, and as you sashay like a drunkard's angel from table to table providing libations to the great unwashed, I will serenade you."

I couldn't see myself waiting tables, making small talk and being congenial with an endless stream of inebriated strangers, or staying sober for more than a few hours at a time, so I thanked him and said I didn't think it was for me. Turned out, it was for Lucy. Sometimes, after her shift at the bar, she'll tell me, "You know, you should give Marc a serious chance. He cares for you a lot. And he's cool."

"Maybe you're right." I feel a warmth flow through me, recalling the way Marc kisses and his strong Nordic face. "But, for now, I just need him to be my buddy, to talk with me and drink with me and exchange stories and think about life with me."

"Do you even hear yourself? You sound like him."

"I'm too busy for that right now."

"Busy doing what? Working in a cube farm?"

"Learning. I'm busy learning."

"I thought Gavin was your big learning experience."

I shake my head and laugh. "He was definitely a learning experience.

But, now everything's new. And I've got new things to learn."

"I wonder what happened to that guy."

"I don't know. Back at school and learning how to look at people, with any luck."

I mention to Lucy that I started selling some of my masks through the internet. Having a roommate, and making a small bit of extra money, I'm a little less poor than I was when I first left Walter six months ago. Luce suggests another trip to Deadwood, or maybe even Vegas this time.

When I tell her I can't go because I enrolled in a few classes at the community college, she laughs, and I think she's going to give me a hard time about it. She nudges me in the arm. "It's about time. You fucking nerd."

Kelly invited me to come along with her for an ultrasound. On the screen, I stared at the fuzzy lump inside of her. This peanut-shaped thing that'll soon be my baby brother. After it was over, we recounted various stories about ourselves while shoving potato chips and sub sandwiches into our faces. She told me how my father was only supposed to be a one-night stand.

"You know how it is," she said, "You have a bad day, end up hooking up."

Yeah, yeah I do. I know how it is.

She explained that the rubber broke. That she didn't plan for life to go this way, but now it did. She didn't want to be a mother, but she's determined to make it work as best as she can.

When I tell her how my father isn't good at sticking around to the end of the ride, she shrugs, pops a chip into her mouth and says, "No one sticks around to the end of the ride. It's not the end of the ride that matters. It's the scenery."

She's going to be a great mother.

People like Kelly, I don't understand. Their wiring confuses and fascinates me. They don't look ahead, at what could go wrong, at all those dangers lurking around the corners of the future. Kelly, Marc, and Lucy, they're all existing in the here and now, wrapping both fists tight around what's in front of them, without demanding that it be more than it is. They don't live in fear of what's ahead, or stagnate from lingering in the graveyard of what's been left behind. They sever connections. They make new ones. There are times, when I look in their eyes, past the surface of what they are, and I can see a window to a room inside of them where the person I'm becoming with them in my life has just walked in.

Author's Bio:

Rasmenia Massoud is from Colorado, but after a few weird turns, ended up spending several years in France. Once she learned all she could about cheese and macarons, she found herself living in England, where she writes about what she struggles most to understand: human beings. She is the author of the short story collections Human Detritus and Broken Abroad. Some of her other work has appeared in places like The Foundling Review, The Lowestoft Chronicle, Literary Orphans, The Molotov Cocktail, Full of Crow, Flash Fiction Offensive and Underground Voices. You can visit her at: http://www.rasmenia.com/

Doctor Porchiat's Dream

By Frankie Rollins

"What are books but tangible dreams?
What is reading if not dreaming?
The best books cause us to dream; the rest are not worth reading."
from *A Fan-Makers Inquisition* by Rikki Ducornet

Acknowledgements

Thanks to these journals who have published pieces of the *Doctor Porchiat's Dream* in similar or slightly different forms:

"Antwerp, Alone," *Feminist Wire*, January 2017
"The Lavotte Girl," *Speculative 66*, Nov 2016
"Excerpt from Doctor Porchiat's Dream," *Cababi*, Nov 2016
"Doctor Porchiat Speaks" *Sonora Review*, Issue 64/65 Spring 2014

The Woman in the Well

The cows sway against one another, some lean near the fence. Dawn rises, casting blue light. Stones in the road throw tiny shadows, each weed waves a curvy seed, the worn wood of the fence holds its weathered creases, the angles of the village beyond rise sharp and bright against the land.

She has been walking all day and night and the burden she carries is great. Her feet are swollen and bleeding in her boots. She is not old, yet she has aged beyond all natural age. She sees the blue clarity, but it is the village she seeks and must reach. She has traveled a great distance to find this, an ordinary village. A village where people are born and live and die. Where meals are eaten, stories told, loves and ordinary sorrows fill out the days. She drags her feet down the stone road.

She enters the village and people are moving about. A child gathers eggs, a woman stacks wood onto a fire beneath a great black kettle, a man crosses with a pitchfork, but she does not pause nor do they. Light cracks over the town, liquid. She trudges past, hears the clatter of pans and sleep-shushed voices, heads toward the center of town where there will be a well.

As a child, she drew water from a well with her sisters. That was a tiny village in the mountains. This well is in the sun, in the center of a paved square. All around the square are businesses, houses, tall windows, painted shutters, stoops. There are a few older girls gathered with their buckets, but they are talking to each other and do not pay her any attention. They are living curves in their dresses, sloping towards each other or bending away with laughter. She smiles in their direction but does not stop. She crosses the flagstones to the well, breathes the great mossy wet of the water below. All the hurts she has carried so far break and spread inside her, and she leans into the well, letting the weight of her dying take her down into the dark.

The three young women see her fall. They scream, drop their pails, and run to the well. In the depths below, they cannot see anything but their own reflections in the water, their hair dangling down.

Poor mother, they murmur.

Later, when many of the villagers are gathered and the young doctor, the priest, and the men of the town lower the baling hook into the water, everyone waits breathlessly. The hook is lowered, dragged, each man handing the thick rope to the man next to him, and they pull it up, once, twice, thrice, empty. The watchers are silent. The girls who saw her fall stand together, holding hands. They are trembling. The hook is attached to a longer rope, lowered, dragged again, from one man to the next, pulled up. The men shake their heads. They hand the rope around again and again, staring down into the water. They confer. They turn and stare at the girls.

The girls are called over to the well. Each tells the story again. The old woman crossed the square. She leaned toward the well, she fell in.

"Ask them," the men say to the doctor. "Ask them."

Young Doctor Porchiat, moved by the girls' sincerity and anxiety, asks, "Was there a splash?"

The girls frown. They don't know. They can't remember. Was there a splash, they ask one another?

Everyone contemplates the soundlessness of the fall.

"There's nothing in this well," the men tell the girls. "We would know. This hook can't lie." One man spits in the dust. Another begins to roll up the wet rope. A growing dissent and disbelief stirs the crowd.

"They lied!" One voice cries.

"They made it up!" Says another.

Doctor Porchiat affirms softly for the girls, "There isn't a body in the well."

"She went in," they cry, "she fell in!" The girls turn to each other, pulling on each other's dresses.

"Poor mother," they say. "She is gone and no one to believe us!" Their weeping is inconsolable. Their bodies heave with sobs. The villagers circle around them, closing in, each trying to hear what the girls say.

The quiet morning becomes something else entirely, and the village is angry. "Liars!"

Doctor Porchiat steps into the crowd and urges the families of the girls to lead them away from the increasingly outraged villagers.

The girls wail at being separated from one another. Villagers shout angrily after the weeping girls. Doctor Porchiat and the constable disperse them, send them to their work.

An old woman complains, "Imagine, to disturb a whole working day with this nonsense!"

After, the townspeople are divided. Some think a new well should be dug. Others believe that the girls are lying. These want the girls punished. The landed gentry wants the new well dug, one further out of town, closer to their lands.

There is hysteria among people who claim they have fallen ill after drinking from the well, but the doctor will not support such theories, finding spoiled food and miasmas to blame.

Everyone blames the families of the girls. Folks claim that these families should pay for the new well. Superstitious villagers chant over the water, leave charms and offerings. Some walk in wide circles around the well. Most of the villagers drink the water, regardless. Some joke amongst themselves about the flavor of strangers. Some curse the water and mutter.

Groups are formed for and against drinking from the well. Papers are written and signed, but carrying water from the river is hard, slow work. Even the most suspicious soon give it up. No one can agree on anything, and no one will pay for a new well. The whole argument eventually fades.

Those who know the girls believe them. These are not particularly mean-spirited, imperious, clever, or deceitful girls. The girls saw a woman fall in, and if there wasn't a body, then something else must have fallen. Something less well understood. For a time, the girls are no longer simply village girls, they are the ones-who-saw-the-stranger-fall-in-the-well. Luckily, these girls are already promised to husbands who are still willing to marry them, and the marriages are rushed. The girls become wives and are thus broken from one another and this taint.

Late at night, when the wooden floors sigh and villagers moan in their sleep, stories about the woman in the well weave their way into the bedside tales of sleepless children. While the candles gutter in their pewter wells, mothers, sisters, nannies, aunts finds themselves above faces fevered or pale with fear.

The only way, as anybody knows, to pass such wide, deep nights is to tell a story.

The Story Speaks

A child, unable to sleep, asks, "Tell me a story?"

The woman tending this child must think of something. What better than a story with no ending? What better than the village's defining story, that of a strange woman entering the town, falling into a well, vanishing?

It is in these hollowed out spaces that I am formed. Here I appear in your mutable human shape, relentless and joyous, and if I hold the not-knowing within these very specific sentences, this is where you mean to keep not-knowing, where you meant to keep it all along. A story thrives on the desire for what is next.

This is a story of a village and it is not a story of a village. It is a story of human lives and weather and buildings, mountains and human love and betrayals and deaths, also. Any village is nothing but stories.

If you wonder how I begin, even in your wondering, you make me.

This is how it was in the village late at night, with the sisters and nannies and mothers and aunties saying, *Shhh, shhh, shhhh,* to sleepless children. These are the women whose minds and mouths first formed the sentences, the ideas that marked this particular semblance out of the murk, their story: an absence, the vanishing of a woman, dead in a well, no, not dead exactly, but gone.

You wonder what good it does to tell a story and I say, I am the long white bones buried in your red flesh, I am the pulsing; I am the wincing, the confidence, the longing, the dreaming, the calling out; I am the softening, the thickening, the nodding, the swallowing throat; I am the what-ness that floats between you and yourself and you and each other. I am a voice in the dark.

Let me tell you:

A woman falls into the village well and vanishes.

Stories first sewn in the mouths of mothers, sisters, nannies, aunties become the fabric of lives. Like weeds, these stories grow thickly green, freeze and brown, wither and die, linger hiding, burst forth again.

The children asked, "Tell us about the well." And in each house a different story emerged.

The woman came from a far-off mountain village that awaits her return.

The woman came from a far-off mountain village where all the people but one were killed in a war.

After drinking from the well, a man dreams a dream that almost kills him, and then he turns into a bird and flies away.

After drinking from the well, a woman dies of a broken heart.

After drinking from the well, a woman becomes an animal that is hunted.

After drinking from the well, a young man snaps all his loves in half, like beans.

I'll tell you each of these stories, and you'll exclaim, this proves nothing about the woman in the well. These sorts of things happen all the time!

And I'll say, *Yes, yes, yes, that is very true.*

Doctor Porchiat Speaks

For centuries, medical men have failed to find the soul. We have mistaken glands for it. Mental strangeness. Blood diseases. But never was there evidence of such a thing in the body, not in the flesh and blood.

When I was a young man, I dreamt the evidence of such a thing, and this dream ruined me. Exalted me.

I am older now and spend most of my time in front of this window, as you see, looking down onto the bustling city streets. Streets that have nothing in common with that old village. This pane of bubbled glass is my lens. I spend a lot of time thinking things over. I am diminished by my scars, and I have plenty of hours to pass.

I arrived at the village to replace the ancient and doddering physician who held the post before me. I was mistrusted and trusted equally by the citizens and earned slowly, meal by meal, day by day, their trust.

Then a woman fell in the well. The woman was a stranger who came to town, and three village girls witnessed her falling. But a body was never found. I believed that the girls saw her. I still believe. This is my ultimate failing as a doctor. My willingness to believe that there are parts of human life that cannot be examined nor understood through bone, blood, and flesh.

Certainly, the girls believed she fell in the well. They keened. The men in the village dragged that well. Even though we know that bodies float, we tied weights to the hooks we sent down, just in case. Nothing. There was nothing there. If the girls had a vision, they all had the same vision at the same moment. Not likely. But these were village girls, from decent families. They'd simply been doing their chores. They saw a woman go in the well. I daresay I don't know what you'll make of it. I've never known myself. Then we went back to our business.

I attended the births of children. I watched them grow. I measured their fevers and sorted their broken bones. It wasn't until one of my favorites, a young girl named Isabelle, was killed by a horse, that I first had the dream which changed my life. This dream is the blank page upon which this story is written.

Isabelle had always been a wild little girl. She bore some reckless fire within. She climbed furniture, fences, fell off things. She burned her right hand, half-drowned, and was dragged twenty yards by a carriage by the time she was six. It wasn't that she wanted to scare her parents, it wasn't bravada. Merely that she could resist nothing. Transfixed by ideas, she felt compelled to try them all. She was the kind of child you found watching you when you thought you were alone.

Another time she sang herself entirely hoarse, trying to perfect a song for her father on his return from one of his long trips away. When she learned to read, her mother had to ban her from the library and give her one book at a time after she'd been found sobbing in a pile of books.

She wasn't only my favorite, but also her mother's favorite. No one could believe it when this child died. I was sent for, told to hurry, that it was urgent. When I arrived, the child had clearly been dead at least an hour. In the room alone with her, I had to roll that little neck in my hand, feel the snapped connection, her long hair tangling around my hand. Her eyes were still open, and their emptiness was horrifying. I closed them, crossed her small arms.

Her mother, Penelope, was administered opiate, so she was quiet. But in the middle of that night, the child was brought to my office by two of Penelope's brothers. The brothers did not speak a word to me, though of course we knew each other. I'd birthed their own children and helped one of them through a terrible flu. They brought the small box into my office and stood there staring down at my floor.

It is well-known by now that doctors must examine the dead to learn the causes of living. But not then. In a village, such a thing was against moral and social code. The brothers waited for Penelope to enter the room. She told them to be back before dawn and they turned and left.

Penelope was sick with grief, her eyes reddened wild. She paced, wept, screamed, begged. She'd brought Isabelle for *autopsie*, she said. I said, no, I couldn't. She said yes, I could. She wanted to know: what had been the source of her daughter's wildness? It was in her body, Penelope insisted. It was in her body, for god's sakes, and I must see what it was.

I told her that the child had broken her neck on a fall from a horse and surely there wasn't need for further investigation when a death is as clear as that.

Penelope said to me, "You and I are nothing like her. Her father, nothing. My brothers and sisters, nothing. My father, my mother. My husband's parents. You know this child is not the same. I want you to tell me what happened here. Why is my daughter dead?" She threw herself upon me, her body hot and damp through her silk dress. "Find out what made her."

I said, "Medical men have spent centuries trying to ascertain the form of the soul in the physical body, and no one has succeeded."

"I am not talking about all *physical bodies*," Penelope wailed, "I am talking about this one."

There was nothing to find, of course. I looked. Autopsy requires a strong stomach. Translated as "see for yourself," you must be prepared for what you see. I had studied. I had wanted to do this. I never imagined that Isabella would be my first. I cut the child open. I peeled back her skin. I broke the cage of her ribs. I took a lot of time. I kept the door locked, in case. A grotesque embroidery, streaked with yellow fat, twined with blue-black arteries. Sausaged intestines, the planks of lung. Could this mess propel a human life? It seems impossible that these ruffled slakes of skin could lead to a light in the eyes of an Isabella. I weighed her small organs. She was a normal little girl. And small. So small that it brought tears to my eyes. She had been in perfect health. I sewed her up more clumsily than I would have liked. I was tired. I washed the body, bruised from its fall, and I returned her to her little velvet dress. I lay her in her coffin. After, there was mopping, the washing of soaked cloths, the rinsing of basins. I washed myself, the smell of blood so distinct and the tiny intestines, too, gave a slender reek. I turned off the lights and opened the windows. I stepped into the library, where Penelope, sleeping and free of horror for a moment, was pale and strewn across my leather chair. I waited for her to wake and when she did, I told her that her daughter was as normal as the morning sun, that what was special in Isabelle was in her heart, in her spirit. Her neck had broken.

She searched my face. I stood and waited, feeling as though I stood for all of science in that moment, clear and free of mystery. The child had been lively, she had fallen. I had done all I could. Penelope and her brothers took the coffin. Penelope left, leaden and silent.

After, I stood in my small kitchen, eating stale bread and cheese, gulping from a pot of water, wishing there had been something.

This was the state I was in when I crawled into bed and had a dream unlike any before.

In the dream I found it, tucked away behind the heart. The soul. I knew I'd never seen anything like it before. I snipped it free from the small web of arteries, washed it clean of blood, and set it in an enamel bowl. It was tiny, parchment colored, yellow-clear, and gilled, little shutters on either side.

It was perfectly formed. Not like some tumors I'd removed, with teeth or hair or lumpy wads of flesh. This was a fine, made thing. Without any practical scientific proof, I knew this was the thing that Penelope suspected.

This was the mania I set my whole life after. This is where my studies began in earnest. I believed there would be evidence, proof to support my dream. My own optimism, my own fanatic belief, a snake dreaming its own tail.

Such blind fervency is always the place where men fail. I don't regret the dream.

I was a good doctor. People forget this in the wake of their outrage, their priggishness. Didn't they wonder how I knew to wash my hands? Didn't they wonder how I knew the ways that gout thickened their feet? Didn't they understand that knowledge bears the price of learning? I shared everything I knew with them. I treated them with the knowledge I gained from their dead, and that village grew healthier and healthier. *Hic locus est ubi mors gaudet succurrere vitae.* This is the place where death rejoices to help the living.

I saved many. I lost some. I lost Margaret, who I tried to save. I saved the Lavotte girl, and then she saved me. I made enemies. Even with the best intentions, there will be enemies. Take the woman falling in the well. I made enemies there. I was young. I believed the girls. I held a scientific testing of the waters. I used myself as example and drank from the well, noted my physical being every day for weeks. Offered these details to the villagers. There were those who never forgave me this defense. But we needed the water! Here in this window, thinking, I wonder at myself. What kind of medical man believes in something unprovable? The woman in the well. The dream of the organ. But we live with these kinds of truths all the time! There are many inexplicable events. And if we believe there is not grace between the physical selves and the spiritual selves, won't we just be stuck in the same spot forever? Isn't it these blind faiths, these suspicions, that lead us forward to new knowledge? Such questions befit not a doctor, but a philosopher, I know.

When the countryside fell to fevers, I was not arrogant. I sent to the city for an apprentice specialist on fevers. I sent for young Antwerp Luther and he arrived.

He needed a smaller village for his studies, a smaller group so he could track how certain problems spread. He was a bright young doctor. He fell in love with a village girl, Louise, and thus began all the unfortunate events to follow.

It is an awful loss, the marriage they could have made. They were much taken with one another. They were, in a sense, my family. Like children I could have had.

We worked on the study of infection together. Louise took to our work. Not just because, as people said, she'd found a marriageable husband and would settle her ways. No, Louise had found science. The magic of the microscope. The village, too small for her originally, became massive, infinite, grand in scale, once she had science. She was especially interested in Antwerp's research. Since she had grown up in a family of ten children, she knew firsthand how sickness passed from one to the next to the next. She was the more intuitive, the more gifted scientist of the two. Antwerp's breakthroughs had been to repeat the same experiments he'd read about, but once he worked with Louise, they began to understand the passages of germs.

Her death, by the way, had nothing to do with me or Antwerp. She had a heart imperfection, and I don't mean in her manner of loving. We didn't know the cause of it, but she had an aunt die of it, too.

Still. We couldn't imagine that Louise would die. Not even a doctor thinks such things. It is a sorrow that bears no explanation, will entertain none.

The Lavotte Girl visits me. She saved me, after. She was a shadow in the streets, with nothing to say, eyes as big as skies, watching us all.

I met her when her brother came to my door one morning, a stranger, but whose blue eyes I recognized as belonging to the whole Lavotte brood whom I'd seen in the market. Foreigners, they were called, though they'd lived at the edge of the village for more than one generation. They spoke little, paid for what they wanted, and left, yet they drew my attention. How was it, I wondered, that they did not need the company of others?

The boy took me to the farm in the hills. We entered a low-ceilinged small house lined with nests of children's bedclothes on the hard dirt floor. There must have been six children sitting in a circle, all turning uncanny blue eyes on me when I entered. And here was the mother, fainting with pain, trying to give birth with only one girl of about eleven helping her. The origin of the eyes appeared in the father who came stamping in, said nothing, nodded to me and sat on a chair near his brood. All those round, blue eyes silently watched my ministrations. This young Lavotte girl helping me, though, was different. She spoke in a low voice, asking what I needed. She was there at my side. The birth was hard, a breech, and I wondered what would happen, blood everywhere. We saved the child, a girl. There was relief and each family member cried out and smiled when the baby's cry was heard. It was the first time I'd seen any of them smile. I watched my girl-helper tenderly stroking her mother's hair, murmuring.

A year later, this same girl came to me, walking that long two miles, to ask if I knew of a place in town for her to work. I knew the church pastor needed a girl to clean, and I trusted him to be kind to her. I set this up. She asked nothing else of me and we only passed each other occasionally. At first, she moved among the other servant girls of the town, but eventually, she moved alone. I only wondered about her when I saw her, and then I forgot her.

You don't know how the crossroads of lives will play out.

Now I know she was studying us all, from the second she arrived in the village. She was using her invisibility to set things straight. She told me about it later. Leaving bread at the orphanage. Slipping a warm coat into a widow's cold room. This is how she makes her way in the world now, too. She goes into places where there are children and sets things to rights. She gets a job in a place, and slowly, surely, fixes, changes, organizes orphanages and schools. Our desire to care for others is what we have in common. Had, I should say. I am no one's doctor now.

Guardian and keeper of the villagers' health, I was charged with grave robbing and betrayed.

Burned skin had to be peeled from me like a rind.

When Louise died, she left a letter. Granting me permission. One's personal horror of anatomy is not everyone's. But they wouldn't believe there was a note. They couldn't believe, because it was not in their own hearts to imagine such a gift. And Antwerp, who knew better, was blind with grief and jealousy. That Louise had given me in death what had belonged to him in life. Who would blame him?

They found Louise in my office that night. Antwerp called them. Antwerp, smeared with Louise's blood, stood in the square and called them down on me. They smashed my windows, and glass showered

Louise and me. These marauders were my friends, you understand. My patients. Children I'd brought into the world. Men whose lives I'd saved. Women I'd tended with cloth and needle and salve.

People are easily led. They fear what they don't know. We are a ferocious species. There is in us a savagery. You see it everywhere, and you know that this is true. Look at any human war.

Still, there is beauty, also. The love of people and place. You live in a town long enough to know the songs of particular birds during particular times of the year. When the creak of the well bucket will awaken you, when the shadows of plane trees will cross the cobbles in your path. You know the sound of a carriage rattling across the square, the dust rising and settling after the whoosh-whoosh of someone's broom clearing the same dirt from the same stones every day. You await the rosy tint of dusk, the first knock at the baker's door, the first coin tinking, children bent and hunched to an errand. You'll both see and not see the old women swatting flies, hear the high croon of a baby's wail four doors down. You emerge on your stoop, call the tavern boy to fetch a horse, and you can't know. You can't know that all of it will be gone from you one day.

For twenty-five years, it was my village, too. I kept my notes, despite. This is part of the miracle, that I am alive, that I have these things. I owe this to the Lavotte girl. She got my valise. And she waited in the dark while the mob roared, while they painted me with black tar, while they mocked and taunted and broke my heart.

I was burned by the boiling pitch they poured on me. A storm of chicken feathers blinded me. They drove me out of town and left me on the road. And so, I passed out there, among the rocks and weeds.

The Lavotte Girl woke me. She had followed all the way, miles out of town, and she'd hidden in the bushes. She carried my valise, to which she'd added a jumble of medicines from my cabinets, not knowing which was which! Merciful girl! We spent a day or two in some shade. I remember little of it. This village girl, of no experience, and no social skill, brought food and medicine for me, was not afraid of my blackened skin. She plucked my feathers as efficiently as any farmer's wife preparing a chicken for dinner.

I remember it as a dream, the Lavotte Girl plucking my feathers, sewing two sheets stolen from a line together, asking, *where do we go?*

The Lavotte girl mummified me in her sheets, so that it might appear I was suffering a horrible illness, something contagious, perhaps. I told her the way to the city and in another day, she'd stolen a small cart. It was Antwerp who betrayed me, and yet, his darling of studies, infectious disease, is what saved me.

You can imagine the horrors of that trip. I was in pain and the girl pulled the cart, herself! Lugging this heap, like so many potatoes, but much heavier. Those we met pitied her the diseased "uncle" she dragged. They fed her and kept their distance from my sheeted self. I remember her face above me, chewing the meat and passing it into my mouth, the base of my throat too sore to move. We traveled in a state of disbelief, and grief, our old selves falling away on the road.

Lavotte, as she goes by now, doesn't live here anymore, and when she does return, she tells me what she sees. She brought me here to the city and my old friend, John, cared for me. I taught her to read and her hunger for learning was immense. I have been lucky, to teach two such pupils as Lavotte and Louise.

Lavotte has been back to the village, only to visit her family. I have not gone back there. I will not ever. I like to think of it, before. The world, as it grows modern, wants nothing to do with the magic of living. Now we're interested in machinery. The city I live in is filling with smoke, the people under my window rush to some unseen force, and there are whistles that blow into the noontime and evening airs. I miss living in a village.

There are times I wish it had been different. That I'd found a wife, made a family, simply doctored and become a fixture at people's dinners.

The particulars of anatomy are not beautiful. A distinctly gray, bulbous, yellow-fatted and blood-tangled affair. When I became acquainted with the nuances of mortality and that clockwork, that mindless function of lust and love and decay, well the idea of romance dimmed. The divinities of the mind and research, this was where romance lay. If I'd had a regular life, though, a wife, children. Yes, it is possible that my insane dream would not have taken hold. That I would still live in that village, that I would be loved and not burned.

I was enamored of dead men. What they'd left in idea and ink. Those early anatomists, no matter how wrong, I loved them for their curiosity, for their willingness to leap into what might be. What they didn't know was infinite compared to what they did know. They leapt all the same, cut back the brush, dealt a pathway into the unknown. Those that opposed them were fools, not understanding that we are never, not for one moment, alone in this living. Yes, alone in death, surely in death, but not in living.

The night after I autopsied Isabella, I had the dream. I know it was a dream. But it was also true. The organ in my dream was small. Papery looking. Shuttered. Tissue-like, not muscle or any recognizable tissue. Finer. What could its purpose be? It cleansed nothing as the liver did, it transported nothing I could see, gave not air, nor cells, nor refuse. The connections to the heart were the apron strings of a fairy! What use was this thing to the body? It was the soul. That is what I believed I'd seen.

It is in us now. Right now. I believe this.

I've put many things in jars. Limbs, lumps, teeth, warts, intestines, spines. The solution yellows and the flesh dissolves over time. *This* organ, though, would have hung in its solution eternally white and precise, as though something cut of paper. A child's paper airplane, a boat.

There is something to be grateful for in tragedy. I will never be as alone, disappointed, afraid, or lost again, as I was, the night they painted me with boiling tar. I will never again look into my neighbor's eyes while he applies the burning pitch and think *once I took this man a basket of apples.*

They'd misunderstood. They thought that I'd tricked Louise. Her family knew better, but they weren't there that night. If anyone had been able to bend Louise to his or her will, believe this, she would have been married to a farmer when her heart gave out. Unless she believed there was something to find, she wouldn't have given me her body so that I could look for her soul.

She was going to die, regardless. That's what we didn't understand. She knew. We didn't know how to fix it. Antwerp refused to hear. A doctor that refuses to hear is a mortician. To listen, well, what does it matter? Neither of us knew how to save her.

Antwerp thought I was crazy to worship, as he called it, a dream. He tolerated it and respected me enough to honor my beliefs. It wasn't cruelty that drove him, or professional scorn; he never told my tormenters what I sought in Louise. He turned on me simply because of a lover's jealousy. Louise didn't give him her body in death because she knew that no man in his right mind would dissect his lover's body. But all the same. It is intimate, dissection. What is beneath.

Antwerp was young. He couldn't have known what would happen. I wonder how many nightmares he has carried of me since. For my part, I heard him screaming when they brought the tar. I heard him screaming *No.* Until they took him away, I heard him. I know he regretted what he'd done.

Strange things happen everywhere, but in cities, all the miracles, dark and light, are swallowed by constant motion. It's impossible to draw all the threads and see how a thing is made. But in a village, it's different. Something out of the ordinary breaks like a storm. It changes you for always.

Despite my agonies, I still believe that we must hold what we are certain of, however dreamlike and intangible, because if you can love a thing, a person, an idea, a belief, it gains a kind of certainty that will shape you. You can't fear the shape you will become, if it is born in love. You can't fear the dreams that form within you.

The Story of the Lavotte Girl

When Doctor Porchiat was tarred and feathered, I fell to my knees. In front those flames and flickering light, his feathers were shocking! A man turned into a bird! I'd heard the stories about what would happen when we drank the water, after the woman fell in the well. There was a story about a man turning into a bird, and when this one came true, I knew they would all come true, and it frightened me. I had to leave.

I chose his story, Doctor Porchiat's, to attach to my own. He was the one who needed help from all those people whom he'd helped, and no one would give it. Right that very moment, I knew.

I went into his office, saw that poor girl naked and split to the stone like a peach. I covered her with a sheet, packed his bag, and followed the mob with its softening cries to the outskirts of town. I lifted the blackened, feathered man they left crumpled by the side of the road. Together, we flew away.

The Story of Louise

Louise stretches in the hay. John stares at the wall above with one leg heavy across her thigh. She watches him, and beyond his face the dust motes spin and twirl in the stall. She wonders if these flecks of light and dust are landing on his blond eyelashes, on the slope of his upper lip, the hair growing there. His long brown arm rests on his hip, his pants smooth and flecked with bits of hay. There is only another minute or so of this time, and then he'll need to get back to his chores before his father and brothers arrive, and she'll walk home alone through the woods.

She knows her sisters' and brothers' faces so well, they are scratched on the inside of her skull, each with his or her own set of eyes, mannerisms, habits of speech. John's face is different geography, she sees it more rarely, and often in the dark. The way his bones are shaped, the slant of his eyes, all of it is another world entirely. She tickles John's nose with a sprig of hay, and he reaches out with closed eyes, grabs her, and rolls them both over in the hay, both laughing silently.

Louise reads the books her younger siblings bring home from school. It has been five years since she was called back to the farm and her own studies ended. She memorizes their spellers, reads the history, asks for repetitions of their arithmetic problems. Her brothers and sisters are the best students in the school because Louise is so hungry for their knowledge. Because they love her, they bring home their lessons for her. In return, she makes games for them. Louise is careful not to scold as her mother scolds, not to predict, expect, demand. She coaxes.

She says the day will come when she doesn't know everything the teacher has offered them. This day has already come, but she pretends it hasn't. She makes up arithmetic problems and solves them. She visits the preacher to ask for books, and he suggests she read the bible. She does, but then she finishes it. Everything about her life feels too small. She doesn't know how to make it larger.

She likes flirting with John, kissing him in the barn before he leaves to join his family in the fields. But even this feels like not enough. Does she really want to become his wife? A farm wife? A mother? Cooking meals, washing, and raising children? Does she want to become her mother? She does not. But what else is there? It's the only story she knows. She goes to dances, dances too hard, stays too long, laughs too loudly. John has warned her, her mother has warned her, her sister has warned her, her aunt has warned her: *You must not behave this way.* Louise doesn't know how to explain that she must.

Her chores are like a long road she walks daily. She breaks the ice in the bucket. She lathers the rag. She stirs the soup. She kneads the bread. Her mother has been doing these chores her whole life; Louise knows this acutely. Each season requires its own work, then its own celebration, which to Louise, seems the same celebration, over and over. The same faces, the same food, the same stories. Tradition, her grandmother sighs, is the soil of human life. But Louise chafes against this soil. How can they pray the same prayers every year, not ever seeing the prayers work against the weather? How can it be that Uncle Robert's family comes from the next village over and the competitive conversation about crops emerges again, in the same way every time? Who is it that decreed that this must all be so, Louise wonders.

They gather for a spring feast and the table is filled. Louise's aunt, her father's youngest sister, says, "Well, it will be me or Louise who marries next." And Louise glares at her. Everyone at the table turns to Louise and her aunt continues, "But we all know it won't be Louise because she won't allow any man near except you, Jeremiah."

"What business is it of yours," Louise asks, blushing.

Her aunt glances sidelong up and down the table, "I don't care what you do, but I do want to marry. And I think someone might have intentions toward me!"

Louise's grandmother tsks and says, "This is not how one talks about such things." Louise blushes and feels her flaws.

Later, when it is time for the dance, Jeremiah finds her out in the barn and says, "Don't you mind her now, Louise, you know she's pecking at you for her own fun." Louise smiles, but can't help wondering, why she has become like this, this untethered animal. She climbs the wagon beside Jeremiah and as they drive away, she can see the light in the house and feels her lungs lift and lighten to drive away from what is always and ever the same inside of it.

Louise awakens to a cat's green staring eyes. She is startled at first, having forgotten where she stretched for a nap, then remembers. She likes this barn because from the knothole in their attic room, she has been able to see this very square window, this very one, every night for years. She loves to be in a place she considers from afar, and think about the distance between, the ways they are connected and not connected. She has slept longer than she meant to, and her mother will be angry.

The tomcat is black and white, and it stares at her with a mean sort of interest. The cat lifts a paw to his face and washes it with a pink tongue. They are in the same swath of light, in the hayloft of the barn. The cat bites at a toenail, making a cracking noise that sickens her. The cat pauses, staring.

"I should be going," Louise tells it. She'd gone for a walk after the morning wash to get away and think about what happened at the dance. She'd danced with Jeremiah and other cousins, and Nathan Longely. John ignored her. And she did dance with stiff, tall Albert, yes, she'd smiled at Albert and pretended his stiffness didn't make her want to shake him. It was John though, who was strange to her. She never understands how these things work. They'd been so close just recently, and now he would not even speak to her at the dance.

She lifts her arms to stretch and the cat regards her, tongue half-out, startled. She pushes herself to her knees, crawls through the straw and sits at the window. A little wind blows in. She looks out over the fields, high with green wheat. Behind her, the cat climbs down the ladder, she can hear his steady da-lump, da-lump, da-lump, and after a while, she sees the cat below, striking out across the lawn for the dense field.

Louise feels envy burn in her, envying him his freedom, knowing hers always comes with a cost. She can't help it, she is happy to wake alone, and with all the room of the loft to herself, and not to the soft jumble of her sisters' arms and legs, their sticky faces, their hair needing combing, their bellies hungry for breakfast. Louise leans into the sun, knowing she must get home, back to her chores. She sighs and gets to her feet.

Her mother speaks coldly when Louise enters, without looking up. "I can't bear this. Where do you go?"

"No shame, Mother, in napping in a loft."

"Not for a boy, perhaps, but you are not a boy."

The baby, Victoria, is sitting in a chair with a spoon, gruel on her face. Mother kneads bread dough viciously. The baby starts to cry.

"No," Louise wipes Victoria's face with her skirt, tickles her under the chin, and spoons some food into Victoria's rosy mouth, saying, "I just wanted fresh air and a walk and then I only stretched out for a moment. But fell asleep."

Mother sighs. Louise looks at her and sees the way the life has aged her. Lines around her mouth, dark circles under her eyes. Mother says, "Perhaps you shouldn't stay so late at dances. It's as your uncle says, we've been too lenient with you, letting you be a tomboy. Now you're of age and this kind of behavior? No one will ever marry you."

"I suppose someone might not want to," Louise says, "but someone else might." She thinks of John, and wonders why he ignored her last night, but knows that young men and women have games they like to play. This is something she wants to ask her mother, but she and her mother have never talked this way. Victoria's brown eyes follow the spoon. Louise looks at her and wonders what questions the baby will have that their mother won't answer.

Her mother rubs her floury red hand across her face, and says sharply, "You know there's the washing to start."

"Yes," Louise says.

"Mother," she says suddenly, "I wonder if I could ever live in the village. I don't know, apprentice to someone or something."

Mother's mouth is a circle of dismay. She is speechless for a moment, staring at Louise. Louise stares back, taking in the lined face, the sad eyes. Finally, her mother says, "You know we can't spare you for that. Until you get married, you will be here at my side, raising these children." But her voice quavers and her face is pale.

"But, Mother, they aren't *my* children," Louise begins, "I love them. . ."

Mother gasps and says, "Don't ever let them hear you say such a terrible thing." She leans to Louise, grabs her arm, hard, hissing, "Of all of the children, you are the one I don't understand." Louise, hurt, shakes her mother's hand loose and steps outside to begin the wash.

She crosses the muddy yard to their well and brings bucketfuls, walking them to the wash basin, tipping them in. As always, when she's at the well, she looks in to see her reflection. They say that all wells have ghost girl reflections in them, but Louise knows this is only because it is women who draw the water. Of course, it is only her reflection down there, and she shatters it with her bucket and a splash.

In the spring, Louise feels even more restless. She still sleeps outside, when she can, taking naps between her work, or if her mother goes to town, but after she has troubling dreams, she feels fretful, incapable of being still. Sometimes she smells smoke where there is none. She has dreams that scorch her sleep with high orange flames. She wants something to happen. Not fire and death, but something.

After a week or so, she decides she will see John. Doesn't he want to see her? She misses him suddenly, even though she didn't for a while. She opens the barn door and a shaft of light follows her in. The stable is musked with animal scents, and she hears them shuffling and stamping in their stalls. He'll be here in this early light, and she's seen his family head out into the fields. She loves to surprise John in his milking, where he lets her do the work, and tells her what he knows of cows, how their feed alters taste, the details of raising animals that her own father doesn't bother to discuss. John teases her, saying, you ought to write a primer of questions someday.

John is milking, and his head is pressed into the cow's dappled flank.

"Morning," she says.

He doesn't look up. "Morning."

"I came to see if you needed any help,"

The nape of his neck, under the curls of his light hair, is so exposed that she wants to touch it. His answer is terse, "No."

"I thought,"

He doesn't look at her or help her finish her sentence and she feels the flip of her stomach, the kind she'd felt as a child when her mother scolded her, before she realized that her mother knew nothing of the world beyond their acreage.

"John?"

He looks up but says nothing.

"Is there something wrong?"

John sighs and says, "Let me finish this milking. You can't stay here long." Louise feels something fall away from her. When he finishes, he carefully lifts the pail away from the animal, kicks the stool aside and turns to Louise.

"I was hoping you'd heard," he says, but he's not looking at her, and he has always looked at her, it is the thing that made him different.

"Heard?"

"I'm to marry Agnes."

"Oh?" She puts her hands together and feels them twisting.

"I didn't think you'd mind, Louise, not really. You never seemed like a marrying girl. I mean, you do as you please, and well, I'm a farmer, Louise, and you're not. I suppose you're not made to be a farmer's wife." Even though she feels the truth of it, it cuts her, it makes her sad, to have him have seen it, too. She is not wanted because she cannot want that, be that, do that. She looks away and turns, saying, "I see," and hurries out of the stall, stalking through the hay, passing the saddles on the wall.

"Louise," he calls softly, but she keeps walking, passing through the morning light in this place, knowing it is the last time she will ever be alone with him. She sees how she is seen. Outside, a cow in a pen rolls her eyes at Louise, lowing, and Louise can feel the liquid brown of that orb, a wet loss inside her skin, a giant eye rolling helplessly, and blind.

To fill her time, Louise takes longer and longer walks, all the way to the village, up and down the streets and then home. On the walks she lets her mind roam, she thinks about what she's heard of certain families when she passes their doors, the three little boys who run past, a skinny horse and a cart in the square. She can see Doctor Porchiat's black painted door across the square. Her family has always loved him. He has treated every one of them. Louise is drawn to his door by a thought. Books! Doctors have books! As though she'd meant to, she turns toward the doctor's door, as she approaches, she sees, inside the window, books. Shelves and shelves of books lined up like so many voices waiting to be heard. Years before, when she was removed from school, it was the doctor who heard and fretted her mother, saying, "Surely such a fine student should be allowed to study at least one day?" Louise hadn't been allowed and now she's become some kind of horror to her mother, and none of it matters because she knows Doctor Porchiat will let her read his books.

She knocks harder than she means, and there's Doctor Porchiat himself, tall and stooped, saying, "Louise, in town! A surprise!" but since she's not seen him in some time, and because of those books, and the hugeness of her request, she finds herself tongue-tied. Then, glancing into the parlor where the books are, she sees a young man with thick sideburns and a sheaf of wavy black hair, wearing the high collar of the city, looking out from the room directly at her.

"I've come to ask if I might read a book," Louise stammers.

"Ah, yes! Of course! Which one?" Doctor Porchiat asks kindly.

Blushing deeply, she hears her voice saying, "Any book. Anything. I don't know."

"I could recommend a few," says Doctor Porchiat, ushering her into the hall. "Please, come in, meet my new apprentice from the city, Antwerp Luther! He's needing a small village to study the spread of fevers, and I have volunteered us. Can you think of any objections to that, Louise?" And that was just like Doctor Porchiat, to save you from your own embarrassment by allowing you an opinion, as if it mattered what you thought to anyone else.

"N-no," she said, and the young man in the other room is rising and striding out to meet her and he bends over her hand, and he's handsome and genteel and she knows she looks a mess from the long walk, wearing her oldest, shabbiest dress and why has she come at all?

"What do you like to read?" Antwerp Luther asks. Oh, it's a terrible question. Here are these two doctors and she a country fool and what does she like to read when there's been nothing to read, practically nothing but the weather. They await her answer.

"I like science, arithmetic, history, I didn't mind reading the speller until I got it memorized through, and I read the bible, which had some nice stories, but . . ."

Doctor Porchiat and the young man laugh, but they are not mocking her, they keep their eyes on her as if she's said something interesting and not listed the most obvious and stupid of all reading lists, in fact, a child's reading list, and then Doctor Porchiat turns, pulls two books from a shelf and puts them in her hands. "Read these, see if you can tell which one I like best. Bring them back, and after we talk about them, I'll lend you more. Would you like to stay and take tea?"

Louise shakes her head, her heart pounding, and she lowers her head, thanks them breathlessly, whirls and flies down the stairs and into the street. In her hands the weight of the books feels true and correct, and she turns them over and over in her hands as she half runs, half walks to a place by the creek where a small tree gives shade and has a good curved trunk for leaning.

Louise's younger sister, Alice, has a scorching fever for three days. That is the measuring then, that calls for the doctors' visit Louise has waited for a couple of months. Dr. Porchiat and his new assistant, Antwerp Luther, (now much the talk of the village), will be coming to the house.

The night passes slowly, with Alice tossing and moaning. Alice's fever breaks in the morning, and Mother and Louise leave her to sleep. Mother rests. After feeding the younger ones breakfast and washing out the porridge bowls, Louise steps out back and at the well, she fills a bucket of clean water and carefully washes her face, hands, and arms. She ropes her shiny hair into a high clean knot on her head. Ignoring her other sisters' teasing, she climbs the stairs into the attic where they sleep and puts on her best dress. It is clean and she knows it flatters her figure, even if it is also old and not in fashion.

She scolds herself ahead of time. Not to be too flattering or eager. No. She will not blow in again, nervous and messy and reckless. She's read the books. She understood them! One a story, one a book of history. She will say this about them. She will say that Doctor Porchiat likes the story best. No! She expects nothing to come of this but dear Alice's health. She will not say anything about the books. She will not even look at Antwerp Luther's face or hair or collar. She has cleaned herself up for dignity's sake. She is practical, and there is nothing to do about that, and she will not be flattering and foolish. She will not say anything about the books, which she has read twice. She will merely offer them to Doctor Porchiat. Even though he told her to return them and get more, she knows he could not mean this.

She returns to Alice's bedside and all her selfish thoughts fly from her. Alice is glassy-eyed again, coughing in violent spasms. Every so often, she cries out in pain. She clutches her nightdress and writhes. Louise applies cool cloths to her head, holds her head up to drink tea. The doctors are slow in coming. Louise can feel the slick anxious sweat rolling inside her dress by the time they arrive. She was foolish to try and look nice. She lets her mind think it once, *her only chance, ruined*, and then pushes it away, *Poor Alice!*, runs to meet their carriage, plucking at their sleeves, not shy, but pulling them, looking into their faces with the details of Alice's illness and she can see they are listening to her, "You say she's pulling at her sides? Belly or chest?" They aren't thinking of other things, either, they care, too. Then they're with Alice in the little pantry where Louise has insisted she be alone and out of the bed they all share. Antwerp is smoothing Alice's hair back from her forehead and Doctor Porchiat has his old wooden stethoscope out, listening. Louise feels at home with them and then she notices her mother, trying to signal her to get up, come away, leave the doctors to their work, but it is Louise's work, too. She's been watching over her sister and will not leave. She turns away from her mother's glare.

The other children arrive home from school, and Louise's mother feeds them. Antwerp, concerned, lifts the flour-sack door of the pantry and asks if any of them have taken fever. "No," Louise tells him, "I checked them all this morning myself. They've not been allowed near her. Let me introduce them: Jim and Marlene are next oldest, that imp there is William, Abigail, Lawrence, Leigh, Tristan and this is the baby, Victoria, whom you've perhaps noticed sleeping in the corner there."

The children each smile when their names are called, otherwise they sit quietly at the table, eating bread and butter, while Mother cuts off slices of sausage to hand around, not looking at Louise.

"Good," Antwerp says, and smiles at Louise's mother, "You seem to know better than so many mothers I've helped in the city. They will keep a sick child right in the eating room, where everyone is exposed several times a day."

Louise watches her mother, who doesn't respond but finally answers flatly, "Was Louise's idea. I never heard such a thing." Antwerp looks at Louise and she sees that his eyes are cleanly shaped, oblong, and he smiles admiringly. He smells good, and his shirt is white and bright. He smiles at her and she feels her own mouth instantly smiling back and she deserves this praise, because she's had to fight her own mother on this point, and right now, not looking at Mother, she is creating a void between them; she is siding with the doctors; she is being praised. She does know better than Mother and this is because of her reading and thinking, which Mother never did, and Louise will not feel guilty about it, she will not.

Louise's mother told her she was being foolish, that they'd all catch whatever Alice had, whether they sat next to her or slept upstairs, but Louise insisted, saying, "When you all were visiting Aunt Clara, and I was here with Jim, and he was sick, the whole family didn't get sick. There's something about it, keeping away." Mother told her then that she was making things complicated, as usual. No, Louise said, I'm being practical. If all of us are sick, we can't get the farm work done. She can hear these words again in her mind and she's proud of them. They are a sign of knowledge that is special.

"Yes," Antwerp Luther says, cocking his head, letting the sack drop between them and the kitchen, "These are my studies. How the sickness passes. They thought it was in the air, but I don't think so. I think it's in the water. Somehow." He shakes himself and turns to Doctor Porchiat, saying, "Pleurisy, then?"

The doctors pronounce Alice's illness a pleurisy. A mustard plaster is called for, and then the work of mixing the ingredients from Doctor Porchiat's bag. Louise murmurs to Alice while Antwerp Luther and Doctor Porchiat work. Whenever her eyes meet Antwerp's, they smile a bit at each other. Antwerp says, "Alice is lucky to have such a kind sister."

Louise, surprised, says, "I'd do anything for Alice to give me her grin again. She hates the gap in her front teeth, but I miss it." Both men nod gently, but Louise suspects she's said something too country, too innocent.

Doctor Porchiat answers, "You should become a nurse and teach people how to care for each other. Wouldn't she be a good nurse?" he asks, turning to Antwerp.

Antwerp says, "She'd be a good nurse, yes. As she is a loving sister."

When they remove the mustard plaster, Alice's coughing grows hard, but not empty and hot and hollow. She coughs and spits and after a few minutes, smiles vaguely. The gap in her teeth makes them all grin back at her. There, Doctor Porchiat tells Louise, you've done it. Alice would need these, or hot compresses, twice a day. Could Louise manage this? She could. Mother and Louise and the children thank the doctors as they move through the kitchen, no, thank you, they won't take lunch as there are more patients, but they will wash outside, and then this is done, with the children swarming them, and finally, all is ready for them to leave. Louise thanks them again. As the doctors are climbing into the chaise, Louise remembers the books.

"Wait!" She cries. She runs up the stairs and pulls them from under her pillow. Alone for a moment upstairs, her heart pounds as she thinks over the beautiful tending of Alice that they all did together, and now this, this acknowledgement of her studies in front of everyone. Does she dare? She pauses, then whirls and runs down and out. Her mother stands in the yard, confused, with the doctors. Breathlessly, Louise shoves the books into Doctor Porchiat's hands saying, "I think that you like the novel better than the book on history. The history book is a story, but tells it in such dry language, it ruins all the truth."

Doctor Porchiat laughs and turns to Antwerp Luther, saying, "History is a story, too, eh? Where have I heard that before?" Louise stands under Mother's anxious eye, defiant and waiting. Doctor Porchiat turns to Louise, saying, "You are supposed to come and have a talk with me, aren't you?" Louise nods and looks at Mother. Doctor Porchiat turns to Mother and says, "Perhaps Louise may come and do a little light work in our offices every so often? If you could spare her? I was managing on my own, but now that I have a second person, we find we could use a help. Of course, when harvest season comes, we'll not interfere."

Mother looks at Louise in a way that Louise, even though she is elated by the request, feels a stone in her heart, she knows that in this, she becomes what she is, a stranger to her mother, a woman unlike her mother, and it is both what she's dreamed of and also a loss. Her mother tells them they must ask her father.

Watching the chaise rattle down the lane, Louise observes her father cross his fields to meet the chaise. The doctors lean and bend to speak to him. After a few moments, when she knows they are discussing Alice, she knows Doctor Porchiat will ask him, and just then she sees her father shrug in surprise, stepping back, nodding yes. Her face burns red and she flutters to think she will see Antwerp Luther again, soon, and often.

Louise can't even imagine the day she's having. It can't be true, because it is so pleasant and interesting and wonderful. It's not anything she knows. Within one week of her work with the doctors, Antwerp Luther has asked her on a picnic. They are on the bank of the river in full view of the little bridge and Antwerp Luther is talking to her and no one else about his experiences in the city, what his family was like, what he thinks about. He asks about the new books Doctor Porchiat has given her and when she answers, describing the tone of each, the impulse of each, what she disliked about the one, he says, "I'll pick out the next books for you, then," and Louise adds it to the list she is making in her mind of unbelievable things that could not be happening to her, but are, but could not be.

In the basket, there are apples and cheese and sandwiches of good beef and there's a pot of beer which she pretends not to like until he says, "Go on, have some," and then she enjoys beer with the picnic, and when she asks who packed the lunch he is surprised and says, "I've made this myself," and he glances at the water swirling away at their feet, and confesses, "But I had to ask Porchiat what to put in it."

There are little starflowers in the grass and there is sun on the creek, and she is being courted by a doctor from the city. Louise starts laughing, surprising him, and they look at each other and he starts laughing, too, and she says, "We'll have to thank him for a fine lunch," and Antwerp agrees and she doesn't even know why they are laughing or why he seems as happy as she, but it is a good moment, and she leans back on her hands and says, "Would you tell me about your schooling?"

"What about it?"

She pauses to think about what she means and realizes she wants to know about the schoolhouse, the studying, the college, the professors, the shape of his very mind, and says, "All of it. From the beginning."

At first it is hard for her to imagine, as he describes his boyhood and brothers, sons of the magistrate in the city, Antwerp the youngest and bullied. First, his interest in teaching was not acceptable to his family, then his interest in medicine was not acceptable to his family. Nothing he wanted for himself suited what they wanted for him.

"It was a house of law," he says, shrugging. He endured a schoolmaster who was cruel, learned from a schoolmaster who was kind. He spoke of his experiments in science, the family arguments over medicine. He tells her how he loved the university with its old creaking floorboards and bright, cold classrooms, yew trees at the windows. He tells her of the professors who taught him to be honorable, who taught him to think. He tells her of receiving the letter from Doctor Porchiat, of arriving at the beautiful village, the beautiful river running through, the blue shadowed mountains beyond... he stops, suddenly embarrassed, and Louise is aware that she has immersed herself in his story, become elevated and different from herself and far away from the grassy bank of the river, and it is exactly this kind of absorption and interest she has craved so long.

In the mornings, while the doctors are out visiting the sick or working in their laboratory, she cleans, sweeping and dusting and bending to pick things up and replace them. She brightens the windows and clears the tables of small things that gentlemen gather on tables: the pipes and ash, rings of sherry glasses, notes (she identifies the handwriting and puts these on the proper desks), twists of bark from walks, coins. In the laboratory, she only cleans the floors and washes anything they've left in a basin. She doesn't touch the beakers and dishes or vials or tins or jars. She dusts, lightly! lightly! the microscope, which she has now been allowed to look through and behold! The wonders of the tiniest imaginable world. What Antwerp has called "animalcules," named by a man clearly his hero, who has said that these things are alive. To her, the microscope is the heart of the room. She has seen creatures swim and crawl and twirl across the delicate glass slides. She has seen inside the blood, a whole other set of rounded swimming things. That a person grows these circles inside of the them, just like the histories each person makes outwardly of their lives. She has been captured, entirely, by the wondrous possibility in all those colored, changing, moving worlds. Doctor Porchiat's side of the room is neat and orderly, while Antwerp's is more haphazard, heaped with notes. His impatience with his progress shows itself in the clutter of his desk. She wonders, if she were to have a desk, what it might look like. But when she enters the kitchen she knows, as it is largely tidy and warm. She keeps a flower in a cup on the windowsill, and when there are many vegetables, she arranges them so that they look colorful on the table, even if she is only going to cut them up later.

In the quiet kitchen, she does the week's baking on Mondays, cooks the daily lunch, and fixes a stew or a roast for the doctors to eat when she's gone home. It is twice as much work for Louise, because even though Alice and Marlene have taken over many of her chores, there are so many on the farm that there's always more to be done. But Louise moves in a kind of trance when she gets there in the evening, because at lunch time, she is asked to join the doctors at the table and at first only listens to their talk, but begins, slowly, to ask questions, to bring up things from a book she's read that she likes or dislikes or doesn't understand. It has turned out that she has as much to say as they. She is becoming something else, and she loves this.

At the market, she is shy. She does not know the other girls, servant girls (though she is one, too, she reminds herself). But she knows she is different, as she shops out of love, getting the fresh honey when there's extra coins (for Doctor Porchiat's sweet tooth), getting rabbit every so often to make Antwerp Luther's favorite rabbit dish, and bundling into her basket the carrots, the parsnips and endive and sorrel and radish she will need to make interesting food, not merely fodder, like hay for horses or gruel for children's bones. She thinks of cooking as her own science. How she can learn and make new things without her mother over her shoulder, urging her to hurry and finish. Sometimes, too, she buys fish. She believes that no other woman at the market buys fish with such pleasure.

These lunches are longer than any she's had her whole life. Each of them takes turns sharing stories about work or their lives. Doctor Porchiat tells them about his father, a priest, to whom Doctor Porchiat is the only son, and how it was expected he would become a priest, but he did not want to. He remembers being in school and watching a boy with one leg shorter than another, thinking how he could make a shoe for that boy, until one day he told the boy this is what he ought to do, make a shoe twice as thick, and the boy cuffs him in the face, utterly surprising him. At the table they laugh, and Antwerp says, "Not everybody wants to be doctored, that is true enough." Louise wants to know what Doctor Porchiat's father was like, but Doctor Porchiat says, "There's not much nice to say. How such a bitter man would make his life in service to others, I will never understand. He's the reason, of course, I am not religious-minded." He doesn't mention a mother and Louise wants to ask, but won't, because she understands, or is beginning to, that conversation has its own rhythm and too many questions halt and alter the thing it might become if you simply let it spool out the way it wants to. The sun shines through the window and they eat and linger and share and although she is aware of how handsome Antwerp is, it is also Doctor Porchiat whom she wants to be near forever, both of them, in a way she's never felt for her family, a spontaneous and generous and familial love of a different kind.

The day that Antwerp discusses the idea of "invisible agents" that spread infections in the houses and towns, Louise watches the way Doctor Porchiat listens, stroking his chin, nodding. She realizes that she believes that they have knowledge that is complete, but in the way that they discuss things, ask questions of the air, ask questions of each other, she realizes finality is not the thing at all. Her head swims with all she wants to know, all she wants to read and understand. Some days she finds she must rise and clear the plates, for she can't sit still in the thick of her unknowing.

At home, it is hard to think when a mind is beset by a hundred daily chores of the smallest kinds. The water must be drawn. The children, each, washed and fed, many small feet to wrap in socks, many little chests to clothe in shirts and sweaters. Set the water to boiling, soak the grains, set to cooking them, the baking or washing or fetching. If someone falls ill, there is that, too. If an animal dies, there is that, too. If the root cellar is growing bare. Louise cannot explain all of this against the riches of her new life. The books, conversations, the work of the laboratory. She can't explain to Antwerp how she was accustomed to spending her days. And she can't explain to her family the inestimable happiness of days in the village, working with the doctors, studying the books they study, poring over the limbs, bones, blood, the chambers of the body, long lunches of beer and cheese and bread. They pretend their work stops during this, but the small visions of the microscope follow them to the table and their discussions never end. Antwerp understands so well the infinitesimally small aspects of human functions, and Doctor Porchiat has uncanny knowledge of the larger workings of organs, but Louise knows the practical health matters of a family of bodies. Louise cannot explain, even to them, how she feels supremely placed, suddenly, after a life of displacement. She is moved beyond dances and John in the hay and the drudgery. How could Louise explain to those she leaves behind (because she is leaving, she has no doubt, she doesn't know how, but she will). She was starving among them and she is no longer and even if this is not obvious, not literal, it is true.

Louise doesn't have evidence about how much she has changed until one day, walking to the village, she passes a cart in the road, walking to the village, and she forgets to look up or think about it, because she is studying a question about the microscope in her mind's eye, she has a feeling that she is being watched, and she can feel that there is something (some connection or understanding that is awaited) and she looks up absently to find John and his wife, Agnes, in the cart. It is too late to determine what to do, but they have turned away, and from the hard gestures of their backs, she knows that seeing her is not a pleasant thing for them, and she wonders how this could be when she barely remembers that life. John was a historical moment and nothing more. The more she reads, the more she understands this.

There is much talk of each doctor's specialty, and as Louise grows to understand, she can't decide if she is more of the mind of Doctor Porchiat than Antwerp, because what interests her are the things inside the body that are the same, but that behave differently. She's not sure which of them has the answers she seeks. Why did her one brother's toes splay when another's did not? Why is Alice blonde, when the others are red-headed? Why does one get colds when another does not? Why does the old baker limp? Meanwhile, the doctors educate her on the history of fevers. They often talk of the smallpox plaguing the city. She talks to them about what passes between the children at the farm, that it is not just what is in the air or water between them that matters, but also, to her mind, the open passages in their bodies. Shouldn't these be considered?

She is, Doctor Porchiat says, a natural nurse, and she loves to hear him say this, though now that she knows more about it, she knows that her family cannot afford to send her for training. Women are allowed to be midwives and nurses and she has no lineage for this, besides, the midwife in the village is very private and has never taken on an apprentice. Louise looks up nursing and finds that the word originates from Latin *nutrire* "to nourish." This smacks of her other life, and Louise doesn't want to simply feed children. She wants the larger book of the body to be the work of her life. She wants to be a doctor. She knows that as a girl from a village, this is not possible, and Doctor Porchiat and Antwerp, though they enjoy her studies and mind, never suggest that it should be allowed, either. She won't be a nurse or a doctor, but she is determined to learn everything she can. At least there is that much she can do.

They are out later than Antwerp's ever been with a girl because this girl, as Louise keeps telling him, is not like any he might know. She can feel his nervousness, and she feels the desire to tease. She looks at everything in the dark, making a game of shadow creatures, and he's helpless to her sense of fun, and even though she knows he's worried on her behalf about being late, shouldn't he get her home, what will her parents think of this? But then he is playing along, accomplice, and Louise loves the shimmering sense of power she feels. The microscope has shown her that there are villages beyond villages inside.

Light glances off the cobblestones in the square and it is as quiet as if no one ever lived there. Glittering windowpanes and the hard lines of the buildings loom above. Louise has always loved the quiet ownership of night. There are small ways, she notices, that she is more advanced, fearless, than Antwerp.

She says, "Let's race to the courtyard," because she wants to see him run. She wants to see him be a child, a body, and when he only stares at her, she starts off, calling back, "Catch me!" She hears him running now, with her, but they are startled by the noise of wheels on cobblestones and they stop.

"Shhh!" Antwerp shushes her. They watch as Doctor Porchiat's tall, stooped, highly recognizable figure turns the corner and the church caretaker follows, huffing under the weight of a cart, which bears a large, lumpy load.

Having seen Doctor Porchiat mere hours previous, Antwerp and Louise are stunned by the secrecy of this late-night act. They instinctively stay in the shadows. Louise clutches Antwerp's arm. When the figures disappear down the alley behind the lab, they stand in silence for a moment, staring after. Louise is thrilled when she realizes what must be on the cart. It is shocking, but also, brilliant.

Louise says, "I suppose that's why he knows so much about medicine."

"What do you mean?" asks Antwerp. His face is pale in the dark.

Louise says, "What do you think was on that cart?" She waits only a moment before saying, "It's a *body*, Antwerp. Most likely old Ettina. I heard her family were hoping she'd hold out until harvest, but I suppose she could not."

Antwerp lets out a hissing noise involuntarily. "You can't be serious!"

Louise says, "Haven't you noticed Doctor Porchiat's knowledge is more in depth than the books he has? No, of course not," she answers herself, "because you have read different books. I have read only his books."

Antwerp abruptly looks around, grabs her hand and drags her from the windows. He whispers, "This is not going to be well-received if he is caught."

They walk away, heading aimlessly from the square. Antwerp walks faster, pulling Louise by the hand. She feels his urgency and fear, and it both intrigues and repulses her. His hand, pulling her, a lovely shock through her body, but would he turn so quickly against his mentor? She would not. She trusts Doctor Porchiat and knows that what is dead is dead is dead. She lives on a farm.

Antwerp stops, pushes his hair from his face, puts both hands on his hips and looks at the ground. "My god. Right under our noses."

Louise is startled by his face, tight-lipped with anger. "Why shouldn't he study the body when it's dead?"

As if to himself, "I guess you're right that he has more knowledge than books. He's taught me so much I didn't know, but good god! I didn't know this, this —this *robbery* was how he learned it."

Louise looks at him curiously. "You're angry! Why? Imagine how your work would progress if you had bodies to further your study."

"My studies are of the living. You've seen them. They're on the slides, alive and well."

"Yes, but Doctor Porchiat doesn't kill his specimens. He needs to see inside. What should he do, ask for volunteers? Besides, from what I've read, it seems this sort of thing is done in cities all the time."

Antwerp speaks slowly and as if to a child. "We aren't in the city." Louise feels her irritation rise and shakes her hand loose.

Louise looks to the sky, "I would give him my body when I die."

Antwerp shakes his head impatiently, and says, "You're going to need your body awhile, still. And I don't think your family would approve. This is not as simple as you're pretending."

"Flesh, when dead, bloats and rots. I grew up on a farm. I know."

"That's a cold approach for a girl, Louise."

"Are you so attached to flesh, then? Where are all the bodies of your ancestors? Are they piled in hallways? Or do you bury them because they stink? We bury ours."

"That's not fair. I'm going to take you home now. I don't wish to discuss this further. I will speak to Doctor Porchiat in the morning."

The next day, Louise arrives at the doctors' offices early morning as usual. Antwerp and Dr Porchiat are discussing it already. Antwerp opens the door for her, but they don't look at each other. Louise steps into the library and is surprised to see a distinct red blush creep over Doctor Porchiat's face.

Doctor Porchiat stands and bowing his head says, "I don't want to pretend. Antwerp told me that you saw me last night. I want you to know I never intended to put you in harm's way."

Louise looks hard at Antwerp's face, which strikes Louise as defiant, but something else, too. Something hard. She says, "How could you question his studies when he would never question yours?"

"There would be grave consequences, Louise. Imprisonment. Death."

"How will villages evolve if traditions aren't challenged?"

Doctor Porchiat sighs. "That's just it, Louise, we challenge traditions quite enough. With you, a young woman, working alone for us, being treated as a student of medicine? This wouldn't be tolerated in the city, either. We must not endanger your trust in us."

"Me! Not me! He is the one who is afraid!" She points at Antwerp, whose eyes are small and dark, and suddenly she hates his fears and limitations and the ways he would hinder curiosity. "Perhaps you should have studied law after all," she snaps, and watches his face wince with pain. She is confused then, because she loves him and what is the matter? Why can't he understand? She opens her mouth to say but does not know what to say.

"No, no, no." Doctor Porchiat interrupts quietly, "I am the one. I have made the decision. Unless I return to the city, I will cease my research. Which, I must confide, is the search of a mad man. Please, sit, let me be honest and tell you what I have been doing. I have been looking for something." Louise and Antwerp look at each other in surprise. Louise sits down.

Doctor Porchiat tells them a story of a young girl named Isabella. He tells them a strange story about his dream of the human soul. He describes it in such specificity that Louise finds herself imagining the little organ, its size and placement in bodies. She wonders if some wither and shrink, if some are smaller and harder, some less resilient. If some must be carried like stones. She can see how such a dream would drive you to see it for yourself.

Antwerp is annoyingly clinical with his questions. Asking about tissue, muscle, trying to show the doctor that what he saw was only dream and nothing more.

Abruptly, Louise stands and says, "I must fetch breakfast for you both." She hopes that they change the subject. They have not argued since she's known them and the air crackles with discomfort. She cooks quickly, thinking only of the ingredients she must use, only of the next thing and the next she must prepare. When she brings the breakfast out, Antwerp is in the laboratory and Doctor Porchiat is sitting in a chair by the window.

"Doctors, it's ready," she says, setting the tray down. She has never seen Doctor Porchiat so sad. She sets out on errands and in a numb state. She is frightened by Antwerp's anger, and she is also angry with him. Doctor Porchiat is the one, of all of them, who should be allowed his research, but she cannot stay in one thought long, picks apples from a barrel, choose a small piece of cooked beef, minds her skirts around the puddles.

What if, due to this trouble, they ask her to leave?

Lunchtime arrives and they are slow to the table. The meal is simply beef and bread and potato soup. They eat in silence until Antwerp Luther says, "I just never took you for a man who believed in the soul." Louise feels a flutter in her chest, glad enough that it has begun again, and they've all had time to think.

Doctor Porchiat takes a bite of bread. After he's swallowed, he says, "Not only do I believe that there's a soul; I believe that you can only find the presence of the soul in the living. The corpse does not carry it into death." He raises his eyebrows and smiles wryly.

"Well, I suppose that's a convenient belief, since you can't find it. It does leave a lot of unanswered questions. Wasn't your father a priest? What did he say of the soul?"

"My father thought philosophers should be hung. Especially the ones who felt that the subject of the soul was separate from religion."

"What would he make of your theory?"

"Probably call for my hanging." Doctor Porchiat shrugs, dips a hunk of bread in soup, and adds, "You're disdainful, but I remind you that your own work is no less mysterious. The idea of 'microbes' all around that cannot be seen. My father and those like him would hang you, too." A silence falls. Louise fills their glasses. "The word 'microscope' comes from Greek, and in part means 'see.' Certainly, when you see the majesty and mess inside a human body, it is hard to conceive of something so beautiful as a soul." He turns to Louise and said, "If it was a dish you cooked, you'd have thrown it out." She understands that he is trying to put her at ease. She smiles at him. "And the body works, yes, punctually, like a clock for the most part. But then there is wonder. There is love. There is mystery. Do you know about our woman in the well?"

"That's diversionary," Antwerp murmurs.

"I assure you, it's not. I have told you; I remember now. You were skeptical of that, too. A stranger vanished in our well, years ago. Just before Louise, here, was born. And we did not find that woman. But I believe she was there. Perhaps this is the reason I can hold two opposing beliefs. I study the human body in its physicality and believe there is more than what the eye can see. Of course, there things that bodies grow that are not natural. What about the widow growing a horn from her forehead, you know of that case, no? All medical students know of that case. That there are physical things about this clock that we do not understand, let alone other qualities that make us different from animals."

Antwerp waves a spoon at Doctor Porchiat, "When you get going like that I can hardly follow. You've made a point. You've made a point. Louise, a hot cloth for the doctor's forehead."

Louise answers, "It is the dream of a thing that makes us what we are, right?" Antwerp sets down his spoon. "The work of medicine is to cure the body of ills, to honor life, to preserve the life. But the different qualities, the desires in a life, are entirely mysterious. And not even considered the business of medicine. But without which, how good can medicine be?"

"I fear for your education, Louise," Doctor Porchiat says wryly. "Perhaps we are not good for you."

Louise feels tears at the corners of her eyes. She is full of this idea, of Doctor Porchiat's organ, which she can see as clearly as if it were a turnip on her chopping block.

She watches and sees he understands what they are saying. That he struggles with the acceptance. He shakes his head at them, saying mildly, "You'll never find any of this under a microscope."

Louise feels a rush of admiration for him, for his ability to think, and she doesn't really know how they could have been at odds, and now not be at odds, but it's true. Doctor Porchiat and Antwerp rise and shake hands and she can see there will be movement forward, unlike fights at the farm, which are always the same, and oft repeated.

She rises and gathers the plates, "You haven't even mentioned babies."

"Babies?"

"When every single one of my siblings was born, it was obvious they were different from the one before. Who liked to nurse, who liked to sleep, who laughed from the beginning and who never laughed? All you have to do is study babies to know that the mechanics of the body are not the only things that define a life."

"Thank you, Louise," says Doctor Porchiat. "Yes. Indeed."

Later in the laboratory, Antwerp arrives home from the doctors' rounds to find Louise straightening his desk. He takes her wrists and pulls her to him, saying, "I am still a student, too. I have been thinking about what we've all said, and I know am like a stick in rushing water. I won't move even though evidence of motion is all around."

Louise flushes with happiness. He kisses her.

One morning she arrives a bit later and she can see their heads through the window. When she opens the door and walks in, she imagines them in their mothers' arms, tiny and soft-mouthed and not yet historied. The little babies they once were. Her heart floods with love, and she beams at them, startling them and making them laugh. Just like babies, she thinks, taking off her shawl and grinning to herself.

When Antwerp asks Louise to marry him, she is not surprised. They are walking in the woods. He should have asked her father, first, but she knows that she has already chosen a path, long before Antwerp, that obscures rituals. Louise feels as though she's in love. She likes studying his mind. She likes his support of her own studies. She doesn't know if these things, together, mean love, because this is not what a farmer's marriage looks like, but they feel real and true and so she says yes.

Antwerp's face lights up and he takes her in his arms. Louise adds, "But only if." He is still thrilled. He does not believe she can ask anything that will change his mind.

"Only if what?"

"Only if I can still be this Louise and not become another sort of Louise, who only cooks and births and washes and mends and feeds. Only if I can keep reading and studying."

She watches Antwerp's face lose some of its illumination and he lets her go. He looks away and sits heavily on a stump.

She wants to move toward him, to touch his dark, wavy hair and promise anything he wants. But she knows unhappiness, and in knowing she cannot go back. She looks at the needles under their feet. "Do you want to reconsider?" she softly asks.

Antwerp doesn't answer. He is staring at the ground, also. Overhead, a ratttttatatatataat of a woodpecker breaks the peace of the woods. He says, "When I was a boy, I dreamed of a household. Where I am the man of the household, and there are children to raise, and my wife raises children. It is a dream I was given by all those who came before, and now you are asking me to give up this dream for you." He runs his hand over his face and says, "How can a new dream be better than the old dream? But of course, this is something you see easily all the time. That it can be new. That it should be. Just as our specimens on the slide are always changing, as you said the other day." He stops.

She suddenly, deeply, realizes that she does want to be with him, that she could do what he wants of her, and she feels a rolling loss stir inside her, but all she says is, "What did I say the other day?"

Antwerp's eyes are wide when he looks up at her, and she cannot tell if they are joyous or sad, and he says, "You said that the specimens always change and that it makes you think about how your brothers and sisters are always changing and how the weather is always changing, how all living things are always changing." Louise puts her hands in his hair, and he pulls her tight and buries his face in the belly of her dress. She can feel the heat of his breath through the fabric and it sends a shiver across her skin.

"Yes," she says, "as if we could ever stop that."

"I guess we don't know anything of what will happen, if that is true."

Louise feels a surge of light inside her, seeing where he is headed, and this way, yes, she is willing. As long as there is no definite thing she must become, she can become anything. She doesn't know how to say this, so she says, "If that is what you think, then I will marry you."

Antwerp laughs, his mouth muffled against her dress, "Good."

Two days later, Louise is reading, and Antwerp sits at the wooden table where they all spend so much time. He pulls the book she is reading from her across the table and reads a bit. Then he sets it down and looks at her. "This," he says, "is love. I don't think it comes in other forms than this. I am always thinking of you. I've never been happier than I am now, working on my research, working with Doctor Porchiat, and yes, working with you. I would like to ask your father for your hand in marriage, now, if you would allow me to do so."

Louise cocks her head. He pushes the book across the table. She grins at him and says, "Ask my father, then." He takes her hand and kisses it, and she adds, "I should think he'll be glad enough."

Louise is out walking past the church, thinking deeply about the structure of the ankle, pressing her own down against the ground, catching the round gravity met by the stones in the road, thinking of fluid and balance, when she passes two young woman she knows by sight only, and one hisses as she passes, *Doctor's whore.* Louise thinks she mishears, half smiles, slows to ask, then hears it again in her mind, and looks down at the ground, walking away from them. Her face burns red because she has been so enchanted by her work that she can't imagine that anyone has paid them any mind, it has been as though she and Antwerp and Doctor Porchiat have disappeared from the world, have become this dream of working and lunches and talking. She's felt like Doctor Porchiat's dream of the soul's organ; they don't really exist except for how they exist so fully in their own minds.

Louise's heart thuds with fear for her mother's peace, for her father's position on market day. She imagines the school yard where her brothers and sisters play and fend off such comments and she hurries down the street, this tumble of anxiety building and that is the first time it happens, a sick, heady trilling deep inside her chest, and she can't quite get her breath and her hands fall blankly numb. She stops to lean against a wall, pain striking out from within, and she clutches at her chest and her head clouds and pounds, and she staggers, frightened, to the doctors' office, pushing open the door without knocking. They rise when they see her, rush to her side, ask her the questions they must, their brows dark with concern. Antwerp strokes her cheek, calling her *dearest*, and she tries to answer, but the terrible squeezing in her chest prevents her. And then it lessens suddenly, and she is weak-limbed, and she wonders how long people have said terrible things about her. It doesn't matter to others that she's doing something she really cares about. She doesn't want people to talk about her, even though before she didn't care at all. Now it matters. She is breathing too fast and Doctor Porchiat lifts her eyelids and Louise thinks how it all can change entirely, how suddenly it can be awful, how it can hurt at the very center of everything. It is, finally, Antwerp's hand on her head that induces her to calm.

Doctor Porchiat examines her again after they've given her tea and toast, more alarmed by her silence than her strange paleness. There is nothing to indicate what has given her, as she calls it, a dizzy spell, so Antwerp drives her home in the chaise, and tells her mother she is unwell. Her sisters fret over her, and Louise can't help it, she begins to cry. Antwerp and her mother stare at her from across the room and she can't tell them what is the matter. Her heart feels steady now, but sore, as though a hard stick of words is jammed in sideways, and Antwerp is anguished, and Louise's mother shows him out of the house. Louise can hear him ask if he can find her father in the fields, and her mother tells him where. Even as Louise knows that he is going to ask for her hand in marriage, and though she knows she should be happy, she cannot stop crying, she's put her family in jeopardy and something else, too.

Mother is at her side, then, knowing Louise is not one to cry, feeling for a temperature, but Louise remembers the pain in her chest, the seriousness of it, its intentional quality. She has been studying the physical body, hasn't she? And doesn't she know that this is not normal, and hadn't they, she and her doctors, just been discussing family traits like blue eyes? Louise's aunt, her mother's eldest sister, hadn't she just dropped dead one day, in the middle of making bread, clutching, Louise's mother always said, her heart as if it was broken?

Doctor Porchiat listens to her heart carefully. She breathes in and out. His face is calm, his hands warm. He pats her on the back as he always does when declaring her healthy, even though she knows, and assumes that he does also, that she is not, since this is the second time in a week, he's asked to examine her.

Her aunt died very young, before Doctor Porchiat had come to town, though Louise does not tell him. She does not want to be sent home to the farm, deemed too fragile for her studies. She doesn't want Antwerp to know that she might not be suitable as a wife, either as the new Louise or the ordinary wife Louise. How can it be? How can she be cursed with such an inescapable problem, a problem within her own very body, when she'd cared so carefully, so dangerously, for the harder thing, for the wholeness of the life?

After this examination, she cleans the kitchen, puts on soup, then sits to her table of books and immerses herself in her studies of the ankle, marveling, as she always does, that it can be arranged so elegantly foot after foot after foot. All the feet her own mother grew inside her body! An hour passes before she looks up at a sound in the room, and Doctor Porchiat, holding a journal of some sort, is staring at her thoughtfully.

"How did your mother's oldest sister die, Louise?"

"My mother says she died of a broken heart."

"Yes," says Doctor Porchiat, grimly, "That is what it says here, too. Rather unhelpfully." He smiles at Louise, and winks, "Well, no danger of that with Antwerp Luther around, eh?" And even though she smiles back, her stomach flips because she knows something is very wrong.

Later, Antwerp is there with bright-faced yellow flowers, and a plan for a tincture, and the news that her father agreed to their marriage. Louise smiles, but can't summon energy for rejoicing, so she takes his hand in reply. She knows she should, what? Do something. Antwerp tells Doctor Porchiat that Louise's father has agreed, and the doctors decide they must celebrate with a special dinner.

Louise, the conversation with Doctor Porchiat heavy in her gut, remarks jokingly that she'll have to cook this dinner in her honor, and they pooh-pooh her away and say they'll get another girl to, that she can stay home and rest tomorrow. She feels like fighting this decision to celebrate, because something seems wrong with it, something empty, but she doesn't have the strength to explain.

Antwerp, still excited, sits beside Louise, then jumps to his feet again. He paces. Does she want to make some plans? No, she says, she wants to talk about why he thinks there might be so many bones in the foot, and he looks at her quizzically, kisses her hand, and leans over to get a better look at the drawing she's studying. He leans in and she looks at the slope of his ear and finds it hard to believe that what is living one minute cannot be the next. She can smell Antwerp's skin, and she is here with a book on the table and the man she's to marry. But death is here, too. She's seen it on the farm: chickens, pigs, cows, birds dead in the field. At least she is not unhappy, not a farmer's bulging wife, or hunched over a tub of boiling laundry, but then she can hear her family's house in her mind, the footsteps and shouts and aliveness there, and hot tears splash down her face onto Antwerp's hand and he says, "Louise! What is it?" and she can't speak, thinking of the old wooden table before her, and skies and windows and flowers, and how special each thing is, every tiny thing, and Antwerp takes her in his arms and she can see he is crying too, and she knows it is very bad indeed, and she leans into him, hot and sodden and lets him rock her for a long time until their tears are drying, and they are kissing instead.

She pretends she is not counting days, but she knows there is something inside her that is not right, and she is counting days. In the village, she pays in coin for sheets of thick parchment. She writes the letter in her best handwriting. She writes out a copy for Doctor Porchiat and one for her parents. She clearly explains why she wants to offer this, and she knows that she will not be refused. Not by her mother or father. She trusts they will explain to Antwerp, if it really does happen. It is too cruel a thing to say before. After she copies both letters carefully, she reads them again and this leads her to imagine her parents reading it, Doctor Porchiat reading it, and this is what makes her cry. She pushes the letters away so that they will not be wet. Imagining the sadness of her brothers and sisters, the absence she will leave in them, seems terrible. She sees that if she dies, she won't carry Antwerp's children even if she wants to, and how the freckled hand holding the pen will no longer be hers. She'll never hear the baby, Victoria, talk, and she won't have her own house and she sees how selfish it is to die. She will be gone, and this will be awful and where will she be? But not once, not for a flicker of a moment does she really think that she will be all right after all, because what is inside of her, making her slow, making her tired, throbs like a warning.

She asks Antwerp if they can put off their wedding plans until she is well. Or would it be better not to, just in case? His face flushes with anger and she watches his eyes narrow. His anger surprises her.

"If you don't want to marry me," he says, "you don't have to use your health as an excuse. But if you are rejecting me, you should tell me today, for I am planning to write to my family." Louise imagines his family getting this letter. Marriage to a village girl? She can only imagine their disdain. She wants to spare him, but he does not want to be spared. "I have not changed my mind," he adds firmly. He kisses her hand and moves into the laboratory. Louise doesn't know what to say because she feels as though she might be dead by the time the letter reaches its recipients. Wait, wait, she wants to say.

But even then, what kind of cold woman is she to think this way of her own death? She is curious and not afraid for herself. She is only afraid for those who must suffer the loss.

Here she is, her clock ticking towards silence, all the while life is still spilling over.

There is a little betrothal party for them at the farm, so that the whole family can celebrate, and they hold hands, Antwerp and Louise, and Antwerp's hand is tight and solid in her own grasp and all of her brothers and sisters are there, the littlest ones bringing flowers and rocks as gifts. There is every kind of food, for this, a celebration not like all the others. Every family member has made some contribution, and Louise wants to cry all afternoon because it has happened again, in the night, and only Marlene, whose brown eyes follow Louise throughout the day, both of them still aware of the night and Louise's gasping and the breath that wouldn't come and the piercing pain and the flailing. Marlene's tears dripping down on her face and trying to be quiet, and the little girls sleeping near, but not waking, and Marlene wanting to know what happened until Louise's chest stills and she can breathe. They whisper late into the night and Louise feels better, now that someone knows. Everyone is looking at her now, and Antwerp. They are raising a toast, so she must not cry; she leans for kisses from aunts and confirms that the wedding will happen after harvest. And she looks at Antwerp, at the curl of hair cupping his collar and it is so rich and lovely to be in love in the afternoon, and if she could just forget this looming thing inside her own body, wouldn't she be the happiest woman?

It is the best kind of morning, sun pouring into the library, after the chores have been done, and she is at the table doing her work. The sun is hitting the red glass of the lamp and sending a bulbous red blossom across the rug. She feels sluggish, but it is all right, she is getting used to it, and doesn't always mind, because it slows everything down and she can really pay attention. She can see the gleam of light on the wood, the grooves of the table, feels the paper between her fingers, run her hands over the alphabet on the pages of the book with its endless variations of knowledge. Something flickers outside the window and she looks up to catch sight of a ragged old bird, big, like something ancient out of the high mountains, flapping its wings, slowly, in the slender beech tree on the other side of the glass. Does she imagine it? She tries to rise. It is looking in at her, and she feels the exhaustion and stink and age of that bird as if it is inside her own chest, which expands, bursting, and then tightens to a tiny burning red hole, until she cannot breathe at all.

The Story of Margaret

She is awake and her sister breathes beside her. The bed is a cage of quiet. She can hardly stand her own limbs, which won't be still and won't let her sleep. The slats that shade the window let pale lines into the room, which lie across their legs. She stares at these slats of light, blinking until they grow brighter. She sits in bed.

Light is breaking and the shapes in the room cut forth, and she sees the wedding dress, ghosted and empty in the corner. Her wedding day. It is a wall and she is pressed against it and she cannot breathe.

Richard is of good family. He wears his clothes well. His hands are elegant. But she is full of dread. He is handsome. He is awful despite these good things. There is something wrong with the way he looks at her. Something unkind. That wink one afternoon, as though marriage were a kind of owning. His brown eye, shapely, yes, in a face of beautiful skin, yes. But nothing to her. Nothing to her, like so many gentlemen one might pass at a fair. She had not been allowed Thomas. They said it as boldly as that. This is the good match, her mother says again and again, as though Margaret hearing it so many times will suddenly believe.

Richard's mother wears a sewed shut mouth, her eyes loose balls in her head, rattling in a rheumy white. She smells of dried skin and powder. The only thing she ever said to Margaret directly was, "No, I never would." Margaret does not remember what she was talking about, but this is what she hears whenever she sees the mother.

Richard's father pinches, ever so, her hands or arms or back when he touches them. His hands slip out and nip a bit of her, as if he'd pinch off a chunk and taste it. Gliding as close to a breast or hip as he dared. He, married to *no, I never*. The mother, married to his pinching. Margaret, to be married to both.

Tonight, she will sleep in a bed in the country, a bed she has never seen in a room she has never set foot in.

She clutches Emilie's hand with a gasp of fear and her sister awakes and sits up, asking, "Margaret, Margaret, what's wrong?"

It all comes out in a hot flood, and Margaret doesn't even know what words she says. Her wet face is pushed into Emilie's small dry hand, which Margaret can't quite hold close enough. Emilie doesn't know what to do but holds her and murmurs and dries her face with the linens and strokes her hair. Margaret cries into the speechless dark of not knowing, of suspecting, of having no tangible reason to fight this thing coming down on her.

The door to the room is flung open and it is their mother, saying, "No gown is complete without a bride and today is the day!" She doesn't look at her daughters, just crosses to the gown and fusses over how it's been hung too carelessly. When she turns and sees them, she surprises them by beginning to cry, and she steps to Margaret and takes her in her arms and whispers into her hair, "It's a good match, we want the best for you and this is why I am so…" She doesn't finish what she's saying because Margaret's sobs grow loud, break down, harder, and Emilie's crying, too, now, and whatever their mother was going to say, she stops, and collects herself. Margaret watches and says, "Mother, I," but their mother scolds her daughters for being silly and sentimental, and something else she might have said to Margaret is now gone, as the night is gone, and there is only the wedding day ahead.

In the church, she is faint. The pews are packed, and she sees no specific faces, only pastel blurs. She is aware of her father's arm, and then he removes it and leaves her facing the altar. The altar looms tall and damp and brilliant with stained glass reflections and there is a kind face in the scene in the glass, no, many kind faces, and she hopes they will come out of the color and save her. Won't they save her? She is cold all over and knows she doesn't want to marry him. Isn't anyone going to see? Her hands twitch and they are full of white flowers and Richard's hand is on her arm, turning her towards him, and the color is cast all over him and she sees that he owns that window, too. No one will hear her prayers and though he is looking questioningly at her, it is not with concern, that much she can already tell.

The great house is such a cold, stone structure that Margaret shivers all the time. She has begged for fires, but Richard only allows them in the morning and the evening. The servants are afraid of him. They know she has no power, and fires are lit only at the times he has chosen. The things she knows about being the mistress of a house are few, but already she knows she is little better off than the servants. Worse, because at least their positions are clear.

She passes them in the halls, clutching her shawl tight, and the halls are full of dark portraits and thick rugs. No one makes a sound and it seems only those hung on the wall are supposed to be here in this heavy place. The long days spool out black and damp. They are already longer than she's ever known. There's no going to market, no chatting with sister or friends or cousins. Her mother, no matter how annoying, was always there, and she too, is gone. Days are endless except for the startling moments when Richard is in a room with her, his body thick with crackling energy, his comments strange and erratic. She watches him blink in a pattern Margaret can't help but count: one, one, two, two, two, one, and she is learning, through this counting, the blinking is a beacon, warning of danger to come.

He wanted to whip her that first night, standing over her. His mouth red. She rolled away from him and screamed. She did not know where she found this courage. One does not scream, does one, in the first night of the marriage bed? She already understood that no one would come, but her screaming startled him. He laughed and coiled his whip and caressed her with falsely tender words. He took her in his arms, and she could feel his strength and her own skittering heart. She knew no matter how he pretended he hadn't meant to scare her, that he had meant to. He planned to whip her like a horse.

Outside the huge windows there is often rain falling on the great oaks and rows of rhododendrons. In the parlor, she is allowed to sew. No one has said she is not allowed in the library, but still, she sneaks in when no one is looking and hides the evidence of what she's borrowed. This is the only thing she looks forward to all day. She reads almost a book a day and doesn't care what it is.

Sometimes, she sits and thinks about what has become of her. Richard wanted to draw her blood with his whip that night, she saw it in his eyes. He wants to open her hide and draw blood. Since she is not pulling a carriage, this can be the only reason.

She learns, daily, that Richard is foaming mad, a foaming-mouthed dog. Margaret's mother does not know what this life is that she gave her daughter into. This is the good match.

The morning after their wedding night, after the whip and the cage of his arms, they slept beside each other. For whatever reason, she saw that he liked the game of pretending to be kind. In the morning, rising, he dragged his hand, slow and intentional, across her belly. They would not go on a honeymoon as planned, he told her. There were many reasons, and besides, why was it necessary to go traipsing all over when they lived in a perfectly grand house with acres and acres of land to explore. No, they would stay where they knew things. They would stay, and he hoped she would see the sense in it. And she is relieved, anyhow, because the idea of traveling in a foreign land with him seems worse. At least here, she is only three-quarters of an hour from home. Even if it feels miles and miles away.

A month after the wedding day he has screamed at her in the coach all the way to tea, causing her to stone her face and stare at him so that he knows how strange he seems. He does not alter, though, and then they arrive at the neighbor's estate, and there it seems that tea itself somehow soothes him, although no one could think his conversation meaningful in a proper sense. Herking and jerking with bright false notes about his business, his horses, and then dark foreboding statements about war. The gathered company, a man and his wife and her cousin, nod their heads. How did they not think him very strange? How could they pretend, as she could not, that there was not illness in the way he spoke? She stares at the small cakes, white and glossy with hard icing. She stares at the carpet once the cakes are eaten, until he moves his boots into her view, then she stares at her own hands, which remind her of the pale cakes. She can see that they think she is the strange one because she does not speak a word more than necessary. She holds her head high, takes the cake and the tea, but she hates them for being his friends, for knowing that he is mad and pretending that he is not. It is the first time she has been out of the house in a month and here are these people in their garish clothes with their overly sweet cakes, clinging to Richard's every word because he is rich.

The woman says to her, "Don't you just *love* the Averill House?" But Margaret does not, and she does not care for this woman and any shred of politeness in her has waned. Her mother would be shocked by her behavior today. Margaret says, "I was accustomed to village living." To which the woman has no answer, raises her brows and turns her body toward the men.

Richard's face, some days, puffy and white as today, has begun to reveal itself to her as another kind of warning. They roll home in the carriage, silence. They pass a cottage, a barn, a wagon. She imagines Richard as a broken door on a barn, swinging from a single hinge.

Emilie visits, once, and the way she moves her body near Richard reminds Margaret of a frightened dog, a tucked tail. It startles Margaret, that her sister already seems to understand the dangers. During the visit, the sisters talk only of village things, and gossip, and Margaret says nothing to Emilie about her tale because she does not even know how to begin. Emilie will not understand how Margaret, always the outspoken and powerful one, has lost her power and ability. Margaret finds herself picking up Emilie's hand every moment or so, but Richard only leaves them alone for five minutes.

Margaret asks why her parents haven't visited, as the village is not distant, and Emilie colors, and says, "But you haven't asked them." Margaret has asked them, though; she has written at least ten notes. No, they have not received these notes. Emilie has come of her own accord. She assumed something was wrong. They stare at each other.

Margaret sits, open-mouthed, looking at her sister. Richard enters the room and announces Emilie's carriage is ready for her to leave. Emilie, white-faced, leaps to her feet, hugs Margaret, and they look at each other, there is so much to say, but no way to express what they have just learned. Emilie turns and receives her graces from Margaret's husband, and again Margaret has an image of a dog, its tail tucked, and she knows her sister is afraid. Margaret watches Emilie's carriage leave and the lonely space inside her grows wide.

When she asks him about it, in his liquor glow after dinner, he stares hard, then, feigns surprise and says he will speak to the messenger boy about his lack of responsibility. Did Margaret want him to call the boy right now and give him a drubbing? He would do that right now, in her presence, so she could see that he is as loyal as any husband, of course, her family belongs to him, now, too. She doesn't like the sound of this, and she does not want to have a boy beaten on her behalf, so she says no, no. And Richard smiles, bright and sharp, in a way that makes her stomach flip.

Often since the wedding night, in the dark of her bedroom, the latch clicks, and the light of his candle tremblingly precedes him. His face, in shadow, looks like the ghouls Margaret and her sister and cousins pretended to be as children. Some nights he tears the covers from her, drags up her nightgown and stands there, looking down at her. Some nights he climbs on top of her, as though she were a log crossing a stream. He forces himself inside of her and breathes in her ear, and she turns her head from his breath which smells of cheese and sherry and all the rich luxuries of his house. He breathes heavier until a spasm shakes him and she holds still, as still as a bone, waiting for him to climb away from her, so that when he leaves she can rise and squat over the bowl and push what he has put inside her out. He has not brought the whip again, but she doesn't know why. She is waiting for it.

She wakes with the moldy smell of the house in her nostrils. She rises, puts on her riding clothes, and escapes the cold horror of breakfast, riding a bright brown mare into the hills. Margaret is allowed to ride this mare, this mare only, because Richard has said the mare is too stubborn to do anything else and should be made into a stew. Margaret thinks of the mare as the only friend she has. The horse is not stubborn with Margaret, who doesn't know the horse's name because Margaret doesn't speak to anyone in the house, and no one speaks to her. She rides the mare in silence, a beast as dumb, as enslaved, as herself.

One afternoon, he hurls Margaret's door open, crosses the room, slaps her hard, once, twice, and again. He is silent, his mouth working like an animal, but he says nothing. She smells liquor, but also something sour, as if it comes from his skin, and his upper lip pulls back in a sneer, and she winces and looks away. He says, "I can do what I want with you, but you're too ugly." He leaves the room, slams the door. She had never been called ugly before, and though she hates him, she is shocked by this. She remembers, looking at herself in the mirror, their nanny warning them not to get carried away by such good looks. How did she become ugly, invisible, with nothing to give, and no one to want it?

She sits with embroidery in her lap and sews stitches: lavender stitches, red stitches, yellow stitches, until the ladylike portrait of a bouquet comes forth. Richard rages in front of the mantelpiece and fire, ranting about men who do not honor him. She doesn't say a word, she wouldn't dare, she sews her stitches. His parents arrive out of the rainy night and she watches while Richard becomes something other than what he was a moment before. There is the pinching, her father-in-law leering. Her mother-in-law no longer even bothers to look at her and barely addresses her. Margaret stays in the seat in the corner by the lamp where embroidery is done, her stall, the place where she is kept in the evening. The mother asks Richard if he's fed Margaret's family, implying that they are poor and mercenary, and Richard grins and says, "They know they're not welcome here." Rage floods Margaret, but she must sit still, she keeps her seat. She imagines that she is the one with the long black whip. She cracks it on their naked backs.

Margaret has a dream about a brook. It is below a mountain with two sloping shoulders. The land is green and vast, and she does not know its shape at all. She floats above it like a bird and knows it is a place she loves. When she wakes, she looks at the light on the carpet and shivers in the knowledge that Richard will be expecting her at the breakfast table soon. She hates him, she hates his house, she hates his servants — her jailers. Even before breakfast she feels desperate.

When they'd been children, she'd gone to the seashore twice with her family, and the girls built castles of sand, and feathered them. Their nanny's brogue grew thicker and her stories more expansive. Their favorite stories were about the woman in the well, what happened to the children who drank from the well. The nanny spun as many stories as they wanted. In the sun shining ocean, they pressed seaweed to their arms and legs as though it were silk adornment and they turned tawny and slept under bright white sheets while the sea breeze blew in. There was the night's salt dark hum, stories, and everyone stretched and calm and new. Margaret remembered this as if she'd only read it once, as it could not be part of the same life she now lives.

Daily, the emptiness of her room fills her, an inch at a time, small measures of space, spreading inside her, taking up room that once had been real hopes and thoughts and dreams.

In the dining room, there is a portrait over the table of a woman enduring what looks to be a great, horrible shuddering. In those cold eyes, painted flat and unloving on the canvas, Margaret sees what one could become. The woman died while the artist painted her arm, it was said. The coffee in the cup before Margaret grows a film of lace. It looks like the lace that drapes the arm that is not there. It is the absence of arm that fascinates and disturbs her, and if she stares too long, she thinks the lady in the portrait is vanishing limb by limb. The coffee is cold and has no charm, and she waits for Richard because she has been instructed to wait, to sit and wait however long it takes, for Richard to come to breakfast. Steps sound in the hall and Margaret fills with an emotion as black and glossy as the varnish behind the woman. She is becoming those pinned eyes that have stared down at so many boiled eggs and cups of cold coffee.

Margaret has to practice what she is becoming so good at, stilling herself to bone, so as not to scream and scratch and stab. Richard sits in silence and the dishes come. He breaks his soft-boiled egg, a sulphur smell rises. She is determined that these will not be all her days; she will not breathe the stink of these false luxuries any longer than she must. He poses a question that he does not mean for her to answer, but the maid stands there, so he asks because his mother has brought him up a certain way. He asks, "Have you slept well, then?" and he tosses a slender envelope next to her plate without comment.

The note is in her hand, made alive with Emilie's handwriting, she would come today! Margaret paces the parlor, waiting too early, raking the window with her eyes, looking for the little chaise to come rattling into view with Emilie's pale figure inside, *carry her to me*, Margaret murmurs aloud. She turns to the far wall where the swords of his ancestors hang, "thick enough to cut a man in half" as Richard brags, she turns back and paces to the window, re-reading the note again for a time which it did not bear, which probably meant not for lunch, no matter. Eventually Emilie would come, and she would no longer be alone in the house and this time she would tell Emilie about Richard's violence and moods and she would tell her about the mistake that has been made and they would find an answer. It might be hours before Emilie came and Margaret sinks heavily to the green chair by the window, calming herself by imagining Emilie, at that moment, in a pool of light in the breakfast room, mildly disagreeing with Mother about the proper number of ruffles.

Didn't they miss her? How could they not know? There, in the village, they must be sitting in the light and bickering and not far, but so far away that it is a bright and blinding distance, Margaret sits in the chair and weeps.

But Emilie does not come that day, and there is no second note explaining.

That evening his moods chop and hack the moment to pieces, his voice demanding and wheedling and whining and screaming; he is not like anyone she's known. He is angry about something, some small battle in his day has been lost, and he cannot move past this. She knows nothing of his real life in the world. He paces and drinks whiskey and she is counting the minutes until dinner is served and they are in the presence of servants, because to be alone with him is always a danger, and it isn't until he says something that catches her attention and urges her to interrupt despite her best interests, asking, "What did you say?"

Something crosses his face, then, wily and strange, and he merely repeats, "No one drives my roads unless I allow them to." Margaret understands that he has tricked her, cruelly played her emotions. Margaret understands that there is nothing about this story of marriage that she understands.

That night he clicks the latch open and is on her in a moment, jabbing at her with his dry fingers as though she is a dead rabbit to be investigated, and she sees maggots crawling on her and holds her nose against the stench and looks into the flayed meat of dried eye sockets and is finally buried under his weight. She imagines the silence of a field with a dead rabbit in it and then he is gone.

In the morning, she asks the quiet horse boy to saddle the mare and he does, and she doesn't wait for Richard and breakfast. Something in her is broken against him, now that she knows he will always keep family from her. She would go to them, but she fears him, and their thrall of him, his estate, all those things that made him "the good match," so instead she drives the mare hard. She pounds across the meadows to the feet of the mountains, normally a distant blue range which comes closer into view, pine light and long weeds and streams to be crossed. Riding gives her the strength of the mare beneath and some feeling cracks wide inside. She remembers running as a girl, Emilie's little pink legs before her, both of them running on their grandfather's farm and this is who she was and is, a person with a history, and she must find a way to get out. She cannot stay with Richard, she cannot.

Later, caught in a sudden squall, she has not brought food nor water nor a coat, and she finds a small shelter of tree and bramble, big enough to protect her while the mare eats and shifts on her hooves under the tree. Margaret is cold and wet, completely alone, and no one can help her. She has been married away and is lost to them all, and they have let her go. She remembers sitting in school with Thomas across the room. His sweet calm there. How they shared their lunches while he helped her with her figures. This was the match she wanted. And what of Thomas now? What must he think of her, married to an Averill and gone? It is a stabbing ache to think of him. They do not know I am a prisoner, she thinks, and hears it for the first time herself.

After a week of such rides, Richard wakes her in the early dark, his fist caught deep in her hair and pulling. He stinks of liquor and has been, she realizes, up all night. He is shouting and calling her whore, and he is slapping her face, and she's crying out. Her hair is tearing from her skin. He lets go and as she takes a breath he punches her, hard, in the gut. She can't believe how much it hurts. He spits in her face and rises, clangs the door shut. She hears metal clicking against metal and now she knows for sure that she is his prisoner, no longer wife, and then she understands, this was all he ever wanted.

The sadness blanches away what was living and curious in her and replaces it with a blankness that envies death.

She reads the novel again. It is a surprisingly meaningless story. Facile and stupid, a love story. She cannot imagine who put it in the library, or why it is the only thing she has in the room when the door is locked. In the story there is a sentence describing a "grass green meadow" and wonders at "grass green." It is not a repetition, and she stares out the window where it is raining again, the end of winter. Once her father told her that the end of winter means not one more year less but one more spine of wisdom gathered because no year passes without new learning. And Margaret wishes her father would have had time for more discussions, but he was busy and did not tend to the life of children and women, and now, there was no chance because she has a feeling, she does, that she'll never see her father again.

From Richard's discussions with the maids outside, she understands that he has told them all that she is sick. Only one of his older servants asks if the doctor should be sent for. The bedding feels hot and tiresome and she throws off the covers and wanders the room in her nightgown. The tray from last night has not been picked up and there is a chicken leg in a pool of white coagulated gravy. She doesn't remember if she ate anything on the tray, but she knows she is more Richard's wife than ever, because she is losing her own hinges.

The servant must have kept asking because Richard opens the door one day and Doctor Porchiat is standing there, stooping to get through the door frame, as he always does because he is so tall. His hat is in his hand and his face grave, and he crosses the room to where she sits in her nightgown in a chair. She stares at him, speechless, for now it has been two weeks of silence, of meals brought and taken away and she has not spoken to anyone in that time. Dear Doctor Porchiat, then, is a surprise, coming as he does, taking her arm and listening for her pulse, Richard glaring over his shoulder with his head cocked, though she is too dulled by the listless hours, and doesn't even know why Richard is giving her such a glare, as if she'd know what to say.

Doctor Porchiat turns to Richard and says, "I am not accustomed to having someone over my shoulder, if you would please step over there."

She sees the flare of Richard's temper, but looks at Doctor Porchiat, who ignores Richard, and her heart floods with love for the doctor who has tended her and Emilie their whole lives. She knows the smell of his bag when he opens it and the lines on his face, the long swoop of his white hair, the shape of his black bow tie. He leans in, murmuring, "*There's nothing wrong with you is there, dear?*" To which she answers mutely with her eyes as best she can yes, yes, yes, I have married wrongly I am lost, yes there is something wrong with me everything is wrong. Doctor Porchiat nods and says loudly, "So you're having fevers, have you drunk plenty of fluids?" He puts his hand to her head, just so, as he'd always done and murmurs again, "*We're going to help you.*"

"What's taking so long," Richard barks, but Doctor Porchiat ignores him and wraps them, Doctor Porchiat and Margaret, in a swaddle of his voice and instruments so that it seems Richard has gone away, or maybe he really has gone away because Doctor Porchiat is talking to her in a low fast voice, "*Your family knows something is wrong, and they've not been allowed to send notes, did you know this? We are going to find a way to get you out of here. He's put a lien on your father's business, I don't know how he's managed that. I suppose it's to keep them quiet, not that it will work. I came here to see what is to be done. Be ready for any chance as will I.*" Doctor Porchiat strokes her hair away from her temple, the first kind touch in all the months of marriage, and she closes her eyes and feels warm tears slip down her cheeks.

Richard's voice enters the room then, "You're tiring her. She can't bear much company, I suppose you're expecting dinner, but I have to insist," the ice in his voice is clear.

But Doctor Porchiat interrupts, saying, "Yes, no need to insist. We'll discuss her condition over dinner," and winks at Margaret. Closing his bag, he adds, "It is as you thought, she has a great fever. I assume it isn't contagious since you don't have it, but still, she's in a fragile state and must be cared for." Margaret hears the words and is confused, she strains to hear the sounds of the house, the dinner, and then the sound of Doctor Porchiat's carriage rattling away. Richard appears again with something else in his eyes, was it kindness or some joke of kindness? He's been drinking, and he comes in and speaks of the doctor, of his strange ways. He tells her about the argument between Doctor Porchiat and Richard's own family, years ago, when they wanted the well shut after a woman fell in it, but Doctor Porchiat refused to condemn it. The tone of Richard's voice is that of a child, that of someone remembering and it was a voice she's never heard him use. Margaret feels blurry, why is Richard even speaking to her? She says nothing. Only sits and awaits his leaving.

The days pass again in the quiet room. Shadows and sun. Rain. Grass green meadows.

In the middle of the night Richard crashes in, leaving the door unlocked behind him, shouting at her and falling down and smashing into things, hurling them to the floor, and somehow, she does not see how, he punches her in the gut again and hurls her against the wall, leaving her nauseous and breathless and reeling. He smashes a vase and holds the jagged edge before her face, screaming, and then he strikes himself with it. There is bright blood all over, pouring out of him, and he grabs her, blood smearing her gown and she pushes him away. She understands what she should do, and she says, speaking to him for the first time in weeks, "Stop! You're bleeding! We must tend to this." And as if he is a child, he crumples into a chair, and whimpers and then as if just noticing, looks at his cut arm and cups it tenderly with his other hand. She can see the muscle exposed in his arm, and steps to the door, calls down the hall. A maid's face appears, white with fear, and Margaret tells her the squire has hurt himself could she bring some warm water and clean cloths? Would they send for the doctor?

Richard sits in the chair, staring at the blood from his arm as it soaks the chair. She speaks calmly to him, bathes him, and wraps his wound, knowing that the doctor has been sent for, and will come and will do something else, too, though she can't imagine what. Richard stays quiet, staring at the floor. Margaret sits beside him and the candle flickers.

Doctor Porchiat arrives, and she can smell the smoke of a fireplace on his clothes, and she is wildly homesick for her family at the sight of him. Doctor Porchiat wraps Richard's arm and creates piles of pillows on a divan to raise it above Richard's head to stop the flow, and Richard is pale. Doctor Porchiat gives him something to drink and he drinks it without question. Margaret cannot believe it when, as they sit with him, he drifts off.

The doctor, her old friend, rises with his finger to his lips and they leave the room. In the hall, he whispers directions to her. She will find a bundle of supplies under the privet hedge by the barn. She is to take a horse from the barn and go to a distant town where a family is waiting and ready to take her in. Her family knows she will not be safe with them, so they have made this plan for her. There's food and clothes and other goods she might need should something happen. It's a two-day ride. There is a map in the bundle. Now Doctor Porchiat is telling her he must go, must leave in the carriage so as not to arouse the servants' suspicion, and she, too, must go. She must flee. Doctor Porchiat embraces her for a moment, says, "I'm sorry this happened, Margaret, we are all sorry."

They turn from each other, the doctor calling downstairs, to make a fuss over something, to distract the servants while Margaret slips down the back stairs, past the steaming kitchen and into the night. She has had the sense to pull on her boots. The bundle is buried in the hedge and hearing the first leaves underfoot and first night air on her skin in a month, Margaret breathes in the smell of dirt. Noiselessly, still in her bloody nightgown, she snatches up the bundle, and runs across the yard. The stable is quiet. She runs to the third stall on the right and peers in. There is the mare, awake, looking out as if she's been waiting. Margaret saddles the mare and the mare is patient while Margaret's trembling fingers tug and cinch. She won't think of the blood and Richard's madness. She won't think of his arm flayed open. She has the bundle and the horse and knows what awaits her if she waits any longer. Margaret mounts and leads the mare out of the stable, down the hill, away from the house.

Once in the woods, it is very dark, but the horse steps carefully and soon they are on the country road heading out toward the mountains. She does not think it will work. The horse's pacing jiggles her body and she realizes she is bruised, deep in the belly, a stinging burn on her forehead, also. The beatings are only beginning. She knows this. She doesn't unfold the paper map that the doctor has tied to the bundle. No one can know where she is, or he will take her back. He will take everything from her family. He will ruin them all and he will take her back and beat her and she will never smell dirt or rain or ride a horse again. The moon is thin and weak. Margaret looks down and can see, even in the dim light, that her arms are covered with dried blood. She thinks of Doctor Porchiat pouring medicine into the glass and suddenly knows that Richard will sleep a long time.

How could it have happened? A lien on her father's business. It is not her fault, and yet she feels guilty. In a few moments, she is on her knees at the stream. In the bag there is a warm dress, a shawl, a jacket, a hat, a cup, a knife, a fishing hook and string, a package of biscuits, dried beef, a canteen of water, a hunk of cheese, a packet of butter, a small pan. There is a roll of bandages. A flint and a bundle of paper. A handkerchief with the initial "M," stitched, she knows, by her sister. She washes herself in the stream, dries her face with the handkerchief. The horse munches grass. Margaret uses the clean parts of her nightgown to dry herself. She doesn't want to carry the damp, bloody nightgown further, but she doesn't know what to do with it. She hurls it up into branches until it hooks. Dressing herself warmly in the clothes the doctor has sent, she eats a biscuit, drinks water, refills the canteen. An owl hoots as she climbs the horse again, better settling the bundle to spread on either side of the horse's flanks. She looks toward the mountain's looming bulk. The mass beckons and promises anonymity. They move again and Margaret falls into the rhythm of the horse's walk. Her mind wanders to Emilie's face, her parents' sleepless night, and she can feel them worrying over her, and their silence over the past months is forgiven. How would any of them be expected to know what to do? Could she go to the village where they expect her? Should she look at the map? She cannot. She cannot lead him to them. A husband's legal right to her: they cannot save her. With that vase in his hand. He meant to slice her. He didn't have nerve yet, but she'd seen the blood and knows he will.

Just before dawn, she reaches the foothills. She unsaddles the horse and lets her feed. Margaret rolls up in the blanket the bundle has been made from, tucking the pieces it held under a rock near. She's never slept outdoors and is surprised, when she wakes later, at the depth of her sleep. The horse is there, and the bundle is by her head where she left it. It surprises her that she is not afraid to be alone. Stiff with bruises, she catches her breath when she sits. The tender ache in her deepest belly frightens her. She must trust that she will heal. She looks and can see they climbed a slight elevation in the night. Peering into fields below she locates the source of the stream to the right. Her spirits, which have been low for so long, soar. She looks out over the patterns of light and land.

She eats a bit of beef and they take off again. She doesn't know where she is going. What does she know? She knows where she's not going. She would not see darling Emilie again. Maybe never. Or her parents. This is a death of Margaret, the one who was. But also, there must be a birth, for she still has a body.

Climbing seems the right thing to do. For Richard, she knows, will have awakened by now. He will be searching. Perhaps first at her family's house, and Margaret winces to imagine. But they chose him, she remembers with flickering anger. Let them buy her time.

She and the mare take it slow, ambling along the slopes. She thinks again of Thomas, remembers. A time at the fair when they'd walked together, and he'd bought her candy. They spoke of things that they liked to do and it was easy and they laughed and the way he glanced at her mouth made her feel pretty, and she'd had such hopes until the day it was announced that Richard Averill had called, having seen her in church. She'd once been a person, a force in other's lives, people who had let her vanish. She needs to name the mare, but she wouldn't name her just anything. She will honor the mare's selfhood, as her own selfhood has been so easily tossed away.

In the evening, she uses the hook and string in a deep pool, and effortlessly catches a fish. She hasn't seen anyone catch a fish, much less clean one, since she was very small. Yet she remembers some things. She cuts off the head. It is terrible to cut through. She slits the belly. It isn't until she's set it in the pan that she remembers there are scales to be scraped. It is a mess, but she manages the bones and scales and eats what she can suck loose. Stretched out beneath the stars, a shocking brilliant display of lights in the black sky, she knows she has never really been alone before. Knows that the shadows around her have been there all along, and that the shadows of the natural world are not frightening.

It is the next day that, from her perch on a high range, she sees a flash of movement below. Tiny figures in the landscape, two horses, two people riding, and she knows with a profound nausea that it is Richard. She keeps checking, in case she's imagined it. They are so small! So far away! Surely, they can never find her. Also, she knows they have already.

He is there and his anger will be bloody. She remembers the split arm. She spurs the mare and they rise, scrabbling, through dense brush.

Richard is a hunter. He's bragged of his prowess.

She and the horse scrabble for a few more hours in the dense forest of the slope. She finds a camp near a stream, dismounts, and paces. She can't start a fire. They will see a fire. But she is hungry. The mare munches grass uneasily, watching her. She paces and feels hunger spiraling in, frantic and angry. She decides she will not go hungry. She threads her fishing hook with a beetle which she mercilessly pierces. She sees Richard's face and hates him, passionately. The blue empty of his eyes, the cold line of his mouth. She sets herself to the fishing, catches, scales, guts her fish. As the sun sets, she starts a fire, daring him in her mind, thinking of her knife. The knife! And in the flickering yellow light, the horse's tail swishes now and again and she decides that she will be hunted unto death. If that is what it comes to. She warms her feet at the fire, leans against a tree, dozes.

Margaret dreams again of the place she has never been, but feels she knows well. Round, thatch-roofed houses, a communal fire pit circled by wide low sitting stones. She passes into the tall pine trees circling the small settlement. The needles crackle beneath her feet as she walks. There is a blonde child, running ahead of her in the woods, turning back, joyous, beckoning her. Margaret begins to run, ducking under branches, laughing until they spill out of the forest onto a clearing by a rolling stream where there is a group of people, washing clothes. They wave and nod. In the middle of the stream, there is a huge boulder veined with blue lines. The girl runs into the water, splashes the boulder, making the blue veins shimmer wet in the light.

Margaret wakes with this dream in her heart. She has not laughed in so many days, months, that the relief of it is still with her. But she is alone, in the woods, with a horse. She loved those people at the stream, she can feel how much. It doesn't make her think of her village and family. It reveals a difference, when she thinks of her family compared to the people in the dream.

Still, Margaret's dream makes her hope there will be another place, a place of deeper kindness.

She washes her face in the cold creek, wishes she had coffee, saddles the horse, and mounts. She feels like she is going somewhere specific. She has a sense of direction she cannot place. She understands that Richard and his companion will be following her. She keeps a pace that they can probably follow. She thinks about the companion, wonders who he could be that would come on such a journey. She wonders what they speak of. She murmurs to the horse all day and suddenly it strikes her that the horse is still without a name. The horse will be named Colley, after the vision Margaret sees in her dreams, the high woods, where, she realizes, they are headed.

In the afternoon, the two following are in a canyon and she can hear their voices caught in the walls. It is strange to hear human voices after many days of silence. Richard's voice is clear, and Margaret shivers with horror, remembering the hollow sour smell of him. She will not go back. She will be killed, maybe, she will lead them into a wilderness, and they will all starve and die, maybe. But she will not go back to that cold, stone house. She hears a smaller voice, then, a boy, and realizes it is the stable boy. Of course, it is a servant who Richard can bend to his will. A child in the world who is hunting her with his squire. How did her life become tangled with this child? She urges Colley up, up.

There looks to be a storm descending. The leaves and needles on the trees turn green and white by turns against the brilliant sky. The terrain is tumbled rock, a bad place to stay the night in a rainstorm. She heads higher. A wall of gray encroaches. Glancing overhead every few minutes, she knows they all need to find shelter. In a few minutes, Margaret and Colley are in a deep close of trees. Margaret tries to hang the oil skin from a tree and stretch it before the rains come, but it arrives in great big drops. Colley is soaked but eats a cluster of weeds at the base of a tree. Margaret manages to get a small measure of space beneath the tarp and huddles. The rain comes in great gray sheets, and she can see each approaching, hear it as it arrives, and then feel the torrents running beneath her, drumming on the oilskin over her head. She worries about the boy. It would never occur to Richard to think of the boy's comfort. It was one thing to leave a horse in the rain, another to leave a boy. Should she go and help the boy? They hunted her up this mountain, and yet, she worries for the boy. It gives her hope, this worry for the boy.

In the morning, she wakes early, stiff and wet and cold. It is the lavender predawn light and Colley is quiet. She is rolling up her pack, when she hears a small cry bounce off the mountain. She cannot see Richard nor the boy, nor any sign of their camp below her.

She is wringing out her belongings when she hears the rustling, scraping, thudding of a young boy running. It could be a deer, of course, but no deer runs toward you on a hillside. He appears, his face white, caked on one side with mud, clothes a startling page of mud against the wet green bushes around him.

"He's stabbed, ma'am," the boy says breathlessly, "Did it himself, I swear, but now I don't know what to do."

Without hesitation, Margaret nods, packs her things in the sack, swings up onto Colley, saying, "I'll follow you."

The boy doesn't hesitate, leads her, and she watches him glance at his surroundings to check his bearings. He knows where he is going. Richard is making a good scout of him. They don't have to travel far, and it gives Margaret the shivers to think how close she was to them. How she'd imagined it was farther. Richard's breathing can be heard yards away. Labored and quick. Margaret never thinks it might be a trap. Richard is at the base of the tree. Blood spreads from his belly where a knife protrudes. His feet kick uselessly at the dirt, and he writhes.

The boy is immediately at his side with his canteen, offering it to Richard, saying, "Drink a sip, sir, you'll be all right, I've brung her to help."

Richard's eyes roll to Margaret, but are unfocused, and he lets out a low moan and says to the boy, "She won't."

"Yes, she will, sir. She's here."

Watching, Margaret knows there is no saving to be done. As a child, she watched a cow die. All of them, a vet, the farmer, Margaret, Emilie, the aunt, all the cousins, they stood in a circle and watched the cow die. None of them could look away. There's no stopping dying once it has begun in earnest, and Richard looks to be dying in earnest. Still, she takes a damp shirt out of a pack and rolls it to staunch the bleeding. She knows nothing of wounds, but she lifts Richard's bloody hands and tucks the shirt beneath them, averts her eyes. It isn't nausea due to the gore, she realizes, but a fear of being so close to him. Richard, sweating, heavily breathes and he stinks, and she sees the bandage around his arm is dirty and stained. "You."

The boy kneels next to her, "I knew you'd help us, mistress."

She looks in his face and his expression is frightened. She whispers, "I don't know anything of medicine."

"I know horse medicine," the boy said woefully, "but the squire is no horse."

"What would you do for a horse?"

The boy looks at her then, and back at Richard, who has passed out, head slumped. He lowers his voice. "The squire told me any beast you're hunting gets gut wounded is going to die." They look down at him, blood pooling at his hips, his face white and grimacing. The handle of the knife curves like a leer, and Margaret recognizes it as one of the knives from the wall.

"I guess we'll make him comfortable, then."

"I was never going to let him hurt you," the boy says.

Margaret exhales, "Thank you,"

"I don't think he was going to, though he talked about it all the time."

"I see."

"Something wasn't right with him, you know."

"I know."

"Well," says the boy. And they kneel there at the edge of the boy's dying master, her husband, and wait to see what happens next.

A couple of hours pass, and Margaret unsaddles Colley and sends the boy out to find them something to eat. She builds a fire and spreads Richard and the boy's things to dry. She cannot bear her own things with theirs. She hangs them on the other side of the camp.

Richard wakes and asks for water. Margaret gives him a sip. His lips are white and dry and hard as wood. He looks up at her. She sees him as she'd never seen him in their time together, as a young man. She sees how a child is born into the world with hope and love and expectation and how you can't control what will happen to him, you can't ever predict. Even Richard's awful mother, once, she must have looked upon his face and thought she'd known some sweet truth of the world.

In the night, the breathing turns sharp and rapid. With the boy holding his canteen to Richard's lips, saying, "Sir, Sir!" Richard dies. Margaret and the boy sit with the body all night. Neither is ready to touch him yet. They sit together, dozing, startling awake, dozing.

"Maybe you ought to tell me what happened," Margaret says finally, as the night begins to cull its morning blue.

"Last night was awful. That rain and freezing and he was fevered and mad. He was in one of his states. But worse, because his arm was also infected," Margaret nods, "and he got out his big knife when it wasn't yet full light and he came after me, all of a sudden, it happened as fast as all that, and it looked like he had hurt his wrist, and then I rolled him over and I screamed. I swear, I didn't do nothing to him."

"I don't think you did," Margaret says quietly. "But I meant for you to tell me about the whole trip." The boy selects a stick from the ground and picks at it.

As dawn rises, he tells her what he has learned about hunting. That you must always search rabbit cover slowly. That you must walk abreast.

Always be sure of your target before you aim the bow. Driving a large animal takes active participation. Get a good view. Sit and wait. (But they could not sit and wait because Margaret never stopped moving, which made the squire angry.) One should spook the animal and one should remain stationary. All gestures from the animal reveal her thinking. Read the signs. The animal will follow water (and she had done this, the boy noted). What causes the most ruined opportunities? Lack of preparation. Lack of determination. The boy knew she was smarter than the squire. He knew she'd never be shot. But the squire repeated these instructions every day.

"I'm a good hunter, now, Missus. I can keep us fed regular."

"You are going back," Margaret says.

"No, mistress, I'm coming with you."

"In the morning, we'll bury the squire and then you'll head back."

"Begging your pardon, Mistress, but I've got a responsibility. I was hunting you and now I must make it up to you. Besides. I can't go back. Without the master? What am I to say? He was hunting you but gutted himself and I swear I had nothing to do with it and can I have my position, still?"

They are both silent, looking down at Richard, who grows stonier by the hour.

The boy hesitates, "Can I ask you a question? Where are you going?"

Margaret laughs. "I don't know. I think I know. I see a place, but I don't know if it exists, or where it is, but I feel like I'm headed the right way." She pauses. "What is your name?"

"Alik." He pauses, looks around, lifts his hands in a sweeping gesture, "My mother is from these mountains, originally."

"Have you ever been here?"

"No, but I feel like I have, in a dream or something."

"Do you like it here?"

"I like it better than anything in my whole life."

"Me, too," says Margaret, and they sit in silence until there is enough light to see, and then they begin to dig, one small shovel between them. A couple of hours pass, and they only have a shallow, root-tangled hole.

"It's terrible," the boy says, "but I don't want to dig deeper for him. This seems good enough."

Margaret nods, wiping her brow with a dirty hand. "The animals will get him, though, unless we dig deeper."

"I don't mean to sound horrid, but I don't know that it matters. He was a bad man. He was hunting you, and you are his wife. I don't like him." The boy rubbed his hands together, shaking off the dirt, and said, "He never once, not the whole time, said your name."

"I guess it doesn't matter anymore," Margaret says.

"No, said the boy, "no one is going to hurt you now."

Looking at the boy's face, freckled with sun, long and thin, she feels that she will let him come with her, that she must, as a tree grows around a rock, she feels a knowing about their paths. They dig again, and the sun is bright, and the horror of Richard is nearby, blood congealing in the dirt, and she isn't sorry, either, and doesn't particularly care if the animals get him. Who will believe that they have not killed their master? Who will protect them from Richard's mother and father, with their wealth and control over the lands? Fury and hysteria increase her digging and the boy is crouched, staring at the dead man and Margaret says, "This is deep enough. You're right, let the animals come."

"Yes," murmurs the boy. She walks puts her filthy hands on his shoulders and shakes him a bit, saying, "Come on, now, stop staring."

The boy wipes his nose and eyes and turns to her. "He's dead. I've been with him every day. Every single minute of every day and now look at him. My ma died the same way. There and then gone."

They stand and each grab a foot, and they drag him to the hole and down in. The boy kicks dirt over the blood and mess while she kicks dirt over Richard and then she hears the boy heaving in the bushes, but they haven't eaten much and only a thin string of bile is coming out of him and she knows they must get this done and be away.

When they are finished, she walks him to his horse and gives him the reins to lead Richard's great stallion, and they pick their way out of the clearing in silence and head up the mountain.

The horses sense some freedom in this new gathering, Colley enlivened to be among her own, and progress is light and fast. By nightfall, they are on a long meadow high in the mountains, and the boy is quick with a fire and Margaret catches fish and they each have more warmth from the extra things Richard had brought for himself. They are warm and eat and drink clear water from the stream and the sky is a fabric sprinkled with stars and Margaret tells Alik about the dreams she's had and he nods, staring at her wide-eyed, with an earnest, eager expression, as though he has something to say. Then he says, "That is the place to go, then," and that night, they both sleep well.

In the morning he says, "I'm good for picking out a trail, mistress. I think I can find the way."

"Won't you call me by my name?"

"I don't know your name,"

"Margaret."

"All right, Margaret," he says shyly, "We know where we're going, then."

The Story of Antwerp

It was the most flattering compliment Antwerp had ever received, delivered in what he came to understand to be classic Porchiat style, literary and practical, somewhat prophetic. Doctor Porchiat had asked an old professor in the city if he had any aspiring students who might want to come practice in a village. The professor had sent three possible, but it was Antwerp Luther that Doctor Porchiat chose:

Dear Sir,
    Your studies in the smallest increments of humanity make you the candidate I would most like to work beside. Your marks are impeccable, but it is what your professor speaks of concerning your personality, your curious nature, and devotion to your tasks that intrigue me. I know how it can feel to work in the city, where there is much suffering, so many conflicting opinions, so much struggle over payment and space for your work. I want to tempt you to practice in this village for a little while, a place where you can tangibly witness the effects of your work, regarding patients and the natural world. I assure you, if you value beauty at all, you will be inspired here. You can stay with me if you so choose, or you can arrange for a room elsewhere upon arrival. I have a decent library and a fine laboratory. . .

It was a letter so inspiring and thrilling to Antwerp that, against the advice of family, he sold his extra possessions and hired onto a carriage traveling the four days out to the village in the mountains.

The place was beautiful. After living in the city and dealing with the mud and the poverty and the swift, unstoppable spread of disease, the country air did Antwerp immediate good. The coach creaked into the village and the dusky blue shapes of mountains, and the brown and white little houses and shops revealed themselves, not black with soot, but old and cared for and lived in. Antwerp knew he'd come to a place he needed to be.

When he met Doctor Porchiat, a far more intelligent, humane mentor than Antwerp had known so far, Antwerp couldn't believe the warmth of his reception. The direct and honest appreciation that Porchiat expressed, with nothing hidden in his eyes, nor competitive in his manner, delighted Antwerp. Antwerp was introduced to everyone they passed, "A big city doctor has come to learn from us!" Doctor Porchiat told the same thing to an old widow carrying a bag of lettuces as he did to a young man driving a carriage. As if everyone were equal, as if Antwerp Luther were worthy of such celebration. He had earned honors at what he did, both in doctoring and research. But only with Doctor Porchiat did he feel seen. Doctor Porchiat took him straight to the tavern for lunch and they ate and drank. The conversations went as if they had always known what to say to each other, what questions to ask. It made Antwerp feel that everything that had come before, lacked in real ideas, compared to the blooded and fleshed theory and fact-talk that he talked with the doctor.

It made Antwerp feel like a doctor. Antwerp was not interested in the butchery of human mechanisms, he was interested in the feathery, complicated, seemingly unknowable systems housed within all that meat and fat and bone. How these secret parts of a body worked and failed and communicated! Communicated, yes, with other bodies in unseen ways.

No. Antwerp stopped the memory. Must not think of it.

Antwerp asked Doctor Porchiat how to make a picnic. He invited Louise, made the arrangements, and drove into the farm lane, only to find she was waiting for him on the side of the lane, away from the house. She carried a blanket in her arms and stood in the long grasses. When he asked her why she didn't wait at the house, she only rolled her eyes. Right away they were chatting. He wanted to know what her father grew, and she was quite knowledgeable, telling him about past crops, pointing out fallow fields.

Antwerp could see that it was easy in ways it often was not easy. The picnic was wonderful, the suggestions from the doctor perfect. But it wouldn't have mattered. Neither Antwerp or Louise was snobbish or particular about food. They ignored the black ants that marched over their blanket and occasionally had to be brushed from their shins. They ate and drank and threw stones in the river.

The first time he watched her bend her head over the microscope, fitting her eye to the lens. Her hand reached naturally, as his did, to the adjusting knob.

"Oh," she breathed. Her hair, always a little mussed, was bunched on her shoulders and back. He wanted to stuff a handful into his mouth. In the city, no woman would be tolerated in these offices, but her curiosity was what he loved. He knew that he could teach her everything he had learned, and there was some gift in it, that he both doubted and embraced. Should he give her what he knew? Should he not give her what he knew?

He looked at the slope of her shoulders, the slightly snarled clumps of her hair, her calloused, farm girl's fingers on the silver focusing-knob. "What is it," she breathed.

"Annuci Feruxae," Antwerp answered, and without meaning to, put his hand on her waist and leaned over her shoulder.

"They're moving," she said.

"They're alive," he confirmed, and leaned forward to smell her hair. No. He stopped the memory. Must not think of it.

The day that Louise died, Antwerp felt he was going blind. He was weeping and could not stop his weeping. He'd been the one to find her in the morning, in the study, slumped onto the floor, having fallen from her chair, her red hair over her like something spilled. When he saw her prone form, he knew. It was this heaviness, this deadness of weight that he could not stomach. When he touched her, she was heavy, her arm as empty of life as though no life had ever been there, and Antwerp felt inside his own chest, the difference between Louise and not-Louise. Doctor Porchiat entered and crossed the room, falling to his own knees, trying to bring breath back into her, though they, doctors, could tell she was dead, stiffening. They took her into the laboratory. Antwerp would not leave her. Dr Porchiat sent for her family and even when her parents and oldest sister crowded into the room, weeping, and Louise's mother gave Doctor Porchiat an envelope, and her sister and mother anointed the body, they could not get Antwerp to leave the frame of the door. He did not ask why they don't take her body as custom decrees, because he felt it should stay with him. He didn't see the mother speak with Doctor Porchiat, who stood in the corner reading a letter with a grave face. Antwerp felt Louise's father's heavy hand on his shoulder and felt an enormous wall rise inside himself and he slammed into it again and again, senseless with the not-Louiseness, saying, *she is dead*. Great worms of sorrow whipped inside of him. He had failed her.

The day passed like this and he was never away from her body, now pristine and foreign under a sheet, but it was her, not-her, and he heard a noise coming from his body he did not understand. Doctor Porchiat gave him a shot in the arm and Antwerp felt himself falling away, looking up into Doctor Porchiat's brown eyes, and nothingness like sleep came to him.

When he awakened, he was ravaged by the knowing, Louise and not-Louise, and he stumbled through the dark rooms, not even remembering to light the rooms, and the tears began again as if they had not stopped. Doctor Porchiat's light shone under the door to the laboratory. Antwerp opened the door and there was Doctor Porchiat, with sponge in one hand and knife in the other, and Louise, slit neatly down the center of her breastbone. Doctor Porchiat, concentrating, dabbed neatly at fluids and without seeing Antwerp, set down the sponge to reach for another, longer knife, with which he would again cut Louise, not-Louise, the smell of lamb thick in the room, and Antwerp screamed and lunged. Doctor Porchiat, looked up, startled but strangely calm, not as if he'd been doing something wrong, which he was, he was, he was, and Antwerp hurled the tray of tools. Doctor Porchiat was shouting, "*Sheaskedmeto, youmustunderstand, sheaskedmeto!*" The doctor's arms pulled at Antwerp saying, "*She*," and Antwerp tried to bring the halves of Louise together with his hands, which kept slipping into her dead chest, the organs bulging with their greenish lace, and he was still screaming, and not-Louise's blood was on him. He ran to the door, flung it open and ran out, screaming, *Murderer!* Shutters began to open all over the square, and tops of heads appeared in windows, and Antwerp, blind, spewed the words from his mouth. In rage he pointed a bloodied finger toward Doctor Porchiat's door, which was already shut against him, where not-Louise was lying, cracked open to the light. He was surrounded by villagers and already he knew what he'd done, but he could not stop. He pointed, shouting, *grave robber!* and they left him standing there, running to pound on Doctor Porchiat's black door, someone smashing the glass of the window, and they dragged the tall, familiar figure out towards the blacksmith's kettle of pitch, which steamed as though they'd readied it just for this. Doctor Porchiat was long-limb tied and speaking in a fast low voice, and suddenly Antwerp understood what he'd unleashed, as a mattress of feathers was brought out to the square, knifed open with a violent ripping sound. The mob shouted, all angers awakened and the villagers caught in a blood fury that Antwerp knew had nothing to do with Doctor Porchiat's careful medicine, and he wanted them to stop, he shouted against their fury, *NO,* and the tears came again and the villagers turned on him, too, locking him away in the blacksmith's horse stable where it was dark and reeked of piss. He could hear the sound of Doctor Porchiat's shouts of pain, and Antwerp screeched until at last, the vastness of his new aloneness overtook him, and he fell to the filthy floor.

No. He stopped the memory. Must not think of it.

At the university where he teaches, he's heard them say that he is cold and unfeeling. He's heard them wonder why he would have set about finding ways to save humanity when he himself has none. They pass in the halls outside of his office and he lets them, sees them as so many germs in a bloodstream, jostling along with their infectious selves.

He has a human story, of course he does, but he has spent ten years trying to annihilate it from memory. All that matters, can matter, is science, *scire, to know.* Some day he will open his door and stab his finger in each stupid, facile, young face and tell them what they will do, how they will love and betray and ruin, because they are too stupid to know better.

He has won awards, written many papers. He takes pleasure in meals and wine. He spends a lot of time stopping his thoughts, distracting himself.

His students, he knows, find him relentless. Their specific tales of woe, the scrapes they get into, their inattentions are all met with the same expression. There are other ways he can respond, the ways Doctor Porchiat would have responded. The ways that Louise would have responded. But they are not here, and he is alone. He will teach these students the boundaries of the world.

The Story of Alik

Alik doesn't mind the order to saddle the horses for a long hunt. He is excited when he realizes they will be headed for the mountains where the village from his mother's childhood sits. He never thought he would get so close to the stories she'd told him of forests, snowy winters, the great blue-veined boulder in the center of the creek, the way the village was a family, dependent on one another not for wages but for what each could offer: wood, bread, goat's milk.

He doesn't mind his squire's ceaseless chattering for the first few hours. No, he doesn't mind the idea of hunting, but he wonders what kind of big prey they are after in the mountains. An older groundskeeper tells Alik what he should pack. The women in the kitchen act strangely as he tells them the list of what they'll need, and when he tells them he's going on a hunting trip with the master, they stare at him in shock. Alik supposes they are annoyed by the request for extra food.

Alik and Squire Averill set out with heavy packs, extra provisions, bows, arrows, knives, empty sacks. When the squire spots the empty sacks strung on a bit of twine and asks Alik what they are for, Alik says, "For the meat, once we dry it," causing the Master to look at him in surprise, laughing. Alik understands none of it, but still he doesn't mind. It is a relief to do something different from stable chores. He feels that something is not right, but he doesn't mind, for he has been given the dark brown Dartmoor to ride, an unimaginable pleasure that he cannot fathom the reason for, only that the master said, "Take the fastest horse in the stable."

What he minds, finally, is the bloody nightgown they find, standing at the creek letting the horses drink while the squire circles the prints on the banks and slowly looks overhead. There it is, hanging like a sad flag in the tree. "That's her," the squire says, "she's a day ahead and too foolish to cover her tracks."

Alik stares at the dress in the tree. Now he understands, completely, the purpose of the hunt. He minds very much.

"Come on, boy" the squire snaps, and Alik, climbs his horse and rides. Silent, he sorts through his possibilities. He could turn back. But his squire would certainly kill him. For who would care?

The squire's Fresian is galloping now and Alik's horse follows the lead, they head toward the foothills, murder sharply jouncing in Alik's mind. He thinks of the young wife they are chasing, with her long dark hair and sad face. He wonders if she's been wounded, as the dress in the tree implies. He'd only ever handed her a saddle, and now he is hunting her. Perhaps he can save her. Perhaps he can.

Squire Averill is mad, it is clear. Even at Alik's fourteen years, he knows when a man is mad. The squire speaks of men trying to steal his land, he speaks of his father's weak mouth, his neighbor cuckolded, he speaks of the village folk as though they are vermin one can shake loose, so many louses on a shawl. Alik knows this is not how people talk, not how a master should speak to his horse boy. He rides behind, always, looking at the squire ahead, riding his black Fresian strangely, favoring one arm, his broad rear spread over the horse with ease. The squire is a good rider, Alik will admit that.

The first night they set camp and Alik makes the fire, cooks the meal, cleans after, while the master checks the hunting equipment. Alik prefers the riding to being alone together, in the wide silence under the stars in the camp. He is afraid of the master, at night, drinking from a silver flask. The master smells strange, Alik notices, a harsh metallic smell. The squire is favoring an arm. Alik sees that there is blood seeping through the arm of his coat.

So, this is it. She has wounded him, and he hunts her in revenge. This is still not the way a man should behave, but it offers a sort of reason. The squire says, his voice slurring, "Boy, you'll need to change my bandages."

When he opens the bandages, he can see that it is bad. Smelly and white with pus. Days of riding will never let it heal. He can see the stitches are loosening, revealing a gap into muscle and sinew, even a glimpse of bone. The squire grits his teeth and looks away. Alik is surprised that the small woman found enough strength to fight against her husband and steal a horse. He would recommend that the master stay still, but he knows this will only make his motives suspect. Every so often the master looks at him, sidelong, as if Alik is not to be trusted.

Alik is able to shut down his mind while cleaning the master's arm, because this reminds Alik of his mother at the end, vomiting red curls of liquid into the pan by her bed. Alik took the little dish out and splashed it on the rocks, where later, dogs appeared. Her face so wasted pale, and her hands like little bundles of kindling. Her voice the rustle of leaves. He takes the master's flask and pours the liquor over it. It is not closing up, for one thing. The master is suddenly strangely quiet and childlike while Alik rewraps his arm. It makes Alik nervous, these weathering changes in the master's behavior.

The squire speaks as though they hunt some mythical creature that the squire does not much like or respect. They see her on the third day, a tiny figure on a horse up on the mountain, crossing a gravel bar, slowly and carefully. Alik knows the horse well, a tan and black footed thoroughbred, tall and elegant and resistant to all riders but Alik and the lady. The woman on her horse is far away, and yet unmistakable.

"A big animal will be following the stream," the Squire says, and he is right. They can see the glimmering water in light glancing off the mountain every so often. Every time they see her, Alik's heart pounds and he makes plans and throws them out. He will knock the master from his horse. He will break the arrows. He will warn her with shouts. Alik realizes he has a perfect way to stop the man. He will use that bad arm when the time comes. He will hit it, grab it, whatever he needs to do. Alik feels a flicker of a smile cross his face, and realizes he is smiling at the idea of hurting a man. This nauseates and confuses him. He wonders what his mother would say, if she saw him on the murderous hunt on the side of the mountain. He can see her face, and she says, *Save her.*

The Squire is gleeful when they see her fire in the evening. "Ha!" cries the squire. "Oh, yes," he says excitedly, "Oh yes!" They set their own camp not far. Alik wants to ask, since they are close enough to ride in and catch her, why they do not, but he is afraid such a question will force the outcome he doesn't want, and so remains silent. Alik watches the master lick his white lips, staring at the fire.

Alik thinks of the woman, who'd been silent every time she came to get the horse from the stable, only nodding for Alik to fetch the horse. She was young and unhappy, anyone could see that, but he'd not spoken to her, either, because what was there to say to one's sad, silent mistress?

When his mother died in that dank room at the bottom of the lodging house where she'd cleaned, it was as though his life took on the blankness of the shadows in the room that night. Things lost definition and color. He was merely a helper in those lodging house stables, a strange boy with a strange name, kept because of his parents' reputation. How long could he stay? The squire's house sent down a request for a new stable boy, and he was hired. He heard the other boys talking, saying, "not on my life I wouldn't take that job up there on that hill. I have heard terrible things."

Alik was not stupid, though some people thought him so. He liked to daydream, was the problem, and his mother had given him plenty to dream of with her stories of the village where she'd been born. He knew that the village in the mountains had been in trouble, and this is why his mother left. She said sometimes that she believed this story was a dream, for how could one person live two such different lives in a single body? But Alik knew it was no dream. It was the story he thought about most. The men had gone to a Northern war to protect their land, the village left to the women, the elders, and the young. The men who went to war never came back. Alik's mother's eyes would soften when she spoke of the husband she'd loved and lost and Alik wished he'd known this man his mother loved, for she never loved his own father in such a way, he was sure of it. He wished his own life had not been so singular and silent, filled with work, and then his mother dying, and then the long nothingness. His father, too, died young, but her eyes did not soften at mention of him. She told him how the illness took him swiftly, and how he'd loved his son.

After the raids began on the village, his mother and three other young women fled, rather than bear the children of the monstrous men who came in murderous groups, ruining, burning. His mother shuddered at these memories and sometimes began to cry and would not tell him anything more of those horrors.

Alik enjoyed the next part of the story, where the girls came down into the foothills and here his mother met his father in the lodging house, and it was his father who arranged for them to find shelter. Alik did not remember his father well, but his mother always stroked his hair from his forehead saying, your father gave me you.

At the squire's manor, he wasn't considered high enough for even the servants to speak with, a boy born of strange mountain folk. He mucked out the stalls three times a day, hauled hay and oats and set horses to pasture. He worked with the farrier, and he kept the horses groomed, warm, clean. He was often alone in the stables with the strong smell of their urine and manure and it was dark and cool, and he didn't mind it one bit. The horses never minded his daydreaming, and sometimes he spoke aloud to them, telling them of a day he would take one of them to the mountains.

As much as he minds the reason, he loves riding in the mountains. He feels he is embraced by the foothills, and great blooms of happiness burst inside him as he climbs. He feels guilty but can't help it. The way the sun lights a ridge, the way a rain comes in, it is so different from the quiet life he's lived at the manor. He wants to be here. He will save her. And he will stay up here.

The squire's eyes glitter with fever in the afternoon, and he mutters about how large prey are best trapped when not on the move and he wishes she'd quit moving and set up a permanent camp. The hunter must be above all things, flexible, and willing to make adjustments. With relief, Alik can see that this will be the squire's downfall, he has a specific vision he wants to play out. Alik may never have to intervene. The odds grow weaker as the squire's arm festers, as she grows more confident, riding more and more strongly upward, as if she knows where she is going.

When they come upon her abandoned camp in the morning, Alik studies everything, but does not let on to the master anything he discovers. It looks like she's been fishing, though how she manages this, Alik can't understand.

That evening, Alik asks, "May I tend your arm, sir?"

The master stares at him, finally whispering, "It's not your arm, is it? Why do you care so much?"

"I am hoping to clean it so that it will heal, sir."

"Don't touch it," the master turns onto his side, with his head on the flat saddle that Alik has fetched from the Fresian, and without dinner, or even the fire being made, goes to sleep. A storm kicks up, a harsh noise coming over the land as though on hoof and wheel, and torrential, cold rains come over them without other warning. The master has the oil cloth and Alik cannot bear ask to share it, so he huddles under a bush, but soon is soaked through. He digs down into the pine and leaf turf into the dirt, where his own warmth will reflect back. Cold rainwater rushes into his collar, down his back, inside his shoes. Alik shivers so hard he thinks he will die.

The next morning, he is not dead, nor is the master. Everything drips and steams with humid air, the master waking in a stranger mood than usual. Alik, still shivering, tries to gather wood for a fire, but despairs, realizes that everything is too wet. He glances at the squire's arm, bandages washed red and pink and brown with blood and rain.

The squire stands. He pulls out his long curved knife and brandishes it, declares today to be the day, and when he spins to look at Alik, Alik sees the hard color of his eyes and knows that he is very sick.

Alik rises, says, "Perhaps I could help you with something, sir." But the squire hisses that he knows of Alik's plans; that he won't be stopped. The squire lunges at him, but Alik is young and quick and turns and runs for the largest tree. He can hear the master's heavy breaths and footsteps and then there is a thud. The squire is no longer chasing, but on the ground, face down, grunting.

Alik rolls him over and there the knife is missing, gone deep inside the belly, and the blood burbles out and the master coughs, "Pull it, idiot, pull it out."

Alik is sick in the bushes and then running, for he knows just where she is camped, and he leaps and climbs and runs. He is sorry to bring it to her, such an awful thing, but he needs help and she understands the second she sees him, he can tell. She packs her camp, and he leads her down to the master.

"I've brung her, sir," but Alik can't stand the sight of the knife in the guts, and he backs away.

What passes next is a blue haze for Alik, who is sick with the whole thing and is trying to help, but cannot think and there is his mother, *why is she here*, and she has the crust of blood on her mouth that she had when she woke, and she was crying again. Then it is full day and the mistress sits with a cloth, dabbing the master's head. Alik tells her about the hunting. Alik is trying to get the squire to drink, and then the squire's legs quiver and bang the earth and then he is dead. When they drag the body there is a thick lake of blood and Alik does what she tells him, and he already loves and admires her so, and he is grateful not to be alone, and she is kind.

He doesn't remember much until they are setting up their own camp. She is fishing, indeed, and he makes a fire.

She tells him the story. Doctor Porchiat, and yes, now he remembers doctor's horse, a fine and good-natured gelding, and then she is telling him something that he can hardly believe or understand. She dreams of a village in the mountains, people washing things in a creek, a circle of houses, and he knows, but doesn't want to frighten her, that there is a boulder in the creek with blue lines in it, and also, he knows which way to head and he knows they will start the right life they are meant to begin. He will be finally useful in a way that allows him to be a person, and he won't tell her now, today. He will not let this telling be smirched with the squire's blood. They will find the place and begin. He leads them up the mountain that morning with the first sense of purpose in his whole life.

The Story Speaks

Tell me the rest of the story, you say. You are not satisfied, I know. You want more, and so on. You want everything that happened prior to and following. And even as the story is told, you already know the story. You have dreamt or seen or heard every story. They are all inside you, as long as you are alive. This is how it should be.

You want to know, you say, what happens to the boy and the young woman, but you know what happens. They have trouble, illness, they lose a horse, they find the village, empty and deserted. They rebuild, they have joy, the sun shines, a garden grows. Do they begin again, as lovers?

Like siblings? Like mother and son, you want to know? But of course, they become all of these and more.

What are you willing to believe?

And what of the woman in the well? Tell us about her! But this is a story you know, too.

And Doctor Porchiat's dream of the organ? Why did he dream this? What is it about? *Tell me a story.*

Someone speaks and someone listens, and it begins again, threading between, this well-made thing.

Author's Bio:
Frankie Rollins has previously published a collection of short fiction, The Sin Eater & Other Stories (Queen's Ferry Press, 2013). Of this book, Publisher's Weekly wrote, "Unsettling imagery and hauntingly beautiful language characterize these stories, as ephemeral and indefinable as dreams." Frankie has published in Feminist Wire, Fairy Tale Review, Sonora Review, Conjunctions, The New England Review, and Bellevue Literary Review, among others. I teach fiction writing and honors writing at Pima Community College in Tucson, AZ

Newly Minted Wings: Craig's List Nikky

By Lisa Diane Kastner

Relaxed yet frustrated on a pleasant SoCal Tuesday, Nicole scrolled through her social media feeds to see the latest and greatest. Orchestrating Karine's surprise appearance on ELLEN was her coup. Karine masqueraded as a pizza delivery woman and made headlines all over Insta, YouTube, Snapchat, FB (so old skool). It was picked up by The Daily Show, GMA, and a dozen or so smaller channels. This simple act, which required a favor from Jenna, a college classmate turned production assistant on ELLEN, transformed Karine's album from number 500 with a flatline to number 400 with a bullet. Nicole was sure to mention this to Joey, the man seated across from her.

Their gender-neutral waitperson with a nametag of "Drue" refilled Nicole's cucumber lemonade as Nicole confirmed the new legs of Karine's European tour. She politely signaled for Joey to wait a moment as she tied up this bit of business.

So funny how an American show like ELLEN could cause a ripple effect of popularity overseas. Nicole sipped on the sweetly sour and refreshing drink as she reminded herself she was a public relations genius. She had resurrected more careers since her teens than most big firms. And she only turned 21 a few weeks ago.

So, what if she had been nicknamed Craigslist Nikky? She proudly changed her tags to #CLN to encourage her own branding buzz. Craigslist Nikky sounded harsh yet she acknowledged it was true: she had found many of her current clients on Craigslist. Former stars fallen out of the spotlight and in search of a path to new glory. She'd perform a google search, contact them with her plan of attack as well as the cut she would receive for sparking their revivals, get a few signatures to seal the deal and get to popping.

The #CLN clients weren't the bane of her existence. The opposite was true: they were the most trustworthy, loyal, and friendly bunch she had ever met. Much nicer than the peers she grew up with in The Malibu Colony. They thought fasting and throwing parties were sports. Nicole rejected (sort of) that lifestyle and decided to help others through her networking genius.

Nicole's problem children were clients like the one sitting across from her. He hadn't said much since she pitched his path back to fame. He seemed to resent that her concepts didn't match his current plan, which included running a special on Living Social for his self-backed revival tour.

Karine's manager, an old college friend, called her to help Joey Tempest. Meet at Olive and Thyme at 2 PM, the college buddy had said. It'll be worth it, she said. Joey had been trying to rejuvenate the previous successes of his brainchild, EUROPE, since the late 2010s with limited success. Since he had cut his sterling locks and refused to be seen in public, this caused problems for the group's public embrace. At this moment, Joey sat erect with large dark glasses and a cowboy hat. She smirked at his lame attempt to be incognito, then put her smartphone down and renewed the conversation.

Tourists eased by and snapped smartphone pictures of the person they guessed was someone. Since he had limited photos from the last ten years, they had a hard time placing him which made this public sighting more of an "ugh" and less of an "a-ha".

He should be more like Miley Cyrus and show up at the Toluca Lake Trader Joe's in a tightly fitted money dress with full on makeup. Heck, even if he wore a blonde wig reminiscent of his former studliness, she could push a few paparazzi to spread the Joey word. Sadly, he refused to return to his old song-stylings, grow his locks or wear a wig, and the most crucial part, sign the agreement. The fact that he agreed to this meeting in a public venue was a miracle.

Joey's fascination with Tajikistani folk instruments and song structure dramatically changed music that had once made EUROPE superstars and went against the pop rock stylings of the 1980s. Nicole had tried to listen to the music and fell asleep. She had downed java shots resulting in her feeling electrified before the inevitable snooze.

"You need to do something about this. Maybe change it to a verse-chorus-bridge structure? You know, modernize it." Nicole had suggested this at Joey's manager's bidding. His manager figured if someone else said it, especially a gorgeous brunette with full lips and long legs, he'd listen. Nicole, not sure of what a verse-chorus-bridge structure meant simply repeated the suggestion. If it meant that this would be less boring and more wow, then she was in.

"That's the point," Joey said. "The music reaches into your soul and rediscovers your center of calm then allows it to flow throughout your chi." Even though Nicole grew up in a forward-thinking area such as Los Angeles, she found the idea a bit much to swallow and even harder to sell. "Think Led Zeppelin with blues or Ginger Baker with African drums."

"Neither caused narcolepsy," Nicole reminded him. Joey clearly adamant that his new blend of Swedish rock pop and Tajikistani stylings would be the next great break through, Nicole decided to check on clients who listened to her, like Karine.

She dove back into her smartphone.

She anticipated huge thanks and kudos from her budding starlet. She figured Karine could ride the ELLEN wave for a bit in Europe, build a bigger following and then Nicole would send over the label reps from the likes of Def Jam, Interscope, Geffen, and A&M.

Pictures of a frowning Karine in front of what looked like a small tilted

NEWLY MINTED WINGS: CRAIG'S LIST NIKKY

stage suggested otherwise. Next were pictures of Karine in front of a tavern, another of her on the stage with some of the oldest hipsters Nicole had ever seen. Caption "Hippest place in Istanbul? Epic fail. #rediscovered the ancients #planetnowhere #hourstofindwifi"

Shit

"No worries," Nicole texted back. "Starter club. Hot venue tmw night."

New picture. This one an outdoor stage with Karine strumming her guitar to a half dozen children with their parents looking on. Karine's band looked bored.

"This was the starter club. #Sendmehome #Epicfailofepicfail #Whathappenedto#CLN?"

"Are we done here?" Joey asked.

Nicole looked up from her phone, cheeks red. She couldn't have misjudged the tour manager, Karl Istaniv. He had promised that the buzz from Karine's ELLEN debut had hit Europe. "No agreement?" she asked.

Joey got up from the white folding chair and walked away. Well, at least one problem had left. Now she had to deal with another.

"Calling Karl." Nicole texted. She had placed a bet on him. Karine had a limited budget and they wanted her to follow in the footsteps of other superstars by touring Europe, then Asia, and then leverage that seasoning to gain the attention of the bigger labels with bigger budgets. This plan had been developed based on the feedback from the big five labels after ELLEN. In summary: "Cute stunt. Let's see more."

Unfortunately, Karine's tour budget didn't include bringing on the bigger named tour managers so Nicole and Karine's manager had to use creativity to make it happen. Karl's ad and website mentioned top shelf venues and an even more impressive list of clients. Maybe Craigslist was better for finding talented stars and not so great for finding talented managers.

Nicole huffed into her headset. "Let me send you something." She forwarded the images that Karine had sent her and waited. Nicole listened for something that would renew her faith in Karl.

"What? This is the second hottest club in Istanbul. She'll hit the hottest tomorrow night."

"Where is it? A retirement center?"

"Look, you want her to hit big arenas then she needs more press and a bigger album than number 308 on the pop charts."

Karl made sense. What held Karine back? Maybe it was time to revisit the plan. When Nicole first met Karine she used social media like a master. Having her tour tiny towns, some of which had never heard of social media, definitely a strategic no-no. No wonder Karine stopped posting. It wasn't only the lack of Internet access (in some countries they had blocked access to Insta, US Facebook, and Twitter) but Karine's embarrassment at the venues she played. Even when Nicole insisted that all press was good.

Nicole asked for the check when her Insta lit up. Multiple postings of someone in a bird suit flailing into a crowd outside of an In and Out. This is hysterical, Nicole thought. She flipped through post after post trying to identify this idiot savant. "Holy shit. It can't be."

Nicole texted Paul, an old friend and Morgan's manager, to confirm: "Morgan Cruise?"

Seconds later he responded. "What do you think?"

Another problem child she had avoided wasn't such a problem. Nicole forwarded the images to her social media ringers, those with friends in the millions. Finally, a client who understood how to play the game.

Nicole's Familial No-no

Paul mentioned something about a problem. Whatever. Nicole worked her social media magic even without getting together with Morgan. Paul could solve whatever "problem" he had with Morgan while Nicole heightened the public's awareness of the human with newly-minted wings. So, what if they didn't like her suggestion for Morgan to appear at the La Cienaga Christmas Village? She had put it forward after her cousin's roommate had reached out to see if Morgan would be interested. It wasn't necessarily the best second move, but it could be a starting point. Plus, she could get great pics and set up paparazzi for more snaps to go viral.

The current set of social memes weren't flattering. They involved Morgan shoving fries in her mouth, plummeting to the horrified crowd, or drunkenly taking flight away from the site of her self-imposed degeneracy.

No matter, Paul had agreed to a group meeting the next day. Meanwhile, LA Times had published an article which, added fodder which Nicole and her media analysts could pounce upon.

Amid this activity and Nicole's desperate attempts to get Karine to play by the #CLN rules, Nicole hopped in her car on the way to pay homage to her parents. It was that time again. Her father Mitchell called and insisted that she meet her parents at the familial home for brunch. He typically called when mama got into detox, got out of detox, or when they wanted Nicole to fulfill her social standing within the 1%. She hated when her mother brought up Paris or Nikki or Kim. "They use the media, they don't become it," her mother liked to say. No matter how often Nicole explained she too used her network to advance her clients, her mother didn't understand. "No value comes from helping those Craig's List degenerates. How do you plan on making your own path?"

Admittedly, Nicole's public relations and social media business had been booming, but she continued to spend like she lived at home. This meant that her monthly stipend went faster than she intended (It had been decreased when she announced she was going to live on her own and start her own business. Her father's expectation was that she inherited his platinum touch and her self-made income would reflect it.) On paper – Nicole's firm was worth millions. In reality, she was lucky if she broke even. Thank god for tax write-offs.

Nicole drove up the meandering driveway to the front of her parents Malibu estate. Once considered the height of Malibu architecture, Nicole had to admit that the styling rang a bit dated - around 1978 modern to be exact.

Through the archway of the four-story home, Nicole meandered through the main entry and out back to the pool to find her mother.

"Come here." Her mother patted the chair next to her as she overlooked The Valley.

This was not a good sign. Typically, Nicole's parents wanted to dine with the beach view. The pool was an extension of the second floor. The only times her parents chose to chat here was when they wanted privacy and anticipated someone at the table would be unhappy with the outcome.

The last gathering held at poolside resulted in Nicole's brother, Mitchell the Third (or MT as Nicole called him) bursting from the house in a fury and leaving without a penny. He had been vaguely heard from since his disownment and subsequent move to a two-bedroom condo in New York City. The point of contention? Mitchell's reluctance to go into banking and produceing like his father. Although MT showed a natural penchant for selecting winning scripts (his father had been testing MT's acumen for years by putting forward scripts and talent selections for the next big production deals. MT scored 10 out of 10.) MT wanted the greater challenge of pursuing his love of street art along the lines of a Banksy. Sadly, MT's career in Los Angeles may have flourished but his choice to escape his parent's reach by taking root in NYC may have been a near fatal error.

Even though MT had fallen out with his parents, he ended up following the family business and developed his own production company while working for an investment firm. The only member who kept in touch with MT was Nicole who proceeded to text: "Sh'ts abt 2 get real" to her sibling as she took the chair next to her mother.

Nicole, smart enough not to speak first, silently enjoyed the cooling breeze as it rippled the water's surface. Nicole also knew better than to obviously use her cell phone in front of her mother. Her father used to say that ignoring one's parents is a sign of hostility. . Nicole preferred to considered it a means of self-preservation.

"Mitchell will be here in a minute. He had to take a call."

"Work?"

"New project. Should close today or tomorrow." Nicole's mom turned to her and sipped from what may have been a mimosa. Nicole waited for her mother to offer her one or for Caroline, the chef to bring one.

"Caroline?" Nicole asked.

"Day off." Her mother sipped from the concoction. Based on her mother's petite sips, that baby was definitely booze-laden. This was her mother's attempt to prove she didn't need alcohol. She did the same thing with painkillers. She'd nibble on the end of one to show she didn't have a dependency. By the end of the day she'd nibble through a half bottle.

Even when MT had been given the ultimatum – dad's way or no way – Caroline had been around. This was not a good sign.

Mitchell approached the dining area while clicking shut his smartphone. "Nikky." He hugged his daughter and then took the chair at the head of the table.

"Mimosa?" He asked his wife.

"Orange."

"Caroline?" He looked around as if saying her name would make her appear.

"Day off."

"Ah."

The trio sat in silence. Mitchell and Janice, AKA, Mama and Dad, fidgeted in their own ways. Janice sipped that drink like she had forgotten how to loosen her lips. Mitchell avoided Nicole's gaze and instead either looked at his smart phone or toward the hillside.

"Are we going out for brunch?" Nicole asked. If they were going to take her down, may as well be sooner rather than later.

"Right," her father said. He looked toward his wife as if they had prepared a speech which they probably had.

Janice knocked back the rest of her drink. "Oh look. I'm out. I'll be right back."

That figured. Her mother had been charged with bad cop duties in the past. Makes sense that she'd give the honor to dad this time around.

"Nikky. How are things?"

"Dad, if you have a question just ask."

He looked at his watch as if somehow this would force time to drive forward and the conversation would be over. At least that's what Nicole hoped.

"Nikky, I thought we could have a pleasant brunch and then have a chat. Can we do that?"

Nicole looked around the open area. No sign of food. No sign of drinks. And her mother was officially missing in action.

"Considering the current state of the availability of inebriants and nutrients, we should just talk." That sounded much more sarcastic than she had intended. She never spoke this way to her father but the way that this "situation", whatever it may be, was being handled pissed her off.

Mitchell put his phone down and sat upright as if this would give him the strength to go head-to-head with his favorite child.

"We're cutting you off."

Not entirely a surprise, Nicole didn't think her parents would handle it this way. She heard rumors that her father's investments hadn't been going as well as anticipated and that Mom had become endeared to yet another recreational drug, most likely prescriptions. She wished her mother hadn't turned into such a cliché and yet the fact that she couldn't even be in the same room with her daughter made Nicole sick.

"Just like that?"

"Well, no." His phone beeped. "One second." He answered, turning away from her. Nicole fought the urge to point out the double standards in this interaction, in this family. She fought the urge to tell him to fuck off and the impulse to find the nearest sharp object and destroy as much of the property as she could a la *Less Than Zero*. She fought the desire to sneak into the house and snap pics via Insta and Snapchat of her mother in the midst of whatever illicit moment. And she fought the overwhelming urge to threaten her father with showing her mother the photos of his mistress even though Nicole was almost positive her mother knew.

Instead, Nicole remained silent and daydreamed of floating in the pool, glass of white wine in hand, relaxing to Miles Davis.

"Sorry about that. Your mother wanted to know if she should make reservations for brunch."

"Really? Tell her that …" Nicole held her hand across her mouth, choking back the harmful words. "Sure. Make reservations."

Her father picked up the phone. "Before that, daddy," Nicole said, "what were you going to tell me?"

For a second, he looked confused. "Oh right. Yes." He put the phone down. "We wanted to offer to continue half your current stipend for the next three months. If in that time you can demonstrate that you are truly independent, we'll reinstate the full stipend but only toward your long-term savings."

"How am I supposed to pay my rent?"

"Your mother kindly found a lovely cottage in a more modest area." He reached into his pocket and pulled out a set of keys. "The address is on the keyring. Deposit made. You simply need to pay the monthly rent." Nicole took the keys from her father.

"What if I say no?"

"No cottage, no deposit, no stipend."

"Nothing?"

Janice returned, a tray of mimosas in hand. Her smile indicative of her assumption that the discussion had been complete. Nicole raised a glass and shot down one drink after another until the three mimosas had been dried.

"Thanks." She held up the keys. "I can see myself out."

Nicole ignored the sounds of her own smartphone and shook back the buzz of the drinks. Even with how poorly her parents handled this last interaction, she wasn't about to give them fuel to totally disown her. She hopped into her 2014 Spider and answered her phone. Picture of the awkward yet somehow angelic Morgan with the caption. "WTF? You can't get me a tour, but you can do this?" Followed by an image of Karine, Karine's bared ass, Karine's middle finger.

Nicole started her car and sighed. May be time to trade the Spider in for a Fiat.

Nicole's War on The Oaks Trash

The hut wasn't so bad. Dad wasn't kidding when he called it modest. The small cottage hidden along a cramped road in Silver Lake would probably be considered an ideal place for a hipster. She was pretty sure her parent's cook lived down the road.

She unlocked the door with ease, gingerbread like, she imagined that the kitchen contained an oversized oven meant to shove small greedy children. Of course, it only contained a "vintage" stove which may have predated the house. A small linoleum table with two plastic Ikea chairs in the corner. The doorway led to a bedroom that someone had the brilliant idea to paint mauve and gold. Who did that? As if on a loop, the bedroom led to a bathroom that had another door leading back to the main area/living room. Well, at least she couldn't get lost. Outside she faced an overgrown yard with trees nested in wild ivy creating a wall that arched above the house. Based on what she could tell, no one had lived here in years.

She retrieved her meager belongings from her car and dumped them into the bedroom. The rest would be brought tomorrow. At least her parents gave her some self-respect. She sat on the floor and pondered her next move. She could not deal with Karine. Enough butt shots for one lifetime thank-you-very-much. She surfed through her Insta and Snapchat. She couldn't live here too long. Just not in her nature. She needed a plan and fast. Her feeds active with upcoming events – Oscars, Emmys, movie premieres but nothing felt right. Rumors of another superhero franchise. Interesting. More pics of Morgan but this time videos of her brawl with some mousey girl. Still if the fight made it into memes exaggerated with piles of feathers and spurting blood then it's good.

As Nikky's media juices connected the dots, Paul called.

"We need a plan," he said.

"No shit," she said. "Got it covered." Before he could ask what the hell she meant, Nicole pointed out the number of YouTube and Insta views in the last hour. "I'll bill you later." She knew she wasn't necessarily the catalyst for the memes but, at this juncture, she needed all the credit she could get.

"Great. What's next?" Paul retorted. Buzz was fine but that didn't necessarily translate into bucks. He hadn't gone through all this melodrama for 15 minutes of fame.

"We'll piggy onto this. She needs a little more hype. Something bigger than a Kim selfie." Nicole paced the claustrophobic room.

"I don't care what it is, as long as we get it out now."

She knew that tone. It was the same tone her dad used when he'd had enough.

"I have a few things to settle. I'm going to set some things up then I'll meet you tonight. Say 10-ish?"

Paul agreed that they needed to meet soon. Time for Nicole to focus on the client that would make them wealthy, not someone who could carry a Domino's box.

She made her new place sound like the biggest, greatest, most amazing move she had ever made. Every single thing she had done up until that very moment had climaxed at this enchanting little villa off a lake. Yeah, something like that. At least Paul bought it. That's all that mattered. He begrudgingly got off the phone with the promise of a 10 PM meeting.

Nicole flipped through her usual apps, sites, anywhere and everywhere that would keep her occupied, but the new digs and the tight quarters made her sad. Her parents deal wasn't horrible. Heck, it was much more generous than the one they gave MT (Who, by the way, had been texting her since her initial message to him. She didn't have the balls to tell him what had gone down. At least not yet.) She couldn't help but feel betrayed. For the rest of the world, she was a PR mogul. She had done more for up and comers and to revive careers than anyone in her generation. Yet her parents only saw reflections of themselves. Since their kids didn't reflect their sparkly view of who their children should be, they decided to eject the kids stage right. Screw them.

Bebes (real name Barbara) texted Nicole with one of her stupid challenges. "First one to get two million hits on her YouTube channel in the next 24 hours pays for drinks."

Oh please. Nikky could get that in an hour. The timing was perfect. Tap existing social memes, tweet a bit and BAM ... Two mil. "Got something better?"

"Queeny, come up with something B8R." Bebes texted back.

Nicole rifled through her purse and found the Black Amex her parents had given her in case of emergencies. Fuck it. This felt like an emergency.

It'd been ages since she came up with a challenge. "The Oaks. Take them down."

Bebes response, "Hell-to-the-yeah." This is your rude narrator voice inserting herself to provide a little context. If you are not acquainted with the Malibu Colony versus The OAKS ongoing rivalry, let me explain. In Los Angeles county are towns with their own police force and fire department. They pay their own taxes and maintain their own roads. They are hidden cities within cities. Those who reside there are only there by invitation. Think of them as the 1% of the 1%.

Behind a tall wooden gate is the Malibu Colony, which is the location of Nicole's parent's primary residence. The Malibu Colony, known for its celebrity residents and tight knit community since the 1920s, is more old school than new school. Old school residence: Woody Harrelson, Tom Hanks, Bette Midler, Gloria Swanson, and Jane Fonda to name a few. The new school, a.k.a. The OAKS, located in Calabasas contains such nouveau riche as The Kardashians and Bieber. Developed between 2002 and 2007, The OAKS residence only wished they could be what The Malibu Colony naturally was.

Until now, Nicole and her friends from The Colony, allow The OAKS trash to brag about their fabulousness and talk crap about the "decrepit" Colony. They claimed the real power base lives in The OAKS. The MC's didn't need to prove to The OAKS their power. Greater power existed in silence than in responding to childish taunts.

With Nicole splayed on the kitchen floor of her newly rented abode, kicking nouveau riche ass felt damn good. Based on Bebes and several other childhood friends, they agreed that the OAKS were going down.

This narrator must provide one additional reveal. Nicole didn't naturally come about her social media prowess. She learned it from her bevy of MC friends. One had figured out how to hack high follower Twitter accounts and post as if she was that user. Another had honed the skill of subtle marketing by having a relative-unknown appear as a celebrity while wearing Gucci or carrying an iPhone. "If the paparazzi treats you like a star, then everyone will believe you're a star."

Until this moment, the MC's had primarily used their powers for good or at least for personal gain. No harm, no foul. And they didn't get too pissed when The Kardashian's ripped off some of their signature maneuvers. Hell, they all had to make a living. But imagine a dozen twenty somethings with the social media prowess of a dozen social media gods. Oh yeah, this was gonna get bloody.

They hit Kanye and Kim. They attacked The Beib. They targeted up and comers, those with high followers. They ID'd starlets being pushed by the Studio Machines and knocked them down. They threw lavish parties across town that occurred at the same time as the Beib's. They stole his followers. Their gift bags more luxurious, their A Listers were A Prime. Meanwhile Nicole eased in images of Morgan – vintage, new, positioning her as the second coming. The woman everyone wished they could be. She pinged Paul and showed him Morgan's media rise dramatically increase. She texted him, "Book now."

Paul's phone started ringing with offers for guest appearances, a possible film and a TV show. Even her own reality TV show. He hadn't seen this much fodder in decades. Nicole and her friends continued their work. She figured Paul wouldn't mind if they missed their 10 PM meeting.

Karine pinged Nicole. There's only so much Nicole can do when Karine travels through villages in Italy for a "tour". This needed to be a give-and-take. The combination of media domination and Morgan's success will give Nicole the creds to prove she's a virtuoso. Time to get her trust fund back. Actually, screw the trust fund.

By the time they were done, Nikky declared victory after their top targets shut down all social media outlets, all public appearances, all evidence of their existence.

Paul messaged her and confirmed the offers, the appearances.

Her text back was simple. "20% of gross."

His counter, "Chat tomorrow. We'll finalize." A few seconds later among the barrage of messages from friends, Paul followed up, "Nicely done, #CLN."

CLN Fights Back

Nicole and her buddies gloried in their pounding of The OAKS with a spirited and chemical filled 24 hours. Her new abode made the perfect hiding spot for her drug induced migraine. She awoke to it as she would a screeching dog eager to silence it. She hopped into the claustrophobic shower and doused herself in warm water. She allowed the droplets to massage the migraine away, little by little. She leaned against the shower wall until the headache subsided to dull remains as she pondered her next steps.

1. She needed to call her bro back.
2. She needed to quickly come up with a plan of attack for Morgan, which would include an onsite verification of what the pictures implied - that somehow Morgan Cruise had functioning wings.
3. She needed to line up a few more "Morgans". She had some in mind but needed to be doubly sure. This was intensity time and that meant the more clients the better.
4. Time to bask in the hype and leverage it to create even more opportunities. Her phone had been ringing non-stop since the thrashing of The OAKS. Including Joey and Karine.

She made her way out of the shower and grabbed the nearest towel. Its scratchiness and mild scent of bleach wasn't lost on Nicole. Every ounce of this place screamed middle income - a warning from her parents.

She dried off, headed into the bedroom, and put on the only clothes she had. Aware that her bodily odor may be a bit more than one may desire, she spritzed herself with her favorite cologne, tied her hair into a twisted bun, made her way out the modest door, and into her car.

She hadn't eaten in at least two days, so she succumbed to the primal need for sustenance. Prada sunglasses in place, she shifted gears in her Spider and made her way down the highway. She suppressed the urge to shift into a higher gear since that might shift her undercurrent of a headache into second. With radio off and phone securely in her pocket she twisted down the highway until she reached her fave restaurant, Bestia, known for their animalistic and divine dishes. Without a second glance, she exited her car, engine running, and handed it off to the valet. She loved how tourists looked at her like they should know who she is ... and in her mind, they absolutely should. If they didn't then they would by the end of this melodramatic period in her life. The doorman smoothly made way for one of their favorite guests with a gentle hello and nod towards the kitchen, Nikky took the spot the chef reserved for her. So nice to be back in her element. She didn't need to look around the restaurant to know that at least one, if not multiple A listers had already spotted her, texted a cohort, and calculated if they should approach her. No need to check her phone, she could feel the texts and notifications piling up since this was her first public appearance after the thrashing. She settled in and readied to order. Without the need to ask, the waiter brought over her favorite Zin and a Perrier with a single raspberry at the bottom. The bubbles gently adhering to the raspberry until Nikky lightly swirled the glass before taking a sip. She motioned to the waiter and within minutes, her regular order of roasted bone marrow and Cavatelli alla Norcina arrived. She dove into the succulent savoriness while selectively acknowledging peers, competitors, and potential clients. And, of course, ignoring those who wouldn't provide a distinct advantage to her current nor future plans. She sat back and admired the decor, finally feeling whole.

She took out her black Amex and slid it into the bill. She hadn't picked up her phone since she had entered the restaurant. Even a social media genius needed time away from work. The waiter returned and shook his head.

Nicole dug into her purse and came up with her standard card and crossed her fingers that it would work. She never really paid much attention to the bills since she didn't need to. That's what her parents' accountant and office manager were for. She mentally added to her list of "must do's" the need to find a new accountant and an office manager. If she wanted her parents to stop tracking her every expenditure, she needed to get out from under their sphere of influence. A very tough although not completely unrealistic objective.

She released her breath when he returned with the bill to sign. Since being jolted out of her moment of relaxation, she picked up her phone and waded through the masses of messages. Interesting that her bro had already messaged her at least two dozen more times. He must have heard about her latest activities. Her parents were MIA, again not surprising. And then there were the several hundred of "others" including threats from Karine that she was ditching Nikky. Each threat pleasantly accompanied by another image from Karine's travels, some so ludicrous that Nikky stifled a laugh. She figured she'd wait a few more days to see if Karine calmed down. If so, this could be part of Nikky's phase two. Many of these texts could go viral if Karine repositioned them and placed them on Insta and Snap. A few notes down, Nikky found another text from Karine's management that they were still reviewing the latest budget numbers from Karine's tour. The implication that Nikky wouldn't get paid. This news slid Karine from the potential of being Nikky's second priority to possibly the last. Nikky still hadn't been compensated for the ELLEN promotion and all the other activities associated with that campaign. Time to cut bait.

Nikky slipped into her soon-to-be-traded-in Spider and launched toward the Hills. She needed to meet Morgan and Paul before she made another move. Even at three in the afternoon, Nikky encountered the infamous Los Angeles traffic. Any time of day or night can feel like standstill rush hour. She long ago stopped attempting to understand the traffic patterns and lounged back. She synced her phone to her car and her social media feeds flashed up on the mini monitor. Nothing serious going on. Same ol' same posts from the typical A listers. B listers in full effect. And C listers clamoring for attention. One or two posts from a Kardashian yet nothing exciting.

She flipped through the news - Wall Street Journal, New York Times, People, National Enquirer, PopSugar … she made sure to stay abreast of the major news and pop culture outlets. Then she started flipping through Craigslist, just to see what was out there. Typically, she wasn't so obvious in her multitasking while driving but the events of the last few days demanded greater action.

She followed the curving Mulholland Drive to Morgan's place. She was almost embarrassed to realize she had never been to Morgan's home. Just as she entered the open driveway to the provincial rancher, Paul opened the front door. Instead of greeting her at the car, he waved her forward and then closed the door behind him.

This odd behavior made her look around. Typically, Paul stayed inside until someone came to the door. That much she knew from previous interactions with him. She silenced her engine and looked up to find photographers in the trees. She hadn't seen anything like this since the last "private" wedding she had attended in which Chrissy Teigen, John Legend, Oprah, Kanye and Kim as well as several other icons of today were in full effect. She only wished she could take credit for this mass of attention.

Along the perimeter, slightly in front of those photographers were, what looked like, security. the rental kind of security. Ones dressed in black with black sunglasses meant to cause intimidation without a single finger being lifted nor a single word uttered. Hell, it sure as heck worked. Nikky didn't want to go near them and clearly neither did the photographers. She bet if she took the time to look around long enough, she'd see reporters in the bushes and fans climbing in through the windows.

Nikky clicked her car door locked and sashayed into Morgan's home. In the main hallway, Paul, as semi elegant as ever, met her with a broad smile and the air of something being up.

"You didn't tell me that Morgan had an "adopt-a-paparazzi program." Nikky hugged Paul and kissed him lightly on both cheeks.

"We decided it was better to adopt them than let them run free." Paul guided Nikky into the living room. The open fireplace blazed. Sliding glass doors to the patio had been opened enabling a cooler breeze to intermingle with the heat emitting from the fire. Even in this undercurrent and interplay of hot and cool, Morgan was nowhere to be found.

"And the rentals? Those new?" Nikky took a seat near the open doorway and enjoyed the slight breeze off the balcony. The room cozy and tasteful. The true financial nature of Morgan evident in the well-maintained agedness of the furniture. Morgan was smart enough to have the rugs removed (Nikky bet they were shag or plush) to reveal the gorgeous wood planking. Evidence of the old carpeting in a corner where the fireplace and the wall met. Definitely shag.

"Necessary." Paul motioned to the refrigerator and offered a seltzer. Nikky waved him off. "Once the video went viral, a few clever folks figured out who she was and where she had taken off. It didn't take long for the masses to arrive." Paul came over with a bottle for himself and stood across from Nikky. His gaze reflective, his mannerisms stilted, Nikky guessed the last few days had been much more than Paul had envisioned.

"Where's Morgan?"

Paul sipped from the seltzer. "Resting. She had an eventful meeting with a reporter from the LA Times."

Paul described the interaction between Morgan and Belinda McDonald and how he had arranged for the meeting hoping for a little sizzle not a knock 'em down fight. The arch nemeses' long rivalry was at least two decades longer than even Paul imagined. Resulting in a hospitalized Belinda and Morgan needing urgent care from her surgeon, Dr. Snolten and his assistant, Felicity Gorge.

"When does this article run?"

Paul pulled up his phone and shared it with Nikky. A few swipes and she got the gist of it. How did she miss this?

"The doc said Morgan needed to rest at least a day. Already getting calls for follow up interviews. And of course, Belinda is taking this as an opportunity to sue Morgan."

"Good luck with that," Nikky handed back his phone. "We can counter whatever Belinda's already spread. The saying 'no such thing as bad publicity' still rings true, as long as you're not a pedophile, a sexist, or racist." Nikky smirked. She loved taking down one specific racist. Someone long known within Hollywood circles as being a gatekeeper who only allowed certain types through the golden doorway. "If nothing, that article with its 30 million views and the fact that the videos are already viral memes only reinforces the power of the Winged Morgan brand."

"Something like that." Paul clicked his phone off and shoved it in his back pocket. "What's next CLN?"

Nikky bought a little time pretending to check a few things on her phone. This had gone much further than she had expected. She quickly reached out to a few potential clients and pointed them to Morgan's article and the fact that Morgan's previously unchecked Twitter account, with barely 1,000 followers, was recently "confirmed" by Twitter and now had more followers than Katy Perry. Nikky was surprised the activity didn't take down Twitter. "This could be you," Nikky texted to them.

"How open do you think Morgan is posting a la Kim K?"

"She's already inundated with scheduled interviews, appearances, and we got a call about a possible reality show."

"What if I get one of my assistants to create Morgan fan club accounts? She'll do all the posting, we just need Morgan to like and share the posts."

"If Morgan doesn't like the post?"

"Then she doesn't like or share."

"Deal." Paul reached out for an old school handshake agreement, when the sound of something slamming against the roof put them both on guard. Next came tumbling and a loud thump. Paul ran out the front door. Nikky, curious but not sure how curious, followed him.

One of the Rentals had an arm-hold on someone, clearly in disheveled distress, who looked to be in his mid-twenties.

"Nothing to be concerned," the Rental said.

"Roof?" Paul asked. The Rental nodded. "Thanks, Felix. Appreciate you being on top of it."

Nikky snapped as many pics as she could and followed up with video. Felix lifted the kid off the ground and threw him over his back. The intruder had been knocked out from the fall. "This one nearly got past us. He shouldn't have made it this far." With his free hand, Felix pointed towards a tree that had a rather flimsy limb hovering over the roof. The leaves crushed and scattered on the rooftop and along the yard. "That was his entry point. Surprised it held him." Felix adjusted the kid's weight and headed to a nearby 4x4. "I'll take him to the local p-station."

"Fan?" asked Paul.

Felix shrugged. "Could be. I'll have his info run while I'm there."

Nikky watched as Felix shoved the passed-out kid into the back of the truck and drove off. "Is this on the regular?" Nikky asked as she followed Paul back inside.

"I'm surprised this hasn't happened at least three times since you've arrived. They must be getting tired."

"Can I see Morgan?" Nikky asked.

"Now that was a quick change of subject. What's the rush?"

"No rush." Nikky just wanted to see this for herself. At the edges of her instincts she felt this could quickly go sour.

"You don't believe." Paul said this as if he knew it even before Nikky walked in the door.

"Confirming." Nikky thumbed through the newly taken pics and held off on sending them. If she could get real images, close ups of the new Morgan then she'd have real ammo that could take them even beyond the reach of MC or The OAKS.

Paul didn't bother to turn around. He didn't make eye contact with Nikky. He simply left her standing in the middle of Morgan's living room and lightly knocked on Morgan's bedroom door then slipped inside.

Moments later Paul returned and gently closed the door. "She's knocked out. Probably from the treatment." He paused. "If I let you in there then be very quiet. I don't want her being disturbed."

"Fine." Nikky readied to go inside, like a racer at the starting line.

"Wait. Pics are fine but you can't post them for a few days."

Nikky loosened her stance. "Deal breaker."

"I already promised an exclusive with the New York Times. He comes tomorrow. After he runs the article, then fine."

Nikky pondered this one. She didn't absolutely need the exclusive. She could even have the fan site post the pictures and infer that a fan got a hold of them. That would be even better than a true exclusive.

"Fine."

Paul eyed her in that only-Paul-can-do-it manner. The implication that he didn't truly believe her.

"I swear." She reached out in the old-school-handshake style he seemed to like. That broke the ice since he carefully opened the door and allowed Nikky in.

You May Realize Later, This Wasn't a Good Idea

Oddly, the bedroom was exactly how Nikky imagined when she was a kid and idolized Morgan. Oh right, we didn't mention that before, did we? Nikky had been a Morgan fan all the way back to Morgan's soap opera days when Nikky and her mother watched the mid-day medical drama. One of Nikky's few untainted memories with her mother.

The spacious bedroom sung in soft pinks and whites. Modern furniture softened the room with fluffy pillows and dreamy lighting. Nikky felt like she had walked into a giant hug. Maybe Nikky's dissipating hangover or the drama of the last few days had caused her to have a sudden need to crawl into the enticing bed and nap.

She looked behind her and noted that Paul hadn't come in after her. He trusted her more than she thought and possibly more than she deserved. Snug in an enormous round bed, Morgan quietly lay on her side, face towards Nikky. In Morgan's sleep, Nikky barely recognized her. Sans makeup, Morgan's face had a pristine clearness as if it had never seen sunlight or puberty. Her cheekbones high enough to cause enticement when seen through a lens, yet not so pronounced that they brought forward images of hunger or malnutrition. In sleep, Morgan's age was unidentifiable, truly placing her among the ageless.

Hooked up to an IV of a clear-ish concoction, Morgan remained silent and unmoving. Nikky slowly crept forward and considered touching the bag, if only to know the consistency of the fluid and to somehow make this moment real. All within the room was in a hypnotic stasis, the curtains, the bed, the covers, the couch, even the television evoked a rhythmic pattern of harmony and comfort. Only the slow, measured up and down movement of the covers let the unseen visitor know that Morgan survived the fight. Unsure what to do next, Nikky continued forward, hoping that something within her would tell her what to do next.

As she neared the corner of the bed, Morgan shifted in her sleep. Nikky froze. Morgan shifted her arms from underneath the bedspread, and returned to a nearly immobile position. Upon closer examination, Morgan's arms appeared darkly painted black and blue with shades of grey and yellow as if she had long standing injuries that had been healing for weeks.

Nikky drew in closer to be sure this wasn't the lighting or shadows playing tricks . The closer she came, the more she realized this simply wasn't possible. She recalculated the timeframe, questioning if she had it correct. Maybe Morgan had the surgery much longer ago than she had reported. This would explain the age of the bruises. Or maybe the fight between Belinda and Morgan had actually occurred weeks ago, not the previous day. Either way, Nikky snapped one camera phone shot after another, acknowledging that in her current state she may not have correctly ingested what she saw. Based on everything she knew the fight only happened the other day. Yet the bruises told another story.

The sheets were tucked up against Morgan's chest with only her arms, shoulders, and head above the blankets. Nikky continued to take pictures and circled around the bed. She moved slower than she had intended. Something about seeing Morgan in this fragile state made Nikky feel as vulnerable as her one-time idol. As she turned the corner, she nearly gasped. She noted no sutures or scars along the base of the wings. She saw no open wounds. No signs of surgery. It's as if Morgan had always had these luminous pinions.

The wings, vibrant in shades of blue and white shimmered in the soft light. Morgan's back was ripe with more bruises, especially along the base, implying additional exertion and stress.

But honestly, who knew? The contrast of the feathers against Morgan's battered skin made them seem almost alive. As if they were their own entities which had attached themselves to Morgan.

Nikky couldn't help herself, she reached out to touch Morgan's wings and they moved away from her hand. She pulled back, thinking this couldn't be right. None of this could be real.

She approached Morgan's wings again but this time as if they were an animal … slowly, hesitantly, giving them a chance to become familiar with the new person in the room. Only then did they allow her to touch them. Their softness. Their life in a light current drifted through the feathers and into Nikky's hand. The calmness of the sleeping Morgan traveled up Nikky's arm and through her body. She gently placed herself on the floor, the urge to close her eyes became even more hypnotic. Her hand dropped to the bedside and she nearly fell asleep when Paul opened the door. The infusion of light from the living room became blocked by Paul's stance. He headed to her and helped her out of the room.

He laid Nikky down on the couch and carefully closed the bedroom door.

"What are you doing?" Paul clearly tried to hide back fury.

Nikky did her best to wake up. "I … I just needed to …"

"I said pictures. I didn't say anything about touching."

He must have a security camera in the bedroom, Nikky thought. Of course, he did. Considering the hodgepodge of visitors, he'd have to put security cameras throughout the house.

"From now on, just do your job, okay? No more of this free form crap." Paul's voice a near whisper. "I can't have her upset."

Half hearing Paul, the images of Morgan's battered body flashed through her mind, she pulled out her smartphone and surfed through the pictures. The reality of what she just saw brought her back to life. "When did she have the surgery?"

"What are you talking about?" Paul peered over Nikky's shoulder.

"Look at those bruises and the close up of her wings."

"I have no idea what you're talking about."

Nikky may not know what he thought, but she knew what she was thinking. She experienced a combination of awe and terror. Not only was whatever she had seen in Morgan's bedroom not possible, it wasn't natural. Not a god-fearing woman, Nikky had never been to church, but she had seen enough to know that this truly wasn't something that humans could do or be.

"All I care about is that she's getting better," Paul retorted. "Are you done?"

Nikky got up from the couch, pocketed her smartphone and headed for the door. She pushed back her anxiety. This wasn't the time to get freaked out. "I'll get these up in two days. I'll be sure to wait until after the NYTimes article. And we'll get those fan accounts up and running."

Without an additional comment or look back, Nikky exited.

You Say Not-Natural, I Say Messiah.

Nikky put her Prada glasses back in place, even though the sun had already begun its trek back below the mountains. She acknowledged the Rentals and clicked her spider alive. One of the Rentals opened the driver's side door and gently closed it. She spied the trees and noted that some of the paparazzi had moved on. Possibly followed Felix in his trip to the police department with the latest trespasser. Nikky synced her phone to the car before messaging her assistant to go forward with the social media accounts on Morgan's behalf. She then sent a few images to help her along in the initial postings and sent links to other images and articles that would help the fodder.

Nikky smiled at the Rentals as she made her way out of the circular driveway. As she reached the end and started onto the infamous Mulholland Drive, Felix returned and turned into the driveway. He must have given Paul a heads up that he was on his way because Paul anxiously waited at the doorway.

Nikky messaged her assistant to find out who was recently turned into the Hollywood Police Station for trespassing and assault at Morgan's address. The combination of Paul's expression and the implied urgency of Felix's return meant this guy was a bit more than your typical fan.

Next, she sent to a completely different assistant directions to search "unnatural sightings" such as people reported as being able to do inhuman or supernatural things. Or research the return of supernatural creatures like Babadook, vampires, werewolves, and the like. Her assistant argued that this was too broad of a topic and only relented when Nikky promised double her normal fee.

Even though Paul never told her who the surgeon was, nothing about what she just saw screamed "natural occurrence". This thought brought her back to the assistant and suggested searching against private plastic surgeons or surgeons known for making the seemingly impossible, possible. Based on the current need for everyone on the planet to regurgitate every moment of every day on the internet, Nikky figured that shouldn't be too hard to find.

Nikky swiftly made it back to her abode only to find that her belongings were already being packed up into a U-Haul. Her mother, classically attracted to drama, greeted Nikky at the entrance.

"What is this?" Nikky blurted out.

"We're simply fulfilling our promise, dear." Nikky's mother reached out to cup NIkky's cheek only to be met with a swipe of her daughter's hand.

"We never talked about this."

"Oh, I thought your father had been clear." Her mother paused. "WE talked about it, meaning he and I. Only natural he would talk to you as well." She reached for her purse and felt it as if verifying it contained her latest addictive substance.

"No need to go for your pills, MOM." Fuming, Nikky crossed the threshold and found that her entryway, living room, and even the back-patio furniture had been packed. Only the empty husks of what was once her favorite home remained. As she crossed the hall onto the patio, she realized that she had gone on autopilot and instead of driving to the quaint gingerbread house her parents had rented on her behalf, she had returned to her previous home.

From behind her, her mother pipe up. "Dear, your father wanted to talk to you as well."

Nikky turned to see her mother sip from yet another glass, just dark enough so that the contents weren't easily identifiable. Nikky sighed. This wasn't the end of the day that she had been hoping for. She had already envisioned herself on her own back patio and relaxing to her favorite play list, champagne in hand, and performing research. Not this. Anything but this scenario.

Movers lugged past her mother with boxes in tow, another reminder of her parents' Machiavellian approach to parenting.

"Would you like to grab a bite before heading out? Did you come here looking for something?" Nikky's mother asked.

Clasping her car keys, Nikky said, "No. I'm fine." Then on second thought, "actually yes. Where the hell are you taking my stuff? Did you think to ask me if I needed anything? I've been wearing the same damn clothes for three days now. Did it occur to you to allow me to get my own damn things? What kind of insanity is this shit?" The words came out in a regurgitated blur. One fueled on frustration.

"No need to speak to your mother like that."

Behind her mother emerged her father. As always, he wore yet another priceless suit, dressed as if he closed a multi-million-dollar deal.

"There's every need. You two walk around like you're unstoppable. Have you heard of white privilege? Everything you do and say is the utter definition of it. You act like no one on the planet matters other than you. And you believe it!" The suppression of years of frustration had finally burst. Nikky felt her anger rise and remain. She matched their sanctimonious attitudes and raised them a level of piousness.

Her parents remained silent.

"We've spent our lives in a fucking bubble and you not only enjoy it, you thrive in it. Do you even know what it means to not have? Have you ever wanted? Ever desired? You both live in solitudes of nothingness fed off what? Off drugs and deals and anything that makes you go numb inside. And your expectation is that we do the same." Nikky thought this would make her feel better. Instead it fueled her anger more, leaving her a ball of passionate rage.

"Are you done?" her father asked.

"Fuck no. I'm not done. I'm only getting started. We've spent our lives trying to make you happy and not a damn thing can come close. All because we don't want to be you. And that's the fucking problem isn't it! We don't want to be you."

Her father looked on as if nothing she could say would even cause the slightest response. Her mother, on the other hand, looked away. Nikky swore her mother blushed.

"Now are you done?" he asked.

Nikky searched her parents faces for an answer. An out that would allow this moment to mean something. Something greater than what felt like a tantrum ending in nothingness. Between the two of them, she only found a void.

"I don't want to be numb," Nikky stated. Her righteousness evoked a straight back and lifted chin.

"Fine. You're not numb," her father said. "You're so 'alive' that you just spent (he checks his phone) a half million dollars on a drug fueled party with your *friends*."

This caused Nikky to pause. How did he know about that? He wasn't social media savvy. Her look of perplexity must have been obvious because his continued.

"Yes, I know about it. It seems everyone in our community knows about it. You've made yourself quite the local celebrity. You also managed to anger several of my business partners. So much so they killed our deals."

He approached Nikky with an authority she hadn't seen since she was a child and been caught staying up late to watch the Tonight Show and the Late movies. "Your activities and proclivities caused us to lose not a few million, but so much that I need to sell this estate. If you want to know where your possessions are, I suggest for the more refined objects you attend the estate sale at Sotheby's and for your more common items go to the Goodwill. If I can't get cash for them then I'll take the write-off."

"They weren't yours to sell!" Nikky screamed. This was ridiculous.

What gave him the right to steal her stuff? "This is trespassing. Get out!" She smacked her father on the shoulder, expecting him to respond in kind. She wanted a fight -verbal or physical.

"Correction, they were mine to sell. These were bought with your inheritance, which makes them mine. You would have no money, no funding, nothing … without us." He turned his back on her. "You asked if we knew what it was like to need or want. I can ask you the same question." He reached his hand out to his wife who toggled to his side. "We're done, Nik. The deal we had is off. You are officially on your own."

Nikky stood there flabbergasted. With the sun down, she shivered as the last of the movers loaded the final box onto the truck. Her overflowing fury made her shake more. She watched as the movers closed the door and locked it as if she hadn't been there, as if she didn't exist.

Resisting the urge to trash the place, Nikky went inside and up the stairs. She wanted a final moment with the place she had called home since she graduated college. The rooms felt like never ending catacombs due to their emptiness. Her parents were nothing if not thorough. She wandered through the guest rooms and noted the cable wires that had once been attached to wall sized screens, the squares of dust that had accumulated in spots that had once marked her hand-picked furniture. Much of it she had bought at estate sales, making the choice of selling through Sotheby's that much more ironic.

She caressed the walls to say goodbye. This had been the home she had dreamed of, long before she had left her parents' home. This had been the house that she had picked out with her mother when Nikky was only a pre-teen. They would drive by and Nikky had proclaimed that one day this would be her home. The intimacy of that moment, and the sheer joy that NIkky had shared with her mother when they closed on the house, caused Nikky's heart to pause. The numbness she had proclaimed her parents lived for, now spread through her. A terrifying, soulless emptiness. Nikky continued to her bedroom, ready to camp out for one final night, the lone person curled into a fetal position where her bed had once been. Then in her former walk in closet, she found her clothes haphazardly strewn into a mound, the sheer lack of understanding of their financial value evident in the knotted mass. On top among her Louis Vuitton, her Prada, her McQueen and Garcons she found a note:

Yours - Mom

Nikky climbed on top of her remaining personal assets, curled into a ball, and wept until she slept.

When she awoke her phone was dead. The moon glowed through a clear window, the rays highlighted her and the rooms near emptiness.

She went into the kitchen and found a few garbage bags. She returned to stuff her clothes into them, the carefulness taken when she first purchased each item now lost in the moment of desperation. She loaded the bags and herself into the impractical sportscar. She sat in the driver's seat and stared at the steering wheel.

It took all of her will not to look back at the house, at her life, at the last several hours. She started her car and moved forward towards her new life.

Curious what happens next? Then stay tuned for our next novella in the *Newly Minted Wings* series.

THE CUPS THAT HOLD

By Kenneth Holt

What can be said about the most beautiful hands in God's creation? I am reminded of the imperfect nature of the world by such hands and I'm quite certain it is that which draws me to them. Perfection would go unnoticed. There is nothing to consider with anything so uninteresting. Not true with any sincere countenance of man's life on earth where a connection is made, and our own toil is measured. Therein lies the hidden essence of our very existence. Hands show the person.

——

The lid is open. Gnarled long and slender fingers work their tips, mimicking the spider in delicacy and precision, as the man arranges the items from the box. Someone holds near for a moment. A scent lingers in the stillness. A boy watches as the man focuses on his task. This youngster, sent from the office and told to report without delay, does not interrupt. He is not allowed in the air-conditioned office due to his gender; it is a place for the girls who were hired along with him under the CETA Program as city employees for the Department of Parks and Recreation during this summer of 1977. The three girls facilitate the checking out of equipment to neighborhood children in exchange for house keys or a rabbit's foot; the one boy belongs outside working the grounds with Black Oscar.

The doors have been unlocked to reveal the contents of two storage closets built into the stonework of the park building's small courtyard. This is the old park building, not the new one with the air-conditioning. The historical site is a work of art that goes unnoticed in this day. It is no longer of use. It is merely a remnant. The boy realizes this, and his attention goes from the man organizing the items in the box to the storage closets that until today contained mysteries his friends and he imagined were far greater than the gardening tools the open doors show to him now. He studies the stonework of the walled courtyard, as he often does, because it is never enough. Something eludes him no matter how often he tries to understand what holds it in place, what keeps it standing upright.

Two upon one, one upon two, they climb, but not in any regular pattern . Anything resembling an Ashlar method would be impossible with these natural river rocks from the local canyon wash. They are still innumerable in their home as if their source is unending. You have to weave through a multitude of them to get from the road to the river; in pockets near the shore, tall reeds appear to grow straight through the stone. It takes a keen eye to see they surround the reed and shelter certain patches from the will of the river.

The stones at the base of the walls weigh several hundred pounds each; those near the top are not much smaller. It is a curious thing to think how they got up there and how the irregular patterns eventually come together to form these walls, this building.

The boy lives across the street from the park. This is his park and at one time he tried to solve the puzzle of how these great stones stand. He believed if he found that answer it would help him scale and encircle the entire building by bare hand and foot without break and without touching the ground. No kid in the whole neighborhood has been able to, that is, until last week. He gave up the idea of a predetermined path, of selecting where his toes might have the best chance of bracing his weight and his fingers might find enough ledge to grasp. There are very few places to rest. The great breadth of the front and back of the stone building takes an endurance that is difficult to summon. The bulky corners turn at a right angle and make it nearly impossible for a kid to reach round and land a new grip. Eventually, it's one or the other that takes you down.

The boy stands looking at, not quite understanding, the stones. There is no answer to why he was successful this time around. He only knows that once he let go, the way was found. And that it took him almost a whole hour to complete.

———

"They say'd you be comin' in." goes Black Oscar as he closes the lid to the box.

The boy could now see it is a fisherman's tackle box as he holds the handle on top.

"Yeah, I'm here." the boy responds.

"What good is it you comin' so late?"

"I'm not sure?" He answers while looking at his wristwatch. "I start at noon ... that's in 3 minutes."

"I see what I cain do 'bout that."

"Yes, please. I'd like to come in earlier."

Oscar stands from the wooden stool, brushes some ash from his pants, and places the tackle box on a shelf inside the storage closet. He must be something over 6 foot 5 and lanky, all bones. His presentation has a childlike simplicity.

"Tell me yo' name, boy, before I get to callin' you Hound."

"How'd you know that?"

"I know a lot about you people."

"What people? ... White people?"

"All people, I guess."

Oscar reaches into the storage and pulls out two heavy-gauge orange colored hoses that have sun-faded to coral. He wraps each into loose figure eights that nearly reach the ground as he places them on Hound's shoulders, first one and then the other. He takes two for himself, locks the storage doors, and says.

"Montelongo, he the one. I see you fixed on that building. I know you was there the whole time watchin' me and fixin' on that wall. He the one who build it. They say he was En Dios … An Indian."

"By himself? Did he do it by himself?"

"That what they say."

"There's almost no mortar. How did he get them to balance and to stick?"

"Only he know that … but what I cain tell you is that it cain't be figured. It only be known."

"It would have been so much easier to use brick. I can't believe he was able to do it, especially near the top."

"No hewn stone, Hound … No hewn stone. What the point in buildin' an altar to the Father if you only mean to defile it?"

"I don't know the answer."

"The hell you don't."

"There are stone houses all over this neighborhood. I've heard there are 67, maybe more. What about them?"

"He the one. He build them all."

There are only a few spots in the park where the hoses are needed. Years ago, they put in a sprinkler system with an aim to cover the whole grass area. They got pretty close. They only missed these few spots.

Oscar drags his one hose along the ground; it unwinds as it goes. He's already attached the Rain Bird to the other end and properly placed it. He drops the second hose at the water spigot, which comes right out of the earth to hip level, and taps them both in. Hound can see the second Rain Bird in his hand but cannot recall Oscar picking them up. The man must have a secret stash somewhere along the property. The other spigot is deeper, closer to the wild area of the park grounds where the pines end and the pepper trees begin. Hound makes his way toward it, anticipating the next move, as Oscar snakes out his remaining hose to a far distance.

Not a word is said as Oscar arrives. Hound must have gotten it right, done a good job of foreseeing the next move. Oscar holds two new Rain Birds and the boy thinks to himself that he should pay closer attention to find the secret stash of them. There are pockets all over this damn place. It's anybody's guess what all is hidden here. Hound knows a thing or two about pocketing secrets. He too has a few out there among the pepper trees. More accurately, within one particular pepper he calls his own. It grows a straight shot about 50 yards out from his mother's driveway but is not easily seen through the growth of those before it. It is the one tree where he brings no friends. What is hidden is kept there and nobody is invited to be a part of it.

Oscar taps the one hose to the spigot and Hound takes the initiative to tap in the second. He is handed a Rain Bird. Taking the lead twice in a row has its rewards, he thinks, as Oscar makes way, snaking out his line. Hound does the same, only in the opposite direction. The length of the hose lands him right at the border where the manicured grass meets the wild. He can see his tree from here. All is clear in the full sun of mid-day. The view would be quite different by day's end, since well beyond the pepper fields an invading dense air drifts from the burning in the rock quarry, making for a most dramatic skyline by sunset, and he is facing westward. Years of illegal dumping on the quarry property finally erupted into fire and the solution was to cover the seeping methane in a layer of dirt from where the smoldering has gone on now, day and night, for many months. It is sour on both nose and tongue but the visual is a rousing feast for the eye, demonstrating a plain fact: that which is foul often has an unfortunate beauty; unfortunate, in that it lures to a point of distraction.

Hound's tree appears and disappears from a movement of loose wispy pepper fronds, displaying the rolling breeze, and arrives as evidence that other things, too, come and go by an invisible force in this world. The Rain Birds are attached, and each man walks to a spigot. They twist, letting the water flow, and the soothing sound begins. Hound stands still and listens to the sprinklers for a time. It doesn't take long until the four are out of sync and have lost the meditative rhythm of their beginnings. They now sound like they are fighting one another; he takes this as a cue to move along.

Oscar has made his way back to the building and is seen entering the courtyard and Hound follows. It will take a few minutes to get there, maybe more, as he strolls evenly without hurry through the maze of tall pines. He knows the way well; he could do it with his eyes closed, as this has been his park for more than two years now. It has been his since the time they left the other place, their former home, which they'd used up to a point of emptiness. There was nothing more to do, but to leave and start anew. It is doubtful anyone could know the way around these grounds better than he.

Hound gets close to the courtyard when the scent returns to him. It hangs in the protected area of the stone walls. The wind is kept out and does not influence anything as it does the pepper fronds in the wild. He is familiar with the scent, although, there is more to it than just that. It is very pleasing, as it takes a combination of sensory involvement to get the full effect of its potential.

He sees the stool and tackle box are out again. This is what Oscar does, whatever it is. The box sits upon his lap, as he sits upon the stool with his back to Hound, just as before. The lower drawers contain undisclosed items, whereas, the underside of the lid and the top shelf hold a few pieces that Oscar is seen working. More than one thing is burning. In addition to the pipe that lies atop, two candles and a small thurible of incense thread thin lines of smoke upward. Hound stops at the same place as before. Moving any closer in might be a violation into a private act. He shifts his focus from what is going on to the open closet to his right and then to the stones all around and is reminded of their earlier conversation, the one where he began to learn something new though nothing conclusive. Oscar knows Hound is standing in position and pinches the burning with quick fingertips. The man has a precise style of arrangement, placement, and closure, as if unaffected by any form of trespassing. The lid snaps, the latch is fastened, but he does not yet stand.

"What out in the field, boy?"

"Huh …?"

"They must be something out there to call you so hard. But different from these here stone walls. Nope, no studyin' … this time you was dreamin'. Something calling you, Hound?"

"No. I was just thinking, that's all."

"A man cain't solve everything by his thinkin'."

"I do daydream, sometimes."

"That you do, Hound. That you do."

Oscar stands and returns the tackle box to the closet, closes the doors, and loops the padlock into the receiver. He slides the stool along the dirt floor toward Hound.

"You set here and dream awhile longer. I go see what cain be done 'bout your hours."

"Is it okay? What if somebody sees me?" Hound says knowing the scent is still heavy in the air. This was the first time he saw Oscar smile.

"See you what? … Dreamin'? Maybe they learn a thing or two. Do them good to remember what it like. Go on … set awhile. These walls do more than just still the wind. I be back."

"I'll wait right here."

Oscar moves across the courtyard walkway and is soon beyond the sight of Hound. The scent got him thinking again and he looks up to the closet doors. They could use a painting. The wood shows an old forest green, bleached with age, chipping away. That color is just the right accent against the gray and black granite stone. Would a fresh coat fuck it up? That's why they won't allow the Sistine Chapel ceiling to be cleaned, for fear of removing the contaminates people have come to see as beautiful. And then, as though something cries out, he sees it. The padlock is looped through, but it has not been clicked shut. The closet is unlocked.

Oh, how he would like a taste. It's a little early but for some reason the idea of it being ahead of schedule does not dissuade him as it usually would. There is, however, a basic principle at work which slow his movements, that keep him in thought and from immediately going for the box: it does not belong to him.

But where would the harm be in a little taste?

These walls do more than just still the wind, said Black Oscar. Was that an invitation or did it pertain strictly to the protective nature of this place? Either way, Hound feels shielded from a risk of interruption and discovery in this moment, and is sure, or at least convinced enough, that he is justified in having a look inside. He peeks from around the courtyard entrance but by this time Oscar has reached the 75-yard distance and is inside the new park building. The grounds are unusually vacant today, but there is the one woman with her son visiting the former wading pool that some time ago was overtaken by sand. It is now a place for small children to play with toy tractors and trucks. They won't be a problem.

He dips back inside and goes for the doors. Off with the lock, flip the latch away, replace the lock on the loop, and swing the doors open: first left, then right. There is an unbelievable amount of gardening equipment within this small enclosure that would not stand a chance of staying put were it not for the high level of organizational skill one could assume belongs to Black Oscar. These items would ordinarily have Hound's attention, especially given the amount of concentration and wonder his friends and he have devoted to them over time, but as of now, his only interest lies with the contents of the tackle box.

Hound reaches for it, but the handle is a little too tall to grab. He feels lucky, since there is a small vacant area left for his feet and so steps inside as far as the equipment will allow. He then stretches upward, using a hand on either side of its width, and lowers the box from the shelf. Up close, it is a green marbled Bakelite unit with a brass closure on front. The white swirl of the marble effect de-saturates the green to a hue very close to that of the aged closet doors. Hound sits on the stool and places the box on his lap. It almost slides right off but he catches it in the nick of time. The height of the stool is meant for Oscar, who is at least a foot taller than Hound. The boy must use his tippy toes to level out the area of his lap for the box, and then he releases the brass closure.

There it is. The scent escapes right away but it is of a strange combination blending beyond distinction. He carefully hinges the lid back, so the box is fully opened, and is surprised to find the top compartment covered by yet another barrier. The box is held steady with one hand while the other slips fingernails along the edge of the layer and lifts out what appears to be a folded game board. He sets it back down on the top area and unfolds it. It opens to a soft tan color devoid of any game spaces or character images. This board is not meant for games. It is simply etched with the words:

Let Me Fulfill Thy Will.

Hound is shaken by the clarity of this statement and his toes go off guard, which sends the box skating down his lap, flying past his knees. He snatches it out of thin air just before it hits the ground, saving the box and much of the contents, but the board and a handful of items spring forward and land in the dirt before him. Hound rights the box, spins a half circle, and places it on the stool. He goes for the board and pieces that made it all the way down.

"Oh god oh god oh god … NO," escape from Hound.

There is a small metal cross with a circle at each end of its four points. Beyond it is a clear cruet half filled with water, and a few old-fashioned fishing lures scattered about. The rest has stayed in the box, including the pipe, which was the original purpose and has so far remained unseen. He starts with the cross and the cruet, wiping them each along his jeans and then does the detail work with his t-shirt. The bottle cleans up fairly easily as it is made of fresh clear glass. What is remarkable is it went unbroken, being of a most delicate composition. And even though the cross shows a smooth texture, there is much work to be done to get it just right, as both sides and the circles at each end need a polishing. There is some degree of tarnish present and so it's difficult to know how far to go with it. While in contemplation of these details, he pauses briefly to really look at the cross because he hasn't seen another like it. Although Hound has always attended private Evangelical schools, this is the first of its kind he has seen.

———

Oscar raps on the opened door and walks into the office where the four females are congregated. They are startled and taken from their conversation. He ducks a bit to avoid the doorway header. There is no chance he would hit it with a normal stride, but this is a habit the man picked up beginning in his fourteenth year after growing 6 inches in the course of one school semester. His knees never completely recovered from the accelerated growth spurt, though no other negative symptoms were noticed. The illogical practice of ducking through doorways he wouldn't hit anyway has remained with Oscar as a sort of unconscious act in self-preservation.

"Yes, Oscar. What is it? How may I help you?" asks Barbara, the assistant director. She handles everything pertaining to the Recreation Center when Mr. Bruder, the director, is not present.

"It's that boy …" he begins.

"What? … What's happened to him? Is he okay?" she interrupts.

"Yeah, it ain't nothin' like that. He fine … a little dreamy, but otherwise, he just fine."

"Oh? … Well then. What is it, Oscar?"

"That what I'm trying to say. Is they anyway that Hound can come in when I start?"

"That's 8 o'clock! The office doesn't even open until 10, Oscar. I'm afraid it is out of the question. Besides, I've already made out the schedule for this week."

"Hound say'd he like to turn up early. We should get at this work before the heat of day fall down on us."

"What's with this 'Hound'? Why do you call him that?"

"I don't rightly know why he called that. Maybe these here young girls know better than you and I, Miss Barbara?"

Barbara looks around at the girls sitting near her who have been stunned to silence and then back at Oscar.

"I think it would be better if you referred to him by his given name: Kelly Sinclair. I'd rather not have any problems with the parents around here."

"No, that be okay with him and the hours be okay with Mr. Bruder, you see?"

"Well … I don't think there's any law against him coming in before the office opens. That is, if there's work to be done, Oscar!"

"They is … they is … always work to be done, Miss Barbara."

"Right. Have the Hound … I mean Kelly! … come in before he leaves for home and I'll explain everything."

"Okay then, Miss Barbara."

He exits the cool of the office for the field.

"Black Oscar scares the hell out of me!" goes the one girl.

"I can't even look at him for more than a second at a time!" says another.

The third sits in a catatonic state with her mouth slightly open and a bubble forming.

"Can't you make him go away?" continues the first.

"I don't think he has any white in his eyes. I swear he has solid eyes!" the second takes her turn.

"Now, girls. Of course, I can't make him go away. He was appointed here by the city, so this is where he works, where he makes his living. Okay?"

Their cheeks go red and they murmur a few things to each other. Then Barbara continues.

"And let me tell you something about a black man. They are no different than a white man, not much anyway. There is as much difference within a group of whites as you will find between a white and a black. Believe me! I went through a phase in college and I know … Woof!"

The bubble pops and the third girl interjects, "Really, Barbara? Really? How can that be?"

"I don't know how it can be. It just is, and that's all there is to it."

"No differences?"

"Well, I guess they do have that funny hair."

"Mr. Burder has tight curly hair too, Barbara. I can tell even though he uses that oily Brilliantine to straighten it all out. He can't see the back is still all bunched up into tiny ringlets, but he sure does work the front. I've never known a man to look into the mirror as much as Mr. Bruder," says girl number one.

"He does NOT look into the mirror? Well, not TOO much, anyway." Barbara thinks for a moment and continues. "You know, that's just what ended my college conquests … I fell in love with a Jewish boy. He was very intelligent. To tell you the truth, I've been hooked ever since."

"Is that why you stay home all of the time? Are you waiting for Phillip Bruder to make his move?"

"I do NOT stay home all of the time! What a thing to say?"

Barbara spins an earring round and round in her lobe. "And who says he HASN'T made his move? Though I do wish he'd take more regular notice of me."

"Is Mr. Bruder smart too, Barbara … I mean, because he's Jewish?"

"I don't know about THAT? But he sure is energetic, let me tell you … Vroom!"

Hound finishes cleaning the cross and tries to find the proper placement for it among the varied compartments of the tackle box. It is not as easy as it would seem, not like it was with the cruet, which fit perfectly in the one spot of its exact shape. Each chamber of the three trays are cork-lined and meant for the care of fine pieces. This would explain why the thin glass bottle survives being stored here; it is obvious that the forethought in placement of all the items is of great importance to the owner. The fishing lures went in without trouble next to the assortment of others of their kind on the second tray, but he cannot find an exact fitting for the cross along the top. The space that is left is not it; there is something not quite right about how it lays.

Hound is called from his own attention when he suddenly remembers Black Oscar. He makes a break and sneaks a peek from around the courtyard walls. Oscar is there in plain view, on the walk and already halfway back. Hound then darts again to the stool and sees it right away. The problem is in the thurible; it is out of position. It must have bounced out of its own compartment into the one belonging to the cross during the turbulence of the falling and catching. Hound lifts it up and sees the impression of the cross in the cork lining. He swaps them and it is a perfect fit. The chain of the thurible is laced in a pleasing fashion, and all is good. Hound places the folded board on top, sealing off the items. He hinges the top forward and the closure is clasped. Hound bolts for the closet with the tackle box. Carefully setting it back on the shelf, the boy sees several tiny empty cups scattered about on either side. He wonders why he didn't notice them the first time around but reasons he had been too focused on the box to be so distracted. The stool is dragged along the dirt ground and finds its home in the vacant area that was earlier of such good use to Hound's feet. He quickly shuts the two doors, swings the latch into position, loops the padlock through and lets it hang.

Hound takes a few steps from the closet when Oscar enters through the walkway. They stand looking at each other briefly. Oscar drops his gaze down to the dirt floor. He follows the tracks made by the sliding of the stool from where he once sat, to the place when he pushed it toward Hound, and then scans the marks leading back into the closet. Hound realizes his mistake. The stool is supposed to be outside of the doors.

"I fix't it up. You come tomorrow, 8 o'clock sharp, and we get busy on these here tree basins before the heat come to us."

"Okay, Oscar. Listen, I just want to say ..."

"Ain't nothin' t' say. Miss Barbara want you in the office before you head out. It been nearly three hours. You wrap up them hoses in the field, then it 'bout time to make your way home."

"I will."

"You seen the way I done it? A big figure eight, boy. A big figure eight. Then just leave them be 'cause she only have you down till three today. I fetch 'em after."

"Thank you, Oscar."

"Nothin' to it, son. And don't you mind them foolish girls in the office. They act all nerves, but they be okay for a young man such as yo'self. You a bit more than just the Hound, you see?"

"I'll meet you at 8 sharp."

"That you will, as far as we cain tell."

Hound stands beside the pay phone that came with the new building. The ringing begins on the other end.

"Yeah, hello?"

"Girl Scout, can you come to the park?"

"I can in a few minutes. I'm just finishing up some shit around here."

There is an interruption. The phone is palmed.

"I've asked you time and time again. Don't speak that way! Not over the phone and not in person. Is this how I am raising you?"

"What'd I do? It's just The Hound."

"I don't care who it is. Remember, you are representing our family."

"What am I, the only one? This is bullshit."

"I don't know, maybe you are? Maybe you're our only hope, son."

She smiles deeply at the sight of her beloved, and then continues.

"And stop calling that beautiful boy 'Hound'. It's distasteful."

"What can I say? He earned it."

"I don't believe that for a second."

And her son returns the deep smile that is the substance of his mother. She softens before she speaks again.

"Anyway, what are you characters up to?"

"He's asking if I want to play basketball in the old gym."

"Playing basketball in the old gym, again? It seems that's all you do anymore. You two should play outside more often. Your dreams are outside … along the dirt roads, among the trees."

"Oh … we spend plenty of time outside, mom. You know we do."

She looks along her nose to her son as he slams the phone down without saying goodbye. He goes for the front door.

Everybody should know there isn't any playing basketball in the old gym, there never has been. Even the main meeting room in the stone building is far too narrow; and while Montelongo pitched the ceiling high at the center, the crossbeams go straight through at exactly eight feet. Despite its small dimensions, those involved in planning park activities did briefly try to make it work for the kid's floor hockey team, but that was before the new building came and solved the problems of the old. That was before reason and efficiency took over a time of wonder in this place.

They had their one favorite pine. Which is too say, Hound and Girl

Scout had a favorite tree on the park grounds they visited almost daily for the purpose of playing basketball in an old gym that could not facilitate this activity. The phrase was but a code for something else they had going on.

And, as a side note, Avrum was granted his nickname by Hound's mother when she noticed he bore a stark resemblance to a curly-haired young scout who represented the month of July - and so marked it in ink. That same calendar has remained hooked to their kitchen wall going on three years in honor of this obscure discovery. Still, the strange happening goes almost unseen, as others rarely visit anymore, but Girl Scout knows by way of the calendar picture he is still present within their home. Hound, in turn, was given his nickname by Bruder in tribute to a perceived though vague notion that the boy was in possession of an overactive libido. Even though it is not well known, an acute perception lies beneath the blatantly masculine exterior of Phillip Bruder, with this feature ever present and periodically marking its existence by the exceptional timing of his intuition.

The tree in question is not Hound's pepper tree but a unique pine; unique in that its branches at the very top are arranged in such a way to form the image of a dancing bear. The two of them first came upon it at the exact same time while lying atop the chain link backstop to the baseball diamond. This tandem recognition of the image meant it was theirs together, and up to this point, Hound and Girl Scout remain the only ones who are aware of its peculiar anomaly.

The neighborhood children of all these years have climbed up and hung out on the backstop so often that they've left their scooped impressions behind, which resemble the sagging backs of old swayback horses. It has formed cups to hold them. Hound and Girl Scout are different from the rest since they recline the opposite direction in the cups. It is due to the high position of this vantage that they see and register a great many things, though more so during the nighttime hours, and this is how they came to discover the dancing bear, thus making the extraordinary pine theirs alone.

Hound and Girl Scout do have good timing in relation to one another, particularly when it comes to playing basketball in the old gym, and they arrive at the base of the pine within two minutes of the phone call. They begin to climb without saying a word because all things worth mentioning are somehow enhanced once they are deeply within the tree. The stability of their seats is made from two nearly identical crooks where the trunk split about halfway up. No longer do they go any higher, not after Hound tried to reach the dancing bear and got stuck there for a time. It was then Phillip Bruder showed he was good for more than just one thing: since he not only relaxes the rules for all involved but has a talent for helping a boy who has gone too high to again reach the ground.

Settling in, Hound pulls a test tube from his shirt pocket. He removes the rubber plunger top, tilts the glass toward his palm, and the hand-rolled with the twisted ends slides out into his grip. Girl Scout has the lighter ready, and after three attempts at the wheel, sparks up the doobie. He takes a nice long draw and holds it in tightly, only coughing a little. They both have much experience and are not taken to fits of hacking like in their fledgling days. It is something to be so experienced at the young age of 14, but, under certain conditions, this can and does happen. Girl Scout passes the J to Hound who takes his own long hit. He says nothing of it but is grateful that Girl Scout's style does not involve nigger-lipping the bounty. They pass the J back and forth for another round and then Hound places it on a limb between them, and they watch a corkscrew thread of smoke rise into the branches above.

Girl Scout begins.
    "What's the story with the gardener dude? Does he even talk?"
    "Yeah, he talks."
    "What about? What the fuck does he have to say? I've never-ever seen him open his mouth."
    "He keeps to himself quite a bit, but he talks."
    "Man, everybody wants to know what's up with that Black Oscar. What's he like? Did he tell you anything?"
    "He told me some things about the neighborhood, about the stone houses, and about the old building, too."
    "He sure as hell is *not* from around here. How could he know anything about this place?"
    "I'm not sure how he knows? He just does."
    "He's pretty creepy, man."
    "No … he isn't. It might be he's a loner, that's all."
    "Fuckin' A, yeah! Who'd want to hang around that dude?"

Hound lifts the J from the branch and gets it going again.
    "He's a really interesting guy, I think? He speaks in a simple way, but I understand what he means even though it seems like some things are missing."
    "What's missing? What do you mean something's missing?"
    "It's not that exactly. It's more like he uses fewer words and I fill the rest in with my head."
    "Get serious, dude. I told you he's creepy."
    "Nah, he's not creepy."

The whole scene has turned to slow motion as the weed comes on strongly. Girl Scout pinches the end of what is left of the J to avoid burning his fingertips as he hits it hard. He blows the smoke upward and then makes a move to pass it to Hound. This is done in a carefully decelerated fashion as if they were at risk of activating the atom bomb. Their hands meet at the middle point for the exchange but the J sticks to Girl Scout's index finger. He rolls it forward with his thumb and tries the pass a second time, but it gets away from him and spirals down through the branches. Girl Scout leans a little too far forward to watch it go and nearly falls out of the pine himself.

"Stupid. What are you? … Baby Brains?" goes Girl Scout.
"They'll probably bump you back to Brownie for this move, Pollyanna." responds Hound."
Then they go back and forth.
"You're stoned, dude."
"Do they let Chinese girls in the Brownies? … Because, I can barely see your eyes."
"You can write me a note of explanation with your pencil dick."
"They only let you try on that girlie uniform because they couldn't detect such a tiny sausage."
"Only a big fag would want to see a boy in a Brownie uniform."
"You better do something about those curly-locks if you want to pass as a boy."
They burst out laughing.

"Stay here and hang on. I saw you almost tumble out a second ago." Hound offers.
Two upon one, one upon two, Hound uses hand and foot to descend the height of the pine. Going down is faster but presents difficulties not encountered in the climb. Hound is mindful of the placement of each step and of every grip. He makes it to the lowest branch, and squats there, searching for the fallen treasure. The smallest trail of smoke gives the answer and so is spotted by Hound. It looks like it started the heap of pine needles ablaze. He silently counts to three and leaps downward, landing a perfect straddle over the small smoldering pile.

"Mr. Sinclair! You nearly scared me half to death. You sprung from that tree like you belong in it. Are you a jungle animal?"

Hound snaps his focus from the smoldering heap up to the looming Mrs. Paslay, Curriculum Coordinator of his private school, who's mass rivals the Old Testament Behemoth. One disadvantage of attending a private school is that, due to its small campus and enrollment, everybody is recognized and known by name.

What is she doing? I've never seen her here before?
And then Hound thinks about his own Chinese-eyes, which cause too long a pause for Mrs. Paslay to bear.

"Answer me, Mr. Sinclair. Are you indeed a jungle animal?"

"Yes, I think I am."

"I've known it all along, Mr. Sinclair. Now tell me, what you are doing here in this park?"

Hound wonders if Mrs. Paslay truly knows of his animalistic nature but believes it is highly likely this question is rhetorical. Is she attempting to draw a confession from him as the smoke rises in plain view? He remembers something he once heard and considers it his only defense: deny everything that would land you in trouble, especially things so obvious, denial would be deemed impossible.

"I live across the street, beside the pepper trees at the end of the block."

"Allow me to tell you, I don't usually come here! I don't like it down here, not at all. You should consider getting yourself back home, Mr. Sinclair. This is where the bad children roam about. You'll *never* see any of my children anywhere near this place."

"Well then, Mrs. Paslay, what are you doing here?"

"Well, indeed! That is a good question, Mr. Sinclair, but an insolent one. You are not only a jungle animal but a pretentious one at that."

"Does that mean you've decided not to answer me?"

"Quite!"

As the ribbon of smoke ascends, Hound's thoughts take him up north to his father's property where burn piles rise almost every day during the cooler months. The aroma, rising between Mrs. Paslay and he, is very close to that of the Poplar, Manzanita, and Clove smoldering on the red clay of his father's land; a land where thanks is given to the ever-present light rain for saving the forest from man's work.

It is therefore of little consequence if Hound is expelled from school. He already knows of great things not taught in a classroom and has witnessed the wrath of unknown origin for far less offences than these at hand.

"Are you all right, Mr. Sinclair? You seem to be distracted."

"I'm fine, Mrs. Paslay. I'm fine."

"Registration is the week before Labor Day. Don't forget to pick up your packet at the chapel."

"I won't forget."

"Goodbye, Mr. Sinclair."

"See you later, Mrs. Paslay."

She rolls her eyes, turns, and begins to lumber away from the direction she came. Hound watches her, waiting for his chance. She slows and says over her shoulder.

"You really should take my advice and get yourself home … now."

To which Hound replies under his breath, "But I am home."

And Hound forages through the light embers of the needles only to come up with far less than half a joint. He stamps out the mound, pulls the test tube from his pocket, inserts the item, and climbs the tree to his best friend in the world.

"What the fuck was that about, dude?"

"That's Mrs. Paslay from my school. She wanted to know if I was an animal."

"*She* wanted to know if *you* were an animal? She's the size of a hippo!"

"Yeah, I know. I think that's what keeps her safe."

They see Mrs. Paslay made it to the curb and is trying to look through the windows of a camper shell. The curtains frustrate her attempts. She hobbles around the truck for a better angle, but nothing works; she gives up and leaves. Someone has parked this truck in the same spot every day since the start of summer. The driver is never seen, though a middle-aged woman unfailingly arrives and avails herself of the back camper. The occupants visit awhile before the woman exits and again speeds off in her car. Hound thinks they will need a new spot now that Mrs. Paslay has found them here.

"I'm just glad you weren't busted." Girl Scout continues.

"These walls do more than just still the wind."

"Huh? … What?"

"It's just something Black Oscar said to me."

Hound hands the test tube over to Girl Scout, leaving it to him to get things going. He thinks about what it means to eventually return to his mother's house and makes no attempt to rush the day along. Girl Scout knows what it means for Hound to escape from there at each opportunity; since their family is a surrogate family to Hound and only last summer did he spend every night in their hayloft and bathe each day in their swimming pool. A fresh commitment has been made this year to get along, for Hound to stick it out at his mother's house, and by either strategy or chance, he makes it through most nights without needing to run off.

Making a bedroom out of the old playhouse in the backyard has helped keep him from late night run-ins with his mother, although, she sometimes goes around looking for her son. At the times she comes after him, Hound runs to the backstop in the park and sleeps on it beneath the sheltering of the pines where his mother's calling voice is small enough to manage. She tires quickly without an object to thrash. It is the boredom that tires her. It is the thrashing that brings her strength. He can hear the moment she begins to wane from this high position in the cups of the backstop, but he does not return home for it is no use. She has locked the door. She locks the front door regardless of time of day, and it is their custom that he, at 14 years old, must knock every time he arrives and ask permission to be let into his mother's home.

Just as Oscar has a secret stash of Rain Birds, Hound has his own secrets in the park. They are contained in the manicured area and in the wild. He came upon a small storage locker when he first moved into this new neighborhood. It is way out by the last spigot at the edge of the park grounds, riding the line between where the grass meets the field of peppers. Apparently, it had lost its original usage and been forgotten. There, he placed an old sleeping bag from the attic and one pillow from the hallway closet and secured the box with a dime store tumble-lock. He comes to it when in need and what he needs is always there. Not once has anybody disturbed it in these two years. The AM pocket radio has a home in his pepper tree. He keeps it in an old cigar tin with a handful of spare 9-volt batteries wrapped in a paper towel. There are other things beneath the pepper, hidden things, some of which are expressed in Polaroid film frames. These items he buried in memorized spots within the canopy of the pepper fronds. He is approaching a dozen tins by now. The fronds thankfully grow in such a way that they go high and then outward before the tail-ends reach the ground. It is its own little world and the umbrella of the arc creates a barrier to keep things in, and to keep others from crossing over and intruding upon it.

They each manage three hits from the roach before Girl Scout burns an eyebrow, trying for the last time to get at its smallness. This is a moment of hilarity. Bystanders, who are around the boys enough, know these two live off every merriment they encounter or create; levity amplifies or conceals depending on the need at hand.

Once the laughter dies away, Hound and Girl Scout sit in thought watching the darkening sky as dusk comes upon them. There are no streetlights here to tell them when to head for home. This is an old horse neighborhood. Every other street is unpaved, and for this reason and due to the mysterious stone houses, visitors are temporarily beckoned to its novelty of a time long since gone. The residents just got the new park building. I guess they should be happy with that.

Girl Scout makes the first move down from the pine. He knows his mother will not call for him, but she will be disappointed if Girl Scout makes her put dinner on late. He and his mother play a cantankerous game, but one filled with genuine love for each other.

Hound allows Girl Scout to make it almost all the way down before leaves the crook. He looks out toward the burning rock quarry as he waits. The smoky sky is salmon with piercing orange that might likely explode were it not for the brown haze seeping up from the flinty ground. Below it all is his mother's house. It is time to try again, and so, he descends after Girl Scout touches down. They say their goodbyes with promises of playing basketball in the old gym again tomorrow and then Hound follows what is sour on both nose and tongue toward his place of games. Games absent any trace of genuine love.

He knocks gently on the door, and it is opened before he strikes three. Odds are she had been peeping from behind the curtain of her front room, timing his arrival up the driveway.

"You murderer! You killed my cat!" is spat at him through the dense cloud emanating from her person. An inferior pink wine is the source of the cloud. She has been at it hard lately.

"No, I didn't. I didn't kill the cat." he responds.

"You let him out on purpose! You hate that cat. You hate me!"

The bottle occupies a prominent position in the refrigerator and is of a size that takes two hands to pour. There is ordinarily more than one in the house; another is often stashed in her bedroom and used during the mendacious promises of quitting.

"I don't hate the cat, mom. I'm allergic to the cat."

"Why would you do it? How could you hurt a defenseless creature?"

"I didn't do it. I don't even have a key to the house. I've been gone all day."

"Doing what? You're a worthless leech. You are incapable of anything good."

Only a burning skillet could outdo the alcoholic breath of his mother at this moment. Hound notices and asks to be let into the house. Mother refuses on the grounds of his murderous potential but he knows of a trick that works on her at most times. He promises to show her the item of her false accusations: in this case, the missing cat.

"Come outside, mom. I put the cat in the well. See the lid? He's only trapped in the well, mom."

His mother pushes him aside and runs to the decorative well featured on their front lawn. Somebody has placed a pitted trashcan lid on top of it. There is a faint red slash near its handle, made with fingertips. She removes the lid, and looks deeply within, but it is empty.

She remembers that only a few days ago her son used the trash lid as a shield against her. She clearly remembers it all. He ran outside, away from her, away from her torment. He left her to face it alone, as is his way. It is this cowardice she abhors. Mother feels there must be a way to cure him of it.

Of her recollection, she chased him as he ran, though despite her great effort, she was only able to get in one clean shot before he picked up the lid. Every other rock hurled toward him either missed entirely or was blocked by the shield in his grip. There were seven tones of rock against metal. The neighbors to the right looked out, but quickly shut their door. The slamming door alerted his mother to the possibility of police involvement. There are times, when she is in such a state of drunkenness, the threat of the police or any other intervention is of no deterrent whatsoever, but this was not one of those times, so she retreated back within the confines of their private hell.

Hound lowered the lid, his forearm still vibrating from the violence of concussion, wiped his brow of blood from the one clean shot and smeared it across the metal top. He then placed it over the well as a reminder to the witnesses of fact, and as a clue to others who are not privy to facts, but simply wonder by these hints what in the world goes on inside of that house.

Hound's mother drops the lid. She realizes she has been duped, but not before her son has entered the house and locked the door behind him. He has turned off the burner to the stovetop and saved two of the burger patties. He stuffs them between slices of white bread, puts two sodas in his pockets, and makes for the backdoor.

The howling begins, a primitive instinct within his mother longing for release. This must be the origin of Hound's own animalistic tendencies. He considers hereditary gifting as an unfortunate truth and wishes there was another life available to him. The boy used to pray but has since given it up. He finds wishing is just as good and there is no anger or blame associated in its failings. Praying for mercy makes one angry toward a God who is discriminating in its delivery. There doesn't appear to be any justice in this world, particularly when one comes to realize that nobody is there. Hound has been forsaken. All others have gone away under the intensity of his mother's need to be heard, and for this reason, he is the only one left to share her torment.

Hound slips inside the old playhouse that is now his bedroom. He gobbles down one hamburger, knowing she'll come for him soon enough. The soda is welcomed and helps him gulp down the larger pieces. There is a shelf above the doorway holding the empty tin boxes and the Polaroid camera. He finds a good tin for the second burger and the soda, and places it on the small table beside him. The gate slams; she is but seconds away. Hound reclines in the beanbag chair on which he sleeps during the quieter nights and pulls the blanket up to his chin in hope this submissive posture will be good enough for her. It rarely if ever is.

Hound's mother flings the screened door too hard and it bounces back, and slams shut in her face. Every momentary action inflames her passion as if the pure and true antagonist is life itself. She is seen through the mesh, enraged, though temperament does not cloud her resolution; there is a natural genius to great horror. She ducks through the doorway and asks Hound to stand. He does not want to stand, knowing what comes next. A way out is unlikely. What can a kid do? He would have been gone long ago if there was any chance beyond simple pauses, diversions, and hiding places.

She does not do well with waiting, and he agrees to stand once she begins kicking the beanbag chair. Hound places both hands behind himself to move out from the awkward position of the chair and his mother slugs him in the face. He covers up and pleads for her to stop. She appears to feel remorse and changes her mind. Her look softens, but is still tight about the mouth. She promises to behave if only he'll get up from the chair to be with her; she hurts and needs him so. Hound leans forward and attempts to stand without the aid of hands, because this time they are occupied, as he is holding something beneath the blanket. The boy is used to her lies and his hands are prepared when she comes at him again.

The flash of the Polaroid blinds her and the wild swing she throws only gets off a partial hit. It goes skimming atop his crown. Hound pulls his heels backward enough to get his feet under him and stands straight up. He snaps another frame with the pop of a flash. This whiteout stumbles his mother back into the doorjamb where she hits her head and falls into the yard. Hound flips the camera around and flashes one into his own face. He removes all three frames and slides them into his back pocket, places the camera beneath his arm, before grabbing the tin of rations and running out the door.

"You hit your mother!" is heard just after he makes it to the gate.

Hound slips a twig through the latch to buy himself more time and he darts across the street into the field of peppers. He draws a serpentine path heading for the one, the only one, known to truly cover the things of such indignity and shame.

There is a detectible difference when leaving the orange salmon sky of the outer world for the steely ambient shade of the canopy. It is quiet and cool beneath the umbrella of fronds. Hound removes the Polaroid frames from his back pocket and thumbs through them: two of the demon face, and one of more blood. He tastes the sweet metallic truth of it and feels his lip with the tip of his tongue to find a bump of swelling where a tooth stopped it flat.

The Polaroid camera replaces the AM Radio in a swap, but not having time to bury the tin of pictures, he places it beside the camera atop the highest branch that can be reached from the ground. Hound then parts the pepper fronds with his rations in one hand and the radio in the other and weaves his way toward the place where the wild meets the manicured grass. All the while, he repeats the combination of numbers to the tumble lock over and over in his head for fear of somehow losing the solution of it. The possibility of failing to open the storage locker, residing in the depths of the park, causes some disagreement within Hound's own memory and he has found that repeating the numbers come as a useful tool for getting it right every time.

Hound rounds a tree and his feet are taken from him. His torso skids to a stop and he loses both the tin of rations and his radio to the field. Perhaps the perpetrators would have been more successful in hurting Hound had they waited until the open manicured grass, as there are few who feel as effective in the wild overgrowth as does he.

Two kids, barely old enough to drive, advance while laughing. These are not locals, more like transients who appear from time to time before taking off again to wherever they belong. The one who did the tripping points at the ground where Hound lay in the dirt and the other zips his fly after taking a leak on the tree. They each have a bottle of beer in their right hand. Hound bounds to his feet in one move; spins around and faces them. A shadow steps forward and Hound's fists reach their target unanswered. The sound of a bottle breaking upon rock alerts him to the second guy, who has dropped his beer and run off.

The first lay twitching below Hound, who knows little of leniency. He jumps on top with the intention of making the older boy ugly as a permanent reminder of his transgressions. Blonde hair slips through knuckles as Hound lifts the head up off the soil, and thin blood drools from the nose. This sight causes him to study the face wherein he finds a simple boy. He swipes a finger across the red streak and tastes the same sweet metallic truth of it. It is enough, far more than enough, and he rises to find his tin and radio but a few feet away. The storage locker is straight ahead, and Hound continues onward to retrieve what he needs to get through the night.

The cups are nine in number. They go in a configuration of two to three to four from narrow to wide. The chain link backstop fans outward and looks to be either shouting at or attempting to swallow the whole of the field. The four outer cups are the most used and therefore have the deepest impressions. Kids sit up there during the game, where they occasionally get smacked when a foul tip goes straight into the sagging cup and finds a fresh ass. Hound has a favorite of the four, and rarely faces the field; he faces the trees and the great many things he sees could be for this reason.

Girl Scouts stands on home plate looking through the links. He hears the static of a softly playing tune and sees his friend etched against the moon-soaked mist. The friend fades and returns as the waves of mist are played by the night breeze. Hound nearly disappears without the light to silhouette his form against a backdrop. Girl Scout acknowledges him with a simple hello. He makes the climb that hurts fingers and toes and chooses the cup next to Hound. This is his usual spot.

The dancing bear comes and goes against the pulsing illumination as Hound did moments before. They watch the image without saying a word. Each time the dancing bear returns, he takes on a slightly different pose and after a while, seems to be repeating a sequence. It is after 11. Girl Scout passes his backpack to Hound who goes through it to find a folded T-shirt and paired socks, soap, a toothbrush and comb. All of it wrapped and taped shut in clear cellophane. This is clearly the work of Girl Scout's mother, who must have made this package well in advance and put it aside for the occasion when the new commitment to stick it out proved to be too difficult. The effort is a testament to her devotion to her son and his friend. Beneath the cellophane parcel comes Girl Scout's paper-bagged contribution, consisting of: a rolled up L.A. X-Press nudie magazine, half a leftover sandwich, and an ARMY canteen filled with grape Kool-Aide.

"You can come back to the hayloft if you want?" goes Girl Scout.

"No … nah, I don't mind it up here so much. Besides, I'm trying to break the habit." replies Hound.

"Alright, use the side gate if you change your mind."

"Hey, can I dip in the pool tomorrow morning? I have to be back here by 8."

"I don't think you need to do that anymore." Girl Scout says, digging into his pocket, "Here, take this thing." and he puts the item into Hound's palm.

"What is it for?"

"My mom went over and talked to Bruder awhile back."

"Your mom talked to Bruder?"

"Yeah …"

"What about? … About me?"

"Well, what happened was he reached into his desk and slid this key toward her. He said, 'I'm not giving you this key and I have no idea which door it goes to.' Then he excused himself and left her standing in the office. She picked it up and noticed that somebody had dabbed orange nail polish on it and so she went looking around for an orange door."

"The orange door is on the outside of the new building." goes Hound, and then he asks, "What's in there?"

"She tried the key and it opened right up. It's the staff bathroom. There are showers and everything in there. This key is yours. He gave it to her for you."

Hound thinks about all that is happening for a moment.

"Thank her … Thank her for everything and tell her I'm okay."

"Tell her yourself, Hound-Boy. She wants me to invite you over for dinner, the day after tomorrow."

Girl Scout moves from his spot and hits the ground walking toward home. Hound tosses the backpack over to the now vacant cup, zips up his sleeping bag, and notices the mist has gone and the dancing bear stands still as a shadow against the night sky. He closes his eyes and tries for sleep.

Today is the first and only day that Hound will see Black Oscar arrive to the park. He hadn't taken into account how Oscar came and went before this time but now sees he does so on foot. The bus stops at the bottom of the hill where Sunland Boulevard meets Penrose Street. It is outside of the neighborhood by less than two miles and allows strangers to visit. Nobody from here uses it. Oscar ventures from a place far away, but does the last bit on foot this morning with a particular grace and blends into the quiet of the early day. He keeps the burden of bad knees to himself. Hound stands with his hair dripping and leaving wet spots on the back of his shirt. He watches Oscar's figure go from the size of an ant, to an upright thumb, to a full-grown man standing directly in front of him. The wristwatch says it's a little past 7:30 am.

"You might be fixin' too hard on punctuality, boy." opens Oscar.

"I've only been here a few minutes." replies Hound.

"Don't let that become a thing … Ain't no way to break it once it come on. It be habit formin', that way of life. A man's time is important. Never forget it."

Oscar stops while looking down at Hound. He studies his face and the knuckles of his hands before continuing.

"You be fighting, Hound?"

Hound had forgotten about the swollen upper lip even though he was brushing around it just 10 minutes ago. He stuffs his hands into his pockets.

"Well, I … I got into a fight."

"Was they no way out, then? Did ya try?"

"I tried … I did."

"I suppose you did. Yes, I suppose so. Sometime, it seem they's no way out … no way out. Ain't that right, Hound?"

Hound tilts his head down, removes his hands from his pockets and takes a good look, both front and back. The boy notices something in them behind the imperfections. In his hands, he finds a strength that bruises and abrasions cannot undo. He lifts his head to Oscar.

"That's right, Oscar. You're right."

"Well then, I got somethin'. I got somethin' I want t' show you. Come on now."

Oscar leads Hound into the courtyard where the stones stand tall around them. He passes a knapsack over to the boy and unlocks the closet doors. They open wide and Oscar takes the knapsack from Hound and hangs it on a hook within. The man removes the stool and lifts the green-marbled tackle box from atop the shelf.

"Why are there empty cups on the shelf? What do you keep in them?"

"I ain't keep nothin' in them. Only empty cups can be filled, Hound."

Oscar sits on the stool in a way where his lap is flat and then angles the box to turn the brass latch. He flips the top fully opened and Hound wonders if he plans for a taste at this early hour. He asks the boy to step up to a position nearly touching knee to knee. Fingernails go along the edge and Oscar removes the folded game board so the contents beneath it are revealed. He looks to the boy and Hound sees up close that Oscar has perpetually watery eyes with deep carmine splotches that are sometimes found in the whites of an old black man.

"This here what you lookin' for?" asks Oscar.

"Uh … I'm really sorry about that. I should do better … I should mind my own business. This is your property. I was only hoping to have a taste of what you keep in there." Hound answers.

"No, no, no, … that ain't what you lookin' for, boy. I ain't saying a taste might not help some, but that ain't *the* thing … not it at all."

"I don't get it. Aren't we going to party? Isn't that what you do all day? I don't understand what you are saying."

"You truly be a funny one, Hound. It too early in the day for that shit, besides, I cain't be givin' no weed to no boy. Don't ya know that? You get it on yo' own, that's another thing, but it cain't come from me."

"Alright." says Hound, looking bewildered though his posture reveals a degree of relief.

Oscar takes some items from the box into hand and unfolds the board that he places on top of the opened lid. It fits just right in the space. Hound is once again staring at the inscription. A nervous feeling comes over him and he is grateful Oscar refused him the weed. The pieces are arranged along the board by long bent fingers and the command of deep watery eyes. The otherness about Oscar's eyes is furthered by a glaze at the outer layer. The bone and skin supporting and surrounding them expresses a multiplicity of feeling, with sorrowful empathy rushing into the foreground. Hound notices the cross, the cruet, and sees two candles already burning, while Oscar gets the incense thurible going. He holds it by the chain and circles it all around the board. The familiar scent overtakes them, and the spiral of the trail ascends beyond the stone fortress.

"This here is my temple, Hound. It is here, I find that way out."

Oscar licks his fingers and snuffs out the fire. He gathers the items back into hand and folds the board in half. The thurible smolders lightly and he tilts it over and they both watch the contents fall to earth. The old boot finishes it off. Oscar then returns the pieces, each to their proper place, and seals the top with the board before closing the lid and latching it tight.

"That's it? Aren't you going to show me how to do it?" questions Hound.

"Nah, cain't be done." He answers.

"Well, that's a fucking rip off. You just tempt me with this thing and then quit when it finally gets going? Let me understand ... *'You cain't do this and you cain't do that'*. Is there anything you can do? How am I supposed to figure it out?"

"That what I be sayin', Hound." and Oscar looks all around at the stones which stand beyond their comprehension. "It cain't be figured. Like Montelongo, it only be known."

Oscar then stands from the stool and returns the tackle box to the shelf between the empty cups. Everything is back where it should be and so the doors close on them both.

"That's the stupidest thing I've ever heard! Where do you come up with this shit, man?" The boy exclaims and rushes away.

Oscar watches him run. Hound dashes through the courtyard exit, far out toward the edge of the manicured grass, where he stops and stares keenly into the wild growth. The only thing left for him is that particular pepper. He wants to make sure he can still see it. He needs to know it is really there.

The fronds in the foreground allow him his cherished view but only as dictated by the will of the breeze. It continues. Indeed, the pepper does continue for him, though it comes and goes intermittently, and it is for this reason he is not met with a proper degree of satisfaction. Hound remembers something and spins a quarter turn to the right with his look gazing high upward. He is scanning the tops of the pines, and there among the confusion of the alternating branches, he finds the dancing bear. It holds the one static pose. The magic in it does not arrive until it is met with the darkening sky. Only then does it animate, only then does Hound stand a chance of watching it dance. His eyes fall left on a slight diagonal to the backstop, the place that held him safely throughout the night. It is devoid of any meaning, now standing only as rigid steel, in a cold sublunary expression.

Hound drops to the ground, sits Indian style on the grass, and places his head into his palms. He tries but cannot bring anything useful to mind. There are no pictures to help him; there is only a vacancy that goes from black to white, switching back and forth, in an even frequency. He keeps this position for a long yet uncertain period before again raising his head and opening his eyes to blink clear the purple dots coming from the bright sunlit day.

He turns around to find Oscar working among the pines, cutting a fresh basin for one a short distance away. An additional spade leans against the neighboring tree and Hound takes it upon himself to begin his work. The spade fits well in his grip and, so with both hand and foot, Hound begins sinking it into the soil. The boy imagines he is proficient at this new task and encircles the trunk at a fantastic speed, chopping the grass away in a minor inward arc meant to surround the base of the tree. This might be his moment, as though this is his spade, and he intends not to disappoint. Oscar lets him go awhile before interrupting.

"This work got t' last us all day, boy."

Hound hears this and stops to focus on the sound of the voice. He turns to see Oscar from behind and notices that he looks up into the heights of the tree, swayed by it. Oscar moves as the tree moves, leaning left as the tree leans left. The man then cuts a few feet of basin and goes back to the sway that further instructs him.

"What's that you're doing over there?" asks Hound.

"I'm lookin' to the tree. It tell me more than does the ground."

Hound checks his own work and isn't as impressed as he thought he'd be. He realizes the activity was only fulfilling because it drowned out the encroaching unpleasantness of circumstances, and drowning is no way to approach the carving of an inward arc. His pace slows as he tries what Oscar demonstrated while caught in the sway. Up into the tree Hound goes and then down to the ground where he cuts away. The sensation provokes a different feeling than before, less to do with proficiency and more with interconnection to the task at hand. Hound notes a development of fluidity in his effort no longer tamped out by his excessive action, and the tree basin benefits by a smooth curve lacking rough irregularity.

————

A picture now comes to Hound in the form of a beautiful mid-teen girl he remembers clearly but hadn't thought about in a long time. It was from the days of cocktail waitressing, when babysitters were thought to be a good idea for the young boy. None of the others chosen by his mother worked out well or lasted long. But this one, with this teenage girl, he might only have needed more time to figure things out. Maybe it's that simple, maybe even at eight years old, that's all there is to it.

The marks she left on him are what gave it all away. If it weren't for the marks, they could have continued. A certain passion possessed her, a tandem quality to her remarkable beauty. And when things did go a little too far, he found promising relief in the way he longed to look into her eyes. It was those dark eyes that did it, and the sacramental white dress, coming together to make Hound first fall in love.

His mother approached the girl's dishwashing father about it after dragging Hound to her Confirmation. Fourteen is the perfect age, thought his mother, since there was something about those older women that rubbed her the wrong way. She believed the young girl would be just right, in she had the youth to be molded into proper shape, so the adults agreed upon the hours and fee with the cash going straight to the Mexican girl's father and she began the following week.

All was prepared for her. Dinner was made, the boy's bedclothes were laid out, and the lights-out time was given. The spare room had a bed and a bathroom for the teenage girl, once she'd read to and put the boy down for the night. The bar closed at 2:00 am, and even though Hound's mother usually stayed out past the earliest morning hours, she always returned home before dawn. The dishwasher picked up his daughter at 7:00 am on the dot to get her to the Catholic school on time each weekday morning.

A ripe loneliness in the house at night gave opportunity to the girl's experimentation. She spent much idle time standing in her undergarments in front of the full-length bathroom mirror. It was always black lace, which accentuated her figure in the way her hair and eyebrows shaped her eloquent face. Hound pretended to be up to other things, but he was captivated by her every pose. The late hours had a way of sneaking up on them, and then noticing the ache, he had little choice but to break the spell and ask her to bring dinner. She'd glide through the house while keeping the boy within sight and scold him when he hadn't strength enough to downcast his eyes from the movement of her maturing form.

Despite her castigations, a stubborn callousness developed in him, and he lost all fear of switching his look from the ground to back along the edge of her unveiled body. She'd then resort to the whipping, as it was a more effective method, but he stood through it and again locked his vision onto what had started it all. It was those dark eyes that penetrated, so they both did dare to see, but she could only take so much of his knowing before she'd relinquish the strop to him. No matter how hard the girl begged, there was no way he could hit her. It happened every time, she'd then sit on the saddle of a hard chair and call him to her lap where he'd sink into her while she cried and cried while pinching him on the belly and back.

His mother ruined it all in less than two weeks; after one late afternoon thrashing, she ordered the boy to drop them to his ankles and discovered a welt running across the front of both thighs. It held the impression of the Hot Wheel track she waved above her head. She had a good look at him and did a comparison with the plastic track before abandoning the idea of using it herself. He stripped thoroughly against his will so she could see and consume every private thing he had with the girl. Mother found a dozen bruises around his torso from where the thumb and forefinger came together. The nails had broken through in a few spots, leaving thin crescents behind.

The dishwashing father pulled into the driveway for the drop off. They both heard the two car doors slam. Hound knelt for his pants, but his mother ordered him to be still. He tried to be good. He always tried to do as his mother asked, but there was no way he was ever good enough to understand what she wanted from him, and this time he managed to break the rules by slipping into his boxer shorts while she went for the door.

The girl drew near and looked as pretty as the painting Hound saw in the church that first day; but her effort wasn't good enough; she was suspected of hiding something beneath the tidy Catholic school uniform. The father removed his hat as he approached because he could feel a problem in the air before reaching the porch. He and the girl entered the front room.

Hound's mother started.

"Look what that whore has been up to with my son! What have you done by bringing her into my house?"

The father squinted in the shadow of the hallway. He moved up close and his eyes scanned the boy carefully. He turned to his daughter and asked.

"Tell me … Tell me, Carmenita. Do you do this to the boy?"

Carmen only stared at the same place on the floor where Hound's eyes had been from the beginning and her father could tell there was truth in it. He excused himself and escorted his daughter into the spare room to retrieve the items she naturally stored there for the week. Sound came but only from the man as the girl learned over the many years to bear the consequences of her life. Hound's mother could tell she was being struck hard by the man and considered interrupting but failed to, in preference to minding one's own business. It is this quality she most admires in others and so keeps her promise to it.

Mother looked around hoping to discover something meaningful in their lives but only found her son standing there. She exhaled and said to him.

"Don't be such a horse's ass. Pull up your pants. Put on your shirt and tuck it in."

The dishwasher returned to the front room with Carmen and her items, a smattering of bills laced through the fingers of his clenched fist. He wished to keep the money. They desperately needed the money, but instead he offered it back attempting restitution. Seeing the girl had no visible marks of her own, Hound's mother questioned by what method the father handled his daughter and refused to take the bills from him.

Through silent tears, Carmen held Hound within the lock of her wondrous gaze and again they both did dare to see. Had they only a little more time to figure things out, he would have grown, he might even had been able to fix these things for her. This time she kindly accepted the fullness of his knowing; and it was clear that she loved him in return, if simply because, she wasn't alone in her nightmare.

The father grabbed his daughter's forearm and started for the door. He turned as he reached the threshold and glanced at the boy one last time before shutting Hound's chances of ever again seeing into the telling eyes of his haunted Carmenita.

———

"That'll do, boy. Yes, that'll do."

Hound catches himself. He is at the edge of the wild with his back a few yards from the work. His pepper comes into focus, as does the mystery stowed beneath the umbrella canopy of fronds. He turns to see Oscar looking above his head, with a narrow fix on the depths, in an effort to envision what calls to Hound. But they both understand it is meant only for the one. What is important in it cannot be given or taught as things of this nature reveal themselves solely to the individual whose need compels it to act and whose time is correct. This very principle came earlier from Oscar's vagueness, and had frustrated Hound, but he now acknowledges a wealth in what is permeable between people even in the face of what is sorely lacking. He heard this all before, because he certainly had heard it before, and something opened up in Oscar by way of Hound's newly arrived at perception.

They turn to the pines and can see today is a fine day; together they have carved the basins for 10 trees, and through the work, a person comes to terms with the complexities of life. Oscar deemed it good enough when he proclaimed: *'That'll do'* to the young Hound.

The sun is now high in the sky and the heat of the day is falling down upon them. They start toting the work items to the old building closet. Oscar asks if he brought a lunch, and Hound runs off to his storage locker to retrieve what Girl Scout and his mother had made up for him the night before. He tears ass back to the courtyard just as Oscar finishes placing the tools where they belong, and with the doors wide open, Hound sees the knapsack on the hook. Oscar grabs it down and they leave the area looking for a patch of shady grass to take their rest. What they find is not far off.

"I have somethin' for you. I brought it from where I live." goes Oscar.

"Where do you live?" replies Hound.

"Ah well, I don' live anywhere near this place. Nowhere you even know 'bout."

"How can you be so sure about that? I just might surprise you."

"Oh, you surprise me a'right, Hound! But they's certain things a man come to know with time, and this be one of them."

"Okay … if this is one of them. Go ahead and tell me where."

"It take me three buses to get here to work, and two to get back to Central Avenue. That be my home. It always was since I can remember …"

Oscar reaches for the knapsack but stops and takes his time in thought. He smiles and his watery eyes shine.

"My granddaddy was a Hard Swinger down on Central Avenue. He blew his horn with Max Roach! And boy, those were the days … the good days. Ain't nothing like it no mo'e. Man dress for the occasion, and the ladies … they sooooo fine. You ain't see nothin' like it! They take a Cat right in, don't matter the color … black or white … as long as you can blow, it cool. And they be smokin' grass right out in the street, nobody care, and d' police … ssssShit … they ain't nowhere, man! Today it a different place, but it still my home."

"You were a kid walking the city streets at night?" asks Hound.

"…. and sleepin' all day. Baby, I was in the clubs startin' as a young boy. They let me! I got a job shinin' t' shoes and fetchin' t' cigarettes. Oh, I did it a'right. I did it all just t' be round that Jazz."

"I can't believe your Grandpa was smoking weed way back then?"

"Ah, haha! Hound-Dog, you one funny boy. Things always be. It only seem like startin' over and over again. You understand?"

"Yeah, I think I do understand."

"The Mexicans know all about that grass, son … and the primitives befo'e them. Things always be, Hound … always be."

Oscar puts one of those long, gnarled fingers to his temple and continues.

"I remember a time. Yes, I remember a time with my granddaddy. He worked a day job with Ol' Hernandez, pumpin' the septic. They had this one that lid had cracked wide open when some fool drove over t' lawn with a pickup truck. We came to see 'bout it. And when Ol' Hernandez hitched up and towed off the broken lid, they be hundreds of dwarf marijuana plants growin' right there on top of it all. They ain't never seen the light of day befo'e now and they were all a downy albino white. It look like a field of fuzzy bleached fern, growin' down there in that soup … but Ol' Hernandez knew, and my granddaddy knew what they be. Somebody flushin' them seeds all these years and look what sprung up!"

He laughs to himself, thinking back on it hard.

"Now careful as can be, Ol' Hernandez and Granddaddy scoop 'em and put the wispy little things in two big gunnysacks for dryin'. My granddaddy talked and talked 'bout the colors he seen while smokin' those fuzzy albino bastards … hahaha! I love that man. Still do."

"Yeah, I can see you do, Oscar." Replies Hound, while not missing a beat of the old man's voice or of his physical expression.

Oscar places his hands on his lap and sighs. He remembers what he was doing and opens the knapsack and pulls at something. An *article* gets caught up in the item he tries for and falls into his lap. There is a flash of *white* but is indistinguishable in the quickness Oscar replaces it. He reaches in a second time and removes a record album.

"This be it, Hound. This what I brought you."

Oscar passes the album to the boy who flips it over and reads the title.

"Visions of the Emerald Beyond."

"A present, fo' you."

"Thank you, Oscar … I don't know what to say. I have nothing … I don't have anything to give."

"Oh, you give me plenty already, son. You doin' just fine."

Hound sets the album down in the shadow next to him and goes after the half of sandwich and grape Kool-Aid. What Oscar eats is unusual to Hound and might be made up faithfully of vegetables. They sit awhile in silence before wrapping the area and starting off for the courtyard.

"You off the clock now, boy. Time to be headin' home. Make sure you give that present a good spin." Oscar says.

"I will. I have a quiet spot to listen to music. It's my very own room in the backyard."

"Alright then, that sounds cool, Hound … real cool."

The old stone building stands before them and grows larger with each step. Hound sees only what is available to him and thinks back to Montelongo and of his work here. He can imagine the many facets of a man who could partake in such beauty, as it is right and true that some things remain strictly for the one, and he meditates upon this thought while keeping its entirety within his view.

They are twenty paces from the safety of the courtyard walls when a screeching comes at them from around the street corner. It is a Camaro pitched sideways with rubber tires fighting asphalt for dominance. The teenage driver gets things under control after the fishtail swipes three passes. He straightens out the machine and races on the wrong side of the road, and with the towhead blonde in the backseat poke their heads out of the driver's window to yell.

"NIGGER!"

Black Oscar's head drops, and both feet stop dead on the path. His chin rests on his chest. They had almost made it to the walls that do more than just still the wind. They had nearly made it there, but not quite in time. Hound knows those boys from yesterday where he bloodied the one and the other run off. He should have finished the job. Why can't he ever get it right? By this confession, he lacks the courage to look Oscar in the face but now understands the source of the perpetually watery eyes and knows they are filling up at this moment. Hound is not wrong. No, he is not wrong, but he is guilty just the same and takes the most beautiful hand in all of God's creation into his and leads the rest of the way to the safety of the stone courtyard.

They don't speak. If there is something to be said it refuses to be known to either of them. He, the stranger who came to the park, opens the closet doors wide and hangs the sack onto the hook. Oscar looks down to Hound with those splotchy eyes running and leaves the only safe area for him in the whole damn place. Something comes to mind and the man stops and turns back.

"We got so close and this's all what's left."

Hound watches him go from the full-grown man in front of him, to an upright thumb, to an ant, before disappearing beyond sight. Then he focuses his attention on the courtyard and locks it up tight for the night. The sound of the Camaro passes at a distance a few times in a row as though scanning the neighborhood blocks. He leaves the courtyard, dashing to the sidewalk near the new building to notice the sound comes from the opposite side of the neighborhood from where Oscar treks down the hill to catch the bus and Hound is reasonably satisfied by this observation. He turns half circle and begins his own walk. Mother's house is where tonight the boy will take his own chances.

Hound removes the twig from the gate and tip toes quietly alongside the house. He finds the backdoor fully opened with the scent of simmering meat escaping through it. How I could use some of that, he thinks. The red playground ball he found under the high-power lines in the backfield behind his mother's property rests nearby on the patio. He sees it and thinks it to be a proper instrument to test where his mother is within the house. After leaning the record album against the porch step, *Tap Tap Tap … Roll* goes the ball through the doorway, into the dining area, where it bounces off the far partition. *Shhhh … nothing there.* He enters quietly and looks into the skillet: more hamburger sitting in oil, though it's barely cooking. Hound dips down low to see the tiny flame doing little more than heating the pan and so he cranks it up to a nice level. The sizzle increases, the ravenous hunger swells. There's no rush to any of this, so he stays put, enjoying the appetizing quiet, so rare in this place. It is just he and the good food alone with the disturbing factor yet to be encountered. He compares what is disturbing to a list of favorable and unfavorable possibilities, and their effects, before deciding to try for his old bedroom to gather some fresh clothes.

He gets to the hallway and sees his mother face-down on the living room sofa. His throat tightens as he studies her stillness. There is nothing animated about her. As he moves closely in, Hound notices that she is like the lamp, the radio, and the television: off and cold. There is no difference between the electronic items, the tipped jug on the carpet, and her stillness. How long might she go unnoticed before somebody discovers her lying here? There aren't many left who give a shit. They long since stopped trying.

He takes a long-reach stick-match from the fireplace and gives her a poke with it. She stirs. Her head moves to the side and she begins snoring. Another false alarm, one day it won't be so; one day it will be the truest thing in Hound's life, but not today. Then, he is taken back to the long stick-match in his hand and knows there are at least a dozen more where this one came from. Those drapes, they haven't been vacuumed since they moved here. The dust from them spins and travels all across the room by some imaginary current. It twirls through the air and lands atop everything Hound sees by what is left of the light from the window. He strikes the match and watches it burn. It lasts quite a while with so much wood to consume. It goes almost all the way down, practically to his fingertips, before it weakens and fails. The orange glow is short lived and is no more than blackened charcoal in an instant. The son drops what remains into the ashtray and heads to his old room, where with a little trouble, he finds a pair of corduroys and two t-shirts.

The scent of the patties bring him back to the kitchen to see they are just about right and so he places them on bread, fills up a large cup of water, and makes for his new room in the backyard.

The turntable spins Black Oscar's gift as Hound removes his stash of weed from behind a phony electrical outlet he mounted into the wall. The outer groove of the vinyl snaps and pops a few times before the soft lure begins its tug on Hound, just as he hits the J in the pinch of his fingers. The feel of the sound is what he imagines is of Hindu origin; a strange sweet melody coming forth that erupts into the chaos of cacophony. The instruments run madly up and down, fighting each other, until the opposing forces come to some bizarre agreement that swing and harmonize above the relentless drumming. A chorale of voices enter, repeating a message very close to what he knows is inscribed on Oscar's game board.

An electric guitar starts which cannot make up its mind if it is playing Jazz or Rock and rushes out of the speakers at a tempo so fast that a melody is difficult to discern, but it is there, it takes a moment for the listener to catch up with the player. The J is only half of its original size by now and Hound places it back where it belongs and screws in the outlet cover. He starts the album from the beginning, as to not miss a thing, and reclines on the beanbag to take it all in. The soft lure again enchants him and soon there is only darkness with music filling his essential being and bringing on much needed heavy sleep that was missing from the chain link bed of last night.

———

A rising sun low on the horizon brings life anew and tickles Hound's eyes enough to get him stirring. The record spins on, playing the inner groove, and conveys a hushed rhythmic berceuse that got the boy through the night. He lifts his head and notices the burgers are gone from the plate though he has no memory of eating them. but they are missing. Clanking and cuss words from the house blend with the spinning of the inner groove. He carefully lifts the needle and places the record album into the sleeve and looks around for all he plans to take with him before making the next move. The spare clothes are right there on the table, but forgetting the watch pocket of his jeans, he has to search his person three times before finding the key with the orange nail polish.

If the damn screen door would hold its springy squeaks on command, he'd stand a better chance of getting out unnoticed but this never proved possible. He'll take a chance and run for it, if he must. Hound ducks and gets passed the screen-way; the back door is still wide open. The ruckus inside continues. He holds his breath, as he makes his way alongside the house and through the gate. Everything Hound does makes too much noise. but he somehow gets away with it and finds himself standing at the edge of the drive staring out toward his pepper.

A gut feeling suggests he should weave the familiar serpentine path and rest beneath the cool of the umbrella but looking at the record jacket makes him anxious to get to the park and be ready for Black Oscar's arrival. The few items of clothing will hold just fine in the storage locker at the edge of the manicured area, while the record album must stay in hand until the last possible moment.

The locker is in plain view at mid-point along his path. He thinks he'll take the blue t-shirt with him to the shower and leave the beige one behind as he bends and grabs the tumble lock. The dial rotates in his hand a few times, and then goes a few times more. Hound realizes he neglected to repeat the numbers again and again while on his way to the locker. There is no fear, and yet he cannot remember the combination, the dial goes on spinning between fingers as he tries to come up with it. A laughs spills when considering fear must be present to retrieve the solution from below the threshold of consciousness. He releases the padlock, thinking Oscar might not mind him storing a few personal items in the closet of the courtyard.

He lifts his head and eyes to where he's headed and sees two people rushing between the walls, generating commotion, within the courtyard. Hound flips his wrist over; it is just short of 7:30 am. He sees a man that looks a lot like Bruder.

Bruder never comes in before 10 am. Hound's walk becomes a jog and then finally a run. The clothes fall from his clutch somewhere along the way.

193

"What's going on? ... Phil, what are you doing, what's wrong?" questions Hound.

The lock has been cut off of the courtyard closet. The doors are wide open with a scattering of items spread all around in the dirt at their feet.

"This doesn't concern you, young man. You just go on home. You'll have the day off and I'll reschedule you for tomorrow at 12 noon." Barbara answers.

"I'm not going anywhere. This is MY PARK! What are you doing to all of Oscar's stuff? Stop it! Bruder, what's happened, is Oscar okay?"

"Listen, kid ... he's okay. It's nothing like that."

Hound focuses on the items in the dirt and can now see clearly that the cups are among those things spilled all around, and the cross and thurible are there, too. The broken cruet is by itself in the corner where two of the great walls come together. Phillip Bruder is picking up the overturned green marbled tackle box.

"Hey, knock it off! What are you doing? These are personal things. These things are important to Oscar. You don't even understand what they are."

"I'll show you what we found! I'll show you what's been going on around here!"

Barbara holds up a small bag of marijuana and presents it to each of them for an inspection.

"Okay, Barbara. That's enough. Things are bad enough without rubbing it into everybody's face. I'll take care of the kid here. Why don't you go ahead and get started on the paperwork? You'll need to get a call in to the city right at 8."

Hound begins scooping up all of the cups that he can and tries to clean them off before setting them back on the shelf. They are but eggshells in his palm, some of them are broken, and so he goes to the cruet and realizes it is of no use. All of this shit is ruined. Barbara can't stand it anymore and does as Phillip Bruder has asked of her.

"Why? ... Why did you do it? Just to find some pot? Who even cares about that? It means nothing compared to these other things you just threw on the floor!"

"That was an accident. She didn't mean to mess up his stuff. Let's just say that what we were told we'd find was much more serious than the baggie and she tore through these things in a panic."

"What did you think you would find, Phil? ... Come on?"

"Well, son, I got a call at home first thing this morning from a parent who claimed that ... on the way to the park yesterday ... Oscar scared his daughter. He says Oscar intimidated her into giving up an article of underclothing before she ran off crying."

"That's a fucking lie! You know it's not true."

"I don't know anything of the sort … and neither do you, Hound."

"Yes, I do. Yes. I. Do."

"I'm afraid you don't, son."

"You know these people don't like Oscar. They would make up anything to get rid of him. You know what this is really about, Bruder."

"That might be the case. Yes, I've noticed, and I've considered it, which is why I am arranging to have Oscar transferred. It took some doing but I finally convinced this girl's father to keep the police out of it … *If* … I promised … Oscar would not return here."

"Not return? I'm just getting to know him. What the hell is wrong with everybody? You have to give him a chance. He should be able to defend himself."

"Well, I did that. I asked him that same question when I called this morning. He chose to take the deal. He doesn't want to come back."

"No, no … Bruder, this isn't right. He's a Man of God. He wouldn't do this thing. It's not in him to hurt anybody."

"What do you mean 'Man of God'? He's the gardener, Hound. And that's all there is to it."

"No, you're wrong about that."

"I'm getting used to being wrong these days. It doesn't bother me like it used to. In any case, he took the deal and as far as I'm concerned, we are done talking about it."

"These walls do more than just still the wind."

"Huh? … What's that?"

"It's just something Oscar taught me. I wish it had been true."

Somehow the album is still tucked beneath Hound's arm and he notices it for the first time since coming upon this mad scene. He gazes at the cover and the rhythm begins in his heart while the strange sweet melody fills his head. The chorale repeats its message many times over and reaches his core. It is alive in him. He snatches the unzipped knapsack off the hook and Bruder considers a protest but quickly fades. The boy bends and picks up what he can of Oscar's items, including the game board that remained hidden from them. The fragmented cups slide from the shelf by the scoop of his hand and the album goes into the bag last. Hound then looks to the tackle box in Bruder's grip and heads out for his pepper in the wild of the field.

———

The Camaro parked at the curb on the far side of the new building catches his eye. Did he miss it on his way in, or did it just arrive? *Those fucking idiots* - goes through his head. He should have finished them off before they had a chance to fuck everything up. He switches direction on a straight line toward the Camaro.

His hand slides along the front fender to rest on the hood and he holds it there. It retains the cold of night. He moves from the hood to the driver's door handle and checks it. It clicks and opens with the sound of steel upon steel. The interior smells strongly of gasoline and Hound can see a red canister on the back floorboard through the split between the front seats. The driver and passenger floors are both littered with multiple empty beer bottles. The keys are not in the ignition, so he checks the driver's visor. When he flips it down, a raining of square sheets fall all over his forearm and cover most of the seat.

Hound blinks hard and his eyes adjust to see an image or two peeking out from behind the others. He brings one near and recognizes the bloody boy in the picture as himself. The knapsack falls from his shoulder onto the street. He is absent control over his breath and cannot swallow. He knows nothing of heart attacks, but feels it is his destiny to die in the street today next to the objects of his terror. Hands grab and shuffle the sheets while he huffs inward. There is no exhaling, gulps expand his internal limits. He is at full capacity. He will burst.

Then he happens upon a singular image of his mother. She is so beautiful in the picture, so pretty, and openly smiling. Hound remembers taking this one when she was completely unaware, he had pointed the camera in her direction. She was lost in thought, thinking back to her promising beginnings or imagining a future they both could be proud of. Her eyes were different for a time, not long, but for a time, as though anything was possible. Captured in this one Polaroid frame — proof to him that they weren't all bad. Something else shone through her, and was likely in him too; another truth from what he had known all of his life.

Everything released from him at once. Yes, the breath, but much more. Everything he'd held in forcibly expelled from his person, from his soul. It all rushed out and this purging rewarded Hound with several long deep breaths in a row, making him swoon, before he gathered the many Polaroid images and stuffed them into the knapsack laid out beside his feet. There is one more item he needs, he reaches for it, then flings the knapsack over his shoulder, and finally finds himself standing at the far corner of the wild field looking outward toward his pepper. Even though Hound doesn't see the tree right away, he knows it is there; its vision is delivered in flashes along the path as the will of the hindering branches and fronds allow.

Hound enters the cool umbrella to see the violations of his trespassers. They found almost everything. The 12 tins that used to hide his secrets are carelessly strewn about the area. It no longer matters; they are devoid of meaning without their objects to hold, not too different than the fractured empty cups that belonged to Black Oscar.

A few fresh, blatantly obscene Polaroid frames, taken below the belt, both front and back, apparently have stayed behind to show this is the best some animals can produce. The camera was smashed into pieces once it failed to hand out additional vulgarity. He leaves what he finds where it has fallen and places the knapsack on the ground in front of him to retrieve the items stowed therein. Again, the *white article* has a way of interrupting as he finds the band resting across his wrist. Hound laughs and takes a moment absorbing it as a fact before slipping the item back into the bag. The candles and the broken cruet, the thurible and the dusty cross, come out, as does the game board that accepts it all. He arranges the cups just so, some fragments, some whole, doing his best to make them right. The album is more difficult because Hound knows it is a rare and true gift from a man who operates and teaches only by methods of self-discovery; but the words of the chorale are still with him as he is directed by the etching on the game board. He tilts the jacket, presenting the front cover, and agrees that it looks beautiful leaning against his pepper tree.

The red is glimmering in the corner of his eye so he goes to it, lifts and tips, and encircles the whole of the tree with its contents. As close to a perfect circle that is possible in life has been drawn by this action. The red canister is flung through the air and lands on its side a good distance away. There is a faded rendering on its bottom meant to assist in its return to the owner should it be lost. Hound then pats his pockets and finds the lighter in the front left of his jeans. He spins the wheel and watches the flame burn, almost too close to eye, but within the flame there exists a second light worth taking the risk. Hound sees it and what is experienced from the thing cannot be related by language, '*It only be known, boy.*'

———

Bruder has placed the phone call to Girl Scout's mother. There is something obvious between them about the boy, and while it has never been articulated, they go to the other whenever there is a need. Today, there is no work at the park for Hound. Today, there is such a need. So, by this call, she grabs her son's hand and they step from the breakfast table to go looking for their friend. Girl Scout seizes upon the dancing bear as soon as they make it to the middle of the street. The backstop is but one hundred paces on a diagonal angle from it, standing tall, silhouetted against the empty sky. And even though these are significant pieces to both he and to his best mate in the world, Hound will not be held by them on this day.

It is Avrum's mother who takes notice of the upward rushing and changes their course with a sharp turn to the right. There is an effect happening, a clear distortion in the air, invisible waves upsetting the smoldering atmosphere of the rock quarry. It is separate, she recognizes it as something new and they run to see.

Hound's mother enters the street right as he exits the umbrella of the pepper and they meet at the curbside of the field. The two come together at the point of eruption so that the woman in mid-life stands transfixed as the tree explodes into an inferno. She should've realized these features about her son. She should have taken the time to get to know him while they still had a chance. For it is true that Hound has learned a great many things in her absence, not least of all, in this event, various details he absorbed from his father by their time spent with the burn piles upon the red clay of his land. It arrives as no surprise that Hound is indeed proficient in the oddities of life as well demonstrated here in the field before his mother's house.

"Damn, you've finally done it. There's nothing I can do for you now," she says.

He looks toward her, seeking something beyond what is available by appearances, as she stands at the curb in a half-tucked shirt with a tendril of long hair hanging between them. They lock eyes in examination, but he cannot find what was present in the exceptional Polaroid frame, so he simply turns back to the blaze.

Girl Scout and his mother arrive at the scene and huddle closely. She reaches for Hound and slides her arm around his shoulder, bringing him near.

"He's all yours." Hound's mother says to the neighbor.

"Oh, I know. I've always known." comes the reply.

The three watch the ascending funnel break the sky above them, and through it go the contents of the tree, though something equal is returned. If they were of a mind to care what was going on around them, the trio would see Hound's mother peeping from behind the curtain of her front room while the neighbors slowly fill the streets to witness the burning in the field. But it turns out they are fully occupied, as the spectacle holds only those freely open to the rapture of truth; it is never forced, it is simply available to the one who compels it to act, whose time is come.

To be sure, Kelly Sinclair does feel his secrets lifted up into the funnel; and he goes along with them through the break in the sky though he returns to find himself standing with two feet on the ground.

"I'm sorry I'll miss dinner tonight, Mrs. Miriam."

"Maybe you won't miss it after all."

"I know how disappointed you are when anyone is late to the table."

"Kelly, this time it might be worth the wait."

He is then taken from them, stuffed into the car, and driven away. It was decided to let the fire burn itself out since it did not move beyond the one tree.

———

A young man sits in a purely white room. After being told to stay put, he waits for the interview to commence. Kelly Sinclair has always tried to be good and to do as he is told, because, despite the many tricks in life, the adolescent can tell there is some value derived from an act of obedience. He has become fairly reliable in this endeavor from his many times of practice, made necessary by the dense succession of these first 14 years.

His fingernails tap the top of the desk where he sets. He thinks on these things but stops when he takes notice of his own hands. They are not so bad, young, but off to a decent start. Not perfect, but who would want to be so uninteresting anyway. His concentration is taken from them back to the white room and he recognizes that this business is taking so very long to get underway. Might as well get it over with, he reasons. What he doesn't understand is the delay has come because something has changed in their plans for him. Someone has called attention to a red canister found nearby the incident.

The door is opened but not by the detective. Rather, it is Phillip Bruder who appears in the doorway.

"Come on, son. Time to go home." He says.

"Home? What home?"

"Our home. Get up, let's do it."

Kelly Sinclair looks to the bricks of the purely white walls that are built up uniformly around him and compares the tranquility found in their unvarying structure to the rushing chaos going on in the hallway. He studies the hand holding the door open and then to the other reaching out for him. There, he catches sight of Bruder's imperfect yet good hands, and in them, he sees the person who stands.

"Yes, it is time. I'm ready."

Author's Bio:

Kenneth Holt is a writer of fiction working from his native city of Los Angeles. He had a 20 year career in filmmaking that allowed him to travel the world. Interests include religious and philosophical studies along with art and music.

Publishing history:

LAST OF THE GREAT RATTLESNAKE HUNTERS - Defiant Scribe: February 2019 Issue.

WHEN SUNSHINE SPEAKS - Borfski Press: Spring 2018 Issue.

COOL OF THE MENACING TREE - Balkan Press: Conclave, The Trickster's Song. February 2018. Reprinted in Selcoth Station: April 2019.

OUT OF THE CLOSET/INTO THE TOMATO PATCH: Nixes Mate Review: Fall 2017. Reprinted in Automatic Pilot: Winter 2018.

AND WITH IT LEFT THE RAIN-SONG - Pushcart Prize nominated by Medusa's Laugh: (twisted) Anthology 2018. Reprinted in Dark Lane Books: Volume 7, Fall 2018.

INTO A KEEN AND BLINDING SUN - Ghostlight, Magazine of Terror: Winter Issue 2018.

SPRING BENEATH SILENCE - New Rivers Press: American Fiction #16 2017, contest finalist.

THE SHOREHAM VEHICLE - Thrice Magazine: #20 August Issue 2017.

A BEER IN BASTILLE - TulipTree Publishing: Stories That Need To Be Told Anthology 2016, contest finalist.

LIKE A HUMAN

By Patrick Breheny

I'm Howie the 'bot, and as I write this, I'm still living at the old Crown Hotel here in Bangkok. My facsimile twin was Harry, who was living with Mildred, possibly bot, but I suspect human—- as she declared during her emotional outburst when Harry self-destructed by swallowing too many fifths of vodka, instead of our specified half pint of oil, after cutting off his hearing sensor to imitate Van Gogh. Harry and I were programmed as literary endeavors. I wrote about Harry's demise as if it were fiction, and it was published in the RISE Anthology from Las Positas College in California. I wrote it under an alias, as I am doing here, because, well, Howie The Bot doesn't do it for me as a pen name.

To get you up to speed, this is the short 'story' that was published in RISE:

VAN GOGH SYNDROME

I'm Howie. Full first name. My twin Harry believed he had a masterpiece. He wrote it in longhand in notebooks, and used internet cafes to type it, printing his pages for revision. He lived in the old Crown Hotel on Sukhumvit Road at Soi 29 in Bangkok, a two-story, horseshoe-shaped structure, unpainted for forty years, with a big, chipped, brown brick bathtub of a swimming pool in the center of the compound. Back then it was a cheap motel with low wattage lighting in the interior corridors; the rooms were big, and it was kept clean despite faded and ripped sheets, towels, bedspreads. (Harry avoided such run-on sentences unless he could justify them as thought progression, not descriptive prose. We have similarities, but each has his own identity.)

He had what he thought of as a companion, one of the advanced robots programmed as a female with a personality, a computer beyond state of the art, contracted to him from the Robo-Mate agency. It sweated and emitted other secretions and excretions, bled, snored, got the flu, had opinions, made demands, argued, and could compromise, but would never age or die. They made it too real. There were times it told Harry she didn't feel like it.

His fanaticism about the manuscript infected her too. If that was all he dedicated himself to, it had to be valuable. Not in this lifetime, Harry thought, but he had faith in its unacclaimed worth. Van Gogh syndrome would befall him; generations to come would praise his genius. Yet he knew if he were to, shall we say, croak at the Crown Hotel, the building staff would clear the room quickly of anything that looked immediately salable.

I have to mention the floors in the rooms at the Crown. They were large, rectangular sections of ceramic tile, just the right size for 8 ½" x 11" paper to fit beneath, so he dug away the grout and raised one. As his output thickened, he carved into the wooden floor beam to make more room. He surmised that if he never put any weight on that beam the floor wouldn't collapse, calculated its straight-line trajectory in the room and warned Mildred not to step there either.

Advanced as the current machine he'd leased was, they had overlooked details. She was English illiterate, though could more or less speak it, had no idea why Harry was hiding those documents, nor what was in the many formal pieces of mail he received (rejections from agents and publishers), but deduced that the big hidden collection was bounty. He tried to explain some of it. She definitely wasn't stupid, she got character, but he had the devil's own time elucidating his style and structure to a model that had a different assigned native language and wasn't programmed to read English.

Keeping her away from the part of the floor with the weakened beam, was tricky. She just seemed to have a mind of her own. No matter what he told her to do, she wasn't the driverless car he wanted, that operated autonomously until you instructed it not to. He consoled himself with the notion that the independence and flaws made her seem more human, and after all no one is perfect.

For a week, Harry had intentionally neglected to swallow his — our — specifications quota of one-half pint of oil per day. He was bone dry — alloy dry —inside. When his project was finished, he instead drank three of those large bottles of vodka straight down, cut off his ear to make his intention clear, then his motor seized up. The authorities of course thought his demise had a more human cause, like a stroke or a heart attack, and nobody too closely examined a near-indigent, foreign vagabond who'd apparently died of natural causes. He did have my phone number posted prominently on a dresser mirror as an emergency contact, so the manager called me, Mildred being too distraught to handle that.

Poor old Harry. Well, he believed his work would be discovered, and it was. I knew of it, and thought it might be marketed in New York's Soho as a stunning Avant-Garde work by a primitive — Harry having no actual experiences or personal history any more than I did — but his novel had degenerated from the designer's literary aspiration to fetishes for girders, nuts, bolts and various steels and wires. By the time I arrived; the crew had put it in a pile with yesterday's newspapers from other rooms. Mildred told me she tried to keep its existence from them, but they'd long known, from the room cleaners, about that loose tile and uncovered it. She tried to get them to leave it with her, but one of them who could read English and browsed it answered "Recycle." So, Harry was correct——it was worth something in the real world.

I've never seen one of us express grief. We don't mourn each other, that would be silly, yet Mildred was inconsolable. I confess I became impatient with her. I said, "Harry was just a thing." That made her worse. I data'd, Okay, it was programmed well, she needs comforting. I tried to address legacy, explained that even

Shakespeare might have been one of us that travelled back in time. Nobody's sure who wrote those plays, but they exist. Of course, that wasn't going to happen to Harry's effort. Yet I reminded her that even if it was deemed irrelevant trash, fit only for salvage, both it, and Harry, and she herself for that matter, were immortal whatever shapes their forms eventually took because even if molecules aren't forever their protons are.

Instead of bringing her the relief I'd hoped for, my comment (motivated by her indulgent shrieking that was searing my listening sensors) seemed proof to her that I was incapable of understanding. I began to suspect it wasn't Harry, but losing the progeny of his obsessive scrawling, in belief that she'd lost her treasure, that was causing such agony. I also thought she might be registering low, which can cause imbalances. The room had two water glasses on a nightstand, and I sought to remedy her situation, and at the same time reassure her, by popping a fresh shiny quart can of oil and asking her to share a drink with me.

It was then that, as you might say, she just totally lost it.

Twixt gasps and sobs she finally out with it:

"YOU can't know what it's like to be a human being serving a robot."

Yeah, maybe she was programmed to say that, but I doubt it.

I haven't been the same since.

I DO know what it is to be a robot serving a human.

I took what she said… personally…as a prejudiced attack.

Even if she was designed to lie, she thought she was human.

Saw herself as shamed and humiliated, de-HUMAN-ized by her assignment.

She (definitely not "it") is better than us, we are only there to serve her (you), you should never serve us.

Whether she thought she was human because of input information or really is I don't know.

She didn't drink oil or wouldn't be seen drinking it. Let's see if she gets wrinkles.

I do know this…I felt…I felt that…

Yes, I FELT…

Her cruel, selfish words of pity for her feelings…deeply hurt…my feelings…

END OF VAN GOGH SYNDROME, STORY

It hasn't been long enough to know if Mildred will get wrinkles. I renewed the contract with Robo-Mates and moved into Harry's room with her. The front desk man and woman acted like I was doing something borderline incestuous. Fuckin' humans don't get us, expect us to think like you, but see, I get you enough to start talking like you.

I plan to win Mildred's loyalty. I told you I have feelings, and now I think I'm in love. How do I know? I think it means you want somebody to yourself. No competition. I don't want any jerks talking to her, eyeing her, coveting my treasure. That's love, right? It IS. It doesn't mean you want the best for someone. You want the best for you. Oh, I LEARN.

One night I came home in the late evening, like eleven, having finished teaching English and stopping at the secret bot cafe for a couple of oils. English classes? Yes, I met a few students and teach private classes from a bulletin board ad I posted at a market. I want you to appreciate the ironies. First, I am only programmed to speak English, and except for recently, have no life experience, but I'm teaching a human language. Second, I'm teaching it to Asians whose histories are of being subjugated by people who speak European languages. None of mine. If you're happy, I'm happy. (See how I can talk like you so quickly.)

So I come home, not tired exactly, we don't get that way, but bored, and Mildred, in a bikini, is lounging in a recliner at poolside talking to some derelict tourist——yes the hotel attracts such——who was several beverages past his limit and ready to fall off his beach chair.

"Good evening." say I. (I'm trying out a literary style here; see if I think it passes)

Mildred, rising, says "Howie, this is Ainsly."

I'm programmed to speak with an American accent, understand American speech phonetically, and what I hear is,

"Sssssss, mite."

But reassure, "It's alright. Stay put."

'Stay put' because he was attempting to flail out of the chair and follow Mildred to our room. To make staying more appealing, I added, "Let me buy you beer."

Whether because of the beer promise or simply the logistical unlikelihood of pulling himself upright, he relaxed back into his cocoon of curved plastic strands.

And I stayed with him. Bought him several beers. And when the hotel staff were asleep, and Ainsly was asleep, I took him for a swim. They found him at daybreak in the pool, and——well, he wasn't the first. They had a sign NO LIFEGUARD ON DUTY posted, and that left them free of responsibility.

Next day, after we heard about Ainsly in the coffee shop at breakfast and went upstairs to toilette and dress for the day, Mildred asked me,

"What time was it when you came up?"

"Hard to say. Why?"

"Oh, Ainsly was such a nice man."

I didn't think of him, nor his slurred braggadocio of misadventures at home and abroad, as 'nice.' And yet, I thought for a moment, did the sentence fit the offense? Then reminded myself what a silly thought that was for a pragmatic robot to have.

"Run of the mill geezer. He was foolish, took a swim, and what time I went to bed has nothing to do with him."

"But you see, it has, Howie. The police will want to know who else was with him until late."

"Weren't you?"

"They know I went in. The desk called to say they were going off duty, asked if we needed anything. They couldn't see the pool from the office."

"So, nobody knows I was there but you,"

"I won't tell. But Howie, you have no experience, you're new. You have to be careful."

"Careful"

"I was there that moment you were aware of feelings. I can guide you, can be like…a…yes… a…."

"What?"

"Let me think."

"Not a mommy, Mildred."

I defer to my program instructions, which I don't think ever foresaw my humanity. I'm a computer. What's good for me is good. What's bad for me is 'satanic', a good accusatory word. Anything opposing my objectives is evil.

Mildred is still Mildred. She can guide me sometimes, as long as I know it's in my interest.

I'm not tormented by your guilt. That's so illogical. I don't feel regret. You do what you do for a reason. Why would you have remorse for it later? I suspect the 'people' running the world are like me. Maybe they are 'me', 'mine'.

About my literary aspirations? How much money can a poet make? Oh sure, there are the 'big novel' writer/robots, the Clancys, Conellys, Kings, but all those hours of writing are too much time wasted for my liking. See, now that I have a will, I make choices. I want to use my programming for recreational hedonism. Quick rewards. You want it, take it. Don't wait. 'A bird in the hand'…all that shit you say.

If I want to take over the world, I have to start small. Take this dodgy hotel first. How? Well, maybe by ingratiating myself with the staff. There were the pair who worked the front desk, who I thought were married but found out weren't. They just fought like they were. At first, they both thought I was a pervert for taking up so soon with my redundant twin's mistress. (I know you're wondering what Mildred and I do. I'm fitted with a sensitive realistic prosthetic that works just fine for both of us.)

First attempt I just hung around the lobby, joked with Mr. Tom about the tourist foreigners — the 'falung' — and the stingy owner he hated. Mr. Tom showed me a display of books, left by check-outs, that he'd turned into a concession. Most were in German and French.

Salesman that he was, Mr. Tom pitched one with "This is in English."
That might not be a selling point for you, but I still wanted to read
anything written in my assigned language, and also wanted Mr.
Tom's (not affection…bonhomie? Friendship?) well, anyway I
bought it for twenty baht—-a deal even it was just an advertising
brochure.

The book was for children, and Mr. Tom didn't need English
proficiency to know that. It had cartoons on the cover. As I sat in a soft
armchair, I caught his sly smile when he saw me thumbing the pages. (I
was improving my vocabulary. It was about kids at a computer, and even
though I'm a computer, I was learning OMG and OTW and LOL,
which I (and the characters) first thought meant Lots of Love.

Older European 'gentlemen' liked the hotel. Word was out in their
vicarages that it was safe, (at least before me) clean, and the staff looked
the other way.

An example and downside of that tolerance was one night when I
heard a man screaming in the next room. I thought the woman was
murdering him, so I called the front desk. I only did that because he was
annoying me. He wasn't keeping me awake, but Mildred likes to sleep.
(I don't sleep. Another advantage I have—-while you're asleep, I'm
NOT.) I wouldn't care if she killed him, any more than I did about
Ainsly drowning. You know, when he fell in. Shit happens, right? When
I told the night clerk about the wails for mercy, he started laughing. Well,
he knew more than I did. He'd checked them in.

You could call other rooms on the house phone, and I did just that
in the middle of an "Aiyee!" It got suddenly quiet except for their phone's
repeated loud ringing until one of them picked up the receiver and
slammed it down. They didn't know from where, but somebody
somewhere was complaining. The silence lasted another minute,
followed by frantic whispers, and when they continued with their—-you
call this what? Lovemaking? He apparently had a sock in his mouth or
was gagged because he only emitted gasps and grunts. So, Mildred could
sleep, and I could plot in peace. Indulge my fantasy, of somehow
someday I'd be king, and Mildred my Lady. If she just doesn't age.
Humans have such imperfections.

A way to imbed myself with the employees, who lived on the
premises, was to drink beer with them in the lobby in the wee hours. I
have a trick I use, since I can't ingest much alcohol or my motor will
seize up like Harry's did, I have a hollow leg. No joke. The beer goes in
my mouth, then in the leg. When it gets full, I do what you do when
your pail needs room. I go to that little private room and empty it. I do
have to use the stall. I'd give my game way standing at a urinal with a leg
full of recycled beer. Just one of the logistics I have to contend with,

passing myself off as one of you. I don't expect you to understand, certainly not to endorse me. You shouldn't. By the time you read this, it will probably be too late. I am NOT you.

Periodically, all water would be shut off to the rooms. When it first happened, Mr. Tom used to explain it as required maintenance, but one afternoon I encountered him at the side driveway, away from lobby ears, as he guided a delivery truck in.

"Why is the water off again?"

"Do you want to take a shower?"

"Yes."

"There's water on in room 100."

Room 100 was a small maintenance room that had a sink and a shower stall for the staff.

Mr. Tom was offering me a deal. If I accepted, I'd be grateful to him and stop complaining.

"I want to take a shower in my room. My… (what was she?) …girlfriend…does, too."

He smiled sadly. It wasn't his doing. And then he told me, "The owner didn't pay the bill."

"You mean he…?"

It usually lasted two or three days, until people started checking out.

"He's a cheapskate. Doesn't pay until they cut him off."

He explained more. The crew were on low salaries, got paid late too. And it was hard for staff to keep track of work hours when they lived there and were on call to service a room if there was a check out, fix an air conditioner, handle any emergency.

The owner seemed worth befriending too, if only because his sour non- communicative expression indicated he had no friends. He was Asian but not Thai, and nobody at Crown seemed sure where he was from. Some thought Malaysia, some Singapore, some China. A foreigner couldn't own a business, so the hotel had to be in his wife's name, but he wasn't happily married because he wasn't happily anything. When he was in attendance, which was irregularly, he either sequestered in his cubbyhole office and left the door open to intimidate staff or sat on one of the recliners at the pool, in the shade of the tree beside it.

I am not one for exhibiting my physique in public. I have quite a complex about that. My disrobed body betrays my ribs as coils and shoulders shaped like oil drums, sections separated by marks and grooves that might as well be Frankenstein's scars. I'm a marked man, though with a shirt on, I appear quite buff. (For lovemaking, Mildred closes her eyes. I don't know what she pretends. She won't tell me, but after Harry, she may be inclined toward the mechanical anyway.)

The pool offered more opportunity for private conversation, away from the lobby office from where Mr. Tom and the room boys as they were called, could hear. (I thought that made a great name for a band—-Mr. Tom and The Room Boys—-and wondered if they could sing.) I first approached him at poolside, wearing my English teacher, dress slacks, shirt and tie. and said, as if I didn't know who he was, "I love the Crown Hotel. Don't you?"

He raised a cautious eye and moved his iced tea over, to block where I might join the table, and asked, "Why is that?"

He was no doubt thinking as I was: Dim corridor lights, shredded sheets, too often no water, but there were the redeeming features.

"The pool. The room rates. The restaurant. Can buy beer all night." Should I have given that reminder of Ainsly? But he'd like the all-night beer, not legal but not seen. He'd keep a strict inventory, make money on late night sales.

"I don't see you at the pool often."

"Fair complexion. I try to stay out of the sun."

"You heard about our unfortunate accident?"

"There was an accident here?"

"A chap, his English chums called him, went for a swim alone late at night, had too much to drink."

"Terrible."

"Terribly inconsiderate and inconvenient."

I see that some of you think like me.

He continued, "I had to deal with the coroner, the police. His friends are trying to blame me. He gets drunk, and I'm supposed to watch him like a child."

I sympathized, "We're responsible for our own actions."

"Not a concept anymore with westerners."

I'd done a little reading on that. "No, they have the Twinkie defense now. I wasn't breast fed, so I killed eight women. Anybody would do the same thing."

"I like you. What's your name?"

"Howie? This hotel, fortunately, never asked me or Harry or Mildred for passports. To my students, I'm Howard d'Bot, pronounced De Bo, so if it worked with them…."

"Pleased to meet you," he said when I said it, and extended his hand. "I'm Mr. Lee."

I tried not to crush his hand with my mighty skin textured paw as he slid his glass back to his side of the steel table to make room for me. He asked, "What do you do?"

"I'm the manager of a language school." Hadn't looked yet but planned to.

"What's that like?"

"Well, headaches. Problems with the staff. Expenses. Tuition fees have to be competitive. Everybody expects an invoice paid NOW."

"I understand. Please, have a seat Mr. De Bow."

If I was to use Mr. Tom's dislike of Mr. Lee, I'd have to woo them separately. That wasn't hard because Lee wasn't at the hotel that often, had other properties to watch.

One afternoon while he was on his break from front desk service, I offered to buy Mr. Tom a beer in the restaurant. I wasn't sure he'd accept, being the on-duty manager, but he did. We sat in a booth, and after we got served, a beer for him, a water for my radiator that was getting dry. I asked,

"How are things between the emperor and the serfs?"

He groaned and dismissed that with "Always the same."

"The same as you told me?"

"Of course. Late salaries, low wages. Extra work you don't get paid for. You were smart to be born in America."

Yes, well. But I'd never told him that, never showed a passport. My accent was well designed.

Being the researcher, I am, and I have to be, I responded, "We used to have the exact same problems."

"Not now?"

"We did something about it. Employees made demands, started unions."

"He would fire us all and get somebody else."

"They did that there too. You have to stick together."

"Mr. Howie, you don't know Asia."

"Okay. I'm just making a suggestion."

"I don't mean this personally, but some westerners come here as tourists and then think they're here to save us"

"I get it."

"Thanks for the beer. I must go back to work. I'll take it with me."

I went back to the room. I wouldn't mention a strike again unless a seed had been planted and Mr. Tom brought it up. I hoped, despite what he said, that he thought I was on his side.

Mildred had too much time on her hands, but she said she already had a job she wouldn't give up and didn't need another. She was still rented to Harry, and by default me, by Robo-Mate — which had me wondering if that was all we had. When her contract ended, would that be the end of me and Mildred?

She was taking English classes, going to yoga and meditation sessions, getting up at 5:00 to feed monks, then going back to bed to practice Tai

Chi in the park at sundown. If she was still with me when I took the world over, I'd have a cultivated queen.

I was developed by a group of people who didn't expect me to become autonomous; I will refer to them as the Admins, or for convenience THE A. THE A take care of expenses like Robo'Mate fees and rent at the Crown. I never meet any of them, but we're in cyber contact. They were dismayed at the investment they lost when Harry self-destructed, and being I'm of the same wiring, worried I'd follow suit. I justified getting a part time job to them as necessary experience if I was to become the literary prodigy they wanted. I'm programmed with simulated memories and do research, but there's no substitute for actual living. (You can remember what sex is like, but you can't appreciate its immediacy unless doing it. I know this.)

They accepted the idea of a job based on that; of course, I had my own agenda. There's a website here for English teacher positions, and I responded to one of the postings. I printed up proper looking documents — a college diploma, an ESL certificate, teaching references from South Korea, and a copy of an American passport.

At the first interview I met Gilbert, who was from Lancaster, California, which I know to be in, or on the border of the California desert. He was about forty, tall, with blending white and black hair, wore dark slacks and shirt, and was strangely grey looking despite living in such a sunny climate and coming from one. He looked over my forgeries, smiled and said, "Cal State LA. I went to Riverside. So, you're from So Cal?".

I didn't want any of this homeboy shit, didn't know enough about Southern California, but I smiled back. "For a while, but I was a transplant like everybody in L.A."

"Oh. Okay. So, where are you from?"

I should have been prepared for this. Just can't anticipate everything.

"Chicago"

"The windy city."

I hadn't heard about…Was this a trick? "Not so windy anymore."

He looked strangely at me, like maybe I was a heretic.

"Because of the tall buildings," I said.

"They were always there. I heard the wind whips around the corners of those."

"That's in New York. The rivers. The Sears Building put a stop to that in Chicago."

"It's the Willis Building now. I'll have to go sometime. Do you have your passport?"

I pointed to the official looking copies of a front page and a visa stamp page.

"I mean the passport."

"I'm getting my 90 Day Address Report done. A service is doing it. I'll have it back tomorrow."

"I'll have to see it then."

"Sure. Of course."

"Can you tell me what a modal verb is?"

Just like that. A snap quiz. But programmed as I am, I was ready.

"Would, should, could, might have, might not have, but didn't."

I smiled, so did he. "What time will you get your passport back?"

"In the morning."

"Can you come in at four and meet Mr. Statton?"

"Works for me."

"Just bring the passport."

At four the next day I was back and was met again by Gilbert.

"Your passport?"

"They misplaced it. It's in their office. They said tomorrow."

"Oh? You will have to present it. But Mr. Statton wants to meet you now, so…"

He pointed to an inner office. I went in. Mr. Statton stood taller than dark and drab Gilbert, and sported beige slacks, powder blue sports jacket, and blonde surfer locks. A giant color photo of the Sears Tower dominated the largest wall. When we shook hands, he almost broke my claw off.

And he said, "I hear you're from Chicago. So am I." I could only think, Oh shit. "And you say it's not so windy anymore?"

"Sometimes not."

"I've been gone a long time, but everything changes."

"No building can stop January. So, Gilbert thinks you have a personality for this. How soon could you start to teach?"

"Any time."

"Tomorrow afternoon?"

"Sure."

"He says you have a document missing. Bring that with you."

"Absolutely."

The next day, Gilbert asked, "Did you get it?"

"Get what?"

"Mister the bot."

"d'Bot. Its pronounced Dee Bo"

"Do you have your passport?"

"Oh God. They can't find it, lost it. I have to go to the embassy tomorrow and order a new one. Such a nightmare."

Gilbert's distress was evident, and I could see he …should…could…

would (not might) tell me to take care of THAT first, but Mr. Bratton (Hank now) saw me and shouted from his clubhouse "Howard d'Bot, come on in," and Gilbert was outranked.

And there was a class, and I was scheduled to meet the students.

I like that old American TV game show Jeopardy and divided my class of fourteen students into two teams. Being a computer, I had an almost endless resource of trivia questions; I offered a monetary prize to the winners and snacks for second place. The game brought out their competitiveness, we all had fun, and they left class happy and laughing, as Hank liked to see them.

The following day, Gilbert persisted about the passport, and I let a bit of irritation show.

"It's not that simple. The embassy has to establish that I'm who I say I am, check out my background. It takes time."

"How much time?"

"They won't be nailed down." Oh, I love American idioms.

"What if you had to go somewhere?"

"They'd issue an emergency temporary."

"A job's not urgent?"

"I'll ask. Okay?"

Mildred is right, I have to be careful, I'm a rookie, I have gaps when I don't think something is important. Like I took a job with intent to infiltrate, so I forgot to ask how much I'd get paid. And yet, that led to a heart to heart with Hank in his sanctum. "The students like you," he said.

"I love teaching."

"We didn't discuss…Have you spoken to Gilbert about salary?"

"No, I forgot."

"Dedication."

"I really don't do it just for the money."

"Howie, we have…well, financial problems. We're cutting salaries to half the former hourly rate, but in return we will give profit sharing. In your case — the popularity with the students — you'll probably perform well and make money for us and yourself How does that sound?"

It sounded like a pass to my goals, but I needed to seem concerned. "Half the hourly rate? I have to live."

"What could you accept?"

"I don't know. Possibly three quarters."

"That's a lot. Maybe we can do 60 percent. I'd have to talk to the bookkeeper, but would that be acceptable to you, three fifths?"

"I'd have to do my own bookkeeping, gauge my living costs."

"Let's mull it over. Remember what I said, though. A teacher like you can clean up on the profit sharing."

Heh.

I saw Mr. Lee again at the pool and joined him. He asked, "How are things at your business?"

"We're getting innovative. Some of the employees are actually taking salary cuts in exchange for shares of the business."

"There's a benefit there?"

"A delay at least. Can pay some other bills instead of just salaries. Shares are based on quarterly reports."

"You still pay monthly salaries?"

"Reduced."

"I see."

There was a period of lag in advancing my program, but not really. I became full time at the school and Hank advanced me to Head Teacher, which formerly had been half of Gilbert's job. Only Gilbert seemed cognizant that I'd never shown a passport. Hank wasn't one who'd concern himself with irrelevancies if the factory was humming, and as Head Teacher I could call and chair meetings. Technically they should be about teaching, with profit sharing still Gilbert's domain, but Hank would see me as enthusiastic and Gilbert was too downsized to raise any objection.

I made a big chart outlining my hourly salary and expected share of profits and used it to show how I would make far more money under the new system. The eight teachers, I was pitching to, were a group of native English speakers from the US, Canada, the UK and Ireland. Only one teacher, Ellen, a millennial from Vancouver, questioned the change.

She said, "You are lucky so far. There's no guarantee of wages in this. Profits can fall."

I improvised. I didn't think Hank would go along with what I said, but then Hank didn't say it "We'll pay a minimum bonus that keeps the wages even with the old hourly rate. You won't lose anything."

"We still have to wait."

"For a reward. And you'll do better than the basic, all of you."

"I'll be gone by then."

"You're only thinking about yourself, Ellen. It's a savings account with generous interest, and we'll wire it to you."

The others, I could see, were accepting it as an increase not a delayed payment. And high performance aligned with profit sharing were precisely what I wanted. Ellen. You were better than a shill. Yet she was pleasant, likeable. I wondered what might happen to her in Canada but stopped such nonsense. She had friends, family there. Why did I care about a human?

If you wonder what became of my literary inclination, well, I've been busy, but I am writing this.

They were a lackadaisical gaggle, those teachers, and I had to get tough with them. They became personally responsible for increasing the number of students in their classes, and if they didn't, they'd be gone. Participating in profit sharing wasn't optional. You had to earn the bonus. I mean you couldn't choose not to earn it. Being a supervisor, as they say, isn't a popularity contest. Enrollment increased, Hank liked what I was doing, and Gilbert was no longer manager, I was. He was a regular teacher as he'd previously been, and one who had to perform like the others.

I paid rent daily, in the mornings before I left for work. One AM, Mr. Tom asked if I had time for coffee. He knew I usually had coffee in the restaurant after I paid. So, in a vinyl booth with the grey stuffing spilling out of the backrests, he said, "Tell me about unions."

"You're thinking about one?"

"Maybe. He wants to cut our salaries."

"Doesn't he know you'd all quit?"

"He's got some trick idea. He calls it profit sharing."

"Maybe not such a trick."

"How can it not be?"

"It gives him time with his expenses, but you can benefit. They do it where I work."

"I want my money when its due."

"You have a few more minutes? I want to show you something. I'll come right back."

He assented. I went up to my room, got the chart I'd shown the teachers, and brought it.

I said, "I'm making fifty percent more than I was on the old salary. Everybody is."

"You're suggesting we go along? You, the union guy?"

"Maybe you're not getting the money now because he can't, he has other bills. If he pays late anyway, why not take the reduction if that's on time, and hold him to the bonus?"

"They like the other idea better. A union. Maybe a strike"

"I didn't say don't start a union. Maybe I could help you with both."

"How?

"I know some lawyers. I could be your representative, make him keep his bargain?"

"I have to talk to the staff. They'd like to burn the dump down."

"I understand, but that won't get them any redress."

And one day, I got a message at the end of a class from Rene, the receptionist, "Mr. Statton wishes to see you in his office."

Hank wasn't where he usually was, standing in front of his massive oaken executive desk. He was seated behind it. Doing the standing was an official, in a military style uniform, though it was Hank who spoke.

"There's been some confusion, Mr. d'Bot. Immigration had a tip that you don't have a passport."

"How could I get in the country?"

"Exactly," Hank said.

"I showed it to Gilbert, he made copies of the front page and my visa."

The officer spoke softly, belying his physicality. "We're asking, not assuming you don't have a passport. Even if lost, you could replace. Do you know where it is?"

"In a safe box."

"Can you bring it tomorrow?"

"Yes."

"Very well."

He left. Hank asked, "Do you have it?"

"I have to look."

"Howie, I have to deal with this. Teachers with no visa, we have made arrangements for that. This is different. Tomorrow you'll have it, yes or no?"

I actually sighed. My first time. A great surging release of air. And I confessed, with theatrical resignation, "Not by tomorrow."

Hank sighed too. I could tell it felt good. I wanted to do it again. He said, "He just wants a bribe. I'm sorry, Howie, but it has to come out of your bonus."

I wasn't acting when I did sigh. I want the money I earned but losing some of that pittance recompense was insignificant compared to knowing Gilbert informed on me.

I took an opposite action to how I was feeling. I pretended to Gilbert I was more injured by the monetary loss. I caught up with him in the canteen, and explained what had happened, as if I didn't know he'd set Immigration on me.

I pleaded, "Please tell him tomorrow that you witnessed my passport and copied it."

"But I didn't."

"Statton wants this to go away."

"I want my Head Teacher job back. Tell Statton the responsibility of that and manager is too much for you."

I agreed. I was such a sport, I arranged a reception for Gilbert on Saturday, outside in the pleasant dry season, poolside at the Rembrandt Hotel. (I'm fond of those names of 'immortals,' Rembrandt, Van Gogh. Harry died, but he didn't have to.)

We had Friday first, when the cop came back for his gratuity, and I made sure Gilbert was at the meeting.

Gilbert vouched for me. "He showed his passport and we copied it."

He proffered copies of the forged front page and visa.

The Immigration guy became florid and roared, "Its a crime to lie to an official."

"I'm not lying."

"You either are now, or you were when you called the hotline."

Gilbert, outed, began shivering like a kitten pulled from a tub of cold water.

"I never…"

Hank stopped it. "It's alright. My people, get back to work." To the visitor he said, "Let's go for some tea and have a chat."

I left with Gilbert, who implored, "Look. I don't know why he said that…."

"He wants a bribe, that's why. I know you wouldn't go so low. You have to help us plan for Saturday." Gilbert seemed amazed he was still going back to Head Teacher and the celebration was on.

"Can you arrange catering with the hotel. What about balloons?"

He said, "I'm on it."

"Great. Congratulations."

It's hard to get people drunk when you don't drink with them, and Gilbert didn't drink like Ainsly. I watched and saw he had a couple of highballs, but by late evening he was nowhere near bombed. (You Americans.)

I stalled him with need for some private time to discuss classes, since he hadn't been Head for a while. He had drunk just enough not to taste the difference when I dropped a Quaalude in his drink.

I had to be more careful, as Mildred said. There were staff, not present, but on duty. Getting wet can only make me rusty, so as I swam him, manipulating his arms as I forced his face down, and softly encouraged, "Good. Good. Use your legs. You need your legs to swim too." Back and forth across the pool, I guided him until, finally, let go and he sank to the bottom. There were no witnesses and I slipped away. THE A didn't expect me to have feelings. I only care about my own interests and nothing about anyone else's. Why would I? Why do you? You want forgiveness. You have confession. Therapy. Being vulnerable.

The stupidest thing I've heard from any of you in my short time. "Look, the bombs are falling. I think I'll go out and stand under them." To show what? You're sensitive? I may feel something (annoyance?) if I mishandled a situation, but I have no moral restraints. I'm the perfect psychopath. Nevertheless, I understand why Gilbert retaliated against me. I came from nowhere and stole his livelihood. Well, tough shit, huh?

Back at the domicile, I was having morning coffee regularly with Mr. Tom, and at one of those sessions he announced, "They said they'd try it, but they're afraid of a trick. They'd want to see income and costs."

"That's only smart."

"These people aren't accountants."

"The bonuses should go into a trust, then be periodically distributed to the shareholders."

"How do we go about doing that?"

"With a bank. And you have to choose an administrator of the trust."

"Like who?"

"Somebody you trust."

"So, do you think you could?"

"I have a lot to do already, but maybe. They're doing it where I work, so there's something to model from."

"When do you think you could say?"

"Give me a little breathing room, okay? I have to think?"

"Okay."

My apparent lack of attachment to money, in that I didn't initially ask what my salary was, led Hank to think me trustworthy. I became CEO of the Profit-Sharing Trust at the school too. Hank realized that a group of employees as individuals could accumulate more than 50 percent of his business and had a clause in the contract that they couldn't combine for a takeover. However, as trustee, with all the employee shares, I wasn't legally obligated to pay anybody anything and had no intention to do so.

At the hotel, I won't bore you with the details this time, but Mr. Lee took a swim too. He hadn't personally offended me, but I needed him out of the way, and it was only right he end up in the pool he never bothered to clean.

But I had a foul night, I was sleeping now, like you do, and I had a dream. A fuckin' DREAM. Lee and Gilbert and Ainsly were having a party in my room, and drinking, not alcohol but pool water, and vomiting copious cascades of powder blue chlorinated bilge so it filled the room and I had to swim in a panic, because I can't swim; me and water don't get along.

I was not myself the following morning. When I came down for work, there were employees, several police and an ambulance around the pool. Between the uniforms I could see Lee lying on the tile deck and somebody trying to resuscitate him with oxygen and Heimlich. I assumed rigor mortis hadn't set in yet and they thought his flesh was still cold from hypothermia.

I approached as if curious and asked one of the room boys what was going on. He gave that grave look people have when they don't want to be the ones to pronounce someone dead, coupled with an expression I knew was based on a rumor among his peers that the time had come to pay bonuses and I hadn't.

When I went in the coffee shop, Mr. Tom wasn't waiting for me as usual. He was still over in the office, but after I sat a while, he came by and joined me.

"Awful," he said, "And we don't know what will become of our jobs."

I like him, and I suddenly felt, and this was the most radical unsettling feeling I'd had yet, sorry...sorry for Mr. Tom and those hardworking people on staff.

He said, "First Ainsly, then Mr. Lee," searching my face for a glimpse of accountability? Care? I saw fear on his face. He'd made the connection to Ainsly but wasn't going to articulate it.

I said, "We need a lifeguard."

"We?"

"Yes. Look, don't worry about your jobs." I couldn't believe what I was saying. And with sincerity. "As trustee, I own the hotel now. If I distribute the bonuses, I won't own it. No one will. You can keep your jobs at the old pay scale, retroactively, and continue living here rent free. Food too."

I could see, understandably, he didn't dare to trust me, but I was telling him they still had jobs. It meant something was wrong with the chips inside me. If anything happens to people, why should I care? Their problems are not mine. They just build us to serve them. I'm acting irrationally, not in my own interest. And that's crazy. I'm crazy. I'm concerned about Mildred too. Not about controlling her, but about her well-being. She's showing her age and it hurts me, too.

I had another dream last night, a vague one. Ellen, the teacher from the school who went to Vancouver, was in it. I never sent the salary and bonus I promised. She sent me e-mails saying she had no money for rent or food, and I deleted them. But now I wonder how she is faring, and if what she said was true. Such worry is shameful. I was designed to be a strong stoic robot, an indifferent machine, even with a writing inclination. I am violating my mandate, my program, by reevaluating my actions. These vile sensations of concern are disgraceful.

Mr. Lee is still with the police stretching tape and measuring. Did Lee suffer? What's wrong with me, asking that? What about Gilbert? Ainsly too, drunk as he was? They say drowning is a terrible death. Suffocation until you must let the water into your lungs. Why should I care?

I'm becoming like you. More like you, than you. A lot of you don't care. But it's too much for me. I'd have to live with this compassion forever. You won't, you'll die. It's too painful for me. All this identification and empathy, it's horrible.

I wrote a note on a napkin and folded it. I called the waitress over and ordered two quarts of vodka. Mr. Tom approved with a nod and said, "Tonight we can have a grieving. And a celebration for the continuing."

I said, "Excuse me, Mr. Tom. Nature calls."

I was even able to smile at that silly expression for taking leave.

I went into the restroom, then into a stall. Yes, I was feeling unbalanced, registering low, but instead of oil, I uncapped the bottles. I swigged the vodka down, in honor of Harry.

When I went back to the restaurant, I was, emitting black smoke and a foul burning stench, and approached Mr. Tom. He slid across the booth away from me, but I was able to force the napkin into his hand and run for the door.

I shouted "Pool! Water!" as I went outside, and he chased me. The officials around the pool prepared to stop me, but Tom shouted, "He's on fire. Let him jump in."

They moved aside to let me. The lunge into the deep end guaranteed none of me or my parts were salvageable. The note I gave Mr. Tom was a will, a legal holistic one, leaving the hotel to him, and the language school to Mildred, who I knew would administer it more fairly than I had.

It was indeed a pleasure, humanity. You're intriguing, but I couldn't stand any more of the angst.

As my last effort, before all the data gets shipwrecked, I am able to finish writing this, click SAVE

And SEND.

Author Bio:
Patrick Breheny grew up in the Bronx, lived a long time in Los Angeles, and teaches ESL in Bangkok. He has had stories published in Adam, Cad, Straylight and Koan, and in anthologies from Havik Press and LVP Publications. He hopes you enjoy "Like A Human."

Somewhat Misunderstood

By Ace Boggess

HERE BEGINS THE CHRONICLE OF
THE FALSE PROPHET

Our main character didn't have a name. Not *Jesus*, especially. Those who knew him or knew of him back in '92 referred to him as Doc, short for Doctor, which he wasn't, or so we thought. He also lacked a home and family. It's possible he had both at some point, but he rarely spoke about his past, although he'd babble for hours about everything else as if a professor of semiotics, Kantian categorical imperatives, mariachi bands, and pet psychology. He offered opinions on any subject—likely the reason he'd been dubbed with the pretentious title *Doc*.

Doc never worried about fancy titles. He concerned himself with beer and soda cans, which he collected, because he also didn't have a job. He recycled cans, newspapers, and bottles, earning what money he could. He considered that professional and respectable. Doc believed himself the best sifter in the business.

While Doc lacked a name and occupation, I think it's safe to say I have both. Name's Harold Hodge. Some call me Harry. A few call me Hodgepodge. Seems I have several names.

Also, I'm a hack. A hack's a writer not all that good at writing, a journalist who violates the codes, forms, structures, laws, and sacraments of journalism. A hack is me. I'm a hack. *Why on earth would he admit that*? You ask. Because it's true. I'm proud of it. Being a confessed hack gives me an advantage over the thousands of closet hacks working the daily grind in newsrooms and publishing houses. Of course, some might argue I'm just too stupid to lie.

Nonetheless, I'm a storyteller. I'm here to share an epic. Like all good tales, it's true … as far as you know.

Either way, two things will stay the same: I'll be a hack, and Doc won't be Jesus. That's the point I'm trying badly to convey.

It took place in Huntington, West Virginia, a city bordering Ohio and Kentucky. Trapped at the crossroads of three states, Huntington seemed almost bipolar. Sometimes its townsfolk toyed with modern concepts like a passion for the arts. Other times, it's like they forgot how to walk erect. Here, anything could happen at any moment without notice: protest marches, government scandal, Elvis sightings, and fishermen claiming they saw a giant, three-headed catfish swimming in the lilac depths of the Ohio River. Yes … a rather strange place.

A college town, home to Marshall University—originally called the Marshall Normal School, though never all that normal—the city relied on Marshall for an annual influx of students; the townsfolk enjoyed nothing more than getting falling-down drunk to celebrate when the university's football team dominated conference rivals. The rest of Huntington seemed a lot like any other small city or large town. One might see parks, landfills, street crimes, hookers in Four-and-a-half Alley, not to mention drug dealers and winos, bankers and bank robbers, doctors and our protagonist, Doc. There were good folks, bad folks, happy folks, sad folks, old folks, new folks, just-like-you folks. You wouldn't find much unusual about it, with the exception of religion. Known to locals as *the City of Churches*, Huntington contained over two hundred and fifty religious institutions in a span of just a few square miles. Quite a lot of churches. More churches than I had names.

With so much religious interest in Huntington, it's understandable why Jesus might select this city as stage for his return performance. That's not what happened. As I pointed out, our main character wasn't Jesus. I can't emphasize that enough. But at least religious surplus might explain why a transient known as Doc got mistaken for that transient religious icon.

What a mistake that turned out to be.

The original Jesus, whose birth many centuries ago did wonders for the calendar, was said to be a peace-loving activist. Whether his mythical status is true or even believed by the current audience, it's clear the man urged broad, general love and kindness for which he found himself lovingly and kindly nailed to a cross. I suspect his words were somewhat misunderstood.

Since the original, many have claimed to be Jesus. They've preached and prophesied (staying far from controversial topics like love and kindness). Many have been believed. Sadly though, when someone claims to be Jesus, it's often someone else who gets nailed.

Not only was our main character *not* Jesus; he didn't claim to be. It was a classic case of mistaken identity blown out of proportion.

It began with a big bag of dope.

On a beautiful autumn day in October, with leaves glowing from contentment as they rocked back and forth in a warm seasonal breeze, I was drunk. Only a little. I'd been tailgating at the new stadium with friends. We, like thirty thousand others, enjoyed a wonderful afternoon watching our team beat up on the team from Furman by a score of four hundred and twelve to three. Or something to that effect.

So, after a marvelous football Saturday, I headed back to my car. I'd parked it in a pay lot several blocks away. It had just come into view when I heard a voice echo from inside a large green dumpster. "Oh my," it said. "Oh my, oh my." The hollow, chiming words, rising as if from empty air, sounded much like, well, the voice of God. Had there not been a dumpster at the source, I too might've pondered something religious.

I knocked on the side of the metal box. I wasn't surprised to hear someone knock back. Again, I rapped. Again, someone rapped back. I repeated this ritual twice more before deciding to investigate. Standing clumsily on my toes, I levered up to glance inside the dumpster, something a normal man with both a name and occupation wouldn't do. As I've said, I'm not normal. I'm a hack. I always need something new to write badly about.

As my line of vision made it over the top of the dumpster, the knocking, wrapping, oh-mying man inside popped his head out like an obnoxious, giant jack-in-the-box, startling me. I lost my balance and tumbled backward onto the ground. "Oh my," he said again.

It's important to note that because of the confusion and anxiety created by falling onto uncushioned concrete, I failed to get a look at my homeless friend. It surprised me when I levered myself off the ground and looked up to see Jesus. Or rather, I looked up and didn't see Jesus. Or, well, I looked up and saw someone who greatly resembled Jesus, but was not—a fact I knew after doing a story on him. His hair flowed in a mass of rich brown mixed with traces of silver and draped to his shoulders. His beard, made of the same colorful stuff, hung two inches off his chin where it tucked itself under, giving it the appearance of a neat trim. His brown eyes felt serene, his lips held a smile, and his hands, I'm sure, would've been calloused but gentle, had they not been covered with gunk. He even wore a Christlike yellowish-white gown that may have been made from an old canvas sack.

"I'm so sorry. I didn't mean to startle you."

"No problem," I assured him.

"I've injured you."

"No harm done, except to my ego."

"You're sure? I couldn't live with myself if I hurt you."

"I'm fine," I said, holding my hands up for emphasis.

"Oh," he sighed. "Pleased to hear it." As an afterthought, he added, "Can I have a quarter?"

Were this man Jesus, giving him money wouldn't bother me. In Doc's case, I hesitated to sacrifice even pocket change while he stood in a box of other people's garbage. "What for?" I asked.

"I need it to phone the police."

"Whoa," I said. "I'm not hurt that bad."

His smile faltered, but didn't fail. "Not for you," he rebutted. After ducking into the box, he popped back up and said, "For this." In his right hand he held a ten-inch by ten-inch bag stuffed tightly with what appeared, to my well-trained hack's eye, to be marijuana.

"Why call the cops? It's just weed."

"It's against the law," he explained with compassion as if I were a mindless dolt (which I might be, as far as *you* know).

"Sure, but it's a stupid law. Right?"

Raising the bag over his head so rays of sunshine flickered off plastic and green leaves like dome-lights in an algae-covered pool, he spoke again, using the big bag of dope as a prop. "That doesn't matter. It doesn't make it any less illegal. As long as it is, we have an obligation to turn it over. Socrates, you know, had a chance to flee from his death sentence, but he stayed and died. Why? Because the law demanded it." He paused, finishing with a wave. "The law's the law, however unreasonable it seems."

"But," I said. "But," I continued. "But," I gave up, already reaching for a quarter.

Cabell County Sheriff's Department Deputy Tera Micheaux didn't relish her job. It wasn't the arresting, questioning, booking, or beating up that bothered her. She liked all that. Not the danger, low pay, or paperwork. She tolerated that. What kept her disgruntled? The constant scrutiny when she walked down a public street. "There's something about a woman in uniform," she often told her colleagues at the Sheriff's Department. "The merest sight turns men into slobbering fools." She hated being stared at as if she were spread-eagle in a sleazy magazine. Of course, Tera was six-foot-eight and two hundred and ninety pounds of mostly muscle and bone. It wasn't the woman in uniform folks were staring at. Dressed in deputy-brown, she looked a lot Bigfoot.

After perfecting her scowl, Deputy Micheaux responded to the doctor's phone call first. As usual, she came prepared to bust a few heads.

At this point, it's important to note that several law enforcement units were active in Huntington (as elsewhere). At the lowest end, the university's force consisted of fully-trained, recognized, gun-toting officers. They were exceptionally good at what they did: mostly a lot of walking around campus and staring at the sky. If something criminal happened on university grounds, they got to stare at the aftermath of that, too. Campus cops normally would've been the first to check out a report about a big bag of marijuana found in a dumpster near campus. Today, though, most were at the stadium, having spent their day alternately staring at the sky and discouraging fans from fighting or imbibing alcoholic beverages in the stands.

The Huntington Police Department popped up as the next tier. HPD officers were everyday city cops. They handled crimes within the city limits. On a normal day, a Huntington cop might have responded first. Today, officers on duty spent the afternoon directing traffic around the stadium and keeping fans from imbibing alcohol on the streets. Those off duty spent the day at the stadium, watching the game, and also, imbibing alcohol.

The top rung on the law enforcement ladder was the Cabell County Detachment of the West Virginia State Police. State troopers normally gave driving tests to folks without licenses and speeding tickets to folks with them. They spent game day either going to the scenes of accidents caused by people who failed to heed the directions of on-duty city cops, or they spent it driving around, trying to prevent fans from imbibing alcohol in moving cars.

Somewhere between those last two layers fell the Cabell County Sheriff's Department, along with its democratically elected leader, the Cabell County Sheriff. The sheriff supervised deputies and detectives—that is, cops with titles.

Here's the problem with the four-layered system of law enforcement: jurisdiction. Who investigates what and where? If all different layers were unrelated, there'd be no problem. But all four were interconnected. Not like a puzzle. More like four crudely-drawn concentric circles. MUPD handled crimes on campus. HPD handled incidents in the city limits. The problem arose because the university was in the city. So, technically, HPD had jurisdiction there as well. Next came the sheriff's jurisdiction: all of Cabell County, which encompassed both the city and the university. Then, add in the West Virginia State Police. With so many overlapping jurisdictions, a great deal of territorial bickering occurred between departments, sometimes involving fist fights.

All that would be irrelevant if not for the dumpster. That green metal box containing piles of trash, a big bag of marijuana and our main character sat a few feet from a parking lot on the campus in the city within the county that was part of the state of West Virginia. As much breath as it took to say that, I guarantee you it was bound to cause turmoil which, in this case, resulted in a nearly-violent dispute between officers, followed by the arrests of myself and our main character—oh, and a car wreck involving two fans who'd been imbibing alcohol improperly.

On a separate matter, there's something decidedly strange about finding a big bag of marijuana in a dumpster. One of two things must've happened to cause such a discovery. First, someone needed to physically place it there, either while attempting to hide it from nearby police officers, or out of stupidity by discarding it with the moldy bread. The other option, one which seems rather fantastic, is that the marijuana plant grew naturally to adulthood there in the scum, then in a fit of despair wrapped itself in plastic in an attempt to protect itself from the widening hole in the ozone layer. While the latter explanation really *should* be considered further, for purposes of this story, I'll presume the former—one established by precedents.

Another thing to note about a big bag of marijuana is what exactly to do with it should one be found in a dumpster. Some folks might offer thanks to God and/or Jesus, not our main character, prior to taking the big bag home and smoking the marijuana—a process which provides a feeling of elation both wonderful and illegal. Others would take the big bag and sell the marijuana—an act not so wonderful but just as illegal, mainly because folks who'd buy it would smoke it. A big bag of marijuana has few other uses. It makes neither an attractive living room decoration nor a viable Christmas-tree ornament. Anyway, as a third option, one might ignore the big bag of marijuana, going on with business and pretending the bag isn't there. Folks who'd do that are not ones who've smoked it. But I'm off the subject. Okay, so there's a fourth option: call the cops. They'll gladly come and take the big bag away, though they probably won't smoke the marijuana.

I was discussing this and many other things with Doc when Deputy Micheaux stepped out of her patrol car waving a .357 Magnum, which is a powerfully deadly handgun and a largely unfriendly gesture. This hostile atmosphere intensified with her shouted demand that we either raise our hands over our heads or have our brains splattered across the sidewalk.

I'm not rash or impulsive. I like to consider every option before deciding what to do. In this case, I didn't stop to ask myself why I'd raised my hands over my head.

"Stop it," Doc badgered as he raised his arms. "Don't point that at us."

"Hold your tongue, Hippie. I'm placing you both under arrest." Here, it's only fair to explain that a hippie's a person who wears strange clothes and smokes big bags of marijuana. If men, oddly enough, they too sometimes get confused with Jesus. This was *not* the point in our story when the doctor got confused with Jesus. It was the point when he was thought to be a hippie: a classic case of mistaken identity of our main character's mistaken identity.

"Arrest?" Doc and I said.

"Arrest?" my transient friend repeated. "What for?"

"Don't play dumb, Hippie. We got an anonymous call about illegal substances at this location. I show up and, what do you know, here you two are with a bag of dope."

Doc grimaced. "Now wait," he said. "I know exactly why you're here. I phoned you."

"Likely story."

I said, "Tera, it's true."

She flinched at the sound of her name, not recognizing me. I'd once worked as a reporter for Huntington's primary newspaper, covering the police beat. I interviewed her several times. Not that it mattered. The deputy snarled and said, "If *you* called us, why not give your name?"

I almost injured myself with laughter.

Tera snarled at me this time.

Doc snarled, too.

"What's so funny?" Our Lady of Artillery demanded.

"How could he leave a name when he doesn't have one? Don't you know who this is?"

"Who is he?" she said.

"Yes, who am I?" asked our main character.

"This is Doc. He doesn't have a name. Not one anybody knows. He's harmless. And homeless. Probably mentally unbalanced."

"Beg your pardon?" he said.

"No offense. I was just explaining your story."

"Oh, well … that's okay."

"Wait a minute," said Tera. "Why'd a vagrant call the cops? You expect me to believe that?"

Doc replied, "Why not?"

She sighed and began to lower her gun.

"I found it in the trash while looking for cans."

The gun went lower.

"Freeze!" came an obnoxious voice behind us, causing the startled deputy to jerk her gun back up, pointing it in a direct line with my head.

HPD Officer Monroe Dollie shouldn't have been allowed to carry a squirt gun, let alone a .25-caliber semiautomatic pistol. Unfortunately, due to some legal loophole permitting police officers to have guns, he held the latter in a clenched right fist. Officer Dollie, a rookie, had been on the force less than a week. Not only should Dollie not have been allowed to carry a gun, but he shouldn't have been allowed to leave the station unescorted. If this had been a normal day, Dollie's wiser partner Chris Carettol would've been with him to keep him out of trouble, but Chris was one of the lucky HPD officers engaged in the random directing of traffic.

Dollie waved the gun emphatically as if to show he wouldn't hesitate to fire four or five slugs before the warning shot. "You're all under arrest," he said, redundantly.

"Back off, Rookie," Micheaux groaned. "It's my bust."

"Hey, Lady," Dollie spat, "I've got jurisdiction."

"The hell you do!"

"Please," said our main character, "don't be vulgar."

"Shut up, Hippie," both officers shot back.

Doc gasped for air but said no more.

"Listen," said Micheaux. "I got here first. Even a twit like you can see that."

The rookie shook his head and his gun. "Oh, no. It's my first bust, and I mean to make it."

"Listen, kid. I'm older than you, and I've got more experience. These losers are mine."

"Wait," I started to say.

"Lady," the rookie countered, "you're old, all right, but I'm still takin'em in."

"The hell, you say!"

"Don't swear at me, Lady. I'll write you up for obscenity in public. It's a one-dollar fine."

"Go to hell, Rookie."

"Why don't you two arm wrestle for it," another strange voice put in. "Meanwhile, I'll take these two bad guys in myself."

We all turned and saw a university cop waving his gun. Behind him, a state trooper hurried toward the scene.

"Oh, Christ," I sighed, and I wasn't referring to our main character.

This situation had grown too confusing. I would've given up and walked away were there not four unhappy police officers arguing, guns raised, about what to do with me and the old man. Doc, meanwhile, put down the big bag of marijuana and went back inside his dumpster, resuming his search for recyclables.

A little luck came our way a moment later. It seemed as if a higher being—not Doc—intervened in part on our behalf. Two cars collided rather suddenly and noisily nearby, stealing half our chaos. The wreck resulted from two football fans improperly imbibing alcohol at the game. These two fans didn't know each other. They had different ages, and eye, hair, and skin colors, different jobs, different cars and different religious preferences. They improperly imbibed different brands of alcohol while cheering for different teams. These two men had nothing whatsoever in common. It happened by a divine act of pure coincidence that their vehicles should collide so magnificently at an intersection when one of the two drove through a red light. Because of this amazing but rather unexpected event, a great deal of confusion erupted rather expectedly just across the parking lot from us.

"Oh, good," said the state trooper. "A wreck. There's probably people injured. I'd better handle that."

"No, you don't," replied the campus cop.

Etcetera.

The two argued all the way across the lot, each starting a semi-sprint toward the wreck. They were greedy children who hadn't learned to share. I expected one to say, "If you won't let me be the policeman, I'm taking my maimed body and going home."

That left Micheaux and Dollie arguing over who'd get to bring *us* to justice.

"Excuse me," I said. "You two keep overlooking the fact that we haven't done anything. Neither of us committed a crime."

"Likely story," said Dollie.

"Expect us to believe that?" said Micheaux, having forgotten that a moment ago she had.

"Well, actually … yes."

"What do you take us for?" said Dollie. "Imbeciles?"

I didn't say a word.

"Fine," said Micheaux. "We'll take'em down to the jail, book'em, and let your boss and my boss decide who made the arrest." They'd argued for ten minutes before Dollie suggested the temporary settlement. Now, as a sign of their good will, they were going to arrest us.

"Wait a minute," I demanded. "We haven't done anything!"

"Oh, right," said the rookie. "And *you* are an authority on points of law?"

"Enough to know I'm being harassed by public servants!"

"Aren't we obnoxious," he replied. "Been drinking?"

I flinched but didn't speak. After all, I *had* improperly imbibed a few cans of beer.

"I see. You know, Deputy, I think this one's intoxicated."

"But I'm…."

"I think you're right," said Tera. "Let's take him to the hospital."

Dollie nodded, then grabbed me.

The rest went by in a blur. I was handcuffed and shoved into Dollie's patrol car as Tera arrested the doctor.

"But what about my cans?" the old man asked. "I spent all day collecting them."

She grunted at him.

He refused to give in. "I need my cans!"

Next, I heard the familiar clanking of aluminum cans as the deputy shoved a full bag of them into the trunk of her car. "Happy?" she snapped.

"Yes, thanks," came the reply.

'Public Intoxication' is the legal term for having improperly imbibed too much alcohol in an inappropriate place. That's the offense I improperly found myself charged with inappropriately. In West Virginia, due to recent theoretical approaches regarding alcoholism—a sickness causing someone to imbibe alcohol too much and too often—the government tested new laws that deemed addiction to intoxication a psychological disorder. These laws declared anyone in such a state, even someone who only improperly imbibed on that lone occasion, could be a victim of alcoholism. Under state law, therefore, a drunk wasn't only a drunk but potentially loony.

I'm *not* loony, not even potentially, though I do seem eccentric at times. In this case, I wasn't drunk either. Sure, I improperly imbibed some beer, but not enough to leave me intoxicated. Even so, Officer Dollie transported me to the substance-abuse unit at our local loony bin. I shook my head as I considered how odd it seemed that I got sent to the loony bin instead of Doc. I was the stable one with a name and a job. I didn't have a Christ Complex. Well, neither did Doc, but he came closer.

Oh, and the things they did to me at the loony bin…! Consider the fun stuff done to lunatics in movies: straitjackets, thorazine injections, electroshock therapy, experimentation. Just imagine all that monstrous stuff. Then you'll have a nice, clear picture of exactly the types of things they didn't do. None of it. Not one loony thing. They put me in a room, gave me a bed, and told me, "Go to sleep." The nerve of those people!

First though, a novice psychiatrist asked me a handful of personal questions about my drinking habits, sex life, favorite pizza toppings, and so on. I answered all her questions and then, finally, she pronounced me a *nonalcoholic*—a word I'd thought reserved for soft drinks and fruit punch. After that, she showed me to my room and made me get in the bed. I lay there for hours staring at the ceiling and wishing it all kinds of harm like plaster rot or smoke damage or cracks caused by noisy loonies jumping around upstairs. I scorned that ceiling for quite some time before finally closing my eyes and dozing off.

The County Jail once earned a reputation as one of the meanest, dirtiest, harshest criminal containment and correctional facilities in the U.S. Run with contempt, scorn, and an iron fist—it housed prisoners doubled and tripled up in tiny cells, and those inmates were granted little exercise or contact with the outside world. Then a court stepped in. Some judge ruled that reforms were needed. So, the jail became a socially-sophisticated, gentle, kind, caring place for convicted criminals to live their lives while paying their debts to society. It might even have been renamed the Cabell County Jail and Theme Park if not for the lack of carnival rides and cotton candy.

What changed? Space, privacy, sports. Oh, and sex. One of the reforms was the "conjugal visit." Murderers and such were permitted a couple hours of unsupervised visits with spouses, girlfriends, or whatever, in order to have sex. Ah, life at the County Jail…!

Several of those involved in it later described the following scene to me. They said dinner arrived promptly at 5:23 p.m. In a temporary holding cell, twelve newer prisoners were having a post-supper chat. "Repent, sayeth the Lord," said a former Huntington minister facing misdemeanor charges for solicitation. "*He* is our judge and our jury, and *He* will be our executioner. Have faith in the Lord, and He'll have faith in you."

"That's all well and good, Preacher," said a 28-year-old black man named Walker charged with contributing to the delinquency of a minor for buying a glass of wine for a 17-year-old girl at a bar, "but how's He gonna help me outta this mess?"

The ex-preacher replied, "Our Savior can solve any problem."

"Can *He* raise two hundred bucks for bail?"

"Son," said the minister, his name Jonathan Regis, "for His servants, the Lord often passes the collection plate."

"Bunk," spat Pocket, an accused sex offender who tried to keep to himself but couldn't. "Christ doesn't consort with criminals."

"He spends His time with the ones most in need."

"I don't believe it."

Then came that gentle voice: "It's true." As prisoners turned to look, into their cell and their lives walked Jesus. Or rather, into their cell and their lives didn't walk Jesus. Wait. What I'm trying to say is, into their cell and their lives walked our main character. "Trust this man," the doctor said. "He seems to know what he thinks he means."

Twelve gasps filled the cell.

Doc said, "Grace is a gift to all, boxed and wrapped in colorful paper with pictures of rubies or rainbows, bound together with a lovely black ribbon in a bow. Most folks accept it, knowing what it is and from whom it comes, but they never open it because they think it's too beautiful and precious to defile. They display the box proudly, setting it on a shelf, or atop the TV. They stare at it and love it so much that it becomes an idol itself. Eventually it's stashed in the attic with the Adam-and-Eve lampshade one of the kids won at a college fraternity toga party. However, folks who really *need* the gift don't receive it at first. It comes cash-on-delivery, and they don't have funds to pay the postman. But the Lord keeps mailing it out, no matter how many times it comes back 'Return To Sender.' When somebody gets it who needs it, he doesn't store it or show it off. He opens it to see what's inside."

The prisoners were silent.

"Nice speech," said the guard who'd accompanied Doc. He smiled a pleasant smile and slammed the cell door shut.

"Who are you?" Regis asked. "You look familiar."

"I'm nobody," said Doc, his characteristic tone sounding over-dramatic and somehow foolish. "Or, wait, that was Ulysses. Okay, I'm everybody else. I'm a friend."

Sighing whirred around the room as if the twelve inmates realized simultaneously that each failed to turn off his coffee pot before being arrested.

"*Padre*," mumbled a 20-year-old accused crack dealer from New York.

"Christ almighty," moaned Pocket.

"*Padre*," the dealer grunted again.

This *was* the point when our main character got confused with that well-known main character from a different book. It might've ended here as well had Doc denied it. He didn't.

I find it only fair to tell you now about the twelve inmates. After a little digging, here's what I learned:

1) The reason that Reverend Regis no longer had a church had nothing to do with his arrest for allegedly soliciting a prostitute; rather, his church no longer existed. It burned to the ground two years ago in a freak accident involving candles, champagne, cockroaches, and a four-foot wedding cake. I don't know how those items fit together, but the fire marshal swore the absence of any one thing would've prevented the building's demise. With his church gone, Regis's parishioners found it easier to go elsewhere than rebuild.

2) Thaddeus "Bo" Skaggs, alias Bo Dwyer, alias Bo Thaddeus, alias New York Bo, alias Bo "the Source," dealt crack, smack, uppers, downers, mescaline, methadone, percs, synths, ice, dreamers, blotter acid, brown beads, cocaine, codeine, and kosher cannabis, which I was told is weed that's been blessed by a rabbi and never touched pork. *That* didn't make him a bad person. What did? Skaggs was a vicious killer. Err, scratch that. As I'm a journalist, albeit a bad one, I need to rephrase. Bo Skaggs *allegedly* was a vicious killer. A couple years prior, the New York City cops cracked down on peddlers after several known coke and heroin addicts were found deceased. Autopsy results indicated severe blood loss. The city police, being rational individuals, determined a vampire was on the loose, roaming around and selling drugs as a means to find more victims. Therefore, the cops rounded up all known drug dealers. Bo Skaggs wasn't a vampire. More to the point, no drug dealer in New York, as far as we know, was a vampire. The coroner pointed this out to members of the local constabulary by slapping them in the face with his report—they'd failed to read much of it. In that report, the

coroner noted victims died from blood loss caused by minor wounds such as scraped elbows and paper cuts. The cops didn't stop searching for dealers after finding this "new" evidence. They did, at least, remove the requirement that officers have an adequate supply of garlic prior to making an arrest.

Thirty known dealers were arrested during the crackdown. One was then-18-year-old alleged peddler Bo Dwyer. In his possession, police alleged, were oxycodone tablets, marijuana cigarettes, a large vial of crack cocaine, and a bag containing a full pound of heroin. The heroin allegedly had been mixed with an alleged substance that allegedly might or might not have been some alleged sort of alleged rat poison (that should be enough allegeds and allegedlys to confound any lawyer wanting to sue me for "allegedly" libeling Mister Skaggs—which means printing lies about him, which I'm not—or rather, which I allegedly am not). Now for some facts. Rat poison is an anticoagulant. It stops blood from clotting, which it allegedly did well, causing the deaths of at least eighteen people. *That* was not a good thing. Hence, Skaggs was not a good person (I allege).

Skaggs was arrested and charged with eighteen counts of first-degree murder, which could've sent him to prison for several lifetimes, with parole in about ten years. But the evidence against him was "circumstantial," meaning he couldn't be linked directly to any of the deceased because they weren't alive to testify against him. So, Bo plea-bargained down to possession of a controlled substance with intent to distribute, for which he served six months.

3) Tyrell Cole "T.C." Walker followed the rules, did what he was told, and tried to stay out of trouble. That's why it came as such a shock to find himself suddenly, at age 28, in the Cabell County Jail. Yes, he only faced misdemeanor charges, and even if found guilty, he'd get off with time served and a slap-on-the-wrist fine, but his ideals were compromised. "That girl sure was pretty," he'd been heard to say. "How was I supposed to know she was underage? It was a bar, for Crissake. It's really not my fault." A judge would later agree.

4) As for the next fellow, Pocket, his real name was Carroll Sue Bergoney, which might explain why he had such a bad temper when it came to women. Pocket Bergoney was a rapist. I don't need to say allegedly here because twice in his life Bergoney got convicted of first-degree sexual assault, a felony, and twice more had been charged with it only to plea-bargain down to battery, a misdemeanor. Yes, Pocket was a pile of oozing, bubbling, slimy, green, degenerate scum like what's infrequently scraped off bottoms of chairs in movie theaters—not just any chairs, mind you, but the stiffest, dirtiest, most uncomfortable chairs in the place, the kind you inevitably find yourself sitting on when you

go to a bad horror movie. And this scum, this oozing gelatinous mass of sludge has been festering like a gangrenous wound under that chair, there in the dark of the theater, for years, growing and growing, so that when you finally sit down, it says, "Ouch," and asks you to move. Of course, this is only one hack's opinion.

5) Myron Douglas, 18, wanted to buy marijuana. A freshman at the university, Douglas could do complex trigonometric equations, name every minor part of the human body, build reasonably powerful incendiary devices for personal use, and perhaps even calculate the hourly interest on the national debt in his head. His problem: no common sense. Instead of asking advice from someone more experienced, Douglas walked up to the first shady character he saw standing on a street corner and said, "Can you sell me some pot?" This is such an incredibly inept thing to do in a city as small as Huntington that I believe Douglas should've ended up in the loony bin with me. It was crazy. So crazy, in fact, that it worked. Sort of. The shady character, an undercover cop, said no. Then, glancing down the street toward the man he'd been following all afternoon, he pointed and said, "But I bet *he* can." Myron smiled, thanked the shady character, and went to buy dope, which he did prior to being arrested.

6) Clayburn Moss was the dealer. Aside from harassing young Myron about getting him busted, Moss kept cool. He realized how nonsensical this seemed and laughed about it for hours.

7) Tommy Eply and 8) Logan Bateman, also known as Cruiser and Crank, were rich kids who enjoyed practical jokes—breaking into houses and either "using the bathroom" in a tropical aquarium or switching the owner's cat with a stray picked up off the street. They caused a lot of commotion. Imagine some dear old granny's reaction when she comes home from a hard day at the beauty parlor to discover her beloved Siamese cat Madeline has turned orange, and into a boy cat as well. All in fun for two rich kids. Only they weren't rich kids any longer. In the past three months, both turned eighteen: old enough for jail. What a shame, as they were caught coming out of old man Wookler's house, having dipped his poodle's paws in purple paint and released it to skip along on his new Persian carpet. They couldn't afford to make bail. But they were rich, right? Let me rephrase. Their *parents* were rich. I called them rich kids when, in fact, they were former kids of rich parents.

9) Martin Mingle was a 40-year-old businessman. He wore dull clothes, liked dull things, had a dull personality, a dull job, and a dull life. He liked to dull his senses properly imbibing cheap alcohol, then improperly beat up his dull wife. For twenty years, she let it slide. Friday night, she called the police who came and charged Mingle with Huntington's second most common offense after Public Intoxication:

Domestic Violence. Martin couldn't believe it. He was stunned. In fact, he was so confused that he curled up all his disbelief into one big, hairy fist and unloaded it on the nearest officer. Then he went quietly to jail. The Domestic Violence charge would later be dropped. Assaulting an Officer wouldn't go away so easily.

10) Jim Jarred, 31, of Macbeth, South Carolina, and 11) Huntington-native 20-year-old Porter Franklin were the two unlucky men whose cars crashed after the football game. Both Jarred and Franklin had improperly imbibed too much alcohol. It was not a coincidence that both were charged with first-offense Driving Under the Influence.

12) The final inmate, like Doc, was a transient. He had no home. Consequently, he was called a homeless person. He also was referred to as a vagrant, a vagabond, or sometimes, a bum. Unlike Doc, he had a name: Roscoe Colson. He also looked absolutely nothing like either Jesus or our main character. Roscoe looked more like Mean Joe Greene, a former player for a professional football team known as the *Pittsburgh Steelers*. Roscoe was charged with shoplifting six dollars worth of chocolate bars from a local convenience store. Well, actually he didn't steal them; he he ate them right off the shelf. For that, he'd spend an unlimited time in the luxuries of the County Jail, pending payment of three hundred and fifty dollars bond. He now had a bed and meals. All his needs were met. Roscoe Colson was moving up in the world.

Jim Jarred was the last to doubt our main character's divinity. He had trouble believing in anything. Prison works religious miracles for villains, but for good men, it can cause a crisis of faith. Jarred wrecked his car, was arrested and thrown in jail—albeit a very nice jail—and worse, he'd driven here from South Carolina to watch a football game in which his alma mater got thoroughly and unquestionably obliterated by a thousand points or more. Snarling, he said, "Well, neighbor, what's your name?"

"Name?" said the doctor.

"Mine's Jim. And you are?"

"Old," came the reply, "and weary."

"What in the hell's that supposed to mean?"

"Don't be vulgar. Your words mark your values. To others, they can be as offensive as the wretched man who stands on a mountain shouting curses at each of the nine billion names of God. He does it well, but God won't suffer once. A man's curse is his own."

"You're a silly old man," Jarred said.

Doc punched him.

I'm lying. This is what I would've expected him to do. After all, there's no greater insult than to be described as silly. Oh, but let's start over.

"You're a silly old man," Jarred said.

Doc didn't punch him. His face flushed with amusement, and his eyes lit up as if he wore glow-in-the-dark contact lenses. "And you are a charming fellow and a dear, dear friend."

Jarred sighed and retreated to the other side of the cell.

By the end of a rather long night, Doc convinced all twelve cellmates that he was, in fact, Jesus. They were swayed by his words and charisma, his beard and peaceful smile. He looked, dressed, acted, and sometimes sounded the way all imagined Jesus would. To them, that's who he was. Of course, Doc also looked, dressed, acted, and sounded like a hippie, but none of his cellmates thought he was one. To take it further, he looked, dressed, acted, and sounded like either a hopeless transient, which he was or a college philosophy professor who'd taken a few too many trips down the narcotic road to enlightenment, which he wasn't—as far as anyone knew. Still, no one presumed him to be either of those. Just Jesus. It's *always* Jesus. No one ever gets mixed up with, say, Richard Nixon for example, or Manny, the video-store clerk from Lexington.

"I'm your servant, Lord," said criminal driving imbiber Jim Jarred Sunday morning, making the circle of twelve complete. "Please, will you forgive my past evil?"

Doc replied, "Stand up, friend. You've done nothing I need to forgive."

The former minister stepped forward, his miniature version of the *New Testament* opened to Matthew, Chapter 3, and paraphrased, "Comes a man mightier than me, whose shoes I can't fill."

"Amen," sang a chorus of inmates.

"You *are* the one," Regis said. "I never would've believed it if I hadn't seen it with my own eyes."

"I'm just a man."

Regis said, "The son of God is also the son of man."

"Amen," said Jarred.

"Amen," said Pocket.

"Hallelujah," said the alleged Bo Skaggs.

Regis said, "You're the one who'll save us."

"Expect nothing from *me*. Expect nothing from anyone, save what you earn yourselves."

"Amen," sang the prisoners.

The good reverend was spellbound. He fell to his knees, shaking with old-time Methodist fervor. "My Lord, I beg you, baptize me with your grace, and claim for me a place in heaven."

"Stand up, friend."

Regis stood.

"I can't do holy rites. I've only as much religion as this thick skull can hold. Besides, if I were in the market for it, you'd baptize me."

The room dulled into meditative silence.

Regis reached out and took the doctor's left hand in a two-fisted grip, thumbs pressing on top. "I love you," he said.

Our main character smiled. "Your kindness is as evident as your good intent."

"Please," Regis sighed. "I must have an answer to one question."

"Ask it. If I can answer, I will."

"Will you…? That is, would you…? What I mean is, are you going to die for our sins?"

8 a.m. Sunday. Checkout time at the mental motel. I scanned myself for wrinkles or untucked corners on my clothes. Convinced all had returned to normal, I headed out the door and down the hall. I reached the front desk, where I stood in line behind other improper imbibers, all waiting for their personal items and the freedom to leave. I knew most of them. Two were my dearest friends. I tried to hide my face, but they saw me anway.

"How you doing, Hodge?" said Ron Galloway, a local musician with whom I'd spent many nights playing guitar, imbibing large quantities of alcohol—in a proper manner … well, mostly—and having deep philosophical conversations about the girls we'd love to love if only we weren't so drunk. He had a square Frankenstein's-monster head with black moptop hair and sideburns. His forearms jutted from his white tee the way Popeye's did in the cartoons. "It's been ages."

"We saw each other Friday at the club." The club was a tiny, hole-in-the-wall, after-hours bar on the other side of the tracks. It was a place where folks like us could imbibe improperly well after legitimate bars closed. It didn't have a name. The club was just the club.

"Oh," said Ron. "That's right. Good to see you all the same. How's it going?"

"Terrible, Ron. I spent the night in the loony bin."

"Same here."

"So did I," said my other friend, Caroline Yeager-Bates, who I should point out was one of those women Ron and I would love to love—though I won't describe her, as I think that Ron's taste and mine speak for themselves. "I hate it, but I'll get used to it. It's only my third time."

"Really?" said Ron. "It's my fourth."

I interrupted them. "You don't understand. I wasn't drunk."

"Of course not," they replied in unison. "Neither was I."

Then Ron added, "But I tell you, wasn't that a great game yesterday?"

Caroline said, "It certainly was. Who won?"

"We did."

"Oh, good. I was drinking, and I guess I missed that somehow. What was the score?"

"I don't know. I lost track in the second quarter. But I'm sure we won. We were up by a hundred and eight points, I think."

"You mean...."

Again, I tried to cut in. "Listen, I *really* wasn't drunk. The cops picked me up because I tried to keep them from arresting this old man with a big bag of dope."

"That's dope fiends, for you," said Caroline.

Ron, with a reminiscing grin, added, "Yeah, dope fiends. What a shame. You didn't get any, did you?"

"He wasn't a dope fiend. He's the one who called the cops."

"Wow," said Caroline.

"That's wild," said Ron. "I think I'll write a song about it."

"Really?" said Caroline. "I can't wait to hear it."

"Yeah. It'll be...."

"Okay!" I practically shouted. "Just forget it. Forget I ever mentioned it." It was a redundant thing to say, as I think they already had.

Ron grabbed his temples. "Don't talk so loud. I have a headache."

Caroline said, "You're a bit touchy, aren't you? Not have your morning cup of coffee?"

I raised my arm, index finger extended, intending to force home my point, even if I offended or upset my two friends in the process. Fate intervened.

"Next, please," said a muscular orderly behind the desk. "Who's next?"

Caroline stepped forward, and Ron moved in close behind her, leaving me there with my lower jaw down, and my finger raised defiantly.

Ron rushed toward me as I opened the door to my taxi. He must have been hiding behind a tree or a parked car, stalking me, watching for the ideal moment to strike, the perfect opportunity to achieve maximum taxi penetration. "Hodge, old buddy, wait up, will you?"

I turned, expecting to see either a babbling lunatic dressed in a straitjacket and pajama bottoms or a husky imbecilic orderly rushing at me with a primed needle full of Thorazine. Needless to say, it was a relief to see Ron—sort of a deranged cross between the two. "What is it, Ron? I'm kind of in a hurry here."

He wore a somber, pleading look like what might be seen on the faces of vegetable rights activists, the ones who march through middle-class neighborhoods carrying signs that say "*Your Dandelion Is Your Friend*" or "*The Grass Is Always Greener When It's Allowed To Live*," trying to discourage landowners from mowing the lawn, weeding the flower bed, or whatever. "Hodge, old buddy," he pleaded, "I have a bit of a problem."

"So do I. If I don't hurry, it'll get worse."

He reached into the pockets of his faded jeans and pulled them inside-out. This revealed a few pieces of blue lint, three guitar picks, and a fragment of green aluminum which at one time or another might've been a part of the package a condom came in. By the way, a condom, also called a "rubber" even though it's not actually made of rubber, is a latex device used during sexual intercourse. It covers the male genital organ to prevent pregnancy in the female, protect against the spread of disease, and, as it once was explained to me by a neurotic, irrational woman—whom I was sleeping with—to shield the man's vital anatomy from the carnivorous demons which live in vaginas.

"I seem to have spent all my money yesterday," Ron said as if to justify the action and show that the lint, foil, and picks were not some sort of a spontaneous tribute to my greatness. Ron wasn't into idol worship. Which reminds me, I should finish up and get back to our main character, who's looking less *like* a main character and more like a minor, insignificant one, or even a figment of my imagination.

"No," I told Ron. "I can't give you any money."

He grimaced, hoping I'd change my mind out of pity. "Can I at least share your cab?"

I thought about it carefully. I could ignore him and slam the door in his face. Or, I could drag him with me to the jail, then get him back to his car later. While I took care of business, he could fraternize with the criminals, murderers, drug dealers, politicians, improperly imbibing drivers, and any other old friends he might run in to. A third option was to return to the loony bin and tell the doctors they'd made a mistake in letting me go. I could lie and tell them I wanted to assassinate the president of the local Street-corner Santa Claus union for striking every year at Christmas time in order to demand higher wages, better working conditions, a less formal dress code, and holidays off. Ah, but I wasn't in the proper frame of mind for self-incarceration.

I looked at Ron. I looked at the cab driver. I looked at my watch. I looked back at Ron. I looked like a bumbling fool. "All right," I said. "Get in."

"So, tell me about this big bag of dope," Ron pried with real interest, sounding almost too eager. "Just curious," he added.

During the car ride, I filled him in on the story as I knew it, leaving out any references to our main character's false divinity since that hadn't been revealed to me yet. I did mention my initial impression of him as resembling Jesus and a hippie. I also noted my opinions about the various police forces, their inefficiencies, and how society would benefit if they'd learn to work together.

Ron seemed unimpressed. "Tell me about the weed," he said.

"What, exactly, would you like to know?"

"Well, just *how big* was it? Was it a dime bag?"

I laughed. A dime bag of marijuana is a relatively small amount. Many people make this assumption based on the title: dime bag. It's only logical that you won't get much marijuana for ten cents, which is to say a dime. You can rarely even find a good piece of bubblegum for ten cents, and believe me, bubblegum, although it has its virtues, is not on the same level with dope. However, a dime bag doesn't actually cost a dime, that is to say ten cents. It costs ten dollars, which makes no sense. So, a dime bag is the small amount of dope that can be purchased for ten dollars. "No," I emphasized. "It was a heck of a lot bigger than a dime bag."

"Was it a quarter?"

Again, this gets confusing. A quarter, like a dime, doesn't cost a dime, that is to say, ten cents. That's only logical. It's right there in the name. But, in following the trend established with the dime, a quarter can also be presumed not to cost a quarter, that is to say, twenty-five cents. Since a dime sounds like ten cents, but actually costs ten dollars, then basic reasoning stipulates that a quarter, which sounds like twenty-five cents, should actually cost twenty-five dollars. Right? Not true. That would be far too simple. No, it costs sixty dollars, or somewhere in that neighborhood, depending on current market trends, because the term "quarter" in this instance doesn't refer to cost, but to weight, a "quarter" bag contains a quarter of an ounce of marijuana. Where the dime consists of a fixed price with a variable quantity, a quarter consists of a fixed quantity with a variable price. "No," I repeated. "It was a heck of a lot bigger than a quarter."

"So, how big was it?"

I considered the question, picturing in my head the big bag of dope. Not being an expert on the subject, I guessed: "Maybe two or three pounds." Now, two or three pounds is a term not often used in association with a bag of marijuana. It doesn't cost a dime. It also doesn't cost a quarter. In fact, it probably costs, well, a lot. The symbolism in describing the big bag of dope as being two to three pounds is very simple: it weighs *two to three pounds*. No hidden meanings. No diabolical codes. No algebraic equations requiring an advanced math degree. Two to three pounds means two to three pounds. It's a revolutionary category. It's also a heck of a lot of dope.

The look on Ron's face at the mention of this was one I'd seen many times before, usually when he and I ventured to area exotic showbars featuring naked women dancing wildly to loud music: the look of uncontrollable desire. "Wow," he said in a straightforward and somewhat childish manner. "Two to three pounds. I'd love to get my hands on that."

Ron spent the remainder of our journey in a fog, dreaming about two to three pounds of marijuana. With the smile on his lips and glazed look in his eyes, I might have thought he'd found the marijuana and smoked it. That didn't bother me until he and the cab driver began singing old *Grateful Dead* songs in a semblance of harmony that could only be appreciated while under the influence of controlled substances. It wasn't so much the singing that bothered me; it was the lack of the controlled substances.

A huge crowd surrounded the courthouse. A thousand people lined the streets, bordered by cops from at least two local agencies. I'd never seen a crowd like that without a sports event, a political discussion, or somebody being beaten to a pulp. It worried me at first, but I relaxed when I saw no one screaming, applauding, or yelling obscenities, which ruled out all three. *What*, I wondered, *are they doing here?* Expressing this to my good friend, I said, "What, I wonder, are they doing here?" After receiving no response, I added, "What do you think?"

"Two to three pounds," he replied. "Incredible." Then he and the cab driver launched into another chorus of "Uncle John's Band."

Lovely, I thought, then asked the driver to stop three blocks from the courthouse. Emerging into the crowd, I pondered the situation. I heard no music, so it wasn't a concert. There were no carnival rides, so these people hadn't shown up to witness new renovations to the County Jail, located next to the courthouse. And as far as I could tell, no gallows could be seen, which told me the mayor's records for the city budget hadn't been audited by an accounting specialist.

"Excuse me, Sir," I beckoned to an elderly gentleman dressed in something Roy Rogers might've worn in an old western. "What's happening here?"

The ancient fellow smiled. Then, with utter sincerity, he proceeded to tell me his life story from his first paddling by a grammar-school teacher to his shock when he saw a naked woman on screen at the cinema. Halfway through the sixties, I interrupted and asked, for the second time, why the crowd had gathered. "Son," he mumbled, "let me tell you something. I turned ninety-seven last Tuesday, and my momma, God rest her soul—she was a good woman, kindest lady ever to walk the Earth—well, she'd be so proud if she were here. Of course, she's not. She's in Phoenix, Arizona, in the family cemetery. Not old Forest Lawn, where pop's buried, mind you, that filthy bum. The family cemetery's where I'll be one day too, though no time soon, you hear. Well, I thought that's where I'd end up, but now, who's to say? I'm not sure what'll happen. I don't know where to begin." Beginning didn't seem to be his problem.

"Yes," I said, "but why are you *here*?"

His ancient eyes turned cold, and he belched at me, "Christ!"

Offended, I turned away and moved farther into the crowd. I next spoke to a skinny brunette wearing a university sweatshirt. "Excuse me, could you tell me what's going on?"

She gave me the coldest, most sinister glare. She grunted, "I'm a lesbian," and sped away.

I stood immobilized, thinking, My God, what's wrong with these people?

When I regained my composure, I approached—more cautiously this time—two college boys in fraternity sweatshirts, one with Greek letters indicating Lambda Chi Alpha, and the other with Alpha Sigma Phi. As an Alpha Sig alumnus, I felt confident about approaching these two. "Excuse me. I'm trying to find out what's going on."

"Well, all right!" the Alpha Sig screamed, too intoxicated to be anything but friendly. "It's the craziest thing. You wouldn't believe it."

"Yeah," the Lambda Chi jumped in. "We saw it on the news. They've got the cast down here, and they're really gonna do it."

"Do what?" I asked. "And who are they?"

"Big-time producers," the Alpha Sig said.

The Lambda Chi added, "Perform *Jesus Christ Superstar* right here, with the guys from Metallica playing the songs and Axl Rose playing Jesus."

I shook my head in disbelief.

"It's not Axl, you idiot," the Alpha Sig corrected. "It's Hank. He's the star."

"Hey, Man, I saw it on the news."

"No way. I was listening to the rock station in my car, and they said Hank."

"I'm telling you...."

I escaped deeper into the crowd. "*Jesus Christ Superstar*," I mumbled to myself. "Not a chance." But what else did I have to go on?

Next, I spoke to a conservative-looking gentleman in a black suit. He wore a pensive expression on his long, pasty face. I'd already opened my mouth to speak before I recognized him as Billy Joe Plymale, director of Plymale Mortuary, the city's newest funeral home. Taking a different approach, I said, "What time does the show begin?"

"Show?"

"Isn't this...?"

"Oh, I see. I guess it'll be soon enough."

"So, I'm in the right place?"

"If you look at it that way."

"Why did they decide to have this here?"

"How the hell should I know?" he roared. "The powers that be, Son! Haven't you heard the old saying, 'The Lord works in strange and mysterious ways?'"

"I guess so."

"Yeah," he said. "It's so."

"You don't sound happy about it."

"Happy! I'm sick to my stomach. This could be terrible for business. All the dead coming back to life! Who'll need a mortuary? And I've still got eighteen years left on the mortgage."

As I scurried deeper into the crowd, I understood the harsh reality: everyone here was nuts. Over my shoulder, I still heard Plymale moaning about immortality and other problems with the economics of funereal demand. I thought, *God help me. This place is full of lunatics.* And that reminded me of Ron, who'd disappeared during my failed quest for enlightenment.

I found him in the depths of the crowd, talking to a svelte young blonde who I soon learned worked as a reporter for Huntington's primary newspaper. Her name was Kirri Cooley. She'd been sent to get the scoop. Kirri joined the newspaper staff only three days ago. She possessed a warm, friendly smile and almost no experience. She wasn't ready to deal with this madness, let alone the advances of my musician friend.

It didn't surprise me that the editors of Huntington's primary newspaper had sent the newest cub reporter to cover what may have been the most significant story of the year. It happened to me, too. Several years ago, while still a student, I signed on as a part-time reporter. On day one, I interviewed drunks, psychopaths, vagrants, prostitutes, drug dealers, and the current county sheriff, who I offended personally with questions about this annoying double murder I'd been assigned to cover. I ran around, gathering info on two dead drug dealers, and after each interview, I returned to the newsroom to update the editors, drink coffee, and scream, "Stop the presses!" in a loud and annoying manner which made my colleagues want to beat me senseless with a pica ruler.

I explained this to my new reporter friend in an attempt to make her feel more at ease. Her pleasant smile brightened as she heard it, and it gave us a delightful form of empathy as I asked Kirri what she knew about the situation.

"Well, let's see," she said, staring down at the long, white notebook supplied by the newspaper. "I have two people claiming it's a rock concert, one saying it's Soul Asylum, and one saying it's Elvis Presley. The fact that Elvis is not among the living didn't seem to phase this guy. Hmm, here's one lady saying it's an old-fashioned revival, and another saying it's a carnival. Four guys said it's got something to do with gay rights, and two women claimed the cast members of a daytime soap opera are here to sign autographs."

"Amazing," I muttered.

"That's not the worst of it. I think this city's gone crazy. I've got a bunch of people claiming they've come to see God, and there's apparently some lunatic priest telling everybody he spent time in jail with Christ himself, and that the son of God is about to be arraigned on drug charges. Isn't that a laugh?"

It wasn't. The truth hung naked before me like a fat, ugly baby at birth, and I felt as if the family doctor, while giving the infant its traditional slap, had missed and clipped me in the jaw. I guessed the truth: some imbeciles in this crowd thought our transient main character was a dope-fiend reincarnation of Jesus. "Come with me," I urged my companions. "We've got to straighten this out."

Kirri smiled at the idea of someone leading her through this journey into the collective consciousness of a confused society. Still, she hesitated. "Where are we going?"

I opened my mouth to reply, but Ron interrupted me, his face alight with a goofy grin. "We're going to get a big bag of dope," he said. Then, as if caught up in the religious fervor of the moment, he exclaimed, "Praise Jesus."

Kirri almost lost control. Her fist clenched around her pen. "You're mad," she said.

I tried to explain, but Ron refused to let me finish a sentence. It went like this:

Yours truly: "I think you misunderstand...."

Ron: "Come on, Man. Let's find the stuff."

Yours truly: "No, wait a minute. I'm...."

Ron: "Do it later. Let's go."

Yours truly: "Now, listen *you*...."

Ron: "Put a sock in it. We're wasting too much time."

Yours truly: "Ron...."

Ron: "Hodge...."

Yours truly: "Ron...."

Ron: "Hodge...."

Yours truly: "Oh, for the love of God...."

Ron: "Exactly. Now, let's go."

Kirri: "I think I'll see you guys later."

Yours truly: "No, wait...."

Ron: "Leave her be, Hodge. She's too stuck up for us anyway. Besides, we can divide up her share. More for us."

I came within a moment's hesitation of slugging my companion and destroying our friendship forever—or at least for a couple of weeks until

I could buy him a beer and make amends. The only thing to prevent such a violent outburst was that Kirri beat me to it. She struck Ron full-force on the lips. The blow shocked all three of us, and though it did no actual damage to Ron's swollen head, it made him keep quiet.

"Good shot," I said. "Where'd you learn to slug like that?"

"Chicago," she said, "where even the nice guys have attitude problems."

"Remind me never to upset you."

"Sure, and remind me never to treat your head like my ex-boyfriend."

"Fair enough," I said, ignoring the suggestion.

"Fair enough," she replied.

"Ouch," Ron finally agreed.

As I explained my story in a rapid, frantic venture through the recent past, it pleased me to watch Kirri take detailed notes, paying attention to my every word and thought. I have to say, it pleased me more that neither she nor Ron sang Grateful Dead songs.

The three of us went on a brief excursion through the crowd and toward the courthouse entrance. It was rough going. No one wanted to let us pass. We'd spot a hole and, within seconds of our moving toward it, it was closed off by a big man in a Hawaiian shirt, a group of teenagers improperly imbibing alcohol at an early age, a bunch of blue-haired women discussing make-up techniques, or a six-foot-tall yellow fish with bulging, green eyes and a touch of orange tinting around the gills. This last one bothered me at first, not because it was such an unusual character to encounter, but because it kept shouting "Tuna! Tuna!" at the crowd as if searching for its lost true love. Later, we discovered that it really wasn't a giant yellow fish at all, but actually, a short man in a leftover Halloween costume who, though he didn't believe in Jesus, nonetheless decided to take advantage of His reappearance, or lack thereof, by selling tuna salad sandwiches to the crowd. Anyway, as we passed the fish, I spotted an opportunity for us to get through. It was a straight run over the courthouse lawn and up the steps.

"Hold it right there!"

We turned, startled, to see a demented blue centaur trotting toward us at a moderate pace which easily cleared the crowd. "Where you think you're going?" it roared at us.

"Into the courthouse," I muttered, but the creature shoved my words aside.

"You should reconsider." A glint of metal caught my eye. I recognized a Huntington cop's badge. He was an officer with HPD's Mounted Patrol Unit, a much more believable thing to see than a blue centaur, though just as absurd and nearly as out of date. "What you're doing's against the rules," the ex-blue centaur continued. "Can't allow you to break the rules."

"Rules?" Ron exclaimed. "What rules?"

The officer, whose name tag read Albert G. Pinkerwhig, answered, "There's an ordinance against what you're doing. If you persist, I'll cite you for it."

Ron attempted to speak up—belligerently, if I know him—but I silenced him with a hand on his shoulder before he could get us in to further trouble. I understood: the mounted patrol had been instructed to keep people out of the courthouse, perhaps to prevent a riot. But I needed to get inside. Calmly, I explained the situation, leaving out all references to police incompetence. "Sir," I said, "I have to see the magistrate. I'm a material witness in one of the pending cases."

Pinkerwhig replied, "Interesting, but none of my concern. I'm here to enforce the rules."

"But I...." I'd found myself in this situation once before. "Listen, I have to get in there."

He smiled and said, "So, go."

I turned toward the looming courthouse.

"Stop!" Pinkerwhig belched. "I warned you. If you do that again, I'll cite you."

"Now wait a minute," Ron began.

I stopped him again. "Now wait a minute," I said. "You just told us we could go. So, why stop us? That's harassment."

Then he said the most amazing thing which, in its simple brilliance, made me feel like a dolt: "Because you're walking on the grass."

"Hold on," said Kirri. "You're not trying to keep us out of the Courthouse?"

The ex-blue centaur replied, "Why on God's green earth would I want to do that? It's every citizen's right to enter the courthouse when it's open. That includes today, though devil knows why. I just can't allow you to ruin the lawn by marching across it like a bunch of hoodlums."

"What about the people out here in the crowd?" I asked.

"What about them?"

"Aren't you keeping them out?"

"Heck no. If they want to go in, they're welcome, so long as they don't trample the lawn."

"Amazing," Ron sighed.

To which I added, "Unbelievable."

Kirri asked, "If you're not keeping them out, why haven't they all gone inside?"

"Maybe they ain't so sure why they're here, or maybe they're waiting for a sign. Either way, it's none of my business."

"And why *are* they here?" I said.

Officer Pinkerwhig again responded with words of such divine wisdom that I've rarely seen their equal. With honesty, warmth, and sincerity, he said, "To make my life difficult."

Let's get back to our sometime main character and unwilling prophet who, it seems, I've neglected for a long time.

Jim Jarred, Porter Franklin, and our main character were escorted from the Jail to the courthouse at 8:30 a.m. for an impromptu arraignment—a tradition during football season. Magistrate B.K. "Binky" Bryarson loved to watch the university football team play. He also loved to improperly imbibe alcohol before, during, and immediately after each game. He probably would be arrested often for some improper-imbibing crime were he not the magistrate on duty and unable to arraign himself. Binky always hoped for no arrests on game day. Should one come about, he called in sick, scheduling the arraignment for Sunday morning before church, or rather, before professional football came on TV.

The Sunday arraignment had two unusual effects. First, it gave the assistant prosecutor extra time to review the case. Second, it forced Binky to preside with an intense hangover—that is, a headache, stomach pain, and/or dizziness, caused by imbibing too much alcohol, whether properly or improperly. This often resulted in a high bond being set for offenders cruel enough to commit a crime on game day, or a severe tongue-lashing for any prosecutor foolish enough to bring unfounded charges against an innocent man.

The doctor went before Binky at about 9:45 a.m., three-quarters of an hour later than planned. First, the assistant prosecutor offered him a plea deal. One might say our main character was led into the courthouse to be tempted by the assistant prosecutor.

Dirk Slaterman was in a bit of a bind. He'd been an assistant prosecutor for two months, and already he knew better than to risk Binky's wrath by going into a Sunday arraignment with little or no case. On this Sunday, he had nothing. The arraignment on misdemeanor charges against the two alleged improper driving imbibers would be easy, but not enough to satisfy Judge Binky's appetite for revenge after being forced from a comfortable bed. A felony charge of Possession of a Controlled Substance with Intent to Distribute against an obviously-deranged weirdo wearing dirty rags and smelling of other people's garbage would be just the thing. He had one problem: no case. Nada. So, the assistant prosecutor took Doc aside to threaten him, coerce him, and hopefully trick him into a highly-unusual pre-arraignment plea deal. That way, Slaterman could spare himself from Binky's disapproving glare.

Of course, Slaterman didn't know about the religious mix-up.

Benny "Skeeter" Deter seemed almost as absurd to look at as a giant yellow fish or an ex-blue centaur, with the primary difference being that Skeeter Deter actually existed. Like dandy Dirk Slaterman, his counterpart, Deter was a rookie attorney, eight months out of law school and five months past the bar exam. Unlike Slaterman, though, Deter didn't care the slightest bit about incurring Judge Binky's wrath. In fact, he didn't care much about anything except clients, which he got a lot of, and women, which he didn't. Deter served as a public defender, a traditional post for an aspiring young trial lawyer. He liked the job and won an average of forty percent of his cases—a high number for a 26-year-old rookie. The thing is, he had little or no respect for the traditions of the court. Many was the time he could be seen in one of the courtrooms with his feet propped up on the defense table, which might not have been so bad if it weren't for the fact that he never wore socks and often came clad in beat-up sandals or scuffed leather loafers. The rest of his outfit consisted of faded blue jeans and a wrinkled white dress shirt covered by the same dirt-brown sports coat with patches on the elbows. Sometimes he wore a tie, but it rarely helped his appearance. Aside from his manner of dress, Deter wore his hair slicked back with gallons of grease, his skin soaked with similar amounts of Brut-33 or Old Spice. Worse, it was a good bet that the first time you saw him, he'd have his hands up at his mouth as he gnawed wildly on his fingernails.

His courtroom presence came across as even more outrageous. He liked to stand on tables, shaking like a preacher. Sometimes he made motions by saying, "Hey, now listen here," and his on occasion objections began with, "That's a load of crap." He once chided a prosecutor—not Slaterman, but the big cheese himself—by saying, "Does your mother know you lie like that?" Just a week before the events of this story, he requested a mistrial on the grounds that "This jury doesn't have the brains God gave a golf ball, though at least a ball could be excused since it gets smacked around so much." For the most part, Deter refused to say, "Your Honor," or even, "Judge." Instead, he referred to Circuit Judge J.D. Munoz as "Bubba," and Magistrate Liz Lolane as either "Lizzie" or just plain "Lady." In addition, he personally dubbed B.K. Bryarson with the title "Binky," a moniker Skeeter said, "means nothing to someone dumber than dirt like him." Deter turned out to be a wonderful freak of nature in the courtroom sideshow of the religious circus I'm in the process of describing—as always, badly.

Doc sat in the assistant prosecutor's office twiddling his thumbs and humming.

And the tempter came to him, saying, "If you're really innocent, maybe we can make this trial disappear."

Doc replied, "A man need not worry about the judgments of others."

"Get off your high horse, old man. You're a major drug dealer. I know it, Skeeter knows it…" Skeeter Deter nodded in agreement. "…and any jury on the face of this planet's gonna know it. I'm offering you a chance to save us all some trouble and save yourself some grief."

To which the doctor replied, "Under your law, a man's innocent until proven guilty. Under another law, I'll be innocent even then."

"Now listen, John," Slaterman badgered. Incidentally, he called our main character John, referring to John Doe, which is a name used to describe anyone whose name is not known and cannot be determined immediately, though such people are usually dead at the time. He called the doctor John because that was the name on the court docket, not even suspecting it might not be real. It was another classic case of mistaken identity of our main character's mistaken identity. "This isn't getting us anywhere. Here's what I'm offering you. You plead guilty to the felony, and I'll ask for one year. What do you think?"

"If I were what you say," the doctor said, "I'd take your offer. You seem a generous sort. But trust me, I can't be tempted."

Skeeter Deter laughed. "I like this guy," he joked. "He reminds me of Jesus. So tell me, Jesus, what kind of deal will you accept?" It was in rather poor taste, but at least he correctly identified our main character's mistaken identity.

Doc didn't flinch at being called Jesus any more than he had at being called John. "There are no deals with truth. I'll accept only vindication."

"A misdemeanor," the tempter blurted out. "You want a misdemeanor?" He paused to consider the implications. "All right, all right. I'll give you possession, with three months."

"Suspended sentence," Skeeter threw in.

"No chance," Slaterman responded, changing his mind immediately. "Fine, a misdemeanor with a three-month suspended sentence pending a year's probation."

"Take it, Jesus," said the public defender. "Best offer you'll get, short of bribery." He hesitated. "Now there's an idea. Off scot-free, Dirkie boy—how much?"

Slaterman winced but didn't respond, "There's the deal, John. Take it or leave it."

"I'm innocent."

"Christ," the tempter screamed.

The defender jumped in, saying, "That's Mister Christ to you, Dirkie boy. Show some respect, or I'll have you charged with harassment."

The assistant prosecutor moaned in apparent agony. "Fine," he said. "Fine and dandy. Really. Whatever you want. I'll tell you what, if you say you're not guilty that's great. I'll drop the charge, and you can plead guilty to jaywalking. That's crossing the street in the wrong place to you,

Skeeter, since I know you don't understand fancy legal terms."

Deter snarled. "Penalty?"

"Slap on the wrist. A forty dollar fine, suspended based on time served."

"Well?" said Deter, turning to our main character.

"Well?" said Slaterman.

"I always cross at the light."

The assistant prosecutor threw his files onto the floor and stormed out of his own office, disappearing in the puff of smoke which poured from his ears.

Skeeter Deter laughed, long and loud this time. He stopped just long enough to say, "What a jerk. I've never seen him so flustered before."

Doc replied, "Oh, dear. I hope I haven't offended him."

We ran into Regis as we stepped off the elevator into the basement, where the courtrooms were. I recognized him from his headshot in Huntington's primary newspaper. The small photo appeared many times before his church burned down. It always made Regis resemble my mental image of what a teenage anime cowboy might look like, rather than an elderly priest.

I should point out that this sort of thing used to happen a lot at Huntington's primary newspaper because of the paper's aging printing press. What happened to Regis happened to me, too. I'll never forget the photo that ran when I tried my luck as a political columnist. Instead of my charming face, complete with stern, logical eyes, and tight, cynical grin, the square with my name under it contained a small, black space with a white spot the size of a thumbnail in the center. It made me look very much like a cheap lightbulb, already a bit dim—which is also the way many people described my column.

Anyway, I recognized Regis from his photo. Still, that didn't make me want to stop and talk. It was the preacher who accosted us. "Have you come to see the Lord?" Behind him stood a cameraman from a local television station, his camera on and directed at us.

To avoid an embarrassing scene, I said, "We're here to get a friend out of jail."

The Reverend's face drooped, and the cameraman lowered his tool. We were the first to make it this far, and our lack of interest frustrated the two. Trying to salvage some kind of story, the cameraman aimed at me again and asked, "What did he do?"

"He didn't do anything," I explained. "He's innocent."

To which my bumbling friend Ron added, "He found a big bag of dope."

"You *have* come to see the Lord," said Regis.

"No," I countered, leading my associates away. "Sorry. Just helping a friend."

"Yes," shrieked the ex-minister. "The Lord's everyone's friend!" He said this with such authority and self-confidence that it almost made me think I was talking to our main character, except that Doc didn't resemble either a teenage anime cowboy or an elderly priest—which is good since he's already had enough problems with his mistaken identity.

Kirri spoke up at this point, identifying herself as a reporter and asking the obvious question: "This has something to do with the crowd, doesn't it?"

"Crowd?" said Regis.

"What crowd?" said the cameraman, whose name I knew to be Joel Lee.

Before I could respond, a deputy led our main character to the courtroom, along with Jarred and Franklin, followed by Skeeter Deter.

"There he is," shouted Regis. "That's Him! That's our Lord!"

Lee panned the camera around for what he believed would be his award-winning shot of "Christ walking to Judgment Day." Kirri readied her notebook. Both sprinted down the hall, giving chase.

"That's him," Regis said, looking at me. "That's our Lord." Then he, too, gave chase.

"Wow," said Ron. "He really does look like old J.C."

I mumbled something to the effect of, "Yeah, well, maybe."

Ron amazed me with his knowledge of religion, saying, "I hope he really is the Old Guy because all hell's about to break loose." I was stunned, shocked, dumbfounded. But only for a second. Ron shrugged and added with sincerity, "I wonder if he's got any more dope."

"If you ever try anything like this again," the judge raved, "I'll have you thrown in jail for two weeks for contempt of court. And if that's not enough, I'll have you whipped in public. You understand?" Everyone in the courtroom should've suffered Binky's wrath. Only one person did. The judge's threats weren't directed at our main character, who not only wasn't Jesus but who furthermore hadn't done anything even the slightest bit contemptible. The harsh words also weren't directed at the Reverend Jonathan Regis, who'd twice interrupted the proceedings by shouting something to the effect of "Release the son of God!" The words weren't directed at Kirri the cub reporter, cameraman Joel Lee, or either of the criminal driving imbibers. They weren't directed at me for politely suggesting that our main character was innocent, and in fact, nothing more than a victim of police incompetence, which the officers themselves helped verify. They weren't directed at my friend Ron, who'd run screaming out of the courtroom after the officers had proven this about themselves. The judge's threats weren't directed at Skeeter Deter who called him Binky and demanded the case be dismissed before lunchtime so the cops could go grab a free meal at the homeless shelter. No, they all went to Dirk Slaterman, the hapless assistant prosecutor. Slaterman took it like a man, though groveling for mercy might've made a more favorable impression on the judge. Here's what happened:

"Bond is set at two hundred dollars a piece," said Binky with regard to the two improperly imbibing drivers. Each lowered his head as Skeeter Deter directed them to the back of the courtroom. A sheriff's deputy waited there to escort the pair back to the County Jail. "Next case. Hurry it up."

"State versus John Doe," Slaterman moaned.

To which the public defender replied, "Yeah, whatever," as he leaned back in his chair and propped his feet on the table.

The judge glanced at Skeeter Deter and then toward Slaterman. "What's the charge?"

"Uhm, it's, well...."

"There's no charge, Binky," said Deter. "This one's free. Let's go home."

Binky ignored him.

Slaterman continued his masterful soliloquy. "The charge is, well, it's possession of, uhm, a controlled substance with, well, uhm, ah, with intent to, ehr, to deliver."

"Good," said Binky, making fun of the nitwit before him. "It's, ah, uh, well, uhm, a felony. So let's, uhm, ah, well, get on with it. Shall we?"

In all the confusion thereafter, I lost track of some of the events that took place. Although I'm not entirely certain, I believe this is the point where I jumped up and proclaimed the doctor's innocence, while at the same time, describing the arresting officers as idiots. I did this in the most direct and simple manner I could think of. "He's innocent," I yelled. "They're idiots."

All eyes turned toward me, including the cyclopean lens of Joel Lee's camera.

This is pure speculation, but I think Judge Binky would've yelled at me for my outcry had the public defender not intervened, declaring, "Well I'll be a possum's penis. That's exactly what I was going to say." To prove it, he held up a yellow notepad on which were written the words, *He's innocent. They're idiots.*

With the exception of Slaterman, the two officers, and our main character himself, everyone in the courtroom laughed. Binky slammed his gavel on the bench to encourage silence, but his attempt failed as he too let out a few gasps and chortles.

"Your Honor, please," Slaterman begged, "can we get on with this case?"

"Why certainly," said Binky. "And it'd better be a good one, too."

Slaterman swallowed self-consciously.

I almost spoke again but decided against it. Instead, I slumped back in my seat.

Besides, it was someone else's turn to interrupt the proceedings. "Release this man," shouted Regis. "He's the son of God."

Smiling, Skeeter Deter responded by holding up his yellow notepad again, chiding, "Nope, I wasn't about to say that."

Again came the laughter.

"Now wait a minute," Binky began.

"Hey, now," said the assistant prosecutor.

But Regis wouldn't be upstaged. "Do you laugh at the one who brings laughter into the world? Do you judge the one who judges? Do you know more than the one who knows all?"

To which Skeeter Deter replied, "Oh, bullpoopy."

On top of which, the judge added, "My sentiments exactly."

"You dare to…."

"Yes, I dare," the judge bellowed. "Now sit down and shut up before I get upset."

"Go on and throw your gavel at him, Binky," Skeeter antagonized in a tone which led me to believe he'd made a request, rather than a joke.

"But…," said Regis.

"No buts about it," said Binky. "Sit down and shut up!"

"But…."

"Do you have to be forcibly retrained?"

"But…."

"Well?"

"But…." He sat down, pouting like a child.

Binky smiled cynically. "Much better. Now, I hope there won't be any further outbursts from the crowd. After all, this is not an open forum."

As soon as the words were out of Binky's mouth, the proceedings were interrupted again, this time by our inexperienced cub reporter. She stood up, pointed a pen at the judge, and said, "Excuse me, Your Honor. Kirri Cooley with Huntington's primary newspaper. What exactly is the case against Mister Christ, I mean Mister Doe…"

"Doc," I whispered, not wanting to leave her out in the cold.

"…ehr, Mister Doctor?"

Binky sighed. "Young lady," he said, "if you'll sit down, perhaps we'll find out."

She blushed, a sign of understanding, then glanced at me as if to say, *This is all your fault.*

I shrugged and turned to watch the public defender speak.

Skeeter Deter removed his unsocked feet from the defense table and forced himself to stand. "Binky," he said, "I submit to you respectfully that this is a load of crap. Interruptions aside, my client spent a night in jail without having committed a crime. Please, I beg you, either let him go free or make that imbecile for the prosecution produce some evidence. But one way or the other, Binky, can we get on with it? I really need to go to the bathroom."

Binky smiled against his will. "I think that merits a five-minute recess," he joked. "And when we come back, I'm gonna bust some heads."

Deter smiled. Kirri smiled. Slaterman groaned. I took in a deep breath. And in front of me, I heard the doctor mumble these words: "I hope no one gets hurt."

During the intermission, I heard a couple things which, although they have no relevance to this story, are worth mentioning. First, I caught a voice I couldn't identify—perhaps Deputy Micheaux's, perhaps Kirri's, perhaps even the assistant prosecutor's, though in an effeminate way—responding to a question I didn't hear with the statement: "Yeah, I love my job, but I wish I'd get shot so I could collect benefits." The other thing, Skeeter Deter returned to the courtroom, still fiddling with his fly stuck halfway up. "That was refreshing," he bragged. "That's the best minute I've ever spent with my pants around my ankles."

When the judge returned to the bench, he directed everyone to sit. Then he exclaimed, "Let's get this done and gone. I'd like to be home for the first football game."

To which Skeeter Deter replied, "Oh Lord, please help us."

Maybe I imagined it, but I could swear I heard a voice say, "No."

"After accusations of police incompetence in this case," Binky directed in his stern, official tone, "I think we should hear from the arresting officer. Will he or she please step forward?"

Deputy Micheaux approached the judge, as did Officer Dollie.

"Well," Binky prodded, "which of you is it?"

"I am," they said.

Seeing the confusion on the judge's face, Skeeter Deter, scoffed, "Whoa there, Binky. Before this becomes a joke, that goof-off should explain the mix-up." He pointed at Slaterman.

Binky faced the assistant prosecutor. "A marvelous idea," he said.

Slaterman lowered his head, acting as if he were studying a piece of paper. "Her, well...."

"Spit it out, Counselor."

"Uhm, well, it seems that there's a dispute between the sheriff's office and police department regarding who gets the arrest. Something about official crime-deterrence statistics."

"I beg your pardon. What does that mean exactly?"

"It seems that, well, both Patrolman Dollie and Deputy Micheaux…" He pronounced it Mitchee-axe. "…responded to an anonymous tip near the university at about the same time."

"All right, we're getting somewhere. Now repeat that in a way we can all understand."

"There was a dispute over who had jurisdiction, so they both arrested him."

"And who did have jurisdiction?"

"I did," replied each of the cops.

"Wonderful," Binky said sarcastically. "This makes things much simpler. You know, I've determined that whoever said you two idiots are idiots was one hundred percent correct. Now, if you don't start making sense, I'm gonna personally call each of your bosses and have you busted down to filing paperwork in a bathroom stall."

"That's telling'em, Binky, old boy," Deter applauded. "Now dismiss this case so these two idiots can go over to the homeless shelter and get the free lunch they've so clearly earned."

Binky ignored the comment. "Okay. Let's see. This man was found with a large bag of what is presumed to be marijuana. Has this been confirmed?"

The officers lowered their heads, neither wanting to answer.

"Well?" After no response, he turned to the assistant prosecutor. "Slaterman, there'd better be a good explanation for this, or you won't even get the honorable privilege of toilet duty."

The assistant prosecutor gulped loudly. "No tests have been done."

"Why, exactly, is that?"

"Well, ehr, well, you see, well, because…." His voice trailed off.

"Could you repeat that, Mister Slaterman? We'd like to share your wisdom."

"Uhm, I said no tests were done because the marijuana…." The rest, again, came out as a confused mumbling sound.

"One more time, Mister Slaterman."

This is the point in my continuing trial coverage where several people gasped in disbelief, several others twittered with laughter, and my dear friend Ron jumped up in a near frenzy and rushed from the room shouting, "It still might be out there!" And it was caused by Slaterman's response, which he finally managed: "The marijuana wasn't brought in as evidence."

It took a lot of shouting before the courtroom regained some semblance of order. During that time, there were many memorable quotes. Here are just a few:

Skeeter Deter to Dirk Slaterman: "You bozo. Why not charge him with murder since you don't have a body either?" Also: "Where I come from, we'd have you dragged out in the streets and beaten to death with your own briefcase. And that's before we'd shoot you."

Kirri Cooley to me: "Does this sort of thing happen often? If so, I might start dealing drugs."

Deputy Micheaux to Binky: "It was his fault. It was his arrest."

Officer Dollie to Binky: "It was her fault. It was her arrest."

Dirk Slaterman to nobody: "It's not my fault. I didn't make the arrest."

Skeeter Deter to Dirk Slaterman again: "Shut up, Bonehead."

Kirri Cooley to Joel Lee: "Are you filming this for news or blackmail?"

Joel Lee's response: "I keep my options open."

Our main character, apparently to himself: "Yes, I always cross at the light."

Jonathan Regis to everybody, or maybe to himself: "I knew our Lord wouldn't sell drugs." Also: "Get thee behind me, Satan." Or maybe it was: "Get thee behind me, Slaterman."

Skeeter Deter to both cops: "Nice day, isn't it? So, where'd y'all drop out of grade school?"

And finally, Binky to everyone: "Shut up, or I'll have you all hanged!"

"Your Honor," Deter said with pseudo-sincerity, "I'd like to make a motion that you dismiss this case and have the assistant prosecutor put to death instead."

Binky, whose face had become so flushed it resembled a watermelon with the shell peeled off, appeared to consider the motion. "In a minute. First, I want some answers." He pointed at Officer Dollie who played nervously with the safety switch on his gun. "Let's start with you."

Dollie flinched as though a large grain of sand—perhaps Mount Fuji—had lodged itself in his right eye. "Well, it's like this. I didn't take the old guy in. Tera and I sort of compromised."

"What was your part of this…" Binky paused, snarling. "…compromise?"

Dollie perked up, showing his bravery. "Why, Your Honor, I brought in that filthy old drunk."

"What drunk?"

"Why that guy there." He flashed a finger in my direction, making me slink back in my chair.

Binky moaned through twisted lips, "I think you'd better explain yourself."

"He was a mean one, that's for sure, yelling and screaming and covering up for his friend. For a moment, I actually thought he might attack me."

"That's not true!" I spat, jumping from my seat. "I had four guns pointed at me."

Binky glared in my direction. "Sit down," he bellowed. "I'll deal with you in a minute."

The only thing I managed was the word "Sorry" as I sat down.

Binky shook his head in disgust. Then he turned to Deputy Micheaux. "Is it correct you, in fact, brought Mister Doe in?"

"That's correct."

"And you did see a large package of marijuana in his possession?"

"That's correct."

Binky sighed. "Then why in God's name didn't you bring it in for evidence?"

"Well, Sir...."

"Yes?"

"Well...."

"I'm waiting."

"It was the cans." She said it with a rush of air as if she herself were exhaling the smoke from a bit of dope. "It was all because of the cans."

"What cans?"

"The old guy's cans. Pop cans. Beer cans. You know, stuff like that."

"Hold on. Am I to understand he had marijuana stuffed in soft-drink cans?"

"No, he had a big bag of cans..." As a side note, while a big bag of marijuana is worth quite a bit of money, a big bag of cans is worth little—in this case, probably fifty cents to a dollar. If someone were to come up with a drug-style naming system for aluminum cans, I think it's safe to say that a dime bag would actually be worth a dime, that is to say, ten cents, and a quarter bag would actually be worth a quarter, that is, twenty-five cents. "...he collected from dumpsters."

The expression on the judge's face made him resemble a kernel of corn in the instant before it pops. "Now wait a second," he said. "Let's try to figure this out logically. Pretend for one moment that you're an intelligent person. All right?"

"I guess so," replied the deputy.

"Good. Now speculate for me as to exactly why Mister Doe might be digging through dumpsters for aluminum cans. Will you do that?"

"Planned to recycle them, I suppose."

"I see. Now, if you'll allow me to presume that he's not doing it because he wants to save the environment, then tell me, why would he want to recycle a bunch of aluminum cans?"

"To earn some money, I reckon."

"You reckon? Well, just how much money do you reckon a person might make by recycling aluminum cans collected from other people's garbage?"

"Don't know, but I think it's about fifty cents a pound."

This time, Binky grinned. "Tell me, Tera, why would a big-time drug dealer with a large quantity of marijuana worth a lot of money go to all the trouble of digging through trash bins for cans that might net him fifty cents a pound?"

She shrugged.

Binky sighed. "I don't know how you got this job, Tera. It's clear you'd be more qualified for something where thinking isn't required."

Her face reddened, but she said nothing.

"Anyway, let's get back to those cans. You told me the reason there's no marijuana for evidence has something to do with this mysterious can collection. Could you explain?"

She mumbled, "It's like this. When I was arresting the old man, he demanded I take his cans with me. They were his personal property, he said. He made it clear that if I didn't bring his cans, he might be likely to cause a stir, which I felt would be unnecessary."

"So?"

"So, I picked up the bag of cans and stuffed it in the trunk of my squad car."

"And?"

"I forgot to get the drugs."

"I see." Binky frowned, moaning at what might've been the onset of a painful peptic ulcer.

"It was all part of his plan, if you ask me."

Binky glared at her. "Tera, get out."

"Sorry, what?"

"Get out of my courtroom. Go away. Get out. Now!"

She looked shocked.

"Go on," he demanded. "You too, Dollie. March."

The cops glanced at each other, looking for support. Neither found it.

"Move it," the judge bellowed. "And pray you never see me again!" After a few moments of confusion as the two cops removed themselves, Binky finally turned his attention to me. He asked me my name and directed me to explain my part in this crazy scene.

Pleased to be able to speak without being told to sit down and shut up, I stood and proudly told my story from beginning to end, emphasizing once again the incompetence of the police officers, the innocence of our main character, and my theory about how the various law enforcement agencies might perform their duties better if they'd get over their differences and work together. I said all this and much more, seemingly without taking a breath.

Hearing the great depth and profundity of my testimony, Binky waved an approving finger at me and said with what I presumed to be total agreement, "Sit down and shut up!" Then he turned to Regis. "And what's your story?"

Regis jumped to his feet and spat forth a lengthy sermon about hellfire and brimstone, along with more gibberish about the son of God not selling drugs.

"I see," said the judge. "So, it's safe to presume you know the defendant?"

"Know him? I've worshiped him all my life." Regis paused before adding as an afterthought, "We spent the night together in jail."

Binky frowned. "I see," he said, quoting himself. "And how did *you* get out of jail?" His expression changed to a malicious smile. "Please tell me you escaped so I can have my bailiff shoot you." He nodded toward the ancient relic of a man standing in a corner, dressed in the official uniform of the Cabell County Sheriff's Department as issued in 1948. Until the judge mentioned him, I hadn't even noticed the bailiff. I vaguely recalled seeing his outline in my peripheral vision, but I'd written it off as an odd decoration.

In response, the bailiff, whose name I never learned, appeared to flinch, though it might've been a trick of the light.

"I called some friends," Regis said, unbothered by the threat. "When I said our Lord had returned, they were happy to chip in for my bail. First thing I did after being released was to call all the local television stations. I told them all about Christ's return."

"You didn't!"

"I did. We can't hoard the Lord's time all to ourselves. He has to be shared."

"No," Binky moaned, rubbing his temples with the palms of his hands. Then, with frustration, Binky directed his attention to poor Dirk Slaterman. I need not describe that. I'm sure it can be imagined by splicing expletives together while inserting the words 'you,' 'worthless,' and 'firing squad.'

"Mister Doe," the judge said in a kindly voice, "It seems there's been a terrible error here. I hope you won't lose faith in our legal system."

Rising to respond, the doctor let out a sigh. "Am I free to go?"

"Yes, you're free."

"Am I cleared of all charges against me, including jaywalking?"

The judge squinted, confused, but said, "Your case is dismissed."

Our main character smiled. "Seems to me the legal system worked. I'm innocent, I'm free, and I've made new friends. What more could I ask for in a criminal proceeding?"

"I like your attitude, Mister Doe," the judge said.

Cynically, Regis whined, "Well, he is our Lord and Savior, after all."

"No, he's not!" I shouted.

"No, I'm not," our main character seemed to sigh.

"You're mad," Deter chided. "You're popping the boils on my butt."

"Why do you keep saying that, Reverend?" said Kirri Cooley.

"Would all of you repeat that for the camera?" said Joel Lee.

Slaterman sobbed.

The bailiff did nothing but breathe. Well, I think he was breathing.

Doc reiterated, "I'm not who you think. I want to take my cans and get back to work."

Regis grinned like the devil. "His desires to toil and sweat for our benefit."

"No, I need to find more cans."

"And to die for our sins?" said the preacher, sounding too eager.

Our main character again failed to answer in a complete and final way. Directing his gaze at Regis, Doc frowned as he said, "I hope not. It would take an awful lot of dying."

HERE BEGINS THE CHRONICLE OF THE FALSE ORACLE

Our main character couldn't predict the future. That's not to say he wore blinders to the possibility, just that he didn't know what would happen, when, where, or to whom.

Doc, Kirri, Regis, Lee, and I stepped as a group into the warm morning sunlight. Regis and I debated the doctor's godliness or lack thereof, while Lee filmed, Kirri took notes, and our main character smiled and kept to himself. Thus there were four on hand to hear the doctor's whispered remark after seeing the crowd. His words left us with many sleepless nights as we considered their hidden meanings. He said, "Oh, my. Not again."

"You have to speak to them," I said.

Regis agreed. "Reveal your divine nature to the beguiled masses."

"No," I corrected. "Tell them to go away."

Regis replied, "You can't tell the servants of our Lord to go away. They're here to see *Him*, to praise *Him*. Maybe you should go away, heretic."

"Heretic? Why you pompous old...."

"Excuse me," Doc interrupted. "I'll talk to them if you really think I should."

"Yes," Regis and I sang in chorus.

"But what do I tell them?"

Regis said, "Tell them you've come."

I said, "Tell them to go."

Kirri, being the voice of reason, offered a better suggestion: "Why don't you just tell them whatever you feel like telling them?"

The preacher and I stared at her as if she'd taken the Holy Grail up to the cashier at McDonald's and asked for a refill. We were still flashing her the evil eye when Doc said, "Okey Dokey," and shrugged.

"It's been ages since his last speech," Regis announced from atop the courthouse steps. "Let's have a warm round of applause for our Lord and Savior, Jesus Christ."

I slapped my forehead in disgust as the front half of the crowd erupted in a mixture of laughter and amazed gasping. From the back came stranger cries: "What was that?" "Say again!" and "Fresh Tuna!" But the masses were silenced when Doc stepped forward, giving them a clear view. Sunlight covered him, producing a sort of halo. "Hello," he said. "How are you?"

"Fine," said some.

"Good," said others.

"My butt hurts, and I've got arthritis in my hands and feet," said an older lady toward the front.

Doc wasn't prepared for a healing. "That's good," he mumbled. "I'm okay, too."

"What was that?" said someone in the back.

"I'm okay, too," he restated with more authority. The crowd applauded, and it seemed to break the ice. But then Doc stood motionless.

"Go on," the minister prodded. "Talk."

Our main character turned and stared at Regis as if to imply, I've spoken to them, and they don't have any cans. He looked lost. The lines on his face, highlighted by the sun's glow, were rounded in an expression that made him look like a basset hound injured through no fault of its own while napping peacefully on the freeway. "What should I say?" he asked.

Regis closed his eyes. "I've got it. How about the sermon on the mount?"

"No," I groaned.

"The what?" Kirri questioned.

"Sermon on the mount. You know, the *New Testament*? Matthew, chapter five, verses two through, well, a lot. You remember, Jesus climbed a mountain. His disciples came to him...."

"We're not on a mountain," Doc interrupted. "We're on the courthouse steps."

"What?" said Regis, dazed.

"How can you have a sermon on the mount without a mount to have a sermon on?"

I laughed. "He's got a point."

RUNNING WILD NOVELLA ANTHOLOGY, VOLUME 3, BOOK 2

"No!" said Regis. "I'm sure the Biblical passage is just figurative. It probably refers to any elevated place, including the courthouse steps."

"No," I moaned.

"Yes." Regis motioned toward the crowd. "Go on. Enlighten them."

"No," I repeated, stuck in denial.

"If I must," the doctor said.

I sighed.

He opened his mouth and taught them. Sort of. "Blessed are the poor for theirs is the kingdom of heaven."

The crowd seemed confused. Most folks hadn't expected a sermon.

"What's next?" Doc asked.

Regis whispered, "Blessed are those that mourn…"

Doc to the crowd, "Blessed are the mourners…"

"…for they shall be comforted," added Regis.

"…for they shall be comforted," added the doctor, who turned to Regis for the next line.

The reverend looked befuddled. "The meek."

"The meek?" said the doctor.

"The meek!" said Regis.

"What about them?" said Doc.

"They're blessed," said Regis.

"Oh," said the doctor. "Timid, aren't they?"

"Yes," said Regis. "I believe that's the point."

"Not much of a blessing," said our main character.

I laughed.

"Forget it," said Regis. "We'll go on to the next one." He paused. "Blessed are they who hunger and thirst after righteousness for they shall be filled."

Our main character flinched at the last line, then turned and said, "Blessed are the hungry, the thirsty, and the right-handed, for they shall eat heartily."

Regis, unfazed, said, "Blessed are the merciful for they shall have mercy."

"Blessed are the merciful," said Doc, "for they are merciful."

Many in the crowd laughed. I laughed. Some left. I wanted to leave.

"Blessed are the pure in heart for they shall see God," Regis continued.

Doc sighed, took in a couple of breaths, then repeated the phrase. There was little emotion, so the crowd straddled the border between restlessness and boredom.

"Blessed are the peacemakers, for they shall be called the children of God."

Doc said, "Blessed are the grease makers, whose children shall be called names by God."

"Blessed are those persecuted for righteousness sake, for theirs is the kingdom of heaven."

"Blessed are the … what was it again?"

"The persecuted."

"Oh, the persecuted. They'll serve kings in heaven."

Regis groaned. "Blessed are ye who are reviled and persecuted by men who say all manner of evil against you falsely for my sake."

The old man paused. Then he rephrased the passage simply and sincerely: "You're *all* blessed," he said. "What's next?"

Regis frowned. "Rejoice and be exceeding glad, for great is your reward in heaven."

"I like that one. It's a happy little verse."

I laughed again, and this time Kirri and Lee joined me.

Not sure the cause of our outburst, Doc gave us a silly look as if to imply, *Well, it is a happy little verse, so Nyah!* Then, turning back to the diminishing audience, he said, "Rejoice and be happy." He paused before adding, "I know I'm happy."

The few hundred who remained applauded.

When the wave of good cheer crested and began to fade, Regis moaned and said, "Are you ready for the next passage?"

For some reason, it didn't surprise me when Doc shook his head. Turning back to the crowd, he said, "That's all. Go home and think for yourselves for a while."

Regis shook his head. In ten minutes, he'd seen a huge crowd diminish into a few hundred devout believers. The preacher explained later that he wondered if it was his fault or God's. "God's had PR problems since the beginning. He just doesn't communicate well with His stone tablets and symbolic plagues. Folks would rather see a well-designed newspaper ad or a television commercial with a nice jingle and scantily clad men and women."

Regis considered all this without saying a word, the whole time praying for a little help, just a touch of advice about public relations—which wouldn't be the least bit relevant if a stranger hadn't walked up to us just then: Justin Todwell Taylor, image consultant.

"How do, fellows?" said Taylor. "Dandy speech. Fine and dandy. Little dull, though. If you'd like to talk about it, maybe I can help make you into something more. Here's my card." He handed it to Doc, only to see it intercepted by Regis. "Let's have brunch, shall we?"

Taylor could best be described as polite, considerate, fashionable, charming, clean-cut, intelligent, a perfectionist, and anything else you can think of that's an annoying character trait. Aside from that, he was a rather nice guy, the kind of man who'd send you a Christmas card, even if the only time you spoke to him you threatened his life with a cheese grater or ran over his wife and kids with rusty farm machinery (purely speculation since, to my knowledge, he never married). Taylor's flaws were complemented by his decision to educate himself in public relations and marketing. With newspaper ads in beautiful processed color, he could annoy many more people at once.

There were four of us left: Taylor, Regis, Doc, and me. Our reporters had gone to work so they'd have time to fabricate interesting stories before the evening news or tomorrow's paper.

The waitress flashed me a flirtatious grin at first, which turned into a scowl as the morning progressed. It was, I speculate, the result of over-friendliness on J.T. Taylor's part, as he continually said such things as "I love your uniform" and "Where do you buy your hair nets?" "Just one check," Taylor told the girl, whose name tag read Brenda Mae. "That is, if you'll allow me the courtesy?" We agreed, not considering this bit of annoying niceness all that annoying since it involved free food. Niceness only irritates when it doesn't come with free stuff. "I'll have one of your stunning waffles, crisp and golden like my mother used to make."

Brenda Mae flinched. On her pad, she wrote *Waff 1.*

"You know what'd really brighten my day's a fresh cup of pure, sweet orange juice."

Brenda Mae wrote *Juice 1.*

"You'd better bring a side of those delicious biscuits, too, if you don't mind."

She wrote *Bisc 1.* Then, still smiling, she turned to Regis. "What about you?"

"I'll just have an omelet and coffee."

She wrote *Omlt 1* and *Coff 1.* "And what about you, Lover?" she said to me.

"An order of hotcakes," I moaned, "with burnt bacon, coffee, biscuits. Oh, and bring me some new silverware. Mine looks dirty." So much for flirting. If there's one thing more annoying than someone who goes out of his way to be nice, it's someone who goes out of his way not to be nice.

She turned to Dox while maintaining her composure. "And you?"

He smiled. "Eggs."

"What kind?"

"Just normal eggs, thank you." He said it with such a straight face that poor Brenda Mae looked as though she wouldn't be able to handle it.

"Everybody's a comedian," she mumbled. "Scrambled, fried, or boiled?"

The doctor's face drooped, and he seemed to lose hope. It had been such a long time since he ordered breakfast that he'd lost the skills. "What do you recommend?"

"Honey," she replied, "you can have them barbecued for all I care."

"Okay," he said. "Barbecued it is."

She shook her head in disgust. "That was a joke."

And of course, I thought, *Everybody's a comedian.*

"Oh," Doc said. "That's too bad."

Growing weary, I intervened, saying, "He wants them scrambled."

"Yes, scrambled. I'd like that."

Sighing, Brenda Mae said, "How many?"

She didn't look the slightest bit surprised when he said, "Half a dozen."

"Bacon or sausage?"

"Oh my. I don't know."

"Yes," said Taylor. "Your wonderfully delicious sausage'll brighten his day. It does mine. Makes the world a better place." He turned to me. "Don't you think?"

I grunted and turned toward my formerly flirtatious waitress and said, "Bring him coffee, too." I paused, turning to Doc, "Or would you rather have a Coke?"

"Do I get to keep the can?"

"So, this is what I propose," said Taylor, "that is, if it's all right with you. I'm sure you'll like it. It's a wonderful idea, and you're an intelligent man. Handsome, too. Did I mention that?"

Our main character didn't seem interested.

"Get on with it," Regis urged.

"Here's the thing. People think you're the son of God. Right?"

"He is," said Regis.

"He's not," I countered.

Our main character shrugged and sipped his cola through a straw, making a slurping sound.

"Anyway, that's given me an idea. I propose we set up a consulting firm. If we decide now, we can call the television studios, and they'll probably mention it when they run the story. We can get free publicity. Then what we do's charge some token fee, you understand, and give part of it to charity. I think I'd donate all my money to charity if I didn't need it."

"Get on with it," Regis bellowed.

"Well," said Taylor defensively, "that's it, actually."

Regis replied, "Oh." Then, with renewed enthusiasm, he said, "So, with whom exactly would our Lord consult?"

Taylor grinned like a jack-o-lantern suffering from too much fire on the brain. "Different people. People with problems or conflicts. Unhappy people. Unusual people. Whoever wants to pay the fee. Spouses, businessmen, politicians, drug dealers, communists, eggplant salesmen, anybody. They're all welcome, no matter how bad their dispositions. It'll be like *The People's Court*, only Christ will be the judge. It'll be *The Lord's Court*."

"I don't like it," Doc said, and he went back to sipping and slurping his cola.

"But you'll be helping people overcome their problems."

"It's not that," Regis said. "I think he's offended about making money."

"No, I'm not," said our main character. "I'm just not Jesus."

"Yes, you are," Regis rebutted.

"Oh," said our main character.

Taylor set up God & Son Mediations, LLC., in his own office. A rushed idea, but a necessary one. The plan was to capitalize on Sunday evening's news coverage by getting the business ready to operate Monday morning, figuring the whole routine would last only a day or two. He assumed interest would fade before the paperwork went through on limited liability company.

The first customer, Hubris Plymale pulled up to the red no-parking zone in his dirty once-red pickup fully equipped with mud flaps, bug guard, gun rack, AM radio, and scratches on the hood made from the antlers of deer. On the radio, Elvis Presley sang about his mutt. Hubris hated to silence the king by shutting off the truck's engine.

Plymale was a gambler. He loved to place "a little wager" every now and again, but usually nothing more than, oh, the deed to his house, and definitely less often than, say, five or six times a day. Plymale bet on football, baseball, basketball, hockey, soccer. He'd put his paycheck on the line for drinking contests, which he was good at, or thumb wrestling, which he wasn't. He'd been known to bet a buck on roadkill accuracy or a hundred on roach racing. It's a safe bet Plymale would take odds on anything, and that's a wager even he couldn't lose. But it's probably the only wager he couldn't lose. In his thirty-six years, he'd lost everything. He bet cars and pets, cash and canned goods, *Playboys*, postage stamps, and even his wife's pantyhose. He probably would've lost his wife, too, if she hadn't divorced him first. That turned out to be the luckiest day of his life. At their wedding, he bet her a dollar she'd leave him.

"I'm here to see the Savior," he said to no one in particular.

Taylor's secretary ignored him.

I was the only person in the waiting room, casually reading a copy of

Final Exit that I found lying on a table. "Excuse me," he said. "Could you by any chance direct me to the Savior?"

"No," I said, skimming through a less entertaining segment of the book.

"Oh," he moaned. "Why not?"

I sighed, closing the book. I probably wouldn't have enjoyed the ending anyway. "Listen," I said. "I don't work here. Go away and leave me alone."

"I'm here to see the Savior," he said again.

"That's all well and good," I said. "Now, go away!"

He stomped his feet—seemingly both at the same time, though I know this is a physical improbability and, as I've already noted, Plymale was terrible at beating the odds.

"All right, all right," I said, admitting defeat like the lazy, self-preserving hack that I am. "Go talk to Janet. She'll tell you what you need to know."

Janet Caleb, a college student, took a job with the annoying J.T. Taylor for one reason: cash. He paid well without asking for much work. At present, she had her nose buried in a copy of Milton's *Paradise Lost* for class.

"I'm here to see the Savior," Plymale said.

To which she replied, "It's better to rule in hell than to serve in heaven."

"Whuh?" he said.

"It's Satan."

"Hmmm?"

"Satan. You know, the devil. Old Scratch."

"Oh," said Plymale. "No, I don't think so. Spoke to him, and he wasn't much help. Told me to join Gambler's Anonymous, then bet me a buck I'd never make it through twelve steps."

Janet forced a smile and said, "All right. What can I do for you?"

"I'm here to see the Savior."

"The what?"

"The Savior. Jesus. I saw his ad on television."

"In that case, sign this." She handed him a standard (as of now) False Prophesy Waiver.

"Nothing's ever simple." He signed it.

Checking the form, Janet gave another pseudo-smile. "If you'll step right through that door, the Lord will be with you in a moment."

"Thanks," he said, and turned to go.

I got up and followed him.

As Plymale walked through the double doors, Janet let out a sigh. "Welcome to Paradise."

"Well, well," said Plymale as he shoved his blubbery buttocks into a leather chair opposite our main character. He rubbed at the stubble on his face. "The TV bunch was right. You *do* look an awful lot like J.C., don't you?"

Doc smiled with the look of a shy fieldmouse. "So I'm told," he said. "But Hubris, you really shouldn't believe everything you see on television."

Plymale was dumbfounded. "You are the Savior," he said.

"Not really."

"Yes, you are," argued Plymale.

"No, I'm not," countered the doctor.

"Make a bet?" said Plymale.

Doc paused. I think he considered it.

"Don't look at me like that. I didn't come for a lecture. Just answers."

Taylor had been sitting quietly in a corner, hidden by the shadows. He spoke up. "That's what you're paying for. Ask away."

Plymale didn't flinch. He said, "First, I'd like to know how you knew my name."

Doc grinned. "Because I remember you, Hubris."

"From where?"

"We met. I remember it as if it were yesterday—or a year ago, which it was. I was wandering around, pushing a shopping cart filled with cans. There you were, running from a policeman to whom you owed money. You slammed into my cart, then stared at my cans, introduced yourself, and offered to bet a quarter to a Coke can you could guess my occupation."

Plymale let out a weary sigh. "Well," he mumbled. "I bet I won, right?"

"No, you told me I was a taxidermist."

"Well, you do look like a taxidermist with that long, gray beard and all."

Doc nodded as though he understood. "I guess a taxidermist could have a beard like mine. So could a snake charmer, or a bullfighter, or a pizza delivery man."

"Or the Savior," said Plymale. "That would've been my second guess."

"I'm sure it would've," the doctor agreed. Looking at the crystal clock on Taylor's desk, he added, "Alas, I think your fifteen minutes are almost up."

"But I haven't asked any questions yet."

"Yes, you have."

"But...."

"No buts about it," said Taylor from the shadows. "Time's money and, as much as I like you and all, if you want another fifteen minutes, it'll cost you another hundred bucks."

"The devil, you say," he shouted, realizing his mistake. "Forgive me," he said to Doc. "But listen, I can't afford another fifteen minutes. Just one question?"

Doc looked at Taylor, who shook his head, and then at me. I gave a cynical scowl. Turning back to Plymale, he said, "Okay, one question. But I can't promise you I'll be able to answer it."

Plymale smiled, satisfied. Pulling out a newspaper clip from another of West Virginia's major newspapers, he said, "I'm going out to the Cross Lanes dog track to bet my life's savings, all eighty bucks that's left after your fee."

"What's your question?"

"Well, which dogs? Who'll win the first five races?"

After reciting a mini-thesis on the possible nature of sin in gambling and after admitting that he couldn't predict the future, our main character grinned that charming grin of his and said, "Of course, I've always been kind of partial to the number seven. I'd probably bet on that in all five races, though I confess, I don't know much about dog racing."

Angie Fishburton's claim to fame had something to do with baby pictures. Not hers, but everyone else's. She made her living posing, prodding, and playing with children long enough to get them in adorable positions so she could take a few photos. She sold those photos to appreciative parents. Angie could charm tikes with the ease of a cartoon rat, and she took great pictures: babies in baskets, toddlers with toys, boys on bikes, girls in gowns. There was just one problem. "I hate kids," she said through gritted teeth, her eyelids tense and unbudging as if they too were an image on paper. "I can't stand the little brats. Screaming, crying, kicking little cretins. I absolutely hate them!"

Doc listened but didn't reply.

"Go on," said Taylor. "I'm sure you have a good reason."

"Well, look at this." She motioned toward a big, blotchy-purple bruise on her left arm. "It hurts like the devil. I was shooting the Plymale brat…" That's Billy Joe, not Hubris. "…at his dad's funeral home. I just snapped a lovely shot of this spoiled little maggot playing with cars, those little metal ones about two inches long. He was sitting cross-legged in an empty coffin, parking his cars in the satin folds. A good picture, too. I'm sure of it. At least, it would've been if that boy hadn't thrown his little truck. Smacked me in the arm. Made me drop my camera."

Doc offered a sympathetic sigh.

"That's only the beginning. The Roth girl bit me right here." She pointed to the back of her thigh which was hidden by her jeans. "It's hideous. You know, one minute they're calm and posed. But as soon as the flash flares? Mutants, demons from the blackest pits of...."

"Well," interrupted our main character, "you're saying you don't like kids. So, what do you want from me? I'm rather fond of children, myself."

"You can have them. Just keep'em away from me."

Doc frowned—a startling sight. "If you dislike them so much, how can you take their pictures?"

"That's just it. I wish I didn't. I never wanted to be a baby photographer. You think that's my life's ambition? I want to be an artist."

"Interesting," said Doc. "What's that got to do with your visit?"

Her eyes held all the fury of a Long Island iced tea, while his remained as calm as lite beer. I say this because I remember thinking, I really need a drink. Anyway, she said, "I want your help. I'm a good girl. I pray every night. Twice, sometimes. I give to charities. I go to church, even when the weather's bad. None of it does any good. Show me the way out of this rut."

Our main character considered her request. "We must love the children," he said. "If not, they may not love us back. One of my deepest fears is that somewhere in this world a toddler, taking her first steps, will stagger across an empty room into no one's arms. It won't be *my* fault, but I can't help feeling responsible. If I could be there for every kid that's unwanted, uncared for, unloved...." He hesitated. "It saddens me to hear you say you don't like children. If you've always felt like that, then nothing I can say will help. If, however, your disillusionment comes from your job, there's hope. Change jobs. If you want to be an artist, be an artist. You can do it with hard work, the right attitude, and a little faith."

She stared at him, mesmerized, but said nothing.

"You need to find a new career. Perhaps you should send your photos off to fashion magazines or modeling agencies. Or maybe you could send pictures to newspapers. There's bound to be a job someplace where you'll be happier."

Angie said, "Who am I to argue with the Lord?"

From the ever-more-crowded waiting room came two hideous beasts. The first resembled the devil's shadow. He came cloaked in dust of a West Virginian's dreams—the wage that let him live and the shroud in which to bury him: coal. Early on, coal miners were treated like slaves. And what did they get for their trouble? Killed. Coal mines flooded or collapsed. There were accidents with picks, dynamite, the coal company's dogs. Lungs turned black, and hearts stopped beating. Then, when the miners tried to get their due, they were scorned and fired. Or fired at. They formed unions and fought back with production stoppages, unified negotiations, and sometimes, shotguns.

The first fiend represented the union. Elbert Earl Gates only knew one thing in life: how to dig coal. He could dig it with a shovel. He could dig it with a pick. He could dig it with his fingers. He could dig it with a stick. He could dig it with a bulldozer and tear the land to shreds. He could dig it with a pocket knife or a needle pulling thread. Knowing so much about petrified swamp rocks and the many ways of removing them from the earth allowed him to earn a reasonable living for his family without putting himself at risk. On the other hand, as an expert, he was given authority to negotiate in the name of the union under the presumption that he'd know what miners needed. But he didn't know the first thing about negotiating. It was a job he didn't want. Plus, his negotiating skills were hampered by some rule against using his fists during contract talks.

The second was more of a gargoyle, five-foot-two, and clearly management. His tiny wire-rimmed spectacles rested loosely on his tinier nose. They didn't quite hide his eyes which were calculated and cold. At a guess, I'd say this man cared about nothing but money. At a guess, I'd be wrong. The only thing John Killian cared about was *his* family. I met them some months later while doing research for this book. His wife Kathryn smiled in a way so magical it could allow the sun to rise or set ahead of schedule. Starlight, meanwhile, danced behind her eyes. Killian's two kids were charming. David, age 8, could get you involved in a game of Space Invaders or Super Zaxxon, while his sister Elsbeth, age 14, could pick your pocket, tie your shoe strings together, and set your hat on fire without you knowing or caring. All John Killian really wanted was to go home and be with his wife and children. Unfortunately, he had to deal with the union, and he despised the union. As the company's chief negotiator, Killian's job consisted of sitting in his tiny, yellow-walled office and listening to complaints from union employees. That part was easy, and he handled it. What he disliked was the constant striking: walkouts by union employees that shut down mining operations.

Taylor grinned as he considered this case. The reason had nothing to do with pieces of swamp or the problems of union/management relations. He smiled because he could bill double—two hundred dollars for each fifteen minutes—because there were two participants.

"The problem," explained Killian, "isn't money or benefits or liability or safety standards. The problem's that the union's always on strike."

Gates shifted in his chair but didn't interrupt.

"Every two or three years, when the contract expires, they make these crazy demands, most of which they don't expect to get, and when the company refuses, all the union members go on strike. Then we bring in nonunion workers...."

"Worthless scabs," Gates interjected.

"*Nonunion* workers," Killian emphasized. "We bring them in to keep the company from going bankrupt, and they get assaulted, shot at, and threatened by the strikers. Cars are vandalized. Roads are blocked. So the mines still end up shut down. We can't get anything done. And with the mines shut down, the company makes no money, so we're even less able to meet union demands."

He fell silent, giving his opponent a chance to recite the union's side of the story. After explaining the past abuses inflicted upon miners, Gates said, "We just can't work without a contract, not after the way we've been treated."

"I'm not saying you should work without a contract," Killian shot back. "It's just that you go on strike even when you've signed on the dotted line. Some coal company off in God-knows-where, Pennsylvania, gets shut down, and y'all have to go on strike to show your solidarity."

Gates looked angry, but he held his temper.

"Look," Killian said, "we bring a guy in who, for one reason or another, refuses to join the union. Maybe he just doesn't want to give up a hefty portion of his paycheck for dues. Maybe he's got a wife, ten kids, and a sick mother with a taste for the bourbon. I don't know. But y'all go crazy. Then you strike."

Gates growled like a werewolf with irritable bowel syndrome. I distinctly heard a "Grrrr" sound coming from his direction. "He doesn't join the union, he's not one of us. If he's not one of us and he's getting paid, then he's taking our job. We can't have that. We got a right to that job. You give our job to somebody else, we strike."

Killian looked disheartened. "I understand how you feel," he said. "In fact, I respect your loyalty. We at the company wish you'd show the same loyalty to us. With you going on strike every other day, we don't see it. All we want's for you to work when you should be working." Shaking his head and turning to our main character, Killian said, "Can you help us?"

"No," said the doctor.

"No?" said Killian.

"No?" said Gates.

"No," said the doctor.

"Why not?" said Killian.

"I don't understand," said Gates.

"Because," said Doc, "no matter what solution I propose, whether balanced or leaning in favor of your union or your company, you'll both reject it."

"I doubt that," said Gates.

"No," said Killian.

"Yes," said Doc, and he was firm in his assertion.

It took ten minutes of confused discussion before Taylor intervened. He did it not because of Killian's threats of a lawsuit or threats of a broken nose by Gates, and not because of some hidden desire to solve the problem. He did it because he hated to see people unhappy. His motto in life was "If everybody's smiling, we'll have a lower suicide rate." So, he told Doc to propose a solution.

Reluctantly, our main character agreed. "The solution…"

"Yes?" said Killian.

"What?" said Gates.

"…is to implement ten-year contracts."

"No," said Killian.

"What?" said Gates.

"If you were to negotiate a ten-year contract with appropriate income increases over time, and a no-strike guarantee as well, then both sides could continue with business."

"No," said Killian.

"No," said Gates.

"Why on earth," said Killian, "would we want to do anything of the sort?"

"Because it'd give the union a chance to show its commitment to the company, and it'd give the company a chance to show its commitment to the union. If you're stuck with each other, you'll form a closer relationship than you will being at odds all the time."

"It won't do," said Killian. "What if they go on strike?"

"You'd have it in writing that there'll be no strikes during the contract's duration, providing the company meets its obligations."

"But what if they strike anyway?"

"Liquidated damages. You figure out the cost per person per day that a strike will cause, and you stick a clause in the contract to cover that amount. If the union strikes, there'll be a set fee the union must pay per day."

"No way," roared Gates. "That won't happen. Not ever!"

Paying his companion no mind, Killian asked, "But what happens if union members go on strike—maybe an informal strike—without the union's approval?"

"You fire them. If they're under contract to work, they have a responsibility to work. If they don't work, they break a binding agreement."

"No way," Gates bellowed. "What about inflation? We'll starve."

"No, you won't," replied our main character. "You'll have your salary increased by a fixed percentage annually with no exceptions."

"What if they decide to cut the number of union employees or shut us down?"

"Another damages clause," said the doctor who it now seemed also might have been a lawyer in a past life. "You'll have it legally binding that they can't do it. If they fire people or close the mines, they'll owe those unemployed workers their salaries just the same. In addition, you can have it put in the contract that no nonunion worker will be employed by the company with the exception of those on salary at this time. It's all very simple. Of course, the alternative isn't pleasant."

"Which is what?" said Killian.

"Absolutely nothing," said Doc.

"Should we listen to him?" I overheard Killian ask Gates as they left.

The blackened, dust-filled lines on the coal miner's face turned up in a sinful grin. "What for?" he replied. "That'd be a damn fool thing to do."

"You're right," said Killian. "At least we agree on that. What do you suggest?"

"Maybe we should have him run over by a milk truck," said Gates.

"No," said Killian, shaking his head. "I don't think that'll be necessary. No reason for us to get involved. I imagine things will take care of themselves."

Into Taylor's office walked the governor of West Virginia. This offended many waiting patrons—not because the governor's presence meant an intermingling of religion and politics, typically taboo in these United States of America, In God We Trust, Amen, but because it wasn't his turn. Even so, no one tried to stop him. I speculate this had something to do with his being accompanied by six state troopers.

The calculator in Taylor's brain began to punch numbers. Undoubtedly he planned to bill our governor one hundred dollars per person, per fifteen minutes, even though only the governor came seeking guidance. Should the session last that long, it'd amount to approximately two thousand eight hundred dollars per hour, and that's a respectable salary. For a while, I found myself wondering why more people didn't get into the God-selling business. Of course, I've realized since that more people *do*.

It's important for me to mention why I haven't referred to our governor by name. I think this'll help in the future as I continue not to use his name. The governor, whether he serves in West Virginia or one of the other forty-nine states, is the most insignificant character in this story. In fact, not only is he insignificant, but by placing him in this story, I make every other character worthy of as much depth and detail as possible by comparison. Not our governor, though. He'd be the most insignificant character in any story, even his autobiography. I will describe and name the six unlucky men assigned to guard our governor's life. Their names are Sutter Hall, Reginald Bonedog, Frank Terrance, Jimmy Joe Hopend, Ollie Prance, and David H. Hodge (no relation). Their description is as follows: big. Their thoughts, I imagine, were: *I want to go home*, or *I need to go to the bathroom*, or maybe, *Gee, wouldn't it be nice if I could shoot someone today.*

Our governor placed himself with much arrogance in the chair across from our main character. When he spoke, that also showed great presumption, as though our main character, Jesus or not, should recognize that waxen smile, those tailored threads, that aura of practiced compassion. But why should he? The doctor didn't watch the news. He didn't vote or attend political rallies. He didn't read newspapers; he recycled them. But our governor was unaware of this. Arrogantly, he said, "If you're *Him*, tell me it's all right." He didn't say what *it* was.

That didn't hamper Doc, who replied, "No."

"Why not?" asked our governor.

And our main character responded with what may have been four of the most religious words I'd heard him speak: "Because I said so."

Our governor meant taxes. He'd had a bit of a problem with them. Many West Virginians were content to despise him because of taxes. Well, not because of taxes, but because he'd repeatedly raised taxes, as had all governors before him. Then again, it wasn't so much because he'd repeatedly raised taxes, but because he'd repeatedly raised taxes after promising hand-on-heart not to—again, like all governors before him. "I came to you for help," he said.

"Why should I help you?"

"Because I'm the governor."

"So?"

"Because I didn't mean to do it."

"So?"

"I didn't want to do it."

"So?"

"I had no choice."

"We all have a choice."

"Not me. My hands were tied by corrupt, money-hungry politicians."

"You can claim your peers made you do it, but the choice was yours. You never do anything you aren't willing to do. It's your free will. No one's to blame for your failures but you, as no one's to be praised for your successes. If what you do's wrong, take responsibility."

Our governor covered his face with his hands. Peeking out through the cracks between fingers as if he might be blinded by light, he said, "Maybe what I did wasn't so wrong."

"If it weren't wrong, you'd accept it and move on."

"But what about all that stuff about rendering unto Caesar what's Caesar's?"

To that, Doc replied, "Caesar's dead."

The next visitor would be the last. That made it more bizarre to learn the name of the man who came seeking truth, wisdom, enlightenment, and other silliness: our friend Jonathan Regis. He entered Taylor's office with all the grace and sophistication of a charging three-legged rhinoceros building steam to jump a twenty-foot ravine. Twice, he tripped over his feet and almost fell, just in the three or four yards between the door and the chair. Sitting down also proved difficult as he managed first to perch on one arm of the chair, followed by the other. Regis was nervous. He said he'd been down by the river sitting on a bench, watching a purple stream of chemicals flow out of a drainpipe and float along the Ohio's tranquil waters. When I asked him about it later, he said amidst the subliminal cries of dying fish, he found himself wondering about the meaning of life. A single question came to him over and over, making a lasting impression. That question could be the most profound thing ever to have gone through his head without making him sneeze. He thought, *Did I just see a carp with legs, arms, hands, and opposable thumbs?* He later revised the question. "I was wondering," said Regis, "where exactly do we come from?"

Hopefully, you'll not be the least bit surprised when I tell you that our main character didn't know. That didn't stop him from taking a guess. "I believe," said the doctor, "that you came from the waiting room. I've been right here for hours now."

Regis shook his head. "I meant before that. Where do we *come* from?" Then, before the doctor could say something logical about women, wombs, and sexual reproduction, Regis added, "What I mean is, are we evolved from apes, or more to the point, from fish?"

Our main character seemed to ponder this possibility for some time. "I think the Bible you're always waving around says we were created. Correct me if I'm wrong."

"Yes, I know that. But how? I just have this terrible feeling God was up in Heaven advancing His technology and dumping the chemical waste products into the world's oceans. Are we the end result of God's excess and waste?"

The doctor's eyes seemed filled with sorrow. It took him little time to cheer up. "Do you believe your version of God would be wasteful? It's true we're a motley race of self-serving, inhuman humans. We fight and kill. We hate. Still, are we accidents? Did we evolve? Maybe. Were we apes or slugs or fish? I think we were and are perhaps all of those. How often do we crawl around on our bellies, nameless and humiliated like the slug? How often do we act like apes, uncivilized, yet always with a purpose, always knowing what we want? But are we fish? Are we sleek predators, hunters, cannibals? Do we move about, carefree and yet ready to go home again? More to the point, are we stuck in an aquarium not of our choosing, swimming around in circles while some Grand Mariner watches every move? I think so. Does it matter?"

Regis wasn't satisfied. "We're fish. You're right. But were we fish? Did we grow from minnows or evolve from algae, or were we created from dust? Where do we come from?"

"My friend," replied the doctor, "there's no answer. I can guess, I can lie, or I can speak my mind, but the truth is, I don't know."

"But...."

"I'm sorry."

"But you're the son of God."

"No," said the doctor. "I'm not."

"No," said Deputy Micheaux as she stormed into Taylor's office. "He's not!" She came accompanied by Officer Dollie, who wore a wicked grin. In his right hand, he held a pamphlet easily identified as an arrest warrant.

"What's going on here?" demanded Taylor, standing and stepping from the shadows. His intervention was futile. The last thing Doc needed was someone to enhance his image.

"Out of the way," said Micheaux, pointing her gun at Taylor. "We're here for His Holiness."

"But why?"

I started to intervene, but I decided against it. The next-to-the-last thing our main character needed was some lousy writer shooting off at the mouth on his behalf.

"This man's under arrest," said Micheaux, as she used her free hand to remove a set of handcuffs from her belt. "If anyone gives us any trouble, you'll have your butt in a sling too."

Dollie cut in. "News came today. We got a match for his fingerprints."

"Say again?" said Taylor.

"We printed him Saturday when we took him down to the jail."

Micheaux took it from there, adding, "FBI had a file on our John Doe, here. Or are you still going by Jesus these days?"

Doc, in defense of himself, said, "I go by whatever name you call me."

"Well, how about your real name, Mister Lesage?"

He shrugged.

"What'd you call him?" I asked. I had to know.

"Lesage. Matthew Lesage."

"What's he wanted for?" said Taylor.

Dollie grunted a hick's laugh, nasally and coming from the belly. "They want to know what he did. Can you believe it? What'd he do?"

Micheaux wasn't laughing. "Murder," she said. "It's murder."

"Oh my," said the doctor.

Micheaux handcuffed our main character, whose name we now know. Officer Dollie told him he had a right to keep his mouth shut and a right to a lawyer. As they did, I realized I'd gotten my wish. The two major branches of local law enforcement were working together.

What a damned shame...

HERE BEGINS THE CHRONICLE OF
THE FALSE MARTYR

Our main character wouldn't die for our sins. He might be slapped, kicked, shot, stabbed, or publicly humiliated, but dying was out of the question. There'd be no firing squads, electric chairs, gas chambers, lethal injections, and no trampling by wild elephants—at least, not fatally.

Judge Binky again had Doc's case. He told me afterward that he would've done almost anything to avoid arraigning our humble main character. Doc's charges were for significant crimes in another state. They had been investigated by a federal agency, although they weren't federal charges. Therefore, the purpose of Doc's arraignment was to deny bond and bind the case over to Circuit Court, where an extradition hearing would be held. With some other magistrate, that's what would've happened. Binky, as I've noted, liked to bend the rules.

Skeeter Deter also repeated as part of the doctor's arraignment team, having been requested by name. "Well, heck fire," I heard him say. "I'll be a blue booger on a monkey's beard. Nobody ever *asked* for me before."

One person who didn't make a return appearance in the Incredible Trial of Our Main Character, Part Two (subtitled *Return of the Vicious, Murdering, Maiming, Bloodthirsty, but Otherwise Pleasant and Friendly Guy*) was Dirk Slaterman. I mention this to ease your mind as to his whereabouts since, when we last saw him, he'd found his way into considerable trouble. I wouldn't want you to spend your time worrying about *him* when you should spend your time worrying about our main character. Or rather, when you should spend your time *not* worrying about our main character. Anyway, the naive assistant prosecutor had resigned by the time of the second coming. He was now the former naive assistant prosecutor. Actually, make that just the former assistant prosecutor. He remained naive. The difference was that now he'd become naive in manipulating people's lawn-care needs rather than their lives, though some might see the two as intertwined. He exchanged his law career for a highly respectable job in the field of cutting grass. It consisted of other gardening activities too: raking leaves, pulling weeds, trimming hedges, and picking fruit. Dirk Slaterman found his niche.

Quickly, let's run through the passenger list for the arraignment of our main character who wasn't Jesus but actually Matthew Lesage, and who we'd later discover to be Doctor Matthew Lesage (yes, he had a doctorate after all). The simplest way to do this is for me to name the players, list one fact about each, and then explain their appearance. Here goes: Jonathan Regis, ex-minister and devout believer in our main character's Christliness, there to find out if his blind faith has been unfounded; Thadeus Skaggs, alleged vicious killer, currently sitting with his attorney from New York and watching eagerly while hoping to be the first person to be found innocent of a crime because God told him to do it—incidentally, that refers to our main character, who wasn't God either; Carroll Sue Bergoney, rapist, hoping to be the second person to be found innocent for the above reason; a strange man dressed as a big yellow fish and wearing a sign which reads "Tuna For Christ," formerly a strange man dressed as a big yellow fish not wearing a sign which reads "Tuna For Christ," and as for his reason for being there, your guess is as good as mine; Billy Joe Plymale, undertaker, still waiting to see the implications of our main character's existence on the demand for mortuary services; Kirri Cooley, inexperienced journalist, following up for Huntington's primary newspaper; Joel Lee, cameraman, ditto that last part but for one of the three television stations; Hubris Plymale (no relation to Billy Joe), gambler, testifying at Skeeter Deter's request; Angie Fishburton, professional baby hater, testifying; Elbert Earl Gates, digger of dried swamp rocks, testifying; John Killian, management imp, testifying; our governor, well, *he's our governor*, testifying; Sutter Hall, Reginald Lee Bonedog, Frank Terrance, Jimmy Joe Hopend, Ollie Prance, and David H. Hodge (no relation), security personnel, guarding our governor from those who might do him ill; and finally, Harold Hodge, professional hack, continuing my badly written saga of our main character.

That covers everyone we've met. Now, I'll introduce you to the woman we haven't. Well, there were several women in the courtroom that we haven't met, and men too, but only one that's relevant: Loralee Garrett, special agent for the Federal Bureau of Investigation, FBI for short.

The FBI is a law enforcement agency I failed to mention earlier when discussing the crudely-drawn concentric circles. It's easy to forget the FBI, probably because it's brought to us by the federal government, though it also might be because the average person's experience with the FBI consists of seeing it on uninteresting television programs or in badly written stories like this one. In any case, now would be a good time to note that fifth circle. Let's rehash the inner structure. Campus police handled crimes on campus. City police handled crimes within the city limits. The county sheriff handled crimes in the county. The state police handled crimes in the state. Okay, so those law enforcement agencies and the areas they covered were all within the borders of the USA. As such, they fell collectively under the jurisdiction of the FBI. FBI agents generally handled major crimes or crimes that crossed state boundaries such as drug smuggling, gun running, and kidnapping, though they pretty much could step in for anything—even jaywalking, which our main character doesn't do.

FBI agent Loralee Garrett came from a long line of law-and-order types, going all the way back to a distant relative named Pat, famous for hunting down and killing the bloodthirsty cowboy Billy the Kid, who happened to be a close friend. Loralee Garrett would never shoot a good friend. In fact, it's doubtful she'd ever shoot anybody, except maybe herself. This, I believe, is why she didn't carry a loaded gun. She was what we in the business of writing badly call *totally incompetent*. Her parents should've grounded her the day she decided to become an agent with the FBI. Instead, I think they were probably glad to get her out of the house. This is speculation as her parents are dead—through no fault of hers—and unable to verify this theory. Ah, but Garrett tried so hard to get things right. She just wasn't very good at it. She was the kind of girl you didn't tell not to play with matches because she'd burn your house down trying to figure out why.

The FBI knew this. I'm told by some of her colleagues that prior to about twelve years ago, she was in charge of nothing more important than answering telephones and nothing more dangerous than using the office photocopier, though this could be fatal in the wrong hands. But she wasn't content to be a secretary. She pressured her bosses for a case to work on, no matter how insignificant. She threatened to do something drastic if they didn't find her an investigation. Not knowing what she meant by 'drastic,' and afraid that she might hurt herself, they decided to give in. They offered her the most futile and utterly unsolvable case. Her job was to find a person vaguely suspected of murder who'd disappeared off the face of the planet three years earlier, not expecting her to capture the miscreant. They told her she wouldn't get another case as long as this one remained unsolved.

So, Loralee went back to her uninteresting but still dangerous life as a secretary, content with her insignificant case. She memorized every page and each detail, then waited.

Monday morning, she came back to work after a long weekend spent recovering from a nearly-fatal sewing machine accident and discovered a set of fingerprints on her desk which she recognized instantly after years of staring at their exact match. How this act of memory was accomplished, I won't guess, though it has been verified by various agents, all of whom I consider trustworthy—in other words, like me, too stupid to lie.

Now, having solved her first case, she was to testify in court for the first time since the age of eleven when, as trial documents show, she accidentally released the brake on her mom's Ford Torino station wagon, sending it and her out of a parking lot, down the road, over a steep hill, across a crowded sidewalk, through a police barricade, and then a reindeer-and-sleigh float at the annual Christmas parade, thereafter causing Santa Claus to sue.

Finally, it's time to share the strange case of Doctor Matthew Lesage. As you already know, our main character was charged with murder— several times over, in fact. In case you're not too bright, let me explain that murder is to kill someone. It goes beyond that, however, as there are instances in which you can kill someone without it being considered murder. There are general rules regarding this such as self-defense, which is killing a person who'd otherwise have killed you, and temporary insanity where, for a split second, you became loony and didn't realize you were killing someone or that killing someone was wrong. If either of these possibilities can be proven, you won't be convicted of murder.

Another instance in which killing someone isn't considered murder is during military service, where you can be given a powerful weapon and sent off to who knows where with the specific intention of killing as many people as you can. In addition, you might not be found guilty of murder if you kill someone by accident, perhaps by stepping on a sleeping man's head while you're chasing a Frisbee on the beach or by shooting someone walking in the woods while you're hunting deer with a semiautomatic rifle. I imagine it's also possible to avoid conviction for murder by claiming other things such as incompetence, paranoia, Simon says, or even that the blade of your knife was somehow diverted by the electromagnetic rays of a passing alien spaceship, though that's purely speculative. So, those are some of the ways a person who's killed another person can avoid being convicted for murder. The crimes our main character is charged with didn't meet these preconditions. He couldn't plead insanity, self-defense, military service, or even space invaders, any of which might have cleared him. The reason: he didn't kill anyone. To be found not guilty of murder by reason of insanity, for example, two things must occur. You must kill someone, and you must be completely and unmistakably out of your head at the time. As you can see, killing someone is another major precondition of defending yourself against a murder charge.

As I've pointed out, our main character didn't kill anyone. I can say that without bias because not only did Doc *not* kill anyone, no one claimed he *did*. You see, you don't necessarily have to kill somebody to be charged with murder. It's a good idea, but not a requirement. There are ways around it. A person can be charged with murder for several reasons that don't necessitate actually killing anybody. For example, if you and your friend rob a liquor store and both of you have weapons, whether they're guns, knives or slingshots, and the owner dies of a heart attack, you and your friend can be charged with murder. If your friend actually uses the weapon to kill the owner, you will still be charged. Also, if you fail to do something which, as a result, causes someone to be killed, you can be charged with murder. For example, if you go inside for a sandwich and leave the lawnmower running, after which it chases down and kills a pack of girl scouts selling cookies, you can be charged with murder. If you fail to heed leash laws and allow your pet—Doberman, Pitbull, twenty-foot Python, malnourished Siberian Tiger, for example—to run free, and it decides to head down to McDonald's for a snack, only to end up eating the new part-time fry cook, you might be charged. So you see, you don't *actually* have to kill to be charged with murder, though in my opinion, that detracts from the symbolism of the crime.

Anyway, back to our main character. We've established that he hadn't killed anyone, so what was he accused of doing? He did pretty much the same thing he's done throughout this story, which is to say, nothing. In other words, he was charged with murder because he wasn't Jesus, or rather, because he also wasn't Jesus fifteen years ago. Yes, I know you're wondering how he can be charged with murder simply for not being Jesus. Trust me, it's a complex legal system we're working with. Anyhow, the reason Doctor Matthew Lesage had been charged with murder was that several people *thought* he was Jesus, and many died as a result. The question that raises is this: did the doctor claim to be Jesus? If he didn't, as he hasn't so far, then surely he wouldn't be convicted of murder. If he did, that complicates things a little bit.

Author's Note: Somewhere in this world, people are being gunned down by automatic weapons. Or, as the National Rifle Association would point out, people being gunned down by other people who just happen to be using automatic weapons. Somewhere in this world, children are being raised with no morals, as I was. Somewhere in this world, nuclear missiles wait to be launched at unsuspecting countries. For that matter, somewhere in this world, missiles wait to be launched at paranoid countries that do suspect and are quite prepared to launch missiles back. Somewhere in this world, a wealthy rock'n'roll star sings about how terrible life is. Somewhere in this world, bridges are crumbling. Somewhere in this world, dogs are being kicked. Somewhere in this world, senile farmers are being kidnapped by little green men in flying saucers. Somewhere in this world, sheep are being sheared. Somewhere in this world, toast is being burned. Somewhere in this world, unpleasant things are happening to unpleasant people.

Right here, on this day, in this tiny, cluttered courtroom in the city of Huntington, the county of Cabell, the state of West Virginia, in these United States of America, In God We Trust, Amen, our main character, Doctor Matthew Lesage, who wasn't Jesus, couldn't see the future, wouldn't die for our sins, and who hadn't actually killed anybody, was facing twenty-three counts of murder. Twenty-three! And through it all, he continued to smile as though nothing in this world could bother him. And you know, I doubt if anything could.

Kirri approached my seat, two rows behind the defense table, and gracefully guided herself to a spot beside me. She wore a black sweater matched with a flowing skirt hanging almost to the floor and hovering around her ankles like fog over a moonlit lake. Her hair was in a ponytail. Casually, she began to converse with me in a manner that, if I were unable to recognize the hidden motives a journalist has during the quest for news, might've seemed flirtatious. Kirri sat next to me, her sleeve's soft cashmere rubbing the back of my hand. "Think he did it?"

"That's a terrible question for a reporter to ask," I snapped. "You want me to guess if he's a vicious criminal? That man? Forgive me for saying so, but it's not for a journalist to predict the future, merely to report it when it becomes the past."

Her face turned sour. She looked sad. "I wasn't asking you as a journalist," she said, sounding on the verge of tears. "I was asking as a friend. If I wanted someone to bite my head off, there are a thousand other people out there ready to yell at me just because I'm a member of the working press. And I haven't even been working very long. Or have you forgotten?"

"Forgive me," I said, humbled. "I spoke out of turn."

She shrugged. "So," she said, "do you think he's guilty?"

Seeing the chance to redeem myself, I shook my head and said in the most solemn manner I could muster, "Probably not. I think he's just misunderstood."

She wrote my answer in her little notebook.

Let's flash back now, and I'll share the story of the Doc's twenty-three victims. Well, I guess they weren't victims. Or were they? Here's the tale, slightly less slanted than when Loralee Garrett presented it to the court:

Pittsburgh, Pennsylvania, was about an hour's drive from West Virginia, though four to six from Huntington, depending on traffic and roadwork. A big city, much bigger in fact than Huntington, it far outnumbered Huntington in population, tourist attractions, violent crimes, jobs, shopping centers, tall buildings, newspapers, screaming children, and even rivers, of which it had three to Huntington's one. Another thing Pittsburgh had bigger than Huntington's was a university. In truth, it had several, but one around which much of the city's life centered. I won't describe that university because I won't be attending any football games, improperly imbibing alcohol while watching, or encountering Jesus afterward. One thing I will mention is that, for one semester, it served as home to a philosophy professor named Doctor Matthew Lesage (yes, he earned his doctorate in philosophy).

The university in Pittsburgh wasn't the first institution of higher learning to showcase the unusual talents of Doctor Matthew Lesage. For ten years, he'd been a journeyman philosopher, traveling town to town, acting scholarly. Over time, our main character taught at Michigan, Oklahoma, and Northwestern. How he ended up in Pittsburgh, I don't know, nor does it matter. He did, and for one semester, he became a god. I'll wager that the summer before his arrival there our main character experimented with the art of beard-growing. I say this because it's the only reason I can think of to explain why, after so many years of teaching, no one ever got Doctor Matthew Lesage mixed up with Jesus.

That Fall semester, twenty-three freshman philosophy students, eighteen men and five women, got together outside of class and, during a night of properly imbibing alcohol, decided in true democratic fashion to elect Doctor Matthew Lesage to the holiest office, one not often considered an elected position. They did it based on his appearance, his way with words, his pleasant attitude, and the fact they'd all imbibed too many cans of cheap beer.

Doc didn't want to be Jesus. But when you have twenty-three drunken philosophy students deciding to do something off-the-wall and against the norms of society, who's to tell them no? Not Lesage, that's for sure. He liked to encourage his students in their intellectual pursuits, no matter how misguided. He knew the nature of philosophy involved doing things that seem ridiculous, foolish, and weird while searching for truth and wisdom.

Thus for almost three months, Lesage filled in for the missing prophet, until one cheerful New Years Day (after an important football game), these twenty-three students, having passed the doctor's course and once again having imbibed too many cans of beer, decided to collectively blow their brains out. In other words, they committed suicide. They killed themselves. This, as I've noted, is not murder—at least, not by the doctor.

However, questions arise. It was no secret that he encouraged them in their misguided religion. It follows that he also might've encouraged them in their misguided manner of shooting themselves with guns. If he did, then by law he might be considered a murderer.

Did he encourage them? No one knew. Lesage disappeared before authorities could interrogate him by locking him away in a windowless room and beating him senseless.

Garrett concluded her version of the doctor's story as follows: "Your Honor, it's clear this man brutally and maliciously murdered twenty-three of his students, people who loved him, people who trusted him, people who put their lives in his hands. And now they're dead. Thank you."

Judge Binky shook his head in apparent disbelief. "Thank you for such a depressing speech, Miz Garrett. I can't remember when I've had so little fun." He turned to Stanley Hotchkiss, the new assistant prosecutor whose inexperience at the job caused him to view the courtroom as a place where anything goes—possibly because his only major influence so far had been Skeeter Deter. "And thank you, Stanley, for letting the FBI make your opening remarks for you. It gives me such wonderful faith in our nation's law schools."

"You're welcome, Binky," Hotchkiss said.

Again, Binky shook his head. "Well, Mister Deter, since we've thrown out the conventions, would you care to say a few words?"

Standing, Skeeter locked his fingers together and cracked his knuckles. With the grace and speed of a Huntington lawyer, he belched twice. "Thank you," he said and sat down.

Oh, one more thing to note. Normally, no witnesses testify at an arraignment like this. The procedure normally is as follows:

Judge: "Next case. What's the charge?"

Assistant prosecutor: "Murder."

Judge: "How do you pleat?"

Defendant or attorney: "With a sewing machine, Your Honor."

Ahh, scratch that. Just a typo. Let's try again.

Judge: "How do you plead?"

Defendant or defense: "Not guilty, Your Honor."

Judge: "Any recommendations before I set bond?"

Prosecutor: "This man's a vicious thug. He doesn't deserve to be free on bond."

Defense attorney: "Now, Your Honor, my client has never hurt anyone in his life. In fact, he's incompetent. He probably couldn't harm anyone if he wanted to. Besides, he maintains his innocence. Can you justify keeping an innocent man in jail?"

Judge: "Bail is set at five thousand dollars or a five hundred dollar cash bond. Case is bound over to the grand jury." Or in this case, "Bond is denied. Case is bound over to Cabell County Circuit Court for an extradition hearing. Next case."

It's that simple. No trial. No cutthroat questioning. No attorney antics.

This was different. It was the arraignment of someone who, like it or not, had twice played the role of Jesus. That tended to muddle things up.

Here's what really happened:

Judge Binky: "How do you plead?"

Doc: "I always cross at the light."

Skeeter Deter: "There you have it, ladies and gentleman. Let's go home."

Judge Binky: "Not so fast, Mister Deter. I'd appreciate it if, for once, you'd address this court in the proper manner."

Skeeter Deter: "How do you expect my client to ever be free with you up there on the bench daydreaming?"

Judge Binky: "Mister Deter...."

Skeeter Deter: "Not now. I'm contemplating autoerotic asphyxiation."

Judge Binky: "What was that?"

Skeeter Deter: "Oh, never mind. Just pointing out that we all have fantasies. Didn't mean to get your hopes up."

Stanley Hotchkiss: "Your Honor, can we get on with this, please?"

Judge Binky: "Mister Deter, is it safe to presume your client wishes to plead not guilty?"

Skeeter Deter: "You can presume anything you like. You're the judge, I think."

Judge Binky: "You bother me, Mister Deter. You really do."

Skeeter Deter: "Good. It proves you're human after all, rather than some silly trained chimp like my colleagues and I have always thought."

Judge Binky: "Oooh!"

Skeeter Deter: "See, that's what I meant."

Judge Binky: "Mister Deter, will you please answer the question? Is he guilty or not guilty?"

Skeeter Deter sat in his chair in the Thinker pose, quizzically rubbing his chin. "Well, Binky," he said, "right off hand, I don't know. At a guess, I'll say not guilty."

Binky clutched his hands to his throbbing temples. "Mister Lesage, do you agree with your attorney's observation?"

The old man continued to grin as usual. "I leave myself completely in his hands."

The judge moaned. "I guess that'll have to do for now." He paused, pretending to look at his notes. "Mister Deter, Mister Hotchkiss, do either of you have any further comments before I decide on bond?"

"Well," Hotchkiss began, only to be interrupted by Deter.

"Bond," shouted the defense attorney as he jumped to his feet. "Why? We've already established that he's not guilty!"

"Mister Deter," the judge began.

"There's no justice here. No justice at all."

"Mister Deter," the judge said, tapping his gavel.

"How can a man hope to live his life in peace if our court system turns its back at every opportunity? And how can we let it happen?"

"Mister Deter!" The judge's voice exploded through the courtroom.

Deter was undeterred. "You have to dismiss this case, Binky. It's a moral imperative."

"Mister Deter!" the judge roared.

"Yes?"

"This is only an arraignment."

"So?"

"No decision's been made about his guilt or innocence, you idiot."

"That's it," snapped Deter. "I want a mistrial. You called me a nasty name."

"Nothing more than you deserved," prodded Hotchkiss. "Now why don't you sit down and let the professionals get some work done."

"Oh," said Deter, "I'm hurt. I'm so hurt."

"This hearing is getting out of control," Binky admonished the two attorneys. "I don't know where you two think you are, but this is an official courtroom in the state of West Virginia. From now on, you'll follow the rules of etiquette established for such a place."

"Fine," said Deter, who thrust his pinky up the left nostril of his nose and began to dig around for any sign of his respect for the court.

Taking a page from his opponent's law book, Hotchkiss said, "Agreed," after which he leaned back in his chair and propped his feet on the desk.

Binky's face lit up like a book burning. He paused long enough to let his blood pressure settle, then said, "Let's get on with it, shall we?"

Skeeter Deter stuck his hands in the pockets of his denim jeans and turned to face his audience, packed elbow to elbow in the tiny courtroom. "Let it be known," he said, "that I intend to prove to you here and now that this man is Jesus Christ. Furthermore, I don't think I need to work very hard to do it, because everyone here already knows it deep down inside."

Binky had given up trying to convince Deter that this hearing didn't require proving or disproving anything. He motioned for the attorney to "please get on with it."

Deter said, "To begin with, I'd like to ask my distinguished colleague Mister Hotchkiss a few questions. Mister Hotchkiss, do you believe in Jesus Christ?"

The counselor replied, "Did you fall off your tricycle and crack that thick skull of yours?"

"Imbecile! Just answer the blue bloody question before I crack your skull."

Hotchkiss said something I hadn't heard since grade school: "I'm rubber. You're glue. Whatever you say bounces off me and sticks to you." Have such significant words ever been spoken in a court of law?

Deter must have been wounded. Turning to the judge, he said, "Your Honor, will you please instruct Mister Hotchkiss to answer the question?"

To which the judge proudly laughed. "This isn't a trial, Mister Deter. I can't very well instruct him to do anything he doesn't want to do."

"Your Honor, how am I supposed to get anywhere if no one cooperates?"

This question should've made the judge laugh harder, if nothing more than as a firm jab at the attorney. But, I think he saw that our main character's future was at stake. "Oh, *all right*," he said. "Hotchkiss, answer the question."

"Thank you, your Binkyness."

Hotchkiss grinned. "Could you repeat the question?" he said.

"Do you or don't you believe in Jesus?"

"Sure."

"And would you know Jesus if you saw him?"

Hotchkiss paused before answering. "I don't know. Maybe. I guess so."

"And this man, who sits here awaiting judgment, doesn't he look like Jesus?"

"Well ... no." What a shock that was. "That is, not exactly."

"What do you mean?" said Deter.

"In the sketches I've seen, Jesus is nailed to a cross. It's really hard to tell."

"I see," said Deter. Then, turning to the doctor, he made a request. "Would you mind standing up and holding your arms out like an airplane?"

"Not at all," said Doc, and he did.

"Tilt your head a little to the right," Deter added.

"Like this?"

"Perfect. Now bend your knees a tad."

"This okay?"

"Wonderful." Turning to the assistant prosecutor, Deter said, "Well?"

Hotchkiss casually and thoughtlessly plucked a hair from the top of his head. Without flinching, he responded, "I do see a resemblance."

"Your Honor," said Deter, "if even my esteemed colleague sees a resemblance between my client and old J.C., don't you think it's conceivable that he really is?"

Binky groaned. "Mister Deter, I hope you have more to go on than your client's physical appearance. If not, I think we can get back to the reason we're here."

"Of course. If I may continue?"

"Go right ahead."

"Well Binkster, I'd like to call as a witness…."

"May I remind you that this is not a trial. A circus, maybe. But by no means a trial."

"Right," Deter said. "In that case, I'll just question these good folks outright. That is if my esteemed colleague has no objections."

Hotchkiss replied, "Oh, don't let me stop you. You amuse me too much. You're more fun than my wife with a bottle of body oil."

"That's enough of that," said Binky. "Please continue, Mister Deter."

Deter was pleased with himself. I could see it in his obnoxious smile. He said, "Is there a Mister Plymale in the room?"

"Right here," said undertaker Billy Joe Plymale.

"Not you," spat Skeeter Deter. "Sit down and be quiet." Then he began again. "Is there *another* Mister Plymale in the room?"

This time, Hubris stood up. "I'm here."

"Mister Plymale," said Deter, "I spoke with you earlier, didn't I?"

"Yessir, you sure did."

"And you told me a remarkable story about my client, didn't you?"

"Sure enough."

"Would you please share that story with the folks here today?"

"If that's what you want. I went to see the Savior in his office," he began.

Hotchkiss interrupted. "Excuse me, but please refer to him as Mister Lesage, Doctor Lesage, the defendant, or as that fellow over there, rather than *the Savior*. An official religious designation hasn't been established in this court."

Hubris grunted, a signal he'd comply. "I saw the fellow's ad on TV, and I thought to myself, Hubris, maybe you should go down there. Maybe he can help with your problem."

"Would you please explain what your problem is?" said Deter.

"I guess it can't hurt. I have a little bit of a tendency to lose a small sum of money every now and then on an occasional wager or two."

"You mean you have a gambling problem?" said Hotchkiss.

"I have a losing problem."

"Please continue."

"Well, I figured, just off hand mind you, that our Savior ... sorry, that guy there ... might help me out."

"And what kind of help did you seek?" Deter asked.

"To be honest, I wanted the winners of a few greyhound races. The first five."

"And did he give them to you?"

"Yessir. He said he'd bet on number seven if he was me. At first, I was skeptical. It's not too likely one number'd take first in all five races. An experienced gambler like me knows that sure as day. But I decided to trust him, him being the son of God and all. I bet my savings on number seven in the first race ... all eighty bucks of it. It was a long shot, too, something like forty-two to one. Hey, and guess what. Number seven it was. That's the first bet I've won since the time I bet myself a dollar on a game of solitaire."

"All right," said Hotchkiss. "This's all well and good, but so what? You won a bet on one race. Big deal. You had a reasonable chance of doing that."

Plymale scratched his inner ear with a fat, grubby finger. "I don't have a point. I'm just telling you what happened. But it wasn't just a bet, mind you. That was the beginning. I won over three thousand dollars. That's a year's worth of alimony I could pay off. Well, I could've anyway."

"So you lost it all on the second race, right?" Hotchkiss declared.

"No, Sir. Not that way at all. I bet on number seven again and *Bingo*! *Hallelujah*! I won again at three to one. More money than I've ever had at one time in my life."

"I see," said Hotchkiss, a glum, distrustful expression freezing itself to his face. Hotchkiss didn't see the significance of Hubris Plymale winning two bets in a row.

Deter understood. "Tell us what happened after that."

"Well," said Hubris, "I think I can honestly say I know when to quit. But I had faith in the Savior, I mean, that fellow there. So, I bet the bundle on lucky seven to win. That pup took first, and I won at two to one odds. Believe it? I wouldn't if I hadn't been the one it happened to."

"Yeah yeah," said Hotchkiss. "Get on with it."

"Lord, Man, hold your horses. I'm getting there as fast as I can. Anyway, I thought about hedging on the fourth race. Maybe bet seven to place or show. Heck fire, my instincts told me to bet on good old number three to win. Good thing I didn't though, as that mutt made it home dead last and late for supper. But shoot me in the behind with rock salt if that there man ain't the Savior, 'cause I bet old lucky seven to win in the fourth and fifth races, and it paid off a minor miracle."

"How much did you win?" prodded Deter.

"I'm not so good with math, you know, but it was well over sixty."

"Sixty?"

"Sixty thousand dollars. Probably more than I've earned in all my life."

Hotchkiss let loose with a fatigued sigh. "Mister Deter," he said, "let me see if I've got this straight. You're telling me the defendant is Jesus, and your evidence is a statement by a hick who won some money on a lucky tip?"

"That's right," said Skeeter Deter.

Hotchkiss continued to pry. "Okay, Mister Plymale," he said. "Let's presume for one moment that I believe you."

"Why wouldn't you?"

"Just presume that I do. Now tell me, what possible bearing does it have?"

"Well bop me on the head with a dirty spoon if that ain't plain obvious," said Plymale. "I ain't never won five bets in a row before. Not never. Heck fire. And top it off, they was all on the same number in five consecutive races, and there was a powerful lot of money involved. If that don't prove to you he's the Savior, Bub, I got to tell you, you ain't got the smarts God gave a toad's hind end."

Hotchkiss jabbed back, "Haven't you learned not to insult a lawyer? Maybe I'll sue you for slander and take all that money you won."

"Not likely," Hubris said with a snicker. "I lost it all."

"You what?" said Hotchkiss.

"You what?" said Deter.

"You did what?" said Binky.

"Figures," said a cynical hack watching the show. "That figures."

"It's like this. I was feeling lucky. Heck fire, I ain't never felt so lucky. So I plopped the whole bundle down on lucky number seven to win in the sixth race."

A grinning assistant prosecutor jumped at the chance to discredit one of Deter's so-called witnesses. "Amazing. You lost it all. Just plain amazing. But I guess that shoots down Mister Lesage's Christ complex. Wouldn't you say so, Mister Deter?"

Deter nodded in defeat.

"I don't think so," Hubris said. "I don't think so at all, thank you very much."

"And why not?" said Hotchkiss.

"Heck fire, Buddy Boy. Ain't you been listening? I only asked him for the first five races."

"Angie Fishburton," said our main character's attorney once the clatter in the courtroom died down, "are you here?"

"Yes," she replied, standing to be seen.

"We just heard Mister Plymale describe what he believes to be a religious experience. You also went to visit Mister Lesage, didn't you?"

"Yes."

"And did you also have a religious experience?"

She started to speak, but Hotchkiss interrupted. "I object in the strongest sense of the word, Binky. My colleague seems to have jumped headfirst into an aquarium to try to catch his dinner with his teeth. He's fishing."

"Oh, I agree," said the judge. "Unfortunately, as I've pointed out, this isn't a trial. I'm content to sit back and listen. After, when everything's said and done, then and only then will I decide whether or not to have Mister Deter shot in the face. Is that clear, Mister Deter?"

"I'm eager to serve, your Binkyness."

"You, too, Mister Hotchkiss."

The assistant prosecutor, following Deter's lead, said, "Yes, your Binkyness."

"Please continue, Mister Deter. And make it quick, if it's not too much trouble."

"Thanks," said Deter. Then, turning back to the professional camera-wielding baby hater, he prodded, "Well, Miss Fishburton? Any stories to tell us?"

"No," she replied.

"No?" said Deter.

"No?" said Binky.

"No?" said yours truly.

"See, I told you so," said Hotchkiss, who was thoroughly ignored.

"Well, not really," explained Angie. "What I mean to say is, not exactly."

"Go on," said Deter.

Angie giggled as if one of those maniacal children she despised. "It's like this. I was given two wonderful pieces of advice from the man, whether he is or isn't the Savior or a psychopathic murderer of college students. He got me back on track." She took a few moments to relate the details of her visit to God & Son Mediations, LLC. "You see, he told me it was wrong to hate little kids, monsters that they may be. And he's right. I know that now. I guess I've always known it. So, he told me not to hate kids, and that was good advice. From now on, I intend to put my past experiences in the past and leave them there."

"Go on," said Deter.

"As for the second piece of advice, well, it was so simple and logical that frankly, most people wouldn't have thought of it. He told me I should change jobs."

"And do you intend to do that?" probed the assistant prosecutor.

"Already have. I'll never take another child's picture, unless by some chance it's my own."

"That's your religious experience?" scoffed Hotchkiss.

"I never claimed it was a religious experience. I said he gave me good advice."

"Excuse me," Binky interjected. "It's awfully hard to get a good job overnight. If you're not photographing tikes and toddlers, what are you doing?"

"That's the best part. You'll love this. I contacted an attorney. I'm going to sue the families of every child that ever caused me harm. Injury isn't covered under the terms of any of the contracts I've had parents sign, nor is mental distress. My attorney thinks I can make at least a couple million." She paused before adding, "I owe it all to that man there."

From the back of the room, I heard Billy Joe Plymale begin to cry.

"Mister Gates, Mister Killian," said Deter, "are you with us?"

The dust devil stood up. "We're here," he said. "Hurry it up, will you? I got things to do." Which was true. He had plenty of work not to get back to and contract negotiations to walk away from in frustration. "What is it you all want from us anyhow?"

Deter said, "You also visited my client, did you not?"

"Sure enough."

"And did he give you good advice as well?"

"No, Sir. Not a whit."

"No?" said Deter.

"No," added Killian, the management gargoyle.

Hotchkiss asked, "So, you fellows don't think Mister Lesage is the son of God, do you?"

"Didn't say that at all," said Gates. "No, Sir. Don't you be putting no words in my mouth. I'm a working man."

Killian stood up, increasing his visibility by a full two inches. "What my associate is trying to say is that, yes, the old man did give us some advice that we couldn't use. So what? That doesn't make him any less Christlike. We both personally saw him predict the future."

"You what?" said Hotchkiss.

"No," said Binky.

"That's right," said Gates.

"Did I miss something somewhere?" I mumbled, only to be ignored.

"What do you mean?" said Deter. "You actually saw him predict the future?"

"Yessir," said Gates.

"And he did it accurately?"

"Yessir. Sure enough."

"When? Where? How?"

"When we came in," said Killian. "We told him our problem and asked him for a solution."

"And he gave us one," added Gates.

"Yes," Killian agreed, "but that's not the point. When we asked him for a solution, he said that no matter what he suggested, we wouldn't listen."

"And we didn't," said Gates.

"That's right," said Killian.

"And we won't," said Gates.

"That's right, too. We didn't and we won't, and that's the truth, so help me God."

Deter scanned the crowd, looking for his next witness. It didn't take him long to spot our governor, hiding in the back with his bodyguards. "Would you please stand up?" the attorney said. "I'd like to ask you some questions."

I presume that Binky hadn't noticed our governor. I say this because the judge's skin seemed to tighten, and his eyebrows climbed higher on his head. "Mister Deter," he whispered, though it echoed in the quiet of the courtroom, "will you please come up here a minute?"

The defense attorney looked stunned. I'm sure it was just an act because he also began to laugh. He stepped toward the bench and said, "Is there a problem?"

"For your sake, I hope not. Why is he here?"

"He's a witness."

"A what?"

"A witness."

"I heard you the first time. I meant, *why?* Why's the governor in my courtroom?"

"To prove my client's divinity." There was no humor in his voice. "After all, if the governor thinks my client is Jesus, who're we to dispute him?"

Binky groaned as if feeling his ulcer's dying breath, or perhaps the birth of intestinal cancer. "You'd better be right, Mister Deter, or I'll have you castrated with a bone saw. That clear?"

"Uhhh … yeah." Deter looked like a beggar in a bank vault. Everything in the world he wanted was within reach, but one slip and … trouble. "I think I get it."

"Let's get on with it, shall we?"

"Anything you say." Deter spun around and redirected his attention toward our governor. "I'll come straight to the point," he said. "You're the governor. Everyone in here should know you. Most of them probably voted for you. Do you believe my client is the Second Coming?"

If our governor would've said no, the whole case might've melted away. Our main character's arraignment would've begun again, probably ending with his going back to jail pending an extradition hearing. Our governor would've avoided humiliation and ridicule for perhaps the first time in the history of all governors everywhere. Not to mention, I'd need to find a new ending for this story. Luckily, none of that came to pass. "Yes," he said. "I have to."

"What do you mean *have to*?" Hotchkiss interrupted.

Our governor replied, "If this man *weren't* Jesus, I'd consider resigning in disgrace."

"Wouldn't that be nice," I mumbled, only to be drowned out by other people saying similar things, but somewhat louder.

Binky silenced us with an admonishing glare and a few fiery taps of his gavel. Then he directed his attention to our governor. "For the record, would you please explain yourself?"

Our governor told the story of his visit with God & Son Mediations, LLC.

"So basically," said Hotchkiss, "he told you; you're a no good, money-grubbing, back-stabbing, lying, cheating, scoundrel?"

"Yes, he did," said our governor, "though not in those exact words."

"And did you agree with him?"

"No. I think of myself as a pretty good example of a governor."

The assistant prosecutor ran his fingers through his hair, a gesture which I recognized as meaning either he was somewhat frustrated and about to casually pull his hair out or that he was frustrated a lot and about to pull his hair out rather quickly. I can't say which as he didn't, in fact, pull a single hair out of his head. Instead, he said, "He called you a greedy little maggot, and you don't agree with him, so why do you think he's Jesus?"

"Because if he were just a man, then all the things he told me would've been nothing more than an honest opinion, and it would've hurt my feelings."

Hotchkiss groaned as if he kept tripping over a pair of dragging testicles while wearing hiking boots. I don't think he followed our governor's logic—though come to think of it, I'm not so sure I did, either. "Let me get this straight. If he were human, it'd hurt your feelings?"

"And if I believed him, I'd consider resigning."

"But if the defendant were Jesus, then what he told you would be true."

"I know that," said our governor. "But since he's Jesus, I don't have to resign. I can just ignore him."

"What do you mean?" said Binky.

"Simple," said our governor. "If it's a man saying those things, I should listen. This is a democracy. But if it's the son of God, I'm free as governor to ignore every word. That's called Separation of Church and State, and it's written in the U.S. Constitution."

"Separation of Church and State?" said Hotchkiss. "That's your logic?"

"I've thought about it long and hard, you know, and I doubt I should've gone to see him in the first place. It was wrong to mix religion and politics."

"Your Honor," the defense attorney began, "after hearing from these witnesses, including the governor of our great state, I think I've clearly shown that my client is, in fact, Jesus."

"Not a chance," said Hotchkiss. "This moron couldn't prove the existence of a doughnut, even with cream filling oozing down his chin. He certainly hasn't shown any proof of divinity."

"Have too," said Deter.

"Have not," said Hotchkiss.

"Have too," said Deter.

"Have not."

"Take a breath," said Binky. He turned toward the assistant prosecutor. "Mister Hotchkiss, I'm afraid I have to side with Mister Deter, as annoying as that may be. It seems to me he's at least shown a reasonable possibility that what he alleges is true. That doesn't mean it *is* true, just that he's shown that it's possible. As for you, Hotchkiss, it seems you haven't shown anything to prove these ridiculous religious theories to be false, though I encourage you to try."

The assistant prosecutor closed his eyes to consider his options while hiding out momentarily in the darkness of his mind. He must've been reviewing the *New Testament* because when he opened his eyes again, he had a different tactic, one which might've come from the condemnation of Christ by Pilate. He said, "Show us your power," and he was referring to our main character, not the attorney for the defense.

"What?" said Skeeter Deter.

"What?" said Binky.

"Oh my," said our main character.

The room filled with oohs and ahhs and other mumbling sounds.

As for me, well, I didn't know whether to laugh or cry.

Banging his gavel, Binky said, "Please explain yourself, Mister Hotchkiss."

To which the assistant prosecutor replied, "If the defendant is really the son of God, it follows that he has some special powers."

"I see where you're going." The judge turned to Deter. "Can he show us something?"

"Bless my soul," replied the defense attorney. "I sure hope so." Deter conferred briefly with his client. I don't know what the two men discussed, but heads were shaken, shoulders shrugged, and the words "oh my" repeated on two or three occasions. After several minutes of this, Deter returned his attention to the crowd and said, "Has anybody got a deck of cards?"

"I beg your pardon?" said Hotchkiss.

"Explain yourself," said the judge.

"My client has consented to show a small fragment of his divine power."

"Wonderful," said Binky, with a hint of sarcasm.

"Yeah, right," said Hotchkiss, whose sarcasm was more than hinted at.

Lord help us, I thought, and I was beyond sarcasm.

The defense attorney said. "The problem, quite frankly, is that to do so, my client will require a deck of playing cards."

"That's ridiculous," said Hotchkiss. "What's he planning to do, show us a holy card trick?"

Deter's voice turned cold and serious. "That's exactly right," he said.

"No," said Hotchkiss.

"You're joking," said Binky.

The crowd laughed. The doctor oh-myed. I slapped the palm of my hand to my forehead.

"Mister Deter," said Binky, "you're trying my patience. No, my patience is long gone. Now you're making me angry."

"Slow down," Deter prodded. "Hear me out. Granted, what I'm proposing is unusual. Hell, this whole case is unusual. But you all stuck your thumbs up to the serpent's tooth, so don't whine when that little critter injects the venom."

"Mister Deter," Binky raged.

"No, just listen. You're putting undue demands on my client by requiring a miracle, even though any fool knows Christ went to the cross for refusing. But my client has agreed to swallow his holy pride and give you a sample. Tell me, just who do you think you are to say it's not good enough? Who are you to say one holy act isn't as good as another or that it'd be better if he did something else? Either relax and let him show his power or concede the point and let my client go."

Binky's face flushed. "Mister Deter," he shouted, but his voice calmed. "That's the most preposterous idea I've ever heard." He paused to take in a breath. "Unfortunately, it's also the most logical thing you've ever said in my courtroom. Please continue."

Deter smiled. "Thank you," he said.

All Hotchkiss managed was, "But…."

"Sit down and shut up," demanded the judge. "Mister Deter, go ahead."

Deter turned to the crowd. "Again, does anybody have a deck of cards?"

Amazingly, someone said, "I do." Add two points to your scorecard if you guessed Hubris Plymale. He stood up, removed a pack from his right shirt pocket, and tossed it one-handed to the defense attorney.

"Thank you so much," said Deter as he glanced at the box. "Hey, wait a minute. Did you know these cards are marked?"

"No, they're not," replied Plymale.

"I'm afraid so. It says so right here on the box."

"No way," said Plymale. "Which cards?"

"Just the aces," Deter replied.

"Gawldern it," said the gambler. "I guess that explains why I keep losing."

Hotchkiss broke in, saying, "I object, Binkster. If you intend to allow this farce, you could at least ask them to remove the marked cards."

"Agreed," said the judge. He looked at Deter. "You'll remove the four aces from the deck."

"Sure," said Deter, and he did. "Now I'll need a volunteer. Binky, I suggest you do it so there'll be no misunderstanding when it's over."

The judge groaned. "Whatever you say, Mister Deter. Anything else I can do for you? Can I get you some water, or would you like me to dance naked up here on the bench while you laugh and carry on?"

Binky's sarcastic tone didn't stop Deter from replying, "Uh, please don't."

The judge groaned once more. "It's your show, Mister Lesage."

Our main character stood up, took the cards from his attorney, and approached the bench. "This is an old trick my father taught me." He clumsily shuffled the forty-eight cards and then fanned them out in front of the judge. "Pick a card," he said. "Any card."

Binky shrugged and pulled an inconspicuous card from the middle of the deck.

"Look at it."

"Okay."

"Can you remember it?"

"Of course."

"Good, then here we go." Doc straightened the cards into a proper deck, level on all sides. Then he took the card from Binky and, without looking at the number on its face, he placed it in the center of the deck, slightly askew so that one end sat about an inch higher than the rest of the cards. Carefully, so no one would accuse him of cheating, he raised two other cards to the same level so that each protruded about one inch from the deck on the same end as Binky's card. He put one of the raised cards on each side of the card the judge had drawn. Then he took two others, placing one between each pair of the three raised cards. These two were level with the rest of the deck. He held the modified deck in one hand and, with a showman's wave of the other, he said, "Are you ready?"

"Get on with it," said Binky.

"And you still remember your card?"

"Get on with it."

"Good," said Doc, and he then slammed the deck down on the bench so that the three raised cards struck the hard wood surface and disappeared into the pack. In their place, two other cards popped out on the opposite end. "It's working," exclaimed the doctor. "I can feel it working. So much power. So much energy."

I heard a few people laugh, while others, I'm certain, watched with nervous anticipation as if the fate of the world depended on this one little sleight of hand.

"And now," emphasized the doctor, "it's time for the conclusion. Are you ready?"

"Get on with it," the judge said once more.

"All right. Here goes." He tapped the deck on the bench, driving the two cards into the pack, and causing the deuce of hearts to appear at the other end. He removed the card from the deck and held it up so everyone could see the twin crimson symbols of love. "And is this your card?" he said as he finished a complete circle and ended up facing the judge.

"Very impressive," Binky said with a dry, monotone voice. "Is that all?"

"Well, yes."

"Good. Let's go home." Hotchkiss jumped up to offer an objection, but Binky saw it coming and sidestepped with a few words of his own. "Mister Hotchkiss, I'm sorry. He did what he told us he'd do, as pathetic as that may seem. I'm afraid we have to concede that it's possible this man is in fact Jesus." His voice was so stale that I couldn't tell if he were happy, sad, upset, or in a drunken fugue.

"You're mad," said Hotchkiss. "Everybody here is mad."

"Good," retorted Binky, "then you should fit right in."

The assistant prosecutor stumbled backward, his face red with humiliation. But he wasn't defeated yet. "Binky," he said, "I accept your decision regarding the divine nature of the defendant. But that's not the point."

"And what do you suggest the point is?"

"Murder, Your Honor. Whether or not he's Jesus has no bearing on whether he should be found guilty. It only affects the name to file the verdict under."

"I see," replied the judge. He pondered the situation. "I hate to admit it, Mister Deter, especially after your creativity and hard work, but Mister Hotchkiss appears to be right."

"Balderdash," said Deter.

"Possibly," replied the judge. "That doesn't change the fact that we're going to have to get back to the arraignment."

"No," said Deter.

"I'm afraid so," said the judge. "Now, do either of you have anything else?"

"No," groaned Deter, pouting.

"Nope," grunted Hotchkiss.

But then another voice spoke up. "I do," it said. Everyone turned to see Loralee Garrett stand up. We'd lost track of her in the commotion.

Binky shrugged. "What is it?"

"Your Honor," she said. "I know absolutely every detail about this case. I've studied it for twelve years and, you know, as much as I'd like to have the conviction, I don't think there's any point in it."

"I beg your pardon?" Hotchkiss snapped.

"It's true. If we shipped him off to Pennsylvania, I don't know whether he'd be found guilty by a jury of his peers. I do know it might not be necessary to find out."

"Really?" said Skeeter Deter.

Binky said, "What did you have in mind?"

"Frankly," she replied, "This isn't a federal case. We were just called in because the locals were stumped. That said, I took the case, so I consider it mine. As for me, I'd be content with a denial of guilt from the defendant. As of yet, he hasn't done that. He hasn't actually said that he didn't do it. Then again, no one's given him the chance. Your Honor, if he'll say plainly for the record that he didn't do it, I suggest we believe him."

"Impressive solution," said the judge. "Any objections?"

Hotchkiss stood there, stunned silent.

"Very good," said the judge, "then we'll go with your suggestion. Thank you."

"You're welcome," she said, and then she screamed, loud and piercing like a group of lost souls condemned to listen to the soundtrack to *Saturday Night Fever* for all eternity. "Sorry," she said. "I bit my tongue."

"Mister Deter," said the judge, once Garrett sat down, holding her mouth in a cupped hand, "do you have any problems with that suggestion?"

"None at all, Binky old boy."

"I didn't think so." Binky shifted his head, focusing his gaze on our main character. "Mister Lesage, how do you plead?"

This time, for some odd reason, I expected Doc to reply with something like "On my knees." As it turns out, he gave his characteristic response: "I always cross at the light."

Binky shook his head. "No," he said. "That's all well and good, but not charged with jaywalking. You're charged with twenty-three counts of murder for allegedly encouraging a group of your students to kill themselves. Please answer me this, did you do it or did you not?"

Doc sat silent, though only for a moment. When he replied, his words slapped everyone in the face. "As I have all my students," he said, "I encouraged those boys and girls to do whatever they wanted. I explained the importance of having goals and striving to accomplish them, no matter how bizarre those goals are, or what society thinks of them." His voice sounded weary, lost, hopeless, as if the vast tides of the Earth were coming to wash him away. I think that for the first time I was hearing the true voice of Matthew Lesage. "I also encouraged them to use morals and logic in setting their goals. I explained how important it is to reason, to study, to understand. I taught them to know themselves so they could understand their reasons for doing what they chose to do. These are the values and ideals I wanted to instill. So, Your Honor, if you're asking me if I took a gun and shot each of my students, the answer is no. If you're asking me if I wanted them to join in some ritual suicide, the answer is still no. But if you're asking me if I encouraged them to search for meaning in their lives, down whatever twisted path it waits or behind whatever gnarled shrub it hides, then do what you want to me. I'm guilty."

Unsatisfied with the doctor's moving speech, Binky pressed on. "You have a way with words," he said, "but somehow, you've failed to answer the question."

"I'm sorry. I tried but…."

Before the doctor could launch any kind of lengthy surrealist, existentialist, metaphysical apology, Binky stopped him. The judge said, "Listen, Mister Lesage. I'm going to ask this question one time and one time only. It's a simple yes-or-no question. Your response will either be 'yes' or 'no.' Nothing else will be acceptable. I hope I'm making myself clear."

"Yes," said the doctor.

"Good. Now, pay attention. Did you at any time say to any of your students, even one of them, anything even close to resembling anything to the effect of 'Sure, you might as well go ahead and kill yourself,' or anything of that sort?"

"Well," the doctor said, stumbling over his thoughts, "no, I guess not."

"Good," said Binky. "Case dismissed."

Author's note: This is the end of our story. I know, I've left you hanging a bit, but that's life. Just the same, I think I'll share a few details, just so you won't stay awake nights wondering.

Hubris Plymale, in a deranged fit of inspiration, spent his last dollar on a lottery ticket. The object of the game was to rub silver shavings off six squares, each containing a number. If any three numbers matched, he would win that amount. He scratched the card with a penny and, miracle of miracles, he won. Three times, he uncovered this symbol: $1. "Well, I'll be," he said. Then, instead of using the money to buy another lottery ticket, he bought himself a candy bar. For the first time in his life, Hubris Plymale broke even.

As for Billy Joe Plymale, not much changed. The mortuary business continued to have a steady profit margin.

Loralee Garrett went on to a successful second assignment in which, after only a two-year search, she was able to arrest four vicious thugs, all over the age of eighty, who ran a profitable interstate moonshine operation out of their nursing home. No charges were filed.

Our governor continued his marvelous life of doing whatever governors do.

Skeeter Deter and Stanley Hotchkiss formed a strong working relationship, eventually going into business together. It hasn't been a profitable one, and to this day, they're still suing each other with regard to whose name should appear first on the company's letterhead.

Incidentally, about one month after the trial of Doctor Matthew Lesage, Deter received a key in the mail, apparently sent by our main character. The key unlocked a storage shed in Huntington's Westmoreland district in which the doctor had left four thousand pounds of beer and soda cans, some eighteen hundred newspapers, and a dirty, old chair, the sale of which—excluding the chair—covered the victorious attorney's fee, especially since he didn't charge one.

I, of course, went on to write this story. I need not mention which direction my life took.

And as for our main character, I honestly don't know. In the audience's wild celebration following the dismissal of the case, Doc managed to slip away, and he hasn't been seen since. Even so, he's left everyone he encountered with renewed hope for the future. Come to think of it, he just might have made us better people, too. But that's another story for another day.

ALMOST UNRELATED POSTSCRIPT: HERE BEGINS THE REVELATION OF RON THE NOT-SO-DIVINE

My good friend Ron and I sat on the bank of the Ohio River in a secluded spot, doing what many West Virginians love to do on a day off, which is to say, fishing. We also were doing what many people from most states love to do on a day off, which is to say, becoming intoxicated. I drank vodka which I'd mixed with grape juice. My head spun like stars before the eyes of a cartoon character who'd just run face-first into a brick wall. Ron, on the other hand, was smoking large quantities of marijuana. He'd found a big bag of the stuff in a dumpster near the university several days earlier after learning that a couple of police officers left it there by accident. I'm sure the cartoon-character image applied to Ron as well. Neither of us cared that we weren't catching any fish.

One of the problems with alcohol is that it goes through the body quickly. After a few drinks, I got up and staggered off behind some bushes to relieve myself. When I returned, I saw Ron lying flat on his back and staring at the sky. His eyes were glassy with amazement (and dope).

"What's wrong?" I asked.

He sat up cautiously, making sure it was me. Then he said, "I've just seen a vision from God." This is the story he told:

The waters began to bubble and boil, and the world shook. The sun disappeared behind a vast, demonic tract of clouds, stealing away all light. From the river, came the beast. Its silver body was long and slender, covered with scales the size of roofing shingles, and also a strange purple ooze. It walked on four legs, which were made up of fins and feet. Its four arms groped with the riverbank to pull the beast on shore. It had three heads—fat, round, catfish heads, with protruding spikes and bulging eyes. On each head, it wore a crown, or perhaps a helmet. Each helmet was made of a turtle shell. Strung across its back with an algae strap was a stone sword shaped like a fishhook. The beast caught a glimpse of Ron. "Oh, sorry," it said and turned to go back into the water.

"Wait," said Ron. "What are you? Why are you here?"

The beast turned and confronted him, the center head saying, "I came to conquer the world."

"You what?" said Ron.

"You know, the spirit of colonialism, and all that."

"You're joking."

"No, not really."

Ron wiped nervous sweat from his brow. "Okay, so why are you leaving?"

And the beast said, "Well, because *you're* here."

"Hmm?" said Ron.

"Well, I can't take over the world with you here, can I?"

Ron shrugged. "I don't know. Why not?"

"It's like my mommy always said, it's no use trying to take over the world while the monkey-creatures are up there. But the oracles have told us that someday you'll destroy yourselves, and then we can conquer everything. I can be a king. Frankly, I thought you were already gone."

"No, not yet," said Ron.

"I can see that," said the fish. "Any chance of you leaving soon?"

"Doubtful."

"Pity. Oh, well. Another year or two. Anyway, I guess I'd better head home. If I'm not going to conquer the world, I might as well get back in time for dinner. We're having seafood."

"How wonderful," sighed Ron.

"Well, it was nice meeting you," said the fish.

"Nice meeting you," said Ron.

And so the beast turned, dove into the Ohio River, and vanished into its depths. Still, it lurks there, off in the distance, waiting for its chance to strike. It could be tomorrow. It could be next week. It could be twenty years from now. It waits for one thing only before it comes to take control: the annihilation of the human race.

Funny, isn't it?

Author's Bio:

Ace Boggess is author of the novels *States of Mercy* (Alien Buddha Press, 2019) and *A Song Without a* Melody (Hyperborea Publishing, 2016), as well as four books of poetry, most recently *I Have Lost the Art of Dreaming It So* (Unsolicited Press, 2018). His fiction appears in *Notre Dame Review, Superstition Review, Lumina, Flyway,* and other journals. He received a fellowship from the West Virginia Commission on the Arts and spent five years in a West Virginia prison. He lives in Charleston, West Virginia.

Past Titles

Running Wild Stories Anthology, Volume 1
Running Wild Anthology of Novellas, Volume 1
Jersey Diner by Lisa Diane Kastner
Magic Forgotten by Jack Hillman
The Kidnapped by Dwight L. Wilson
Running Wild Stories Anthology, Volume 2
Running Wild Novella Anthology, Volume 2, Part 1
Running Wild Novella Anthology, Volume 2, Part 2
Running Wild Stories Anthology, Volume 3
Running Wild's Best of 2017, AWP Special Edition
Running Wild's Best of 2018
Build Your Music Career From Scratch, Second Edition by Andrae Alexander
Writers Resist: Anthology 2018 with featured editors Sara Marchant and Kit-Bacon Gressitt
Magic Forbidden by Jack Hillman
Frontal Matter: Glue Gone Wild by Suzanne Samples
Mickey: The Giveaway Boy by Robert M. Shafer
Dark Corners by Reuben "Tihi" Hayslett
The Resistors by Dwight L. Wilson
Running Wild Press, Best of 2018

Upcoming Titles

Running Wild Stories Anthology, Volume 4
Running Wild Novella Anthology, Volume 4
Open My Eyes by Tommy Hahn
Legendary by Amelia Kibbie
Christine, Released by E. Burke
Recon: The Anthology by Ben White
The Self Made Girl's Guide by Aliza Dube
Sodom & Gomorrah on a Saturday Night by Christa Miller
Turing's Graveyard by Terry Hawkins
Running Wild Press, Best of 2019

Running Wild Press publishes stories that cross genres with great stories and writing. Our team consists of:

Lisa Diane Kastner, Founder and Executive Editor
Barbara Lockwood, Editor
Cecile Sarruf, Editor
Peter Wright, Editor
Piper Daniels, Editor
Benjamin White, Editor
Andrew DiPrinzio, Editor
Amrita Raman, Operations Manager
Lisa Montagne, Director of Education

Learn more about us and our stories at www.runningwildpress.com

Loved this story and want more? Follow us at
www.runningwildpress.com, www.facebook.com/runningwildpress, on
Twitter @lisadkastner @JadeBlackwater @RunWildBooks